Sunrise Kisses

(Book Two in the Angel Series)

Cheryl R. Lane

Best wishes! Cheryl R Lane

ISBN: 1518807216
ISBN-13: 978-1518807213

Printed in the United States of America

This book is a work of fiction. All of the characters, organizations and events portrayed in this novel are either products of the author's imagination or are used fictitiously.

Cover photo taken by the author at Little Island, Virginia Beach.
Models: Dakota Lane and Bryanna Vesely.
Author photo taken by Sherrie Frontz.

Also by Cheryl R. Lane:

Wellington Cross (Book One in the Wellington Cross Series)
Wellington Grove (Book Two in the Wellington Cross Series)
A Wellington Christmas (A Wellington Cross Novella, Book 2.5)
Wellington Rose (Book Three in the Wellington Cross Series)
Starlight Wishes (Book One in the Angel Series)

Prologue

Virginia Beach
March 2015

Scarlett Juliandra Laurent looked at the ultrasound screen again. It was a big mass. Her breast cancer had come back.

She'd first been diagnosed nearly eight years ago when she found out she was pregnant. She went in for a simple pregnancy test and came out with a cancer diagnosis. The doctor gave her the option of aborting her baby so that she could begin chemo treatment immediately, since it was an aggressive type. She had refused, deciding instead to wait until after her baby boy was born before having the mass excised and starting chemotherapy and radiation treatment. She'd lost all her hair and her mom helped her take care of Tyler during that awful ordeal. It should have been the happiest time of her life, enjoying her newborn baby, but instead she was throwing up, losing her hair, and getting weaker by the minute. She finally made it through and had been in remission for many years. Until now.

She was sitting in her surgical oncologist's office looking at the ultrasound monitor with the doctor, who'd just shown her where the mass was. She'd gone in for a routine mammogram two weeks prior when they'd found one very large mass in the same place the original one had been. She'd been referred back to the surgeon who had excised the first one, and an ultrasound confirmed that the mass had returned. Dr. Gary Mitchell had done a biopsy, and sure enough, it came back positive. She was back at his office a second time to discuss treatment and to do another ultrasound.

"I'm sorry to say it doesn't look good, Scarlett." Dr. Mitchell looked at her gravely. "This is a totally different kind of cancer than what you had before. This one is HER2-positive and is a fast-growing aggressive cancer."

She was barely listening and didn't understand what he was saying in that medical language. "What..." she coughed to clear her suddenly scratchy throat. "What does that mean?"

"It means we have to act quickly. There is a medicine we can try called Herceptin, which may slow or even stop the growth of the cancer in addition to chemotherapy and radiation therapy as before. But I strongly recommend a mastectomy since the cancer came back and because it's so aggressive."

Mastectomy?

"A double one, just to be sure. Otherwise, Scarlett, without that, you might live a year, even with the chemo."

Her eyebrows rose. "A year?" she squeaked.

"Without the mastectomies." He put a reassuring hand on her shoulder and gave it a squeeze. "It won't be so bad. You can have reconstruction surgery after all the other treatments."

Scarlett tried to absorb what he was saying.

"I'll send the nurse back in here, and she can explain in more detail what needs to be done. Decisions need to be made quickly."

He turned off the ultrasound machine and quietly walked towards the door, pausing to give her a sympathetic yet reassuring smile, and left the room, closing the door behind him.

A year. She was devastated. She'd have to have the mastectomies, of course. It was her only chance of survival. *Damn it!* She would lose her boobies. She could have reconstructive surgery like her mother did.

Her mother had also had breast cancer and died from it last year. She'd had the surgeries, but it came back in her lungs. She and Tyler had moved into her mother's big five thousand square foot home on ten acres of land in south Pungo to help take care of her for the last year of her life. At a certain point, her mother made the decision that she didn't want any more chemo. She wanted to enjoy her last days.

Scarlett wiped the goo off of her breast and put her clothes back on. Soon the nurse lightly pecked on the door and came back into the room.

She handed Scarlett pamphlets, paperwork to be filled out, prescriptions to start taking, an organic diet to follow and other precautions, and a business card for a psychologist. She spoke in a quiet voice, trying to reassure Scarlett, but she felt numb. Her life was about to change. Again. And this time, she wouldn't have her mother to help her through it.

She made an appointment to come back in for blood work and then left the office, the door closing with a resounding thud behind her. She walked down the hallway towards the main glass doors of the building and stepped out into the cool, blustery air. As she stepped out onto the sidewalk and headed towards her car, her dark green scarf blew across her face, momentarily blocking her view. She stumbled, but a pair of hands reached out to catch her.

"Oh, mon Dieu!" she exclaimed in her French accent. Her father was French and her mother was of English descent. She'd been born and raised in the U.S., but her father spoke French, having been born in Toulon, France, and he taught her French at a young age.

She found herself in the arms of a tall, muscular man with brown hair and eyes the color of dark chocolate. Her hands rested against his chest and she looked up into his handsome face.

"Are you all right?" he asked.

She found her senses and backed away from him. "Yes, I…I wasn't watching where I was going. Thank you for your help…"

He smiled and said, "Call me Jackson."

"That's a lovely accent you have," Jackson said. "Are you French?"

She eyed him curiously. "Half-French, half-American."

"Ah. It's pleasing to the ears."

"Thank you."

She started walking towards her car again, and halfway across the parking lot, his voice called out to her. "You're not going to make it through this time."

She whirled around and faced him. "What are you talking about?"

"Your condition." He pointed to her breasts. "You need to prepare yourself."

"What do you know about my condition? Are you a doctor?" Who did this guy think he was?

"No, but I am aware of your situation, and I can help you through this."

"I don't need your help. I've done this before, and I'll do it again. Thank you very much for your concern," she finished, in a hateful manner.

He actually grinned at her. "I admire your determination. I'll be seeing you soon, Scarlett." He turned away from her.

He knew her name? "Wait. Do you work for my doctor? What do you know?"

"I've already told you that I'm aware of your situation. Your doctor won't be able to help you this time. You might as well forget about the surgery."

"How dare you tell me I can't do something! I beat this once before and I'll beat it again. I'll have the surgery, take the chemo and radiation, and I'll beat it. You wait and see." She wiped a tear, rushed away to her car, and locked herself inside quickly. Before she started the engine, she looked for Jackson, but he was nowhere to be seen. She looked all around the parking lot and at the front of the building, but he had just vanished.

Chapter One

November 1, 2015

Scarlett pulled into the parking lot at BayBreeze Farms produce stand and quickly opened the door to throw up. During the past eight months, she'd undergone double mastectomies followed by chemotherapy, radiation therapy, and then removal of scar tissue and implant-reconstructive surgery. She was still in the healing stage from the last surgery and on antibiotics to prevent any infections, but they made her sick. She'd never been so tired of taking pills in her life. She was sick of it all. Sick and tired of being sick and tired.

She'd given it her best shot, but her body failed her. Her last visit at the oncologist revealed that despite all the surgeries and treatments, there was now cancer in the lymph nodes. She was so damned mad, she cursed in French at the doctor's office. She decided then and there that she didn't want any more treatments, pills, or surgeries.

She closed the door of her car, wiped her mouth with a nearby tissue, and then pulled back on the curvy road that led to Sandbridge Beach. It was an early Sunday morning, the day after Halloween. She had attended a big party at a neighbor's house the previous night and drank a little too much deep red wine, which could be adding to her nausea.

She'd been shocked to see Jackson at the party.

"Scarlett," he'd said in his deep rich voice. He was dressed like Dracula including a painted white face and ruby red lips, hair slicked back and wearing a very nice old-fashioned suit and cape. He picked up her hand as if he meant to kiss it but turned her arm sideways and pretended to bite her on the wrist, revealing long fangs.

It made her laugh. She couldn't remember the last time she'd laughed.

"Jackson, what on earth are you doing here?" she'd asked. She was wearing a black and silver flapper dress with long fringe and black feathers tucked into a headband around her neck-length wig.

He ignored her question. "How are you?" he asked sincerely, like he knew the ordeal she'd been through. She had lost a lot of weight, so she probably looked anorexic compared to the last time he'd seen her.

"Not too good," she confessed. Since he worked for the oncologist, he probably knew what she'd been through anyway and was just asking to be polite.

"I'm sorry to hear that. Why don't we sit down in the parlor and catch up?"

Sitting down had sounded good to her, so they spent the next three hours sitting on an old Victorian couch that had been reupholstered in a beautifully decorated room, sipping wine. She told him everything she'd been through.

"I don't mean to bore you with all the details," she said later. "I'm sorry. You must hear this kind of thing all the time at work. It's the wine."

"It's not boring. I'm truly interested in you. I'm sorry that the cancer has spread. What are you going to do?"

"Nothing. I'm sick of it all. I'm so tired."

He nodded. "I understand."

She looked into his dark eyes and remembered that he'd told her that day back in March that she wouldn't make it this time. She'd been mad at the time, but now she realized he was probably right. She felt so defeated. She nearly spilled her wine in an effort to place it on the coffee table. Jackson helped her to steady the glass and then surprised her by pulling her into his arms and hugging her. She cried until her mascara ran.

"I was so determined. I did all the right things," she said through her tears. "I guess you were right, after all. How did you know?"

"I didn't want to be right, you know." He let go of her, and seeing her face, pulled out an old-fashioned handkerchief and wiped her eyes for her until the white cloth turned black. "You gave it your all, and you are to be commended. It's just your time, that's all."

She sniffed and studied him. "I don't want it to be my time. Don't I get a choice in this?"

He shook his head. "No, you really don't. I'm sorry," he said, as if her condition was his fault.

She took a deep breath and then picked up her wine glass again and took another long drink. He found a carafe nearby and filled both their glasses again.

"Who's going to take care of my son?" she asked, bewildered.

"You should find his father."

She looked at him, startled. How would he know that his father had not been in the picture?

"He deserves to know," Jackson said.

"Are you a mind reader?"

He smiled, but then she realized he must have gotten the information from her records at the oncologist's office.

"I don't want to live in my big old house anymore," she said suddenly, changing the subject. "I want to live someplace happy for the rest of my time, surrounded by my friends and family."

"That sounds like a good idea. Where would you like to live?"

She thought of her father, who lived in France. Her parents had divorced when she was eight and he'd moved back to his homeland. He was in the French Navy when he met her mother while his ship was anchored in Norfolk, Virginia. They fell in love, got married, and she moved to France with him for a while, but she missed home. They found a big old house in Pungo, which her father paid to have remodeled just the way her mother wanted it, and they'd been happy for a while.

Their arguments started when her mother had a miscarriage. She never got over it. They eventually divorced and her father had moved back to France.

Scarlett would love to see him again, but she didn't really know him anymore, and she didn't want to spend the rest of her days in a foreign country.

That's when she remembered that her friend, Catrina, whom she worked with at the State Farm Insurance office, had a beach house in Sandbridge. She'd been to her house before and remembered Catrina saying she had a neighbor who was real estate agent.

"The beach," she told Jackson. "I'd love to live in a little house on the beach. To wake up and see the sunrise on the ocean every morning. That's what I want to do."

"Then you should do it," he said.

So here she was, driving on the curvy country road to find the real estate agent's house and see about getting a beach house. She'd texted her friend Catrina the night before and found out the agent's name was Maggie Reynolds. Catrina gave her all of Maggie's contact information, and Scarlett typed the address into her smart phone for directions. She didn't know if Maggie was home or not, but she'd called her home phone number and left a message. She'd also called her cell phone number, but Maggie didn't answer that either, so Scarlett decided to drive over and see if she was home. If she wasn't, Scarlett thought she could at least drive around and look at the houses, maybe park somewhere and take a walk to the beach. She'd not been to the beach in quite a while.

She found Maggie's blue and white house a few minutes later and pulled into the driveway. There was a black truck in the driveway, so hopefully she was home. She got out of her car and knocked on the downstairs door, but nobody answered. She looked at a steep staircase nearby and decided that she would try the door up there and see if she could get Maggie. If not, she'd just walk to the beach.

She was out of breath by the time she reached the top of the stairs. She took a moment to take in the view of the ocean over the top of the tall sand dunes and breathed in the salty air. *Yes.* This was where she wanted to be.

She walked to a screen door on a screened-in porch that stretched from the front of the house to the back, and she turned the handle. It was locked. She knocked and waited.

Finally another door opened and a pretty blonde woman came out to the screened porch.

"Can I help you?" she asked. She had a pleasant, friendly face, looked a little flushed, but mostly looked happy. Scarlett was immediately envious.

"Are you Maggie?"

"No, I'm afraid not. This is her house, but my husband and I…" she paused and smiled. "Well, we're on our honeymoon. We just got married last night."

"Oh, mon Dieu. Pardon me. I didn't mean to intrude."

"It's okay. We're leaving today for Savannah. We just spent our wedding night here since we had the wedding out there on the beach." She pointed behind her.

For the first time, Scarlett noticed that there were tables on a deck on the other side of the screened porch that had white tablecloths draped over them, and there were pumpkins and black lanterns on each table.

"It must have been a beautiful wedding," she said.

"I'm Jen," the lady said, unlocking the screen door. "Would you like to come in?"

"Oh, no. Thank you. I've intruded enough."

"Maggie will be home sometime later this afternoon. She spent the night at my house with our kids."

"Oh, I see. I'll come back later then."

Scarlett turned to go when she heard someone else coming to the door. She turned around and saw a very good-looking man with sandy blonde hair hanging down straight across his face. He wasn't wearing a shirt and only a pair of dark blue loose shorts.

Luke? she wondered. It couldn't be, could it? What were the chances of seeing him here?

"Hey, what's up?" he asked, putting his hand around Jen's waist and finally looking at Scarlett. When he did, he looked surprised, confused. Did he remember her?

"This lady…what was your name?" Jen asked.

"Scarlett. Excusez-moi. Forgive my manners."

Jen smiled. "It's fine." She looked back at her husband. "Scarlett, this is my husband, Luke."

So it *was* Luke!

He did not recognize her though, she could tell. That made her a little angry, but she couldn't really blame him. They'd both been drunk, and it was only one night. They'd been strangers to each other who enjoyed drinks and then went back to his house for sex. She'd left in the middle of the night.

Jen looked at Luke. "She's looking for Maggie. I'm guessing about a house?" She looked back at Scarlett.

She nodded, suddenly felt slightly dizzy. "Yes, but I can come back later." She turned to go. "It was nice meeting you," she said to Jen. She looked at Luke and then turned to leave.

"Nice to meet you, too. Good luck with your house-hunting," Jen said.

Scarlett turned back at the top of the stairs before going down. "Have a nice honeymoon," she said, forcing a smile.

She herself had never been married in her young thirty-one years. At this point, she never would be.

Chapter Two

"Would you like me to email you information on some properties, or do you want to come and talk to me in person?" Maggie Reynolds was sitting in her best friend Jen's antique shop, making some phone calls and tending shop while Jen was on her honeymoon. As a real estate agent, she could take her work with her anywhere. She had her trusty laptop with her and all the information about houses available at her fingertips. While Jen was on her honeymoon, Maggie would spend half the day at the shop helping customers, and then the other half, she would show houses to interested buyers.

Right now, she was talking to a lady named Scarlett who had a different accent, maybe French or Spanish. She said she'd been to her house that morning and met Jen. Maggie normally didn't work on Sundays if she could help it, but her neighbor, Catrina, told her that she had a friend who would be calling her about a beach house. She called Scarlett right back as soon as she looked at her phone sometime after breakfast and saw her missed call.

"I'd like to come and talk with you in person, if that's all right," Scarlett said.

"Of course. As Jen may have told you, I'm shop-sitting for her while she and her husband are honeymooning, so you can come here this afternoon if you'd like, or tomorrow if that's more convenient."

"Today would be great. My son is staying at a friend's house all day. What shop is this?"

"Jen's Antiques. It's a white house with black shutters in Pungo, not too far down from the red light."

"Okay, great. I'll find it. What time should I come?"

"I'm here until 5:00, so come on now if you'd like."

Scarlett was a pretty, dark-haired woman who showed up twenty minutes later driving a white BMW convertible. This woman must be loaded, Maggie thought. She had on dark sunglasses, had chin-length straight black hair, and wore what looked to be a cashmere dark purple sweater and tan wool slacks. She pulled out a burgundy Michael Kors bag, which she shrugged onto her shoulder and walked carefully to the porch.

She pushed the door open and took her sunglasses off.

"Are you Scarlett?" Maggie asked, standing up and walking around the counter.

"Yes, I am," Scarlett said.

Maggie reached out to shake her hand. "I'm Maggie. Nice to meet you. Let's go over here to this table where we can talk." She pointed over to a corner of the shop where there was a round table covered with a white lacy tablecloth surrounded by four French bistro folding chairs.

"How charming," Scarlett said, walking over to the table.

Maggie picked up her laptop, a notebook and pen, and joined her at the table. They both sat down and Maggie opened up her computer, flipped open her notebook, and began to write.

"How do you spell your name?"

Scarlett spelled her first and last names for her.

"What's a good number to reach you?"

She wrote down Scarlett's cell phone number.

"Now, are you looking to buy a house or rent?"

"Rent."

"On the beach, the bay, or somewhere in between?"

"Beach, definitely."

Maggie smiled. "I agree. Did Catrina tell you that we're neighbors?"

"Yes, she did. You have a nice house, what I saw of it."

"Thank you."

"I've always wanted a house on the beach."

"The view alone is worth it. How big of a house will you need?"

"A small house, two bedrooms is fine. There are only two of us, my son and me."

"I see." Maggie kept writing. "How long were you thinking of renting for?"

"I don't know…maybe six months?"

Maggie looked up at her and could've sworn the woman's eyes were watering. Maybe she had allergies. "Six months?"

Scarlett nodded.

Maggie put her pen down and looked closely at Scarlett, noticing now that she had dark circles under her eyes, was very pale, and extremely gaunt. She tried not to judge people or get in their business too much, but this woman looked like she'd been through a lot.

"So you're not looking for a vacation rental or a permanent home?"

"No, I just need a place to rest. I've been sick recently."

That explained the dark circles and weight loss. "There aren't too many homes in Sandbridge that are rented for that long of a period of time, unless they rent on a yearly basis. Otherwise, people rent the vacation rentals for a week or two, a month tops, and most people would have already booked something in the next six months, especially with the holidays coming up. Are you sure you don't want to rent for year, or maybe buy a house? You could always sell it again in six months if you needed to, or you could rent it out when you don't need it anymore."

Scarlett looked down at her pale un-manicured hands, which she rubbed together nervously. She looked back up and spoke softly. "No, I don't want to buy a house, and I don't know exactly how long I'll need it. You see, I'm dying."

Maggie gasped.

"I have terminal cancer. I live in a big lonely house out in the country that I have to hire a maid to clean. I want to spend my last days in a small comfortable house on the ocean where I can watch the sunrise every morning."

"Oh, Scarlett." Maggie reached across and squeezed her hands. "I'm so sorry." She hadn't imagined Scarlett's tears earlier. "Of course, I'll see what I can do to find something that will suit your needs."

Scarlett sniffed and said, "Thank you."

"How soon would you need this?"

"As soon as possible."

Scarlett got into a 2010 silver Audi with Maggie, which was pristine on the inside. Maggie had looked up some beach houses and came up with one in particular she thought Scarlett might be interested in.

"This house just came on the market this morning. It has three bedrooms, is right on the ocean, and the buyers are eager to sell quick," Maggie said. "I haven't even seen the house myself, but the picture from the back deck shows that there are big sand dunes between the beach and the house. That would be a good sound barrier from all the people who walk up and down the beach, and it deters people from getting too nosy about what your house looks like on the inside. My house has big dunes in the back, too. I guess you saw when you were out there this morning."

"Yes, I did notice that."

They drove along the curvy road that emptied out at a big water tower, a fire station, and a market across the street from the beach. Maggie drove right past her own house and kept going maybe fifteen houses down when she stopped in front of an overgrown yard. Her phone announced that they had arrived and she looked up at the property. "There must be a house in there somewhere." She laughed.

Scarlett couldn't see it very well and got out of the car for a better look. Maggie did the same. The house was built up on top of a dune so it was elevated. The house was hidden by an array of foliage, flowers, short palms, banana leaf plants, small pine trees, cacti, and even some dreaded Virginia creeper. Upon closer inspection, Scarlett saw a porch with white railing behind some bushes, but it was in bad need of a coat of paint. Since it was up on an incline, there was no need for the stilts that so many beach houses had. The roofline had an A-frame, the siding was pale yellow, and the front porch wrapped around the house. A sign across the bottom of the A-frame read, "Kissed by the Sun."

There was some Bermuda grass and weeds but mostly sand for a yard, and tall yucca plants lined the sidewalk. Maggie and Scarlett walked up to the porch, and Maggie got out the key while Scarlett looked around the corner to see how far the porch went. It stretched all the way to the back where she could glimpse the ocean beyond. It was a beautiful view.

"I'm sorry, this one needs a lot of work, it seems. Let's take a look at the inside."

The inside wasn't much better than the outside. The smell of cigarette smoke and mildew hit them as soon as they opened the door. There was outdated dark brown paneling on the walls. A staircase covered with dingy tan carpet was to the right of the doorway. To the left across the foyer was a small bathroom, which had pink tile everywhere. Down from that was a small kitchen with cabinets covered with several layers of thick white paint. The white appliances were smudged with fingerprints, and sand and cigarette butts littered the floor. The room opened up to a decent-sized living room at the back of the house with a vaulted ceiling and a loft up above. Three big windows at the back of the room were covered up with old cheap blinds.

Maggie immediately pulled up the blinds, one of which broke in the process.

"Oops," she said, laughing. She opened the other two slower and remarked, "Now, that's a lot better. What about that view, huh?"

It was gorgeous. Scarlett could see the ocean over the dunes, and could imagine herself watching the sunrise every morning, just like she'd envisioned. "It's wonderful," she said softly.

"I'm sorry about the condition of the house," Maggie said. "Some people just don't know how to sell a house. This is where I usually come in and have the walls painted, have maids come in and clean the place from top to bottom, and borrow some nice pieces from Jen's shop to make it look homey."

"It does need some work," Scarlett admitted.

"I wanted to show it to you right away, though, even if it does look rough. I already asked the owners about renting indefinitely, told them your situation, and they're fine with it. It has been neglected for the past two years. The couple that lived here were military and moved away but rented it out through another company. We have just now acquired the property. Obviously, the other company didn't keep it up very well or maybe some renters have trashed it."

They walked out the back door to a nice-sized deck, which was empty. Scarlett would like to put a table and chairs out here for dining and some nice cushioned deck furniture for relaxing and gazing. They went back inside and walked through one bedroom downstairs and another one upstairs along with a small loft overlooking the living room, and another bathroom. There were beds in the bedrooms, a queen in the one downstairs and two twins in the upstairs one, and a couple of tables, but otherwise sparse decorations.

It was old, musty, and needed a lot of work, but Scarlett still loved it. It had potential. She loved the view and even liked the hidden area at the front of the house. She didn't want any nosy people invading her privacy. She could see herself having coffee every morning on the deck overlooking the dunes and ocean beyond, and watching her son play on the beach with friends.

"So what do you think?" Maggie asked her.

"I love it."

Maggie looked surprised, but then she smiled. "Really? Even with all this mess?"

"It needs some work, but I think it could be beautiful. Peaceful. Just what I need."

"The sunrises are unbelievable on the ocean. Just wait and see! I think you're going to be amazed."

"I'm sure I will be."

"Are you sure you don't want me to look for anything else?"

"No, this is it."

"Great. That was easy." She laughed. "I'll have a cleaning service come out and get this all cleaned up for you first thing in the morning. After that, I could call a landscaping service to come and clear out some of that mess out front if you'd like."

Scarlett thought she could do some of the gardening herself. She used to enjoy doing that at her house in Pungo, when she was well enough. It was relaxing to her, to feel the dirt in her hands, seeing something ugly turn into something beautiful.

"No, I think I'd like to work on that myself. I kind of like the idea of being hidden from the busy road, too. The cleaning service would be nice, though."

"Of course. How soon would you like to move in?"

"As soon as you get this place clean," she said, smiling for the first time that day.

"Sounds great. Let's go back to the office and sign some paperwork."

Chapter Three

A week later, Scarlett was at her big house deep in Pungo, trying to decide what to take to the beach house and what to keep at this house. She wouldn't need everything, and of course there wouldn't be room for it all anyway. This house was nearly five thousand square feet, was made of stone on the outside, and was Victorian in style with a turret on one side of the long front porch. The formal rooms on the first floor were opulently decorated with French and English furniture from the nineteenth century, and a few from the eighteenth. There were brass chandeliers in each room, statues, grand vases filled with flowers, and portraits of bygone family members.

She had only recently inherited the huge house and surrounding ten acres of land after her mother's death a year before. She hadn't changed any of it, and even left her mother's room exactly as it had been before she wasn't well enough to go up the stairs anymore and stayed in a small parlor downstairs instead. The house had many fond memories, especially when both her parents had been happy when she was a child, but was also full of sad ones. She was ready to move to a happier place.

She was folding some clothes into a suitcase when she heard the doorbell chimes. Her housekeeper, Blanche, a light-skinned black woman, came up to her bedroom and knocked on the door a few minutes later.

"Forgive me, Miss Scarlett, but there's a gentleman here to see you," Blanche said in a pleasant Virginia accent. She was widowed and had a grown daughter who lived in nearby Ghent in Norfolk. She'd served the family since Scarlett was a young girl. She was like a second mother to

Scarlett and the two had grown close in the last year after her mother's passing. She had been a close friend of her mother's during school. When Scarlett told her she was moving to the beach, Blanche cried and protested, but in the end decided that she would go live with her daughter in Norfolk.

Scarlett wondered who the male visitor could be. "Anybody we know?" she asked.

"No, ma'am," Blanche said.

Scarlett sighed and put the sweater she was folding into her suitcase. "Thank you, I'll be right down."

"Shall I send him to your sitting room upstairs, ma'am? That way you won't have to go up and down those stairs."

Scarlett nodded. "That'll be fine. Thank you."

When Scarlett walked into the sitting room at the far end of the second floor overlooking a gazebo and surrounding rose garden, she was surprised to see Jackson. He was looking out the windows at the garden.

"Jackson," she said. "What are you doing here?"

He turned around and smiled at her warmly. Walking over to her, he reached out his hands and took hers. "Scarlett, you're looking as lovely as ever." He kissed each of her hands.

She smiled. "You're a liar but thank you for the compliment."

"Have you found a beach house yet?" he asked her.

"I have," she said, sitting down on a beige velvet curved sofa.

"You have an exquisite home. Why would you want to leave it?" he asked.

She sighed and looked at her hands. "I've already told you I want to live someplace happy. This house has some good memories but also some sad ones. I don't want to think about the sad ones any longer."

Jackson sat across from her in a chair covered in tapestry beside an ornate fireplace made of mahogany. He looked like he belonged there, so regal and yet so comfortable. He was quite handsome in gray slacks, a dark gray V-neck sweater, and a white collared shirt peeking out beneath it. His dark eyes were warm and friendly, his lashes long and eyebrows dark to match his neatly combed hair.

"How did you know where to find me?" she asked.

"I have my ways," he said, smiling.

She guessed the oncologist's office must've given her address to him to check up on her.

"Do you need help moving?"

"Oh, that's not necessary. Surely you have better things to do with your time."

"Really, I don't. I'd love to help."

"Well…if you're sure. I could use a man's strong arms."

He smiled at her and she smiled back.

"I was just trying to decide how much to take over when you arrived. I have nearly one suitcase full and another one already full of my son's things. We can start with those if you'd like."

"What about heavy furniture?"

"Yes, I'm going to take all of my bedroom furniture and also my son's. I'll use the casual sofa and chairs from there for the parlor in the beach house." She sighed. "I'll confess it exhausts me to think of everything I have to do to move over there. I may as well just hire some movers."

"Nonsense. I'll help you."

She showed him the things that needed to be moved, and then he told her to sit back and relax while he effortlessly moved all the furniture and boxes out for her, singlehandedly. She'd never seen a stronger man. How he moved the sofa by himself was beyond her. She hadn't actually witnessed that part, as she had been in the bathroom, but she saw it later in the back of a small panel truck out in the driveway.

She drove her car ahead of him and they took it all over to the beach house. She unlocked the front door and led the way inside to show Jackson before they got down to moving stuff in. The first thing she noticed was the smell of fresh paint. All of the walls had been painted off-white, the carpets on the floor had been replaced in a warm beige color, and as she walked through the house, she saw that the bathrooms had been cleaned, the window treatments had been laundered and nice new plantation blinds had been put up. It was a vast improvement to the hellhole it had been before.

Back in the kitchen on top of the bar was a fresh bouquet of sunflowers in a green vase, a bowl of cinnamon-scented potpourri, and a card from Maggie, welcoming her to her new home and thanking her for her business. Maggie also wrote down her cell number to call for anything she needed, anytime. She also left her brochures for businesses, restaurants, and pharmacies close by, a gift card to Baja Restaurant just down the road, and some coupons.

While she was looking at the card and brochures, Jackson had slipped out and started unloading her furniture. "Where do you want this?" he asked, carrying the sofa over his head.

"Jackson! How in the world are you carrying that sofa?" She was astonished at his strength.

"If you'll tell me where it goes, I won't hurt myself."

She pointed into the family room where it should be placed. She followed him out for more furniture, and in the time it took her to roll her luggage in, he had made three trips with heavy furniture. When she went back for Tyler's suitcase, he had completely filled the house with furniture.

Her eyes bulged. "How did you do that so fast?" She looked across into the family room, and the furniture had been arranged exactly how she'd had it in her bedroom, very neatly. It looked like home to her now. She felt tears well up in her eyes and she quickly blinked them away.

"Did I do something wrong?" he asked, seeing her expression but taking it the wrong way.

"Oh, no. You've been wonderful. It feels like home now."

She walked over to him and felt his biceps. "You are the strongest man I have ever seen," she said, and then laughed.

He laughed, too. "Thank you."

And then he pulled her into his arms like it was the most natural thing in the world.

Jackson held Scarlett for a few moments, feeling like he needed to comfort her in this changing time of her life, trying to deny the fact that he was attracted to her. She was doing something to him. He wasn't sure what was happening between them, but he felt a strong connection to her.

"Would you like me to go grocery shopping for you?"

"Why are you doing all of this for me?" she asked meekly.

He wondered the same thing himself. He pulled away and gazed into her big green eyes. She was so beautiful. He'd seen countless women but none compared to her beauty. She had porcelain skin on her face as if the sun had never touched it, dark hair that he knew was a wig but was reminiscent of the color of long lustrous hair she used to have, small lips that perched perfectly on her face. He shrugged his shoulders. "Just trying to be helpful."

She pulled away from him and smiled. "Well, I do appreciate it, but you must have other things to do, other clients to see."

He shook his head. He wasn't ready to leave her just yet. "No, really. If you want to come with me, we can shop together. I can show you how you should shop from now on."

She raised one eyebrow. "You're going to show a woman how to shop?"

He laughed. "You should buy all organic foods, nothing processed. Drink pure water, no faucet water. Drink kefir every day, get some amino acids and other natural supplements. We could get you a bread maker for fresh bread, a Nutri-Bullet for homemade smoothies." He looked down, not realizing he was rubbing her arm. He stopped and put his hand down to his side. "Do you like honey?"

She nodded.

"You could put that in some tea and drink it two or three times a day. It's the perfect natural sweetener, and tea has lots of antioxidants."

"What good is all of that going to do me when I'm going to die anyway?"

She had a sad look on her face that he wished he could erase. He wished he could change her fate. As an angel of death, he'd had to tell many people they were dying and usually told them right away. He'd held other women before who blubbered on about their upcoming demise. But Scarlett was different. She was both vulnerable and strong at the same time. Weak in body but strong in mind and determination. He'd been watching her, checking in on her from time to time and had seen her slowly lose hope. When he saw her shaking at the Halloween party, the emotion she was trying to hold back when she realized he'd been right about her condition, he had a strange desire to comfort her. Really comfort her. And when he'd held her in his arms, he began to feel a warmth inside of him, an unusual feeling compared to his usual coldness and nonchalance. Oh, he could laugh and have a good time, flirt a little, but he'd never felt compassion like this before. It intrigued him, made him want to spend more time with her.

She was the first person he regretted telling what he was and why he was really there, which was why he would put it off for a little while longer. He wanted to get to know her better first.

"You're right, it doesn't matter," he said, answering her question, "but it might make you feel better, might extend your life a couple of months. Wouldn't it be worth it to be with your son a couple more months?"

She reluctantly nodded and let out a deep sigh.

"It also might help you feel better, not so sluggish, especially if you incorporate walking thirty minutes every day. And get up and watch the sunrise every morning that you can."

"That part I can do for sure." She looked at her phone. "All right, where shall we go shopping? Walmart?"

"Might I suggest some place more like Trader Joe's or Whole Foods? The farmer's market would be good, too."

"The farmer's market is closer. Let's start there."

"All right. Après vous, mademoiselle," he said, motioning for her to lead the way.

She smiled brightly, warming his cold heart, and said, "Mais oui, bien sûr."

Chapter Four

"Catrina, it's good to see you," Scarlett said, hugging her friend and co-worker. Catrina was a tall blonde woman with deep dimples in both cheeks.

It was the following weekend, and Maggie was throwing a housewarming party for Scarlett. She had invited a few of Scarlett's co-workers and some of Maggie's friends and neighbors.

"Which house do you live in again? I forgot," Scarlett asked Catrina. They had been co-workers for a couple of years but really hadn't hung out much outside of work.

"It's about, oh maybe four or five houses down from here towards the red light, a two-story green house with white trim. It's called *Beachcomber*."

"Beachcomber. Okay. I'll walk down there soon. Come on in."

"I don't think you've ever met my daughter before, have you?" Catrina introduced her daughter, Arianna, who was also blonde and wore stylish black-rimmed glasses. She was carrying a big white box.

"So nice to meet you. What's in the box? Not a present, I hope. I don't need anything, honestly." She looked at Arianna and then at Catrina.

"It's pastries for the party. I thought you might like something French. I remember you talking about the pastries you used to get in France, so I looked up a recipe."

"Oh, patisseries?! What kind?"

"Chocolate éclairs. I hope you like chocolate."

"But of course. Who doesn't?"

They both laughed.

"Thank you so much. You can sit that down on the bar right over there," Scarlett said.

A nice looking man with short dark hair and a nice full beard ran up to the door.

"Hi, I'm Jim, Catrina's boyfriend."

"Nice to meet you. I'm Scarlett."

A couple of other co-workers from State Farm also came, as well as a few more neighbors, names Scarlett would soon forget, and each with a dish in their hands. Maggie had insisted upon everyone bringing food so Scarlett wouldn't have to do anything.

Luke and his pretty new bride came in a few minutes later.

"How nice to see you again, Scarlett," Jen said, surprising her with a hug. "I'm so glad you found a beach house. This place is great."

"Thank you. Maggie was kind enough to send a cleaning service out here to help. It was a mess when I did my first walk-through. I still want to get out there in the garden and get rid of some of the weeds."

Luke was holding several containers and couldn't shake her hand or anything. He just smiled and said, "Hey, nice to see you again, Scarlett."

"You too, Luke. Come on in."

"Sorry, baby. Let me take one of those," Jen said, taking a big bowl out of Luke's hands.

"Just put them on the bar," Scarlett told them.

Luke walked past her, laid the bowls on the bar, and looked back at her again. She thought he was still trying to figure out where they'd met before. He wouldn't recognize her name, though. She never gave her first name to strange men, but her middle French name instead. It was more exotic and harder to contact her again if she didn't want to be, if she didn't like them well enough for a second date. Luke would perhaps remember her as Juliandra.

Three teenagers walked in, and Jen introduced them to Scarlett as being Luke's daughter, Cassie, her boyfriend Skyler, and Logan, who was a son that Jen and Luke had together. Behind them were another teenage girl and a man. Maggie introduced them to be her ex-husband, Steve, and Steve's daughter, Emily.

The names were beginning to swim around in Scarlett's head, and she was beginning to feel a little overwhelmed. She smiled pleasantly and looked at Tyler, who was already getting acquainted with Arianna. She excused herself to go to a private bathroom upstairs. She used the facilities and then sat down on one of the twin beds in Tyler's room for a moment to rest and collect herself before going back down. She nearly fainted when she looked across the room and saw Jackson standing outside on the balcony overlooking the ocean. She got up and opened the French door.

"Jackson! What are you doing up here?"

"You know, you're going to make me think you don't want me around if you're always so surprised to see me. I think that hurts my feelings a little bit."

She laughed. He could always make her laugh. "Don't be ridiculous. Why would I not be surprised? Everyone else is downstairs, and I didn't even know you were here. When did you get here?"

"Just now." He was grinning at her. "Do you need a moment alone?"

She sobered and said, "I did, but…I'm glad you're here."

He smiled. "That's a much better greeting." He pulled her close to him and kissed each cheek like the French do. He was such a charming man. She'd better be careful. He was starting to do funny things to her heart.

"Is there a reason you're up here alone instead of entertaining your friends?" he asked.

"Well, for one thing, I heard of the dreadful news of what happened in Paris last night," she said. There had been several terrorist attacks in Paris and many people were dead. Since her father lived in France, she was naturally worried.

"Oh, yes. That was terrible. Do you have family over there?"

She nodded. "My father, yes, but he doesn't live in Paris. He lives in Toulon."

"Have you talked to him?"

She'd called him on the phone last night. "Yes, he's fine."

"I'm glad." He pulled her into his arms again for another hug and asked her, "Have you told Tyler's father about him yet?"

"No."

"He's here now, why don't you do it?"

She pulled back and looked at him, her eyes wide. "How do you know who Tyler's father is?" She didn't know how he could know that. Information like that wouldn't be in her medical records, unless he had access to her hospital records.

"It's true, isn't it? Luke is the father?"

She nodded her head reluctantly. She was beginning to get a little suspicious of him but also nervous about telling Luke about Tyler. She walked across the room and sat back down in the corner chair, straightening out her dark green lacy dress. Jackson followed and stood beside her.

"It's time he knew, isn't it?"

"But he's newly married. I don't want to mess up his life."

"He deserves to know. You have to think about Tyler. Do you want him growing up without a mother *and* a father? One is better than none."

"You're right, of course." She looked down at her hands and then out towards the ocean. "It must be fate bringing us back together like this. I haven't seen him since Tyler was conceived. I didn't know how to contact him. We were just strangers in the night." She hadn't even remembered his last name.

Jackson nodded. "Would you like something for your nerves? Valium? A joint?"

She laughed.

"I'm not joking," he said. He patted the pocket of his navy blue jacket.

She shook her head. "No thank you."

"Okay, maybe I'll fix you a drink, something to calm you a little and give you courage. Do you have drinks set up downstairs?"

"Yes."

He offered his arm and helped her up, and she led the way back downstairs.

Luke Callaway looked around the room and watched his bride talking and laughing with her best friend Maggie. God, he loved that woman. They'd just gotten back from their honeymoon, and he'd never been happier. They'd explored the historical town of Savannah on foot, took romantic carriage rides, and toured a couple of old houses. Then they'd relaxed on the beach at Tybee Island, listening to the waves and falling deeper in love with each other. And in bed…that woman was a wildcat.

He blinked his eyes, looked over at the staircase, and saw Scarlett walk down with a dark-haired tall man who looked familiar. Where had he seen him before? Maybe at one of Cassie's cross country meets?

The two of them walked over to the kitchen where the man fixed up a drink and handed it to Scarlett.

He was wracking his brain trying to remember where he knew her from. She looked familiar, too. He was almost sure they'd had sex in the past. He could never forget that accent. He didn't remember her name being Scarlett, though. He thought it was something more French.

She took a long deep sip of the drink, looked around the room and her eyes rested on him. He smiled faintly, worried that Jen might see them and get the wrong idea. The last thing he wanted to do was make Jen jealous. She could be a fireball when she was jealous.

Scarlett walked over to him. "Luke, I was wondering if we could speak privately for a moment."

He looked at Jen, who was talking to a blonde woman, and he nodded his head. "Sure."

She led the way to a back deck, and after she closed the sliding glass door, he asked, "Have we met before?"

She nodded. "Yes, we have."

"Did we…" he asked, bumping his fists together two times to insinuate having sex.

She nodded again and smiled a little. "I was wondering if you recognized me when I came by Maggie's a couple of weeks ago."

"Honestly, I didn't. I knew you looked vaguely familiar but it didn't hit me until just a moment ago that we'd…been together before. How are you?"

"I'm okay."

"Was there something you wanted to talk about?" She seemed to be stalling, and her expression looked worried, nervous.

"Yes…but not here, not now. I don't want your pretty wife getting mad at me. Could we talk sometime, maybe have coffee? I promise it won't take long, but I have something I need to ask you."

"Sure." He wondered what that was all about. Maybe she just needed help with something around the house. "Is your name really Scarlett? I thought it was something more French."

She smiled. "Juliandra – that's my middle name. That's the name I give to strange men in bars."

He laughed. "I see. Your hair looks nice that way, but didn't it used to be a lot longer? I seem to recall it touched your butt."

She looked down, "Yes, I…I have cancer," she whispered, and at the same moment, Jen walked out onto the deck.

She must've heard what Scarlett said because she gasped. Luke and Scarlett both turned and looked at her.

"Oh Scarlett, I had no idea. I'm so sorry," Jen said.

Scarlett smiled faintly and said, "I asked Maggie not to say anything. I was just telling your husband that we had met before. He didn't remember me at first."

"Oh?" Jen looked like she didn't know what else to say.

A young boy with straight blonde hair came running out the door past Jen and rushed up to Scarlett. "Maman, look at this!" He was holding up a dinosaur. "Logan gave it to me."

"Tyler. How many times have I asked you not to interrupt me when I'm talking with grown-ups, hmm?" She smiled at him despite her scolding.

"Sorry, Maman."

"Let me introduce you to these nice people."

After she made introductions, she pulled Tyler's back against her and wrapped her arms around him. "Sorry for the interruption. Shall we all go back inside?"

Later when Luke and his family were leaving the party, Scarlett slipped a business card into his hand discreetly. He looked at it later and read her name and phone number with a State Farm logo at the top. On the back was written, *Coffee @ Margie & Ray's 11 am tomorrow?*

He put the card inside his wallet before getting in the bed with Jen for the night. He again wondered what Scarlett wanted to talk to him about. Maybe she just needed someone to watch Tyler for her while she underwent cancer treatments or something like that. He nuzzled up to Jen, and Scarlett and her little boy were quickly forgotten.

Chapter Five

Sixteen-year-old Cassie Callaway was sitting with her boyfriend Skyler on the upstairs covered porch overlooking the backyard of her house. It hadn't always been her house, but she had stayed here a lot over the past ten years whenever her dad traveled with his job. It was where her Aunt Jen – now her stepmom – lived and owned a shop downstairs. Jen and her dad recently married and since her dad lost his job, they sold their other house and moved into this one with Jen and Logan.

Cassie didn't know until recently that Logan, whom she thought was just her cousin, was also her half-brother. He was also sixteen and was the product of a teenage romance between her dad and Jen that until recently no one else knew about. Jen had kept it a secret because of Luke being married to her sister, who died ten years ago, and later, because she was just plain scared of losing him. Cassie was happy the whole family was together now.

She and Skyler were sitting in a swing bundled under a blanket while an electric fan circled above their heads, moved by the wind. It was early Sunday morning, and he had come over as soon as his dad would bring him.

"Did you see Jackson at Scarlett's?" she dared to ask Skyler.

Jackson and Skyler were angels, and although Skyler was now human – permanently – Jackson was still an angel of death, and he was known to punish other guardian angels and their humans when they didn't obey the rules. Skyler had been punished for, among many things, spending too much time with Cassie, kissing her, falling in love with her, and for performing a healing through her of another human. His punishment was that he had to go back in time and take the body of a little boy – the son of Jen's ex-husband Brad, who also used to be a guardian angel, and his wife Juliet. Skyler had to wait ten years before he could speak to Cassie again, to the point where angel Skyler was going to go back in time. Angel Skyler and human Skyler couldn't be in contact with each other or else there would be more punishments. Skyler had just recently turned.

Skyler nodded. "Yeah, I saw him."

Cassie pulled his arm into her lap and she looked at him. "What do you think he wants? Do you think he knows that I remember everything?"

Jackson and Skyler both had tried to erase all of Cassie's memories of all things related to them being angels, but she remembered everything. She had been afraid to say anything about it until Skyler's mom, Juliet, approached her about it. Her theory was that true love was the reason she didn't forget what Skyler was. They both agreed that it needed to be kept secret, but Cassie had wanted to tell Skyler that she knew. She wanted him to know how much she appreciated what he did to be with her and how much she loved him all the more for it. They talked about it briefly at her dad's and Jen's wedding, and this was only the second time they had talked about it.

"I don't know." Skyler looked worried. He blinked and looked at Cassie, leaned over and kissed her lips. "Don't worry about it. I'll talk to him and find out what's going on."

"Maybe my time is up. Or yours," she said, still worrying.

"I don't think so. He would have said something to us by now. It was probably someone else at the party."

Cassie hoped it wasn't her dad. He'd been in two car accidents in his life, one that resulted in her mother's death, and his latest one resulted in a coma and a broken ankle. He'd had enough brushes with death for her liking.

"Did you notice how much older he looked? He could be in his thirties," Cassie said.

"Yeah, I did notice. Maybe whoever he's helping is older, then. That may be our first clue."

She looked out at the yard thoughtfully, barely noticing that the leaves on the apple tree were changing into shades of deep yellow. "I guess so."

Skyler turned her to look him straight in the eyes. "We're not supposed to talk about this, remember? I'll talk to him, I promise. Next time I see him."

She nodded her head and he kissed her again, pulled her against him, and she forgot all about Jackson.

Jen and Luke were downstairs in the shop, moving things around, getting new products ready to sell. Luke had suggested that they expand the shop and maybe add in some things that local horse ranchers might need – saddles, brushes, spurs, that sort of thing. Jen had agreed it was a good idea. There weren't many shops in the little area of Virginia Beach called Pungo, where she lived and worked. It was the house she and Luke had inherited from Jen's mother, and she now had an antique shop called Jen's Antiques downstairs while living upstairs.

It had been a fine arrangement until two more people moved in. Now the four-bedroom house with only two bathrooms was a snug fit, though Jen couldn't be happier. She was finally married to the love of her life, and so she overlooked having to share the bathroom more, having to cook more, and not having much privacy. She wouldn't trade a minute of it for anything.

They'd only been back from their honeymoon a week and already they were setting up the new things, trying to make a "horses" corner of the shop. Luke was let go from his last government contract job, so he was helping out in the shop for now until he decided what else he wanted to do. After years of going from one government contracting job to the next, he was sick of that line of work and didn't want to return to it, so he didn't know what else he could do to make a living. He was also the lead singer and guitarist in a new-country band called Renegades but they only played occasionally at local restaurants and didn't make enough money to pay the bills.

Luke was polishing a saddle while Jen was setting up stationery sets with drawings of horses on the front. They worked companionably side by side in silence for a while.

"It's sad about Scarlett, isn't it?" Jen said. She had been looking for Luke at Scarlett's house when she'd inadvertently heard Scarlett say that she had cancer.

"Yeah, it really is," Luke said.

"Wonder what kind of cancer she has? Do you know?"

"Nope, she didn't say. I heard it for the first time when you did."

She finished putting price tags on each box and then asked him, "Where do you know her from?" She'd been dying to ask him that since the previous day, but she didn't want to seem like a suspicious wife. She loved him dearly and trusted him, but he'd had a lot of girlfriends and one-night stands in the past.

"Uh," Luke said, "the thing is…I've slept with her before."

Jen stopped cold. Her worst fear had come true. That gorgeous French-speaking woman had been intimate with her husband. Even if she did feel sorry for the woman for having cancer, it still made her extremely jealous. She felt tears but blinked several times to keep them at bay. "You did?" she asked, her voice a higher pitch than usual.

"Yeah. You know my history with women?"

She nodded sadly. "Yes, I do."

"Well, this is one of those women."

"She's very beautiful. I can see the attraction." Jen fought hard to keep jealousy out of her tone.

"She is, but that's all in the past. You know that, right?" He laid his polishing rag down and then walked over and took her in his arms.

"Yes, I do."

He looked in her eyes. "You're the only woman I'll be sleeping with for the rest of our lives."

He kissed her on the lips.

"Thank you for telling me," Jen said.

"There's one more thing. Something I want to ask you."

"What's that?"

He let go of her and pushed a strand of her hair off her forehead. "Scarlett asked to speak with me privately. She wants to meet me at Margie & Ray's this morning at eleven. Would that be okay with you?"

Jen looked at her phone for a moment. It was ten o'clock. While she was still jealous, she felt like she could trust Luke to just be cordial with the woman and not be tempted by her. She nodded her head. "Yes, that'll be fine. I appreciate you asking me first."

Luke let out his breath like he'd been holding it. He took her back in his arms again and said, "Thanks for understanding. I can't imagine what she wants to talk to me about, but I didn't want to keep any secrets from you."

She smiled. "Thanks, baby."

He kissed her lips tenderly and then passionately until her knees were weak.

"I've got the best wife in the world," he murmured.

She smiled. "And don't you forget it."

Chapter Six

"Thanks for meeting with me," Scarlett said. She was sitting at a table at the back of the restaurant when Luke walked up to the table. Margie & Ray's was a quaint restaurant that served mostly seafood as well as a good breakfast, located on the long road that led to Sandbridge Beach.

"Of course," he said, shaking her hand before sitting down across the table from her.

"I've taken the liberty of ordering coffee for both of us," she said, motioning to the carafe. "Do you take cream in yours?" She pointed to the little containers of half-and-half in a small bowl.

"Yes, thanks."

He poured himself a cup and she watched as he fumbled with the little container of milk and cream. He must be nervous, she thought, and wondering why on earth she would ask to meet with him.

The waitress came up to the table and asked if they wanted anything to eat, breakfast or lunch, whatever they wanted. Scarlett asked for a spinach and feta omelet while Luke ordered a country ham biscuit.

"My…I guess you'd call him a hospice worker, I'm not really sure what he does…he told me I should eat fresh food and avoid processed foods. So, I'll be eating this omelet but wishing I had your biscuit," she said, smiling.

He laughed lightly. "Is that the man I saw you with at the party?"

She nodded. "Yes, his name is Jackson."

"I think he might work at my daughter's school or something. He looked familiar."

"Oh, I don't think so. He works for my oncologist."

"Hmm," Luke said, looking thoughtful. "Does he have any children?"

Did he? She wondered. "Not that I know of." She had only known him a short time and just realized that he never talked about himself.

She took a drink of coffee and decided to get right down to the reason she'd asked him here. "Luke, I told you I had cancer…but I didn't tell you how serious it is. I'm dying. This is my second time with it…it's gone into the lymph nodes. I've had chemotherapy, mastectomies, reconstructive surgery, everything, but it won't go away. I'm terminal." She had to stop to swallow a sob.

"Oh God, Scarlett. I'm so sorry," Luke said. He reached out with both of his hands to cover hers. "There's nothing else they can do?"

She shook her head, sniffed, and closed her eyes momentarily. "I have a bit of news for you that's going to come as a shock – a bigger one than this cancer."

"What's that?"

"Tyler is your son."

She watched the color drain out of Luke's face. He withdrew his hands and pushed his hair back with one of them. "What?" he finally managed to say.

"I am so sorry. I didn't know how to get in touch with you. I couldn't remember your last name, if you even told it to me. I even went back to the same bar and asked, but they didn't know either. I figured it was just as well, anyway. We were only together one night, and I didn't think you'd want this burden."

"But how? We used protection. I always used protection."

"Sometimes it doesn't work. There could've been a little pin-sized hole. Believe me, I've been through all the scenarios myself."

"Are you sure I'm the father? I know how that sounds, but are you?"

She nodded, understanding why he would ask the question. "Yes, it's yours. You can have a DNA test if you'd like, but I didn't have sex with anybody else in the few months before or after I found out."

Their food arrived and was a nice distraction for a moment. She didn't feel hungry anymore, and the smell of the spinach nauseated her somewhat. She pushed it aside, determined to keep going. She poured more coffee into her cup, blew on it, and took a sip. "I suspected that I was pregnant after missing a period after you and I had sex. So I went to my doctor for an exam, and he confirmed that I was pregnant but also said that I had breast cancer. They did an ultrasound and found it. I remember them telling me they couldn't do a mammogram or X-ray because of the pregnancy. That was crazy, huh? I just went in there thinking I was pregnant and ended up finding out I had cancer. They said I had two choices. I could wait until the baby was born before doing chemo, or that I could abort the baby since it was small enough, and start chemo immediately." She shook her head. "I could never abort a baby, so I chose the life of my baby and to wait for the chemo, despite the risks."

Luke finished his ham biscuit and said, "What an awful decision to have to make. Did everything work out okay? Tyler looks like a healthy boy."

"Yes, I delivered a healthy boy and then began chemo immediately after. It was rough, but I had my mother to help me." She took a bite of the omelet, feeling the need for sustenance. After chewing and swallowing the cheesy egg, she said, "My mother passed away recently, so I don't have her to lean on this time."

Luke's hand went on her arm. "I'm so sorry." He shook his head. "You've had a run of bad luck, it seems."

She nodded. "That leads me to my important question I wanted to ask you. Are you interested in having a relationship with your son at all? I need someone to care for him when I…when I'm gone."

Luke couldn't believe what he was hearing. One night many years earlier, he'd had casual sex with a woman he'd just met, and now he found out he'd impregnated her. This was the second time he'd found out he had a son, the second time he learned the consequences of his past actions. Tyler was a lot younger than Logan was and would need a lot more care.

What was Jen going to think now? Would she be as forgiving after he told her he had another son?

"You don't have anyone else in your family who could care for him? I'm not saying no, but, man this is bad timing. I just got married."

"I know and I'm so sorry to do this to you now. I do have a male cousin who lives in Nashville, so if you don't want anything to do with Tyler, I totally understand. I'm not trying to trick you into anything. I just thought that you would like to know that you fathered a terrific…" She choked on her words and had tears in her eyes. "...little boy, and I wanted to give you the choice. I made a difficult choice before. I could have easily aborted him. I was unmarried, I didn't know how to contact you, and I had cancer. But I chose life. If there was a chance that I could care for a precious baby, I wanted to take it. Now it's your choice. You can choose to be part of this boy's life, or you can carry on as you were, and I won't tell another soul who his father is."

Luke took a deep breath and let it all out. He sat back in his chair, wondering what to do. "I don't know, Scarlett. It's a huge decision, and I'll have to talk to Jen about it."

"Of course, take your time." She took another sip of coffee.

"How old is Tyler?"

"Seven."

That would've been three years after his first wife, Josie, had died. He was in his drunken didn't-care-about-anything, mad-at-the-world phase. If he'd only known then that Jen still had feelings for him, he would never have had sex with this woman. Would've never fathered a child out of wedlock. But then, it seemed that Tyler had been a good thing for her while she was going through cancer. Maybe it was a blessing in disguise, meant to be.

Except now she was dying, and he didn't know what to do.

"Have you and Tyler been happy? Have you needed anything? God, I could've helped finance things."

She smiled at him. "We've been very happy, and don't worry, we haven't needed a thing. We lived with my mother until her passing, and she made sure we were well taken care of. My father...he's not well. He lives in France, and I haven't seen him in years. He's unable to care for Tyler, so I don't even want to ask him."

More bad news. This woman truly had a long string of bad luck.

"This cousin of yours...would he want to take on a child? Is he married? Does he have kids of his own for Tyler to play with? I have two kids, but they're both teenagers."

"My cousin is unmarried. He's a music producer. I don't know how he will feel about Tyler, but he's family, so I'm sure he would take Tyler if he had to. His parents live in Quebec, so they're also a possibility, but they are getting on in age."

He nodded his head.

She took her last sip of coffee. "Just one more thing, and then you can go home to your wife and talk about it. You may think this is the worst thing that could've happened to you and regret our…liaison, but to me, it was a blessing. I didn't know when I made that decision to have my baby and waited on the chemo that he would be my only child. So for that, I thank you. It's not something I have been proud of over the past seven-and-a-half years, but the outcome was wonderful. It taught me a valuable lesson about myself – in fact, I haven't had sex since. It also gave me my miracle baby. I hope you'll give this decision a lot of thought and realize that I only want what's best for my son…our son. Again, if you want nothing more to do with him, I'll understand, and I'll contact my other family. I only want him to be with you if you want it. I don't want you to think of him as a burden." She put her hand on his arm. "But I think it was meant for you to have him. All this time, I haven't known how to contact you, but now here you are out of the blue again at a chance meeting, and I think it was meant to be. Please, let me know if you need me to talk to Jen. I'll be happy to do that for you."

She got up, paid for her bill, and walked out the door.

Chapter Seven

Scarlett was out in the front flowerbeds pulling weeds when she heard a voice behind her.

"Need some help?" It was Jackson.

She turned and looked at him through her dark sunglasses. He was holding two big yellow mums in his arms.

"Jackson! How nice. Are those for me?"

"Yes, they are. Where would you like me to put them?"

"They're gorgeous!" She laid her digging trowel in the dirt and stood up. The flowers looked like they were in full bloom. "Where did you get these? I thought they were all finished blooming at this point."

"I have my sources," he said, grinning.

She smiled back. "On the porch would be fine."

He sat them at the top of the steps, one on each side.

"Wanna help me pull weeds?" she asked, hoping he could pull one of his magic tricks like he did when he helped her move, maybe pulling weeds just as quick. He seemed to have magic hands, and she momentarily wondered what it would feel like to have those hands on her. She blinked away such thoughts.

"I would be happy to help you."

They pulled out many weeds including Virginia creeper, clover, and some Bermuda grass. Scarlett also trimmed the dead blooms off the yucca plants along the sidewalk, while Jackson dug up a dead banana plant, and then raked up the pine needles from the small trees and bunched them around the plants as mulch. He did quick work, just as she'd hoped. He certainly seemed to have a lot of energy.

It was late afternoon by the time they were finished.

"Wanna come back tomorrow and help me paint the house?" she asked him, hoping he'd say yes. She hadn't known him very long, but she was beginning to like having him around to help her do things, and she enjoyed his company.

"I would love to. What color?"

"I'm just teasing," she said, realizing he was going above and beyond the call of duty. "All of this can't be in your job description. Helping someone move, maybe, but yard work and painting…this is too much."

"I'm not doing any of this for my job."

"You're not?" she asked meekly. He shook his head slowly. "Then what are you doing it for?"

He looked at her intently and glanced down at her lips. He looked almost like he wanted to kiss her and her heart started racing. Then his expression changed quickly back to a pleasant smile. "I simply enjoy your company. Where's Tyler?" he asked, looking around, changing the subject.

She took off her gloves and walked up to the porch. "He's over at my friend Catrina's house a few houses down. She has a daughter who is twelve, and they get along pretty well."

"That's nice."

She opened the door and held it open. "Won't you come inside? Maybe we could have a little supper on the back balcony and relax a little." She wondered if she was taking a risk inviting him in. If he stayed longer, would he look at her again as he just did? Would he want to kiss her? She was a little nervous about that but decided she needed his friendship, if nothing more.

"Sure, that sounds nice." As he walked past her, his eyes followed hers, and he stopped as she closed the door. "Are you all right? You look pale."

She was more tired than she wanted to admit. At his observation, she realized she did feel a little dizzy. "I must confess I am pretty tired."

"Have you had anything to eat or drink today?" he asked, placing his warm hand on her arm.

She shook her head. "Not since about eleven-thirty." Not since she left Luke at the restaurant. She briefly wondered whether he had told Jen about Tyler yet.

"Come on," he said, pulling her gently into the kitchen. He sat her down at the bar and then opened up the fridge and poured her a glass of cold water. "Drink up," he ordered, a concerned look on his face.

She did so and watched while he pulled out some deli meat, cheese, lettuce, onion, tomatoes, and a loaf of fresh bread and made some sandwiches for them. He then cut up some apples and put them on plates beside the sandwiches.

"You seem right at home in my kitchen," she observed, smiling.

He smiled back. "You don't mind, do you?"

"Of course not. There are some veggie chips in that cabinet up there," she said, pointing behind him. He turned around, retrieved the chips, and poured some on the plates.

She drank the rest of the water, and he filled it back up with more, along with a glass for himself. He cleaned up after himself and put the water back in the fridge.

"Shall we go outside?" he asked, picking up both plates.

"Sure. There's a tray in that long cabinet door there," she said.

He put all their food and drinks along with some napkins on the tray. She opened the sliding glass door, leaving it open, and they sat down at a round table on some weatherworn Adirondack chairs.

"I'll have to go back to my house sometime and get my outdoor patio furniture with the comfortable cushions. I had forgotten to do that when you helped me move."

"I'll do it for you tomorrow," he said, "before I come over to help you paint."

"Are you sure?" she asked tentatively.

"Absolutely."

They ate and looked out at the waves gently crawling up across the sand, one after another. A line of pelicans flew past and called out a greeting. Scarlett started feeling better after she finished the sandwich.

"I told Luke today," she said.

"Did you?"

She nodded.

"What did he say?"

"He was shocked, obviously. Asked if anyone else in my family would be interested in taking him."

He shook his head. "It will take some getting used to. He'll come around."

She let out a deep sigh. "I hope so. Otherwise, he'll have to move to Nashville or Quebec."

"That would be hard on him."

She nodded, dreading all of it. Dreaded dying, dreaded leaving her son, dreaded him living his life without his mother, all the things she would miss.

"It's not fair," she said with a strained voice.

He stopped eating and looked at her seriously. "What?"

"Why can't I raise my son? I'm being punished, aren't I? For having a child out of wedlock?"

"No, of course not," he said. "Sometimes bad things happen to good people, that's all." He picked up her hand and kissed it.

She watched him, wishing she could feel those lips on hers. Where were these thoughts coming from? She didn't know. It was too little too late. Too late for love. But he looked so handsome, in his jeans and black V-neck long-sleeve shirt, accentuating his dark brown eyes, long eyelashes, and bushy eyebrows.

"I never even fell in love," she said before she could catch herself. "Too late now."

He gave her that serious look again, the one where his eyes looked intently into hers, setting her insides on fire. Her heart began to beat faster. "It's never too late for love," he said softly.

She leaned across the table slowly towards him, aching for him to kiss her, but the front door of the house was suddenly and loudly opened.

"Maman!" It was Tyler.

She relaxed back in her chair, Jackson let go of her hand, and the spell was broken.

"Out here," she said, looking at her son through the windows. He walked outside.

"Hey…" He started to say more but stopped suddenly when he realized Jackson was there.

"Do you remember Jackson?" she asked him. The two had met at the housewarming party.

"Yeah, sure. Hey," Tyler said casually. Looking back at her, he asked, "Can I have a sandwich please?"

She laughed lightly. "Well, since you said please."

She started to stand up, but Jackson motioned for her to sit. "Don't get up. I'll make him one. Maybe two. He's a growing boy." He winked at the boy.

Tyler's eyes lit up. "That's right, I am."

"Thank you." She smiled as he walked back in the house with a jovial boy on his heels.

She wondered briefly if he would be interested in taking care of her son after she was gone.

Chapter Eight

"Can you come get me?"

Luke had called Jen around one o'clock after his meeting with Scarlett. Jen had been sitting in the swing on the upstairs balcony when her phone rang.

"Why? What's wrong?"

"I'm drunk," Luke said.

What in the world? Jen wondered. "Why are you drunk, Luke? It's only lunchtime."

"Well, I'm actually more like tipsy, but I don't trust myself to drive."

"Where are you?"

"At Outback."

"Stay there. I'll bring the kids and we'll have lunch. Then we were supposed to all drive down to Chesapeake and walk around the arboretum, remember?"

Luke sighed. "I forgot. Okay, I'll get a table."

"Can you please try to act normal around the kids?"

"I'll try."

Jen, Cassie, and Logan piled into her white Mini Cooper and met Luke at the restaurant a few miles up the road. He did look glassy-eyed and slurred his words a little. Jen ordered him some coffee since he said he wasn't hungry, and the rest of them ate steaks, potatoes, and salads.

Luke acted nervous the whole time, very quiet and reserved. He was doing some hard thinking about something. She was dying to know why

Scarlett wanted to meet with him, but she didn't want to discuss it around the children.

After eating, Logan drove Luke's truck for him while Jen drove her and Cassie down to the Chesapeake Arboretum. They had planned to walk around in the woods and by the big lake while the fall leaves were at their peak. Once there, Cassie and Logan went off by themselves to walk around and take selfies, so Jen and Luke would be able to talk privately.

"Meet back here in an hour and we'll take the lake trail together," Jen told the kids before they walked away. They agreed.

Jen and Luke held hands and walked in the opposite direction under a canopy of colorful changing leaves.

"So what happened that made you want to get drunk?" Jen asked. "Does it have something to do with your meeting with Scarlett?"

"Um, yeah. It's a long story. I'm so sorry, Jen."

Her heart began to beat faster and she wondered why he would apologize. "What about?"

"I slept with another woman and got her pregnant," he said in a rush.

"You did what?! Who? Scarlett?"

He nodded. "It was almost eight years ago."

She felt her blood boil with anger but tried to calm down since it was in the past. "You mean that little blonde-haired boy?"

"Yeah. He's mine. Or so she says."

"Do you think she's making it up?"

He shook his head. "No. She said she didn't know how to contact me before now. It was one of my one-night stands. We didn't catch each other's last name. I never saw her again."

"I can't believe this," Jen said angrily. She was torn between being mad at Luke for sleeping with another woman and getting her pregnant and with the fact that Scarlett had cancer. It was hard to be mad at someone who had cancer.

She stopped in the trail to let some teenagers go around them. "I'm just wondering how many more children you have out there, Luke. Am I to expect any more little Luke's running around?"

"I hope not, Jen. I'm so sorry. I've always used protection – I told you that before."

"Well, Luke, as you now know very well, it doesn't always work."

"You know I've not been perfect. You knew my history when you married me."

She sighed. She certainly did, but she never expected this.

They found a fallen tree trunk off the main trail and went over to sit down on it.

"You have every right to be mad, but you have to know by now that I love you more than life, Jen," Luke said. "This was all before you and I got together again."

She softened, agreeing that it was in the past, and yet it would affect their future. "So, now what?"

"She has terminal cancer, doesn't expect to live very long, and she wanted to know if I wanted to be part of Tyler's life. Essentially, I think she was asking me if I – we – would take care of Tyler after she dies."

Jen put her hand over her heart. "Oh my."

"Do you realize this is another boy I didn't know I had? First you and now Scarlett. Why do you women think you need to keep secrets like this from a man?"

Jen flushed, embarrassed. She had kept the secret about Luke being Logan's father for sixteen years. "Yes well, as you say, that's all in the past now. How do you feel about raising Tyler?"

"I don't know how I feel. That's why I wanted to get a little drunk. I didn't want to think about it," he said irritably.

Luke had a terrible habit of drowning his worries and sorrows with booze. It was something he'd done since Josie died.

"I wish you had just come straight home and talked to me about it first. I'm here for you. That's why we got married, to love and support each other. You have to let me support you, talk to me about things."

"What do you think I'm doing right now?" he said, his voice a little high-pitched.

It was hard talking to a drunk man sometimes.

She pulled his arm around her and cuddled up against his chest. "It's going to be all right. We don't have to make a decision right away."

He squeezed her tight and kissed her head.

She tried not to think selfishly…about how much care this little boy would need and how much it would cost them and be inconvenient for them. About all the activities a child his age would require – soccer practice, going through puberty…missing his mother. On the other hand,

Cassie and Logan should be able to help out a lot. Cassie especially, since she'd also lost her own mother when she was young.

Jen didn't know if she could ever look at that little boy and not be reminded of Luke in another woman's arms. Would she eventually forget? Only see the boy as Luke's? If Luke chose to care for him, then Jen knew she would have to if she was going to make peace about it.

"So the first time she saw you was at Maggie's that day, on our honeymoon?" she asked.

"Yeah. She recognized me, but I didn't know her. She looked familiar, but I couldn't place her until that party yesterday. She used to have really long hair."

The way he talked about her hair made Jen a little jealous. "Oh?"

"She said it all fell out because of the cancer. I'm sorry," he apologized again. "What a mess I've made. What a way to start a marriage."

"We'll figure it out," she said encouragingly.

"Is it going to make you feel weird to raise another woman's son?"

"At first it will. I mean, we don't even know him. It's not like Cassie – she was family from the beginning. But at least Tyler is your son. There's no mistaking those blue eyes and that blonde hair of his."

"Yeah, I guess you're right."

"Are you feeling any less drunk?" She did get him to eat some bread and butter at the restaurant.

"A little." He was quiet a moment and then said, "Who's going to watch him when he comes home from school? Or in the summer? You work in your shop – we both do."

Sometimes he seemed to forget that he didn't have a job to travel for anymore.

"I can still keep my eye on him, same way I did Logan and Cassie," she said. "And they can help watch him, too."

"Can we afford to feed another mouth?"

Jen sighed. "I'm sure we'll manage just fine. You'll have a nest egg soon when the sale of your other house goes through." The other house had sold while they were on their honeymoon.

"That's true."

They were still in each other's arms, and Jen reached up and kissed his neck. "Are you ready to go walking with the kids?"

He nodded and then leaned his head down and kissed her lips. Smiling at her, he said, "Thanks. You're always able to steady me, help me make sense of things. You're right, I should've come straight home. I was scared you'd throw a hissy fit. I wouldn't have blamed you if you did, by the way. It would've been well-deserved."

She smiled. "I wanted to throw one, believe me. I think the fact that Scarlett has cancer softens the blow."

He agreed. He stood and pulled her up. "Let's go spend time with our kids while we only have two of them."

Chapter Nine

Cassie felt the warm sunshine on her skin, heard the ocean waves coming and going, ebb and flow. Above all that, she heard him whisper her name. She turned and saw Skyler walking down the empty beach towards her. He was wearing the light blue flowing shirt she had seen him in the first night she met him, along with loose white pants. He carried a lit lantern, even though it was daylight. His dark hair hung in curls that touched the top of his strong shoulder muscles. She smelled him before he reached her, smelled what he used to smell like…when he was her guardian angel.

As he walked towards her, a fog followed him, and soon they were both encased inside the fog. He sat the lantern down in the sand, which illuminated through the fog across their faces. He lay down on the blanket beside her and began kissing her. His lips felt velvety soft on hers, and his hand caressed her arm, up and down slowly. The kissing became urgent quickly, tongues teasing, breathing heavy, and hands exploring. Cassie sat up and took her shirt off. Skyler did the same. She smoothed her hands over his strong chest, over his nipples, and down to his rock-hard abs. She bent over and kissed his neck and followed the same path her hands just took with her lips.

While she was busy with that, Skyler reached around her and unsnapped her bra. She looked up at him, mid-lick, and he slowly eased her bra off her shoulders. She sat up straight so he could take it all the way off, and he cupped and caressed her breasts. She closed her eyes, lost in the sensations of arousal all over her body. This was the first time he'd done this to her, the first time he'd seen her without a bra or a bathing suit top on. Yet she felt no shame, no embarrassment. It felt like the most natural thing for them to do. When he bent over to take one in his mouth, she cried out in enjoyment and pressed his head harder against her.

"Skyler," she said breathily. "Please don't stop."

She felt her insides, her female area, swell and tingle, aching for his touch. Skyler moved to the other side and showed that breast due attention while one of his hands eased down her abs, across her navel, and down towards her nether regions. She gasped and arched, alternately opening and closing her eyes. He eased her back against the blanket, following her every inch of the way. His tongue teased its way back up from between her breasts, across her collarbone, up her neck and then kissed her like mad. His hand crept up to her jeans, unzipped them, and then slid down inside to caress her nether regions more personally, and she moaned under his kisses.

"I love you, Skyler," she whispered under her breath.

A loud banging noise startled her, and she opened her eyes wide. It was dark except for a nightlight in the corner, and she realized she'd been dreaming. *Damn!* She sat up quickly and suddenly realized she wasn't wearing anything up top. She looked down and saw that she was still wearing jeans, but they were unzipped. *What the hell?* She then remembered that she had fallen asleep in her clothes while studying for a history test. Her closed book was beside her along with her laptop. She looked around the room and saw her shirt and bra in the floor. Wow, that was some dream.

She heard another loud noise, which sounded like it came from the attic and it reminded her of something Skyler told her when he was an angel…that sometimes he and the other guardians would play cards up in the attic while their humans slept. He said if she ever heard noises that go bump in the night, it was probably them, getting carried away. She wondered if that was her new guardian up there.

It was at a time like this that she missed Skyler being able to appear in her bedroom anytime she wanted him to. Especially after such an erotic dream. She was still aroused…dazed, confused…and not from any drug she'd ever had in the past. She wished it had been real. They'd never gone that far before, even though she wanted to, more than anything. She was still a virgin, but she had done other things with other boyfriends including one named Kerrick, who broke up with her after she refused to have sex with him. With Skyler, she wasn't sure she would want to stop. She could see going all the way with him. He was her one true love, and after a dream like this one, it would be hard to stop anything now that she knew – sort of – what it would feel like with him. In the past, after he told her he was an angel, he wouldn't let them go too far, fearing punishments. Now there was be no such obstacle.

The noises in the attic stopped, and she reached for her cell phone to see what time it was: 3:45 a.m. She opened up her phone, the bright light hurting her eyes, and she texted Skyler to see if he was awake.

Hey, r u awake?

There was no reply. *Double damn!* She would like to flirt with him over the phone. It would be hard to get back to sleep. She got up and went to the bathroom, her body still aroused, and it felt sensitive when she wiped. How in the world had she gotten so turned on simply from a dream?

She went to her closet, took off her jeans and pulled on a short gown. When she got back to her bed, she heard her phone vibrate. She quickly picked it up, but it was only a junk email. She opened up her text app again and wrote to Skyler, *I had an erotic dream about us…wish you were here.*

She turned the phone off and rolled over, pulled one of her pillows up and hugged it tight, wishing it was Skyler. She tried to remember everything about the dream in hopes that she could go back to it again and pick up where it left off…

When Skyler got up the next morning, he looked at his phone first thing and saw the text from Cassie. His heart beat faster, thinking about her having a sex dream involving the two of them. This was one of those times he missed being an angel when he could appear at any time and he was always with her. But then again, he wouldn't be able to have sex with her as an angel…not without punishments. He'd had enough punishments to last a lifetime. Now that he wasn't an angel, he didn't have those restrictions on him anymore. It got him to thinking about them being together, and he felt excitement that she was thinking about it, too.

He quickly texted her back: *I wish I'd been there, too.* He sent that and looked at the time she had texted him; it had been in the middle of the night.

She texted back: *I can't wait to see u,* followed by heart emoticons.

He texted her: *I'll see you at school.*

She greeted him with a full-on, heart-thumping, enthusiastic kiss when he met her in the hallway at school. He felt himself get aroused as she pressed herself up against him hard, pushing him into the cold wall. That must have been some dream.

He spent as much time with her as he could at school between classes and at lunchtime, and recently he had joined the cross country team. They met up again after school to run with the team, and she pulled him into a bunch of bushes halfway through their three-mile run to kiss him again. Once they started running again, he started coughing. He felt something stuck in the back of his throat. It was a weird feeling, and his throat felt kind of raw suddenly like he hadn't had a drink of water all day, even though he had just drank some right before they started running. It was more than the feeling you get from running. He thought it was really weird until he described the symptoms to Cassie.

"Sounds like you're getting sick."

"Don't get too close to me, then. No more kissing."

"Uh-uh. I don't care if I get sick."

He whispered, "I can't heal you anymore."

"That's okay. We'll be sick together." She smiled and kissed him again.

"I've never been sick before."

"Really? Not in the ten years since…"

"Nope." He shook his head.

"Aw, I'll take care of you," she said.

They walked their last mile and when they reached the coach, Skyler explained that he thought he was getting sick and that's why they had walked. He and Cassie parted after cross country. His mom picked up him and his sister, Danielle, and they went to Walmart for some groceries. Skyler walked around a corner to look for his favorite cereal when he saw Jackson and the lady who had the housewarming party, Scarlett. He watched them for a moment, as they hadn't seen him yet, and noticed that Jackson was very attentive to her, almost flirty. Skyler had spent plenty of time watching Jackson as an angel when he flirted with Cassie. It looked like he was up to his old tricks again. He wondered if Scarlett was the one whose time was up.

Jackson finally looked over and spotted him, said something to Scarlett, who looked his way and waved at him. He waved back, and Jackson walked over to him without her. Skyler noted again how much older he appeared. The last time he'd been an angel, when he'd been up on the roof of that treehouse waiting for lightning to strike, Jackson had looked to be in his twenties, but now he could easily be in his thirties.

"Hello, Skyler," he said very formally.

"Hey," Skyler said warily. "You've been around a lot lately."

Jackson glanced at Scarlett. "Some, yes."

"Anyone I know?" Skyler looked directly at Scarlett.

Jackson whispered, "Since you're no longer an angel, that's really none of your concern."

"Fine, but I think I can figure it out pretty much on my own."

Jackson's dark eyes got a shade darker, if that was possible. "Stay out of it," he warned.

Skyler held his hands up in surrender and then started coughing again.

"Sounds like you need to see a doctor."

Skyler suddenly had a terrifying thought. "You're not here for me, are you?"

Jackson smiled slightly. "No, I can honestly answer that question. Have you, uh, ever been sick before?"

Skyler shook his head.

Jackson frowned.

"What's wrong with me?"

"I'm not sure but something or someone may be messing with you."

"What?"

Jackson turned and looked at Scarlett again, who was walking away from them slowly, looking at cereal boxes. "Let's just say that it's highly unusual for a guardian angel who became human by entering the body of a half-angel to get sick. Grant even had healing powers. Did you inherit those?"

"No, unfortunately, I didn't."

"That's understandable, but getting sick for the first time in the last ten years is, as I said, unusual and a little disturbing, quite honestly. You might want to be careful, be on your guard."

He walked away from Skyler to join Scarlett again, and Skyler found himself confused and curious about what was going on with him. He hoped it wasn't another punishment.

Chapter Ten

Scarlett rolled over in bed a few days later, feeling tired, lethargic, and didn't want to get up.

Tyler came into her bedroom. "Are you okay, Maman?"

She smiled at his concern. "I'm fine, sweetie. Did you eat breakfast?"

"Yes, I did." He walked over to her and kissed her cheek. "I've got to get to the bus stop."

She panicked. "What time is it?"

"Seven fifty-five."

"I'm sorry that I slept in. Do you need money for lunch?"

"No, I have enough. Bye," he said, running out of her bedroom.

She heard the front door slam a moment later. She sighed and stretched. It wasn't going to be a good day, she could tell.

She forced herself up to go to the bathroom, and when she came back, she was even more tired. She knew she needed to eat or at least drink something, but she couldn't summon the energy.

She awoke with a start sometime later, realizing she had fallen back to sleep. Someone was ringing her doorbell. Wondering who that could be, she forced herself to get up. On days like this, she was glad she had decided to make her bedroom downstairs and let Tyler have the one upstairs. She pulled a deep purple robe around her and tied it as she walked through the house to the front door.

It was Jackson.

He smiled upon seeing her when she opened the door. He had a big plant in his arms with light pink blooms on it.

"Hey, I brought you a camellia. You want to help me plant it, or at least tell me where you want it and I'll plant it."

"That's very sweet of you, but I'm afraid I'm not feeling too well today, Jackson. Plant it wherever you like, preferably some place I can see it easily."

He sat the plant down on the porch, walked into the house, and slid his arms around her. "I'm sorry to hear that you're not feeling well. What can I do? Have you eaten anything?"

She shook her head and glanced at the clock on the microwave in the kitchen. It was after ten o'clock. She couldn't remember the last time she'd slept that late.

He looked at her face and she saw the pity there, something she'd gotten tired of seeing in other people. Just for a while, she wished she could forget her problems and not see pity on everyone's face every time she entered the room.

"Would you please not look at me that way?" she asked him, knowing she could be candid with him. They'd gotten fairly close and she felt totally comfortable saying anything to him.

He changed his expression to one that looked like he was going to reprimand her. He sighed and shook his head. "Why can't I be concerned about you, hmm?" He rubbed the back of her arm, making the skin tingle, the hairs stand on end.

"You can be concerned, just don't pity me."

"Okay, fine. What would you like to eat?"

He pulled away from her and she instantly wished he hadn't. She felt warm and safe in his arms.

"You don't have to go to any trouble. I'll fix myself some oatmeal."

"Go sit down on the couch, and I'll fix it for you. How about some eggs and bacon to go along with it?"

"Sounds good, and some coffee would be even better, if it's not too much trouble."

She walked over to the family room and sat down on the couch, stretched her legs out across the couch, and looked out the windows at the ocean. Tyler must have opened up the blinds. She wished she had the energy to go outside and sit on the deck, but today she just didn't.

Jackson brought her food over to her in no time at all…scrambled eggs, crisp bacon, oatmeal that smelled of cinnamon, and a steaming cup of black coffee all on a tray.

"I'll be right back," he said and left the house.

He came back inside about fifteen minutes later, dirt on his hands. He washed them out in the kitchen sink.

"Where'd you plant the camellia?" she asked him.

"Right out front between the porch and the sidewalk. You can't miss it."

"Thank you so much," she said between bites of oatmeal.

"After you eat, you should do some yoga. It might help you feel better."

"Aw Jackson, I really don't feel up to it today."

"Come on, I promise it won't be anything strenuous."

She finished the last bite of food, and he took the tray out of her hands. She looked down and realized she was still in her bathrobe. She really should go and change clothes.

"Ready for some yoga?"

"Jackson, I can't even muster enough energy to change my clothes. How am I going to do any yoga?"

He disappeared for a moment into her bedroom and came back with a pair of comfortable black capris and a bright pink sports bra. "Will this do?"

She sighed but smiled at him. "I appreciate what you're trying to do, but…"

"No buts. Come on, change clothes. Do I need to do it for you?"

She wanted to be offended but he was doing what she'd asked…not pitying her. She had to grin. "Fine."

She undid her robe and revealed to him that she was wearing only a big loose t-shirt with Snoopy on it wearing a French beret and riding a bicycle, and a pair of comfortable cotton panties. She slid the capris on and turned away to put the sports bra on.

She then got down on the floor. "Do with me as you wish," she said, smirking.

For the next half hour, he helped her do stretches, twists, breathing deeply and letting out all her worries. It surprised her how much better she felt when they were done.

He smiled. "You feel better, don't you?"

She nodded. "Yes, I actually do."

"How about a massage next?"

"You're spoiling me," she said, smiling.

He laughed. "Indeed, I am. Here, lie down on the couch. I'll grab a towel."

He disappeared into the bathroom and came out with a big fluffy white towel. She pulled her capris off, and he motioned for her to turn over. He draped the towel over her rear-end and she closed her eyes, waiting for him to work his magic. She heard him open a bottle and then rub his hands together. He started massaging her neck muscles first with something that smelled like lavender.

"Mmm, that smells nice."

"I found it in your cabinet."

"I forgot I had that. I unpacked in a hurry."

He was massaging her back and she felt herself getting sleepy. He massaged her arms next and by the time he got to her legs, she felt herself drifting off to sleep. She shook her head to wake herself up. She wanted to enjoy this. She noticed that he had turned on some classical music, and Clair de Lune was playing.

"Do you want me to work on the front side now?" he asked, his warm breath on her ear.

"No, anymore of that, and I'll be asleep again."

"What's wrong with that?"

"I don't want to sleep while you're here."

He looked at her seriously for a moment. "Would you like me to bathe you?" he asked.

She looked into his eyes, wondering the motive behind that question. Was he asking as a hospice worker, a person whose job it was to take care of people in need? Or was he asking as a man who wanted to pamper a woman, who wanted to see her naked and behold her in all her glory, maybe as an interlude to something more? She found herself wishing for the latter.

"Bathe me?" she asked meekly.

She saw sudden fire in his eyes. He blinked, though, and his expression went back to friendly. "Would that be all right? I don't want you to be uncomfortable."

What should she say? She saw desire in his eyes, if only briefly, yet he appeared to be just asking as part of his job. He was such a nice man and very handsome. It was too bad she couldn't take this further with him. She found herself looking forward to his visits and liking – no, craving – the comfort of his arms, a little too much. Nothing could come of it, so why should she bother? Then again, maybe she could just enjoy it for what it was worth as much as she could for as long as she was able. Have a little fun.

"Sure," she said softly. "That would be nice."

He immediately got up. "I'll go run the water. Do you like it hot?"

There was that fire in his eyes again. She nodded slowly.

He walked away quickly and she heard him turn the water on. She wished she could take a bath in her antique claw-foot bathtub at her big house in Pungo, but this would still be enjoyable. He came back a few minutes later.

"It's all ready for you, mademoiselle."

She smiled and slowly got up and walked ahead of him, through the bedroom and into the bathroom. She let the towel fall to the floor. She was surprised to see bubbles all the way up to the top of the tub and little candles lit all around the rim of the tub.

"Jackson…this is so nice." She had tears in her eyes suddenly. She couldn't remember the last time any man had done anything this special for her. She had to remind herself it was his job.

She wiped her eyes and slowly took off her underwear and sports bra, glancing at him from time to time. He would turn his head away when she did. He probably thought she was shy to undress in front of a man. That wasn't entirely true. It might be a little awkward to take her relationship with him to the next level in this way, but it wasn't the first time she'd undressed in front a man. It was the first time, however, that she wanted this particular man to see her this way. She wanted to feel desired…by him.

She slipped into the bathtub quietly and carefully, and leaned back into the bubbles, which covered her all up. Jackson walked over and sat down on his knees in front of the tub. The bathroom didn't have any windows in it, so it was rather dark except for the light coming in from the open door and the candles. His eyes looked as black as night in the candlelight.

"Do you have a loofah?" he asked her, his voice sounding strained, nervous.

She told him where to find a pouf instead, and he got it wet under the bubbles. She pointed to a bottle of floral scented bath wash and he poured some onto the pouf. He raised her arm and began washing her.

"What's your last name?" she asked him, suddenly realizing that she didn't know.

"Wiggs."

"Jackson Wiggs?"

He nodded.

"Speaking of wigs…I'm wearing one right now." It was the chin-length dark wig that she wore most of the time. Her own hair had fallen out with chemo and was growing out now but was still only a few inches long. It looked like a man, and she didn't like the look or feel of it. It was dry, brittle, and frizzy. She preferred the wig.

"I'm sorry you have to wear one."

She was, too. "No pity, remember?"

He smiled faintly. "What's your full name? Scarlett doesn't sound French."

She leaned up so he could wash her back. Some of the bubbles fell off her breasts. She glanced at him and saw that he was concentrating very hard on her back. What could she do to get him to see her as something other than a patient? Maybe her voice would do the trick. She'd caught many a man's attention with her accent.

"No, Scarlett is not French. My mother was from right here in this area, and she simply adored *Gone With the Wind.* She named me after the main character."

"I love that movie."

"Do you?" That was surprising. Most men found it boring. "My middle name is Juliandra, which is derived from both my parents' names. My mother's name was Julie and my father, André. He's French."

Jackson pulled one of her legs up out of the water next, and she leaned back again. This was rather enjoyable. She didn't have to do anything but relax.

"How do you get here?" she asked him.

"Hmm?" he asked, concentrating hard on her legs but slowly looked over at her face.

"You never have a car when you get here. Do you fly? Are there wings on your back?"

She touched his back, and he flinched. She frowned, confused.

"I'm sorry. Did I do something wrong?"

"No." He cleared his throat and forced a smile. "You just startled me. I'm a little ticklish."

"Are you?" She smiled, thinking she would have to remember that little tidbit of personal information.

"I take a taxi to get here."

"Why? Don't you have a car?"

He shook his head. "No, I don't."

"I guess that gets pretty expensive, doesn't it?"

He shrugged his shoulders and washed her other leg. She wondered if he was concentrating so hard on her legs because he was trying not to look at her naked body. The bubbles were starting to fade away and more of her was showing through now.

"What kind of bulbs would you like to plant in your flower garden? What are your favorite spring flowers?"

"Tulips." She reached for her razor and handed it to him. Might as well take advantage.

He obliged, found some cream and shaved her legs slowly. Why was something she did every day suddenly sultry? He was arousing her desires, something she hadn't felt in quite some time.

"What color?"

"All colors."

He shaved her other leg, and she closed her eyes momentarily, loving the feel of his hands on her legs.

"Why do you speak with a French accent? Because of your father?"

"Oui. He taught me to speak French as a baby along with Mother teaching me English. I've always been bilingual. It was a little confusing in grammar school at times, but I figured it out."

He finished that leg and she raised one arm for him to shave her armpits. He did so, avoiding looking at her breasts, which were no longer covered by bubbles.

"Will you do me a favor?" she dared to ask, biting her lower lip.

He looked surprised. "Of course," he replied, looking at her quizzically.

"Would you make love to me?"

Jackson nearly dropped the razor in the water. He'd been trying to stay professional with her, not allow himself to get too close, but he was failing miserably. All the small talk had been to distract him from her gorgeous, silky, creamy body…her voluptuous bosom, which he had sneaked a peek at several times. Even if they weren't her original breasts, she was a highly desirable woman, and he found that he nearly couldn't breathe around her this way.

He didn't know why he'd offered to massage her, let alone give her a bath. She still thought of him as a hospice worker, though, so he thought he could pretend to be a professional around her while enjoying looking at her at the same time. He was wrong.

Now she was asking him to make love to her. As an angel of death, he wasn't allowed to have sex with a human. What could he say that wouldn't hurt Scarlett's feelings? She was vulnerable at this point in her life. Worn down, beaten, and yes, even pitiful at times. She wanted to feel desirable, he could tell. He wished he could make love to her. He'd always wondered what it would feel like. He would flirt with women sometimes but had never gone all the way. He could imagine, though, as sometimes he felt such sensations that he had a hard time controlling his desires. Scarlett didn't know what she was asking of him, and he wouldn't be able to give it to her. It would break her heart, and he hated to do that to her.

"No pressure," she whispered. "Can we just have a little fun? You've got me completely all hot and bothered."

He closed his eyes. "I can't."

"Why? Are you married?"

"No, I'm not married." He opened his eyes and looked at her, avoided looking at her body and just concentrated on her face.

"So what's the problem? Don't you desire me at all?" She moved forward and put her face directly in front of his. He could feel her warm breath on his mouth.

"It's not right. It's not professional."

"I won't tell anyone. Do you think I'd sue you?"

"No. Look, I just can't, all right?"

"Do you need some help down there?" She reached one wet hand down and touched his groin.

He gasped, eyes widened, surprised at her boldness. He shook his head and moved her hand back to the water.

"Are you gay?" she asked sadly.

"No." He definitely was not gay. She was making him mad with desire.

She looked at his lips and then leaned in and kissed them, gently, tenderly, driving him wild, his heart beating in double time. Why was it so different with her? Why did it mean so much more? Usually he was able to turn off his feelings, but not with her.

"Don't worry, I can't get pregnant," she whispered. "Chemo took care of that."

"It's not that either," he managed to say.

She leaned back and suddenly got mad. He knew he had hurt her. "Oh, I get it now. It's the cancer, isn't it? You're the professional, so you know you can't catch it, right?"

"Of course I know that." She was making it very hard to say no and coming up with every excuse in the book. He very much desired this woman, more than any woman he'd ever met before.

He'd often observed that some humans had sex and others made love. He could tell the difference. Right now, this woman wanted to have sex. She only wanted to fulfill her desires. She wasn't looking for love or a long-term commitment. It might be the last time she ever had sex or ever felt like having sex. Surely he wouldn't get in trouble if he had sex this one time, in this particular case.

He leaned over and kissed her, pulling her shoulders against his shirt.

She stopped him. "Never mind. I don't want your pity, remember? I've seen that look before. My ex-boyfriend had that look when I told him I had cancer – just before he walked out the door and said he couldn't handle this." She laughed bitterly. "Men are supposed to be the strong ones. You all might be strong in muscles but your hearts are weak. Women are the ones who stay strong. My mother was the one who always stood by me."

He felt like he'd just been slapped, repeatedly.

"How can you compare me to this other man? Haven't I been taking damn good care of you? I am fully aware of your condition, and I'm still here."

"Just go, please. I don't want pity sex."

It hurt more than he thought it would, more than he wanted it to, but he slowly got up and walked out the door.

Chapter Eleven

Jen drove her Mini Cooper down the sandy road towards Maggie's house for a visit to talk about Thanksgiving. On impulse, she didn't stop there. She kept going on up the road to Scarlett's house. She hadn't been able to stop thinking about this woman's situation and her saying that Tyler was Luke's. How unfair could that be? They'd just gotten married, finally got together after avoiding each other for seventeen years, finally able to start a life together, when this had to happen. She couldn't help feeling some resentment.

She pulled into the driveway beside Scarlett's expensive car and got out. The house was still mostly obscured by the road, giving the front wraparound porch privacy, but the flowerbeds had been cleared of all weeds, and a nice camellia was now blooming beside the sidewalk. Two rockers stood on the porch, waiting to be enjoyed.

She nervously pushed the doorbell, hoping she didn't catch Scarlett at a bad time.

Tyler came to the door, and Jen was again reminded of how much he looked like Luke. The bright blue eyes, the shoulder-length light blonde hair. The way his forehead had two small creases when he was confused. Like now.

"Hey, Tyler," she said, trying to make him feel comfortable. She wondered briefly if he knew that his mother was dying and if he knew that she and Luke might be taking care of him. Did he even know that Luke was his father? She felt sudden remorse for her selfishness and had pity on this young boy whose world was about to be turned upside-down. "Is your mom home?" she asked him.

"Sure, hang on."

He disappeared into the house while Jen held the screen door open, waiting. The house looked clean, and she saw that the back door was propped open. She could hear and see the ocean very well. She was glad that Scarlett had managed to find a beautiful, peaceful place to spend her last days.

She appeared a moment later, walked in from the outside balcony.

"Come in, Jen," she called while walking towards her.

Jen walked inside and let the screen door close softly.

"I apologize for Tyler leaving you standing here like this. Would you like something to drink?"

"No, thanks. I hate to show up unannounced, but I was wondering if we could talk?" Jen glanced around, wondering where Tyler had gone.

"But of course," Scarlett said in her wonderful French accent. "Tyler," she called out.

Tyler came out into the living room from a bedroom.

"What's up?" he asked.

"Would you do me a favor and run down to Catrina's and see if Arianna wants to hang out? I need to speak with Jen alone for a few minutes."

"Sure, Maman." He ran past them and flung open the front door. He turned around and waved. "Bye," he said before letting the door slam shut.

"So much energy in that one," Jen said, smiling.

"Yes, there certainly is. Luckily, Catrina said he has an open invitation at her house any time I need a break." She sneezed briefly, sounding like a little kitten. "Excusez-moi."

"À tes souhaits," Jen said, hoping that was the right words for "bless you." She took two years of French in high school.

"Parlez-vous français?" Scarlett asked. Her eyes lit up.

"Seulement un peu," Jen answered, only remembering a little bit.

"Très bien! Won't you come outside on the balcony and we can sit and enjoy the view."

Jen followed her onto the balcony where it looked like Scarlett had been sitting on soft butter-colored cushions of a love seat with a book, a magazine, an empty tall hurricane glass with a pineapple slice in the bottom, and a half-empty water bottle on a nearby table.

"It looks like you've been relaxing," Jen said, sitting down on a nearby chair with the same colored cushions. She breathed in the salty air and blew out her nervousness.

"Yes, this is my favorite place in the whole world now. It's very peaceful."

"It is." Jen listened to the distant waves and tried to think of what to say to Scarlett.

Scarlett broke the silence. "Jen, I want to apologize for getting in the middle of you and Luke like this. He told you about Tyler being his?"

Jen nodded. "Yes, he did."

"I'm sure this must be difficult for you, but let me assure you, you and Luke are under no obligation to take Tyler. You must understand how difficult this is for me, trying to find someone to take care of my child after I'm…gone."

"Of course, it must be awful," Jen said.

"I have a cousin that lives in Nashville, on my father's side of the family, so if you're not able…I can ask him. He's coming here for Thanksgiving."

"Oh. I didn't know that."

"I just found out this morning that he was coming for sure. He's in the music business and stays pretty busy, but he said he could take a couple of days off to come and see us."

"That'll be nice. Is he married?"

"Divorced. He produces country music."

"Really? I love country music," Jen said, glad to be off the subject of Tyler and dying for a moment. "Did you know that Luke plays in a country band?"

"No, I didn't. How nice. Maybe he and my cousin will get along well. Maggie said you guys were coming to her house for Thanksgiving. Is that right?"

"Yes. I was just on my way to see her to talk about it but decided to come by here first."

Scarlett nodded. "Tyler and I will be there, too, and James – that's my cousin."

"It'll be nice to have you all there. It will be my first Thanksgiving as a married woman. It'll be such a big change from last year."

"That's sweet," Scarlett said, though she looked away.

"I'm sorry. That was insensitive."

"Don't worry about it. I was thinking of my mother. This will be my first Thanksgiving without her. She died last year right after Thanksgiving."

"Oh, I'm so sorry. I didn't know that. What of, if you don't mind me asking?"

"Breast cancer. I watched her go, so I know what to expect. If she can do it, so can I."

"I lost my mother to breast cancer, too," Jen admitted. "It was twelve years ago. I was living in Georgia at the time, so I didn't get to see her much in her last days." Jen brushed a tear away.

Scarlett reached over and squeezed her hand. "It's hard to lose a mother, isn't it?"

Jen nodded. "Whew, I'm sorry. I didn't mean to make you sad."

"It's okay. We had a lot of good memories. That's what I think about mostly. Anyway, back to Tyler. Like I said before, I never meant to come between the two of you, so if you don't both agree to take Tyler, I will understand. It's a lot to take on, I know."

"It is, but we're definitely considering it. I mean, it's really up to Luke more than me, but I'm willing if he is."

"That's good to hear. Don't be mad at Luke. We were both pretty drunk the night we were together. It's the accent – it attracts many men." She laughed. "And the long hair," she said wistfully. "It used to touch my waist."

Jen realized she had been a little jealous because Scarlett was so beautiful and had that exotic accent, but now that she was getting to know her, she seemed to be a really sweet person.

"It doesn't matter what length your hair is. You're a sweet person on the inside, and your short hair is actually really cute."

Scarlett smiled. "It's a wig, but thank you for saying all of that." She smoothed some of it away from her cheek. "I bet Luke was mad when he first found out that I had his child and didn't tell him. That must've been a shock."

Jen felt herself blush. "Well, it wasn't the first time he'd been surprised about finding out he had a son. I did the same thing to him. I got pregnant when I was in high school, at exactly the same time as my sister – both from Luke. He'd been dating both of us at the same time."

Scarlett's eyes widened. "Oh, my. What a bad boy." She clucked her tongue.

Jen laughed. "He was, wasn't he? My sister found out she was pregnant first and Luke asked her to marry him, so I kept quiet about Luke being the father of my son, Logan…for sixteen years. I was afraid of losing him, even as a friend."

"Wow, so he has two sons he didn't know about."

"Yeah, and they both look very different from each other. My son has dark hair. They do both have blue eyes."

Scarlett smiled again. "I'm glad you came to talk with me, Jen. This has been nice."

"Me, too. I feel much better."

"Good. I'm glad."

Jen felt like they were having a bonding moment. She had more things in common with her than she realized.

They were interrupted by the doorbell, and Scarlett got up to go answer it.

"I really should be going anyway," Jen said, following her into the house. "Maggie will be wondering where I am."

"Let me just see who's at the door first before you leave."

Scarlett opened the door, and Jen thought she got paler than usual. It was her friend, Jackson. She wasn't sure what was going on between those two.

"Jackson!" Scarlett said.

Jackson was holding a little black and white puppy in his arms. Jen thought Jackson looked familiar but couldn't place him.

"What on earth?" Scarlett asked, but she started smiling.

"I bought you a puppy…to make up for…" He turned and saw Jen for the first time. "Oh, I'm sorry. I didn't see you there."

"Hi. It's Jen," she told him, in case he forgot her name.

"You got me a puppy?" Scarlett asked. "Jackson, you know I can't take care of a dog. I can barely take care of myself and Tyler."

"Tyler will help, I'm sure. Besides, puppies are really great distractions. I thought he would be good company, curled up in your lap at night." Jackson looked at her intently.

Jen was sure that the two of them had a little bit more than friendship going on.

"You're so right. I haven't had a dog since I was a little girl. Tyler will be so surprised. He's been begging me for a dog for a few years." Scarlett said. She took the puppy in her arms. "What's his name?"

"Whatever you want to name him," Jackson said.

"Is he a boy or a girl?"

"A boy."

"I'll let Tyler help me name him."

Tyler walked up behind Jackson just then.

"What's going on?" he asked. He saw the puppy, and his eyes lit up.

"I'll see you later, Scarlett," Jen said, walking out the door. "Nice to see you again, Jackson," Jen said.

Jackson nodded.

"Au revoir, Jen," Scarlett said.

"Bye, Tyler," Jen said, but he was already taking the puppy from his mother's arms.

Jen left them to get acquainted with their new family member.

Chapter Twelve

The next Thursday was Thanksgiving, and everyone gathered at Maggie's "Pelican's Shoal" house. Steve came over and basted a big turkey and Maggie cooked candied yams, green beans, and mashed potatoes while watching the parades on TV. Jen, Luke, and the kids came over at noon, bringing two pies that Jen baked – a pumpkin and a pecan, along with some vanilla bean ice cream. Luke brought beer and a bottle of Fireball. Catrina, Arianna, and Jim came, Catrina bringing some crème brûlée she'd made for Scarlett.

"Oh, Catrina!" Scarlett said when she saw it. "C'est magnifique! Thank you so much!"

"I also brought some oysters in champagne sauce."

"Really? Oh…" Scarlett hugged her, deeply touched, and kissed her cheek. "That you would do this for me."

"I get at least one of those," Jim said, "since I helped her make them."

"Did you really?"

He smiled. "No, but I found the oysters."

"You harvested the oysters?" Scarlett said, clearly impressed.

He smiled again. "Naw, I bought them at Whole Foods."

Scarlett laughed. "Such a jokester you are."

Scarlett noticed that Maggie turned away and headed towards the bathroom. She wondered briefly if she was getting sick or if she could be pregnant.

It was a cold blustery day on the beach, and Maggie had the gas fireplace turned on in the living room. The long table in the dining area, which was open to the living room and behind a long sage green couch, was made of pine, trimmed in white with ten matching chairs. On top of the table, Maggie had scattered orange, green and white pumpkins, gourds, and other squashes intermingled with tall tapered orange candles in crystal candleholders, and big conch seashells. It was a beautiful seaside Thanksgiving table.

Derek Jones and his wife Bridget also came. Derek played bass in the Renegades, and Luke had told his friends to bring instruments for some entertainment later. Bridget brought home-baked French bread and some special friendship bread made with yeast that was passed around among friends and allowed to sit and get bubbly.

Scarlett's cousin, James, came at twelve thirty, along with Jackson, who said he had some other business to attend to that morning, and then he'd offered to pick up James at the airport.

"I see you found each other," Scarlett said, hugging her cousin. James was a tall man with dark hair and thick eyebrows over green eyes much like Scarlett's. She hadn't seen him since her mother's funeral last year. "It's so good to see you." His father and Scarlett's father were brothers, and so James was half-French like her. James's parents lived in Quebec, which is where James grew up, and he was bilingual like Scarlett.

"You too, ma chérie. You're looking well."

"Liar," she said, grinning. "But thank you."

"When's the food ready? I'm starving," he said.

Scarlett shook her head and then began to introduce him to everyone.

She glanced at Jackson, who was fixing some drinks in the kitchen, and she walked over to him.

"Did you check on Harry?" she asked, referring to the puppy. Tyler had named him after his favorite character, Harry Potter. She had been reading the books to him at night.

"I did. He's doing fine. I put him back in his crate until we get finished eating, then I'll go let him have a break on the beach for a bit."

She had fallen in love with the cute little Havanese bichon immediately, but she also dreaded the thought of having to take care of a puppy. It was rather like having a child, especially in the beginning, but Jackson had stayed all night the first night, sleeping in the floor by the puppy's crate to help soothe him. That gesture nearly made Scarlett forgive him for refusing to have sex with her.

She still hadn't quite gotten over his rejection yet, but the puppy did help her forget for the moment.

By the time the ballgame came on, all the food was ready and they all gathered around the table for a prayer and then had their fill of delicious food.

After eating, Luke and Derek got out their guitars while Steve got a snare drum and some brush drumsticks, and they played a couple of their country songs. Cassie even played one song with them on her ukulele, the same song they'd played at Luke and Jen's wedding last month.

After the third song, James got up and walked over to Luke.

"How long have you guys been playing?"

Luke told him how they had played for a while years ago and broke up but recently got back together.

"You guys sound fantastic. You know I'm a music producer, right?"

Luke shook his head. "No, I had no idea."

"Scarlett didn't tell you? Yeah, I'm in country music mostly and a little bit of rap. I think I could get you guys a contract with my boss. What d'you say? Are you ready to come to Nashville?"

"Are you serious?" Luke said, looking very excited.

"I am. How soon can you come out? I'm flying back on Saturday. Could you meet me first thing Monday morning?"

Luke and the other band members looked flabbergasted. "We'll have to think about it, of course."

"Yes, of course. Please, continue playing," James said. He had enthusiasm in his eyes that Scarlett recognized. Any time he had a new passion, that look of pure joy came across his face. It was either that or he was seeing invisible dollar signs in the air, thinking that Luke's band could make him more money.

After the guys played a couple more songs, Jackson took the kids and teenagers out to the beach and played football with them in the sand. The women helped clean up the food and dishes while the remaining men watched the football game.

"How much longer does she have?" Skyler asked Jackson. They'd played some football and then the younger ones went to the dunes to play a game of hide-and-seek. Skyler and Jackson remained on the beach alone.

"About six months, give or take," Jackson said quietly.

"Have you told her what you are?" Skyler could tell that Jackson was getting awfully close to Scarlett. It wasn't something that angels were allowed to do with humans, and something that Jackson had berated him for in the past when he had been Cassie's guardian angel.

"Not yet," Jackson said. "Soon…"

"I can tell you've gotten close to her."

"It's really none of your business," Jackson said sharply.

"Hey, I'm just trying to help you out…repaying the favor," Skyler said sarcastically.

"I don't need *you* telling *me* what to do or how to act. I, more than you, am aware of the circumstances and the repercussions of my actions. I'm handling it my way."

Skyler thought that Jackson had already stepped over the line. "You haven't…had sex with her, have you?"

"Don't be ridiculous. Why would I do that? I know it's forbidden."

Jackson stood up to leave, and Skyler started coughing vigorously.

"You've still got that cough?" Jackson asked.

"Yeah. It won't go away."

"You didn't tell Cassie about the fact that you used to be an angel, did you?"

Skyler shook his head. Jackson didn't know that she still remembered, and it was something they both agreed to keep secret, especially from Jackson. "No, I haven't."

"Maybe you've pissed off some angel. It happens sometimes."

Skyler scrunched his forehead. How would he have pissed off another angel? What had he done wrong? He couldn't think of anything. He still hadn't even met his own guardian angel, at least not that he knew of.

"Couldn't I just be sick for the first time in my life? I am human now. Maybe the protection I had over me for the past ten years has worn off or something," Skyler suggested.

"Maybe…but I doubt it. You had the power to heal when you were an angel, and so did the body that you took over – Grant's. There shouldn't be a sick bone in your body. Ever."

Chapter Thirteen

Later that evening, Scarlett and Jackson were sipping wine on the couch in the family room by the fireplace. Tyler had begged to spend the night with a friend who lived near her house in Pungo, so she had agreed. His friend's mom came and picked Tyler up, after Tyler showed off his new puppy. Scarlett's cousin had a hotel room at the oceanfront, so he left to settle down for the night, and so, Jackson and Scarlett were alone at her beach house. The puppy was napping, nestled between the two of them.

"I want to apologize for my behavior last week," she said. It was the first time they'd had a chance to talk about her proposition to make love. "It was silly of me to think that you and I…" she didn't finish. She thought it was foolish of her to think that he would see her as a desirable woman instead of a pitiful dying one.

He swallowed his wine and put the glass down on the coffee table. "No, don't say that. There's no need for you to apologize. You took me completely off guard," Jackson said.

They were listening to a Pandora music station that played modern French and Latin music including Jesse Cook and the Gotan Project. Scarlett listened to a song of a woman singing a sultry song in French with sort a club type beat in the background accompanied by an accordion, violins, and a piano. It was getting her worked up, as well as the intimacy of sitting on the couch so close to Jackson and the thought of being alone in the house with him.

She felt his hand touch her shoulder, and she looked over at him. *God, you're so beautiful,* she heard in her head. It was Jackson's voice but he didn't utter a word.

"Did you say something?" she whispered.

"Hmm? No." He stopped rubbing her shoulder. "Could I move Harry to another chair maybe?" he asked. *So we can get it on,* Scarlett heard again.

She blinked and nodded. He carefully picked the puppy up and laid him gently down on a side chair closer to the fireplace.

He held out his hand to her. "Would you dance with me?"

"I'm pretty tired, Jackson. All that socializing wore me out."

"Come on...please? I'll hold you up if you get too tired."

She took his hand and he helped her to her feet, pulled her in close and began dancing gently, seductively, and they continued that way in silence, listening to the woman singing about love and desire. He even threw in a little tango and some mambo. She was breathless in no time, not only from the physical exertion but also from feeling this man against her body. Smelling his sweet scent, his manliness, his essence. Looking into his deep brown eyes. Just when she thought they were nearly done dancing, he lifted her up in the air, just off her feet, and pressed her against his chest and slowly let her back down. She slid down against him, feeling that he was turned on, which turned her on even more.

"You don't understand what you've done to me," he said quietly as a different song came on, this one sung in Spanish. "I'm more confused than I've ever been over my feelings for you."

Her breathing became hard, her heart pumping fast. "Before you go any further, you're not allowed to have feelings for me," she said in a strained voice, not full of conviction. "I'm not going to live long enough for either of us to have feelings. You've just stirred something inside of me that has been closed off for a very long time."

Did I stir that in you? she heard in her head again. What was happening? Was she reading his mind? How could that be? She'd never had any special gifts like that in the past, though she had read that some people did.

"It's too late. I already have feelings for you," he said.

She tried to get out of his arms, but he held her tight.

"I want to do what you asked of me last week. Does the offer still stand?"

She looked up into his eyes, looking for pity but saw a burning instead. "Maybe," she whispered.

"But I warn you, I don't do casual sex. I'm not allowed."

"Not allowed? Are you a religious man or something?"

"You could say that." They were still swaying slowly to the music, pressed against each other. "I'm thinking of breaking all the rules for you," he whispered.

She wanted desperately to say yes, but not if it cost him so much. "I'm not going to be the one to make you break your rules on casual sex."

"What if I want you to be?"

"I told you I didn't want pity sex."

"You don't want feelings and you don't want pity sex. What kind of sex do you want? Because if it's a one-nighter you're looking for, that might be awkward between us afterward since you don't want feelings involved."

"Don't worry about it. You just had me all worked up with all the yoga, the massage, the bath…"

"Oh, so you're over it now?" He grinned.

She knew she definitely was not over it but was afraid to admit it. "And this dancing…"

"You're beautiful. Can I just make love to a beautiful woman?"

She pulled out of his arms. "I'm not beautiful anymore. You haven't seen my real hair."

"Will you show it to me?"

She shook her head.

"Please?" he whispered, and the look on his face made her knees weak.

She pulled her wig off slowly, dreading his reaction. If this was a mood killer, so be it. He asked for it.

He put his hand through her short hair. "It's like a pixie cut – like Julia Roberts when she played Tinkerbell," he said.

She nearly laughed.

"It's beautiful because it's you."

She felt tears. "It's frizzy," she said, choking on tears.

"I know how to fix that."

"How?"

He reached into his pants pocket and pulled out a brown bottle. He opened the lid and dabbed some of it on his hands, and then he reached over and massaged it into her hair. She closed her eyes, enjoying his touch. It smelled like coconut.

When he was finished he said, "Look in the mirror."

They walked over through the bedroom to her bathroom where she looked at hair that was glossy and lustrous like it used to be when it was longer. Her jaw dropped. "How did you do that?"

He handed her the bottle. "My special oil. Use it after shampooing."

"Thank you," she said, frowning a bit, not knowing what to do with this wonderful man.

Please just ask me, she heard him say in her head.

"Would you just hold me?" she asked.

"Would this be with feelings or without?"

She laughed and rolled her eyes as he took her in his arms and grinned at her.

She felt a little shy but boldly told him, "I've never felt so much at home in anyone else's arms before…never felt so comfortable with another man before."

He raised her chin up to look at him and kissed her with longing. She recognized the desire in his eyes, not pity, and she kissed him back until she was dizzy.

"Are you sure about this?" she whispered, hoping he'd say yes.

"I'm not looking at you with pity, am I? Do these kisses feel like pity to you?"

She knew they didn't. They were filled with passion, with longing, the same as she felt for him. He had lit a fire inside of her, and she didn't want to put it out. She ripped his shirt off, and he pulled her towards the bedroom while they kissed recklessly. They could still hear the erotic music as it got softer and softer.

He pulled her light gray cashmere sweater off carefully.

"Don't be gentle with me," she said, her eyes boring into his.

He tossed the sweater on the floor, pulled her into his arms a little forcefully, and kissed her madly. They finished undressing each other frantically, and he lifted her off the floor and gently placed her on top of her bed. He made her forget everything else for a little while. His kisses, his touch…to all parts of her body…made her forget her short hair, the cancer, the treatments, the shortened life, her short time with Tyler, the fact that she wouldn't outlive the puppy…all of it. Forgotten in his arms.

He brought her to a peak first, and then she pleasured him before they finished together. Their cries of maddeningly wonderful climax were sure to awaken the puppy. Scarlett clung to Jackson's hard back muscles while they finished, and then he lay on top of her until they both caught their breath again.

Jackson was dizzy with euphoria. This was his first time going all the way with a woman, and it was magnificent. He said so out loud. "C'est magnifique."

Scarlett took a deep breath and let it all out. "Oui. C'est ça."

He'd heard her say "oui" over and over again while they were making love. Never had that word had so much meaning to him before. He could be damned now for doing this, he might be turned over to the dark angels, but if so, then so be it. This lovemaking…this woman…was worth the risk, worth the punishments.

Mon amour, he heard her say in his head. He wasn't sure what was going on. She had asked him earlier if he said something out loud, and he wasn't sure if she had heard his thoughts, but now he was hearing hers. It made no sense. The only angels capable of reading a human's mind were guardian angels, so he was confused.

If it was her thoughts, she called him her love. He was definitely stepping over the line here. He felt himself falling in love with her.

He rolled off of her and lay flat on his back to gather his wits before he could stand up to go to the bathroom.

Scarlett got up and rushed to the bathroom, and came back a couple of minutes later with tissues for him. He sat up on the side of the bed, his legs dangling on the side, and she pressed her frail but beautiful naked body against him and kissed his neck. She then hopped up on the high bed, pulled the covers down and crawled under them. She pulled them all the way up, covering everything but her head.

"Are you cold?"

She nodded and smiled. She was still blushed a nice shade of red from their lovemaking. So much life in a usually pale face. He sighed happily and went to clean himself up. Before he could return to the bed, he heard the puppy whine and then bark, and it ran into the bedroom. The little tyke had woken up and probably wanted to go out. He started putting his clothes back on.

"I think Harry needs to go potty."

"Do you want me to go?"

It was the first time she had offered. He had promised her he would take care of the puppy but was beginning to regret buying such a small dog. His reason had been to help comfort her but also to help Tyler when the time came for her to leave this earth. He wished now that he had gotten a dog that was already potty trained. "No, I'll do it," he said.

He walked into the family room to find the leash and stepped into a wet spot on the carpet.

Too late. The puppy had already peed.

"Harry," he scolded. "Come on, we'll see if you've got anything left."

He took the dog out the front door and into the sandy Bermuda grass in the front yard where Harry peed some more and did his business. When they returned inside, Jackson cleaned up the soiled spot on the floor while Harry went to find his mother.

When he finished, he found the two of them snuggled in the bed together.

"Are you going to join us?" she asked him, smiling.

He couldn't resist her anymore. "Absolutely," he said.

He undressed again and crawled under the covers. Scarlett shifted and leaned against his chest, one hand resting on his belly. The puppy was on the outside of the covers and started digging on the comforter, which tickled Jackson's abdomen. Finally, Harry laid down, half on Scarlett, half on him, and cleaned himself.

Scarlett laughed lightly and sighed. "You have made me very happy. I'm about to burst, really."

"I'm so glad, Scarlett." He rubbed her short hair.

I wish you could spend the night, he heard her say inside his head. Would she say it out loud? Should he offer? He was new to this whole affair thing but he knew he didn't want to leave her. Didn't want to get back to his job of telling other people their time was about to end. All he could think about was spending the rest of this woman's time with her…and wishing he could spend eternity with her.

"Will you stay?" she finally asked him, looking up at him with hopeful eyes.

"Absolument," he said without hesitation.

Chapter Fourteen

Scarlett woke up the next morning and heard the puppy whining. She opened her eyes and realized she was lying on Jackson's chest. She couldn't believe what they'd done last night. What was wrong with her? It had been wonderful, but she had to watch herself. She'd told him not to have feelings for her, but she was beginning to have feelings for him. That wasn't a good thing, as it would make her departure all the more difficult.

She blinked and looked up into his handsome face, watching him sleep. It would be so easy to fall in love with him, but that was not a wise choice, so she forced herself to just enjoy whatever this was they had going on and not worry about her feelings.

His eyes fluttered open and he looked down at her. "Good morning, mon petit chou," he said. He bent down and kissed her lips.

"Morning," she said, smiling. He pulled her closer to him into a big bear hug, and her heart fluttered. She sighed happily and said, "I can't tell you how good it is to wake up in someone's arms." She looked up at him. "In your arms."

He reached down and kissed her again, passion in his eyes this time. His lips moved over hers while his hands roamed her whole body from breasts to toes and back up to her pleasure spot. She caught her breath at his touch, longing to do what they'd done last night, including a second time in the middle of the night. She moved her knee up towards his groin, and he growled like an animal, which made her laugh.

The puppy had other plans, however, and barked loudly and scratched on the door of the crate to be let out. Jackson had put him in there when they'd started round two.

They stopped kissing and Jackson sighed, obviously irritated. "I'm beginning to regret buying that puppy," he said gruffly.

Scarlett watched him get out of bed reluctantly and pull on his underwear and then jeans. He walked over, opened up the crate, and picked up the puppy. "I'll be right back," he said, leaving the room.

Scarlett got up and went to the bathroom, picking her phone up on the way to see what time it was. It was nine o'clock. Tyler was supposed to be home by noon. Since it was Black Friday, she thought about doing a little Christmas shopping for Tyler before he came home, but what she really wanted to do was spend more time alone with Jackson. This could get addicting.

She came back into the bedroom, intending on waiting for Jackson to come back when her cell phone rang in her hand. It was her oncologist's office calling.

She pushed the green box on the screen. "Hello?"

"Ms. Laurent?" a woman's voice asked.

"Yes, this is Scarlett."

"Hi, Scarlett. My name is Peggy, and I'm a hospice nurse from Dr. Mitchell's office. I was just calling to check on you to see how you've been doing. We haven't heard from you in a few weeks."

"I'm doing well. A little tired now and then, but not too bad."

"That's good to hear. I went by your house the other day, but you weren't home. I'm sorry I missed you."

"Oh, I'm not living at that address anymore. I moved into a beach house at Sandbridge. Didn't Jackson tell you?"

"Jackson?"

"Yes, the man who's been checking on me from your office."

There was silence for a moment. "Hold on," Peggy said. Scarlett could hear clicking keys of a computer keyboard. "I don't have record of anyone named Jackson authorized to come out to your house."

Scarlett was confused. Why wouldn't they know about Jackson? "I saw him the first day I came out of your office back in March. He said he worked for Dr. Mitchell."

"Ma'am, I'm sorry, but we don't have anyone by the name of Jackson working at this office."

Scarlett started to feel panicky. "His last name is Wiggs. Could you check again please?"

More silence and some paper shuffling. "No, I don't see that name either. Maybe he's with another office. Your primary care physician maybe?"

Scarlett didn't think so, but she said, "Maybe."

"Could you give me your new address so I can add it to your medical record?"

"Sure." Scarlett gave her the address, all the while thinking that something wasn't right. "My cell number is the same. I don't have a home phone here."

"Okay. Would it be all right if I came by to see you? Is today a good day or maybe you'd prefer Monday. I know this is short notice."

"Monday would be better, thank you."

"All right. Any special time? Morning or afternoon?"

"Late morning, around ten would be good."

"Fine. I'll put you down for ten o'clock. I'll see you on Monday then. Take care."

Scarlett hung up the call and looked around for her clothes. She began getting dressed, wondering who this man was if he didn't work for the oncologist. Was he just a strange man who hung around oncology offices, looking for women in need? Just for sex? The more she thought about it, the madder she got. How dare he lie to her, come to her house almost daily, inch his way into her heart the way he did. Having brilliant sex with her.

Something still wasn't right about that, though. Hadn't he told her from the beginning that her time was short? Like he had read her medical record and knew what was wrong with her. It could've been a lucky guess, though, if he was in the habit of lurking around looking for cancer patients. They shouldn't be too hard to find, skin-and-bones thin, sunken eyes, little to no hair. It would be quite easy to spot his next prey. Well, she wasn't going to be his prey any longer.

Jackson came back into the house with Harry and let him loose. They both headed for Scarlett's bedroom. As he rounded the corner, a shoe hit him in the chest.

"What's going on?" he asked as Scarlett hurled another shoe his way. He ducked before it could hit him. "What's wrong?"

She looked livid. "Who are you?" she asked, picking up objects off her nightstand to throw at him next, a wind-up clock, a journal, a fountain pen.

"Scarlett, just stop. Calm down and tell me what's going on."

She stopped throwing things and buttoned up a silk blouse as she walked towards him. She pounded him in the chest with her fists. "You don't work for Dr. Mitchell, do you?"

He marveled at how strong she was, this frail looking woman. He took her wrists so she would stop hitting him. "Why would you ask me that?"

"Because his hospice nurse just called me and said they don't have any record of you working for them."

Uh oh. He'd been found out. How much should he tell her? He'd been dreading the moment when he would have to tell her what he was and why he was there. He was actually there for the same reason – whether he worked for the oncologist or not, he was there to help her deal with her imminent death.

"Okay, you caught me. No, I don't work for Dr. Mitchell."

He saw tears in her eyes. He felt bad that he'd made her sad. After he'd made her so happy the night before. He loathed the look in her eyes right now, loathed himself for being the cause of it.

"How could you lie to me like that? Is this a game to you? Who are you, really?"

"I never actually told you I worked for Dr. Mitchell. I just let you believe that I did," he said, evading her last question for the moment.

He could see her thinking about it, trying to remember if he had ever told her he worked for her doctor. "You're right. You never actually said it. That was a pretty mean thing to do. Is this your game? How many other women with cancer have you done this to?"

"What?" She must think him a shyster. "I have never behaved in this manner with another woman. Only you." That was the truth. Normally, he would have told her the truth right away.

"I don't believe you." She tried to get out of his grip, and he let her go. "How could you do that to me?" He saw tears in her eyes again and then anger. "You're nothing but a liar and a con artist, and I want nothing more to do with you. Get out of my house!" She pounded him on the chest again.

"Scarlett, please let me explain."

Harry started howling, scared of what was going on.

Scarlett stopped hitting him and bent down to pick up the puppy. She handed Harry to him and said, "Take this puppy with you. I don't want to see either one of you right now."

"But Scarlett…"

"Go! Right now!" And then she started speaking in fluent French with a few choice curse words.

He did as she requested, picking up the crate on the way out the door. He would let her calm down a little before he tried to tell her the truth. What was he going to do with the puppy in the meantime?

Chapter Fifteen

Cassie woke up early on Friday morning and found a white feather on her bed. *What the heck?* How did that get there? She picked it up and looked at it. It was from an obviously big bird. It was big enough to be used as a quill like you might find in Colonial Williamsburg. She sat up and looked around but nothing else seemed out of place. She put the feather on the table and got out of bed, wondering if someone had played a trick on her. It was a little unnerving to think that someone had been in her room at night without her being aware of it.

It was the biggest shopping day of the year, and her best friend, Emily, wanted to go to the mall for some good deals, so she got dressed. Skyler was going with them. He hardly left her side, ever since he had been able to see her again after his ten-year separation, after he'd gone back in time. She wasn't complaining; she loved spending time with him. If he wanted to torture himself by shopping with the girls, so be it.

At a little after nine, he showed up at the back French doors, and she let him in. He kissed her deep and long until Jen came into the kitchen and cleared her throat.

Cassie stepped back and looked at Jen, feeling herself blush. She poured herself a bowl of cereal, while Jen did the same.

"Do you want anything?" Cassie asked Skyler.

"No, thanks. My mom made omelets for breakfast."

"That sounds awesome," Jen said. "Wish I had time for that, but I've got to open the shop at ten. Are you still going to Busch Gardens later to see the Christmas lights?"

"Yes, we are. Are you sure you guys don't want to join us?" Cassie was going with Skyler and his family.

"Not today. I'll be too tired after working. Another time for sure. I'll take a day off to go."

Jen went downstairs to her shop, and then there was another knock at the French doors.

It was Jackson. Dread filled Cassie. He had always annoyed her in the past, used to flirt with her, and then he was the one who was responsible for punishing Skyler, so she wasn't very fond of him.

"I wonder what he wants?" she asked.

"Only one way to find out," Skyler said, walking to the door to let him in.

That's when Cassie noticed that Jackson had Tyler's new puppy in his hands.

"Hey," Jackson said, looking sheepish. "I was wondering if you could take care of Harry for a couple of days?" he asked her.

"Wow, I don't know. I'll have to ask my dad and Jen. Why? Has something happened to Scarlett?"

"She's a little mad at me, and she told me to take the dog away. I know she'll want him back soon, but I have no place to keep him right now." He looked meaningfully at Skyler, and Cassie knew it was because he was an angel and had no home, so therefore no place to keep the dog. But he didn't know that she remembered that he was an angel, so she had to pretend ignorance.

"That's too bad," she said. "He's such a cute puppy."

She took him out of Jackson's arms and said, "I'll go show him to Jen and see if she'll let me babysit him."

"I have his crate, too. He sleeps in that at nighttime so he won't pee on the floor or chew anything up. You'll have to help him remember to go outside to potty, though."

"Okay. I'll be right back."

She kissed Harry on its black head and walked down the stairs to Jen's shop.

"So what's going on?" Skyler asked Jackson. "Why is Scarlett mad at you?"

"She found out I don't really work for hospice."

"Uh oh. Are you going to tell her what you are?"

"Yes, I have to now. I'm just waiting a couple of days for her to calm down. I didn't know she had so much fire in her. Passion, yes, but not fire."

"Aren't you breaking the rules? Who's going to punish you like you punished me and my dad?"

"I don't know. I'm waiting for that. I want to apologize to you for all of that. I mean, yeah, it had to be done, but now I understand how you feel about Cassie. I think I'm falling for Scarlett."

"I don't know what to tell you, unless you want to become human. But then, Scarlett is dying. There's really not much hope for the two of you, is there?"

Jackson looked at him darkly. "I don't know."

"You would know better than any other being. You're supposed to be an expert on death, aren't you?"

"I said I don't know." Jackson knew of only one way the two of them could be together, but he wasn't going to say anything about it to Skyler. He didn't need to know, as he wasn't an angel anymore.

Skyler suddenly doubled over and grabbed his abdomen.

Jackson frowned. "What's wrong?"

"I don't know. I've been getting these pains in my stomach for the last two days."

"Hold on a minute." Jackson went invisible to look around the whole house in his angel form. He saw Skyler's guardian nearby, sitting down on the love seat in the sitting room.

"What's going on with Skyler? I haven't been notified of his impending death, so what is it?"

The guardian stood up. He was six feet six with bulging muscles and blonde hair. "He's being haunted."

"Haunted?"

"Yes. I told the other one to go away. He's gone now."

"Who is he?"

"He's another angel of death."

"What's he doing here? If someone in his house was dying, I would know about it. I'm the authority in this region."

"Yeah, but you've been kind of busy lately…with your woman."

Jackson sneered at him. "How would you know about that?"

"Word gets around, you know that."

"It's none of your business. You just keep your eye on Skyler."

He went back to human form.

"What's going on?" Skyler asked him.

"Just checking up on something. Nothing to worry about."

Cassie came back upstairs with the puppy in her arms. "Jen said it's okay with her if it's okay with my dad. I think he's still in bed. Wish me luck."

"Luck," Skyler said. He looked at Jackson again. "Why'd you go into angel form?"

"Someone's stalking you, that's all I can say. That's really more than I should say."

"Stalking me?"

Cassie came back in the room. "Dad said it's fine with him if I take care of him. I'm going to call Emily and tell her I'm not going shopping today. I'll be gone long enough when we go to Christmas Town, so I'll stay here with him until we go. Is that okay with you?" she asked Skyler.

"Sure. You know I just want to be wherever you are."

Jackson wanted to leave before it got silly or he got jealous, or both.

"This will be great," Cassie said. "I've always wanted a dog. Maybe I'll get one soon."

"Maybe you will," Jackson said.

Late that night, after coming home from Christmas Town, Cassie took a quick shower, got into bed, and fell asleep quickly. Sometime in the middle of the night, she began to dream about Skyler in a sexual way again. They were in the woods this time, nothing but trees surrounding them, and sunshine streaming through the leaves. They were holding hands, and then suddenly there was a small clearing near an old abandoned house and Skyler pulled her to the house.

"Come on, let's explore."

She laughed and agreed. They tried the front door, but it was locked. They tried the back door, but it, too, was locked, until Skyler waved his hand over the doorknob and it clicked and the door opened.

"How'd you do that?" she asked, knowing he didn't have powers anymore.

He just grinned at her and pulled her inside. They went from room to room, looking at old dusty pieces of furniture mingled with plastic cups and Styrofoam plates like someone had been in there recently. They found a bedroom, and whereas the rest of the house was dusty and smelled musty, this room was clean, smelled of roses, and looked like it belonged in a brand new house. There was a tall four-poster bed with green, pink, and white curtains hanging from a canopy, like something she had seen at the Governor's Palace in Colonial Williamsburg.

Skyler pulled her up onto the bed and began kissing her, taking her clothes off. Before she knew it, she was completely naked, as was he. He looked at her with a sort of fire in his eyes, very unlike the Skyler she knew. Just as quickly as the look came, it went, and Skyler kissed her and pushed her back on the bed. He was about to penetrate her when a loud scream distracted her.

She woke up with a start, saw that she was naked in her own bed at home, and realized the scream she had heard in her dream was the puppy. He was whimpering in his crate.

"Aw, Harry. It's okay, boy."

She got out of bed, put her underwear and camisole back on – wondering when she had started taking her clothes off in her dreams – and got Harry out of his crate. She pulled on some sweat pant capris and carried him downstairs to the back door to let him out, thinking he had to go potty or something. She looked around the moonlit backyard while Harry sniffed around and peed on the apple tree. She thought she saw something at the very back fence of the property, maybe a figure. Scared, she called for Harry.

"Come on, boy. Let's go back inside."

The figure got closer to her, and Harry started barking at it and kicking his back feet like a bull.

"Come on, Harry. Let's go!" she yelled. Her heart started beating like crazy as the figure got closer, and Harry growled low and menacing.

She boldly ran over to the apple tree, picked Harry up, and turned back around and ran to the house, Harry wiggling around in her arms. Before she reached the back door, she heard a loud growl and felt but didn't see something about to pounce on her. Harry barked like mad, and finally she flung the back door open and slammed it shut, bolting the lock and peeking out through the wispy curtains to see what was out there.

She saw nothing. Nothing at all.

Chapter Sixteen

"Do you have everything you need?" Jen asked Luke. They were at the airport early on Sunday morning. The wives had driven all the band members to the airport for their trip to Nashville to see about getting a recording contract. James had already flown back the previous day.

"Yeah, I think so," Luke said. He couldn't believe this was happening. Couldn't believe his dream of being a country star might actually come true. It was unfortunate that it came at such a time as this though. He and Jen had just gotten married not even a month ago.

"I'm so happy for you, Luke," Jen said, "but I'm going to miss you like crazy."

He pulled her into his arms. "No more than I'll miss you, but this shouldn't take long. I'll be back in no time. We're just going for a meeting right now."

"They'd be a fool not to sign you. You're so talented."

He kissed her. "You may be just a little biased."

She smiled. "I may be. But only a little."

Luke looked around at the other couples saying their goodbyes. It felt almost like when he used to go to Wallops Island nearly every week when he was a government contractor. This time was different, though. This time, he was on the road to doing what he loved…and hopefully would get paid for it. He couldn't be happier. Unless he could take Jen with him.

"I wish I could go with you," she said, as if reading his mind.

"I wish you could, too, but someone needed to stay home with the kids."

"I know." She looked sad. "It's an unfortunate time to be leaving, what with the news of Tyler and all."

"Yeah, but if we eventually moved to Nashville, after Scarlett…is gone, Tyler would be near his cousin – he'd have both of us."

"Have you thought about telling him that you're his dad?"

"I have but I'm not ready for that yet. Maybe when I get back, after we see what happens in Nashville."

"Maybe Scarlett should be the one to tell him first. I know how important that is to her."

"Yeah, you would know." Jen had surprised him with the news that Logan was his, but she had asked to be the one to tell him first. "Okay, I'll wait for her then."

"You brought one guitar. Was there anything else you needed to bring?"

"They told me I could bring a favorite guitar if I wanted to, but otherwise we'll be using studio guitars." He was bringing his worn acoustic Fender Tele that Keith Urban had signed when the band opened up for him years ago.

"Come on, Luke, they're calling our flight," Steve told him.

Luke nodded. "Be right there." He hugged Jen one more time and kissed her sweet lips. He ran his hand through her shoulder-length blondish-brown hair, releasing the smell of her favorite rose-scented shampoo. "Well, this is it."

She smiled. "It sure is. When you come back, you'll be a different man."

He laughed. "No, I won't. I won't change, no matter how famous I get. If I do get famous. I'll never let this music get between us, I promise."

She nodded. "Okay. I love you, Luke."

"I love you, too."

One more kiss, and then he said goodbye to Cassie and Logan, who had been sitting down waiting nearby.

"Take care of the house," he told Logan.

"Yes sir, I will."

"Take care of that puppy," he told Cassie.

"I will, Dad. Be careful."

"I will."

He turned to get in line with Steve, Derek and James to go through the security check and find their terminal. He turned around one last time and blew his family a kiss. He followed his friends, his heart full of excitement.

Jen and the kids left the airport and headed towards Charles City County where Jen's cousin, Sarah Wellington-Barnes, lived. It was in a quaint country area between Williamsburg and Richmond near the James River. Sarah had inherited a small old plantation house five years ago after her first husband Seth died in Iraq as a Navy SEAL. The house had been in his family, and Sarah and her daughter Victoria, Tori for short, moved into the house six months after his death. Sarah longed for a change and time to mourn and get used to living without her husband. The plantation had been in Seth's family, had been neglected in recent years, and so was not in very good condition. As part of the healing process, Sarah had the house restored bit by bit to its former glory. During that time of restoration – for the house and for Sarah – she fell in love with the carpenter, Jason Barnes, who'd been working on the house, and they later married.

About an hour later, they reached the property, which sat on about five acres of land, complete with a main two-story Victorian house, horse stables, and a guesthouse. As Jen pulled into the long driveway, she saw her cousin come out onto the covered wraparound front porch. The house was blue with white trim and four lattice columns across the front.

"Hi," Sarah said, all smiles when Jen got out of the car.

"Hey, it's so good to see you again."

The two hugged, and then Sarah hugged Cassie and Logan.

"Come on in," Sarah said. "Tori should be right down. Are you ready for some horseback riding?"

"I don't know about them, but I sure am," Jen said.

At Jen's wedding, she and Sarah had talked about horses, and Sarah invited her and the family to come anytime they wanted to ride. So when Jen found out that Luke was going out of town, she called Sarah and asked if they could come out and ride. Sarah agreed that it would be a good time to get together since they hadn't been able to see each other for Thanksgiving. Sarah and Jason also owned an inn, which had been booked up for the holiday, but their guests had gone home that morning. Jen was glad because she didn't want to be alone to think about missing Luke so much.

"Yeah, sure," Logan said.

Cassie agreed, too. "I'm ready."

Tori came down a moment later. She was a beautiful young lady of twenty years old, with long dark brown hair, a rounded face with nice cheekbones, and green eyes like her mother's. She was wearing a white turtleneck, a tan blazer, dark jeans, and long riding boots.

"You look ready to ride," Jen said, hugging her.

"I'm always ready to ride," Tori said.

"It took both of us a while to get the hang of it, didn't it?" Sarah said. "Jason taught us both."

"That's great. I helped teach Luke when we went to Georgia back in September."

"Did he enjoy it?"

"He did. By the way, where's Grayson?" Grayson was Jason's son from a previous marriage.

"He's been with his mother for the whole weekend. He'll be back tonight. Would y'all care for something to drink first before we head out?"

The kids shook their heads, eager to ride, and Jen said, "No, thanks."

"All right, then. Let's go."

They found Jason out in the stables, saddling up the horses for them. He was a tall well-muscled guy with slightly curly dark brown hair, brown eyes, a mustache, and neatly trimmed beard and sideburns. He greeted Jen and the kids.

"It's good to see you again," he said to Jen. He had a rich deep voice.

"You, too. Are you joining us?"

"No, not this time. I've got to fix a broken shutter at the inn. Y'all have fun."

They each got on a horse and Sarah led them to a trail that ran parallel to the old two-lane Highway 5. The trail took them through the woods all the way down to the Rappahannock River, which was where they turned around and headed back. Jen enjoyed the peacefulness of the area where few cars traveled and birds of all kinds chirped and flitted about. The sun was shining brightly, warming the air even though it was a cool sixty-one degrees. Jen missed living in the country and having access to horses like she had when she lived with her dad in Georgia. The house she lived in now was in a somewhat busy section of Pungo with quite a bit of traffic, which seemed to grow more each year. She'd like to have a house more out in the country. Maybe now that Luke might be getting into the music business, they could find something bigger deeper in Pungo.

Then again, he had already talked about moving to Nashville. She wasn't sure she wanted to do that. She had her shop here and her best friend, Maggie, and was now getting back in touch with her cousin, Sarah. It would be hard to leave them, but of course, she would do it for Luke if that's what he wanted to do. If it all worked out and they got the recording contract.

When they got back to the stables, they put the horses in the field to feed, and then went inside. Sarah and Jen made some sandwiches along with chips and hot chocolate for the young people, coffee for the adults. They sat in a dining room off one end of the house that was inside a turret and had curved windows all around with sweeping views of the woods and the field.

"I love that sweater you're wearing," Jen said to Sarah.

She was wearing a green plaid shirt that made her eyes pop and an off-white cable sweater over that.

"Thank you," Sarah said. "I got this in Ireland. Jason took me there for our honeymoon. I had been doing my genealogy when we met and did one of those DNA tests and found out I have a lot of Irish in me. We spent some time in the areas where my three times great-grandfather lived – Dublin and County Meath.

"Oh, that sounds interesting."

"If you'd like, I can show you the scrapbook I made. I bet you have some Irish in you, too."

"Maybe I do. Sure, I'd love to see your book."

They took their coffee to the big front parlor, which was decorated in golds and purples, and already had a Christmas tree in one corner.

"Wow, that is a gorgeous tree!" Jen exclaimed. "This whole room is so pretty."

"Thank you. I do enjoy decorating. I started this on Friday."

"I'm impressed. You got a lot done."

"Thanks."

Sarah got her scrapbook off the lower shelf of a round antique table. The two spent the next hour looking at the pictures and family names in the genealogy, a few of which were also Jen's ancestors. She downloaded an ancestry app on her phone and started putting some of the names on it.

"I warn you, this is addictive. Once you start getting hints about other relatives, you end up spending way more time on it than you intended," Sarah said, laughing. "Jason and I spent many a night up late looking at this stuff." She smiled, making Jen wonder if she was remembering some romantic interludes in addition to looking up ancestors. It made her miss Luke.

Even more so when Jason came in the room and kissed Sarah.

"Did you get that shutter fixed?" Sarah asked him.

"Yup. Piece of cake."

Jen looked at her phone and noticed it was nearly five o'clock and that the sun was going down.

"I guess we better get going. It's a long drive back home."

"Aw, I know it is. I'm so glad you guys came to visit. Come back anytime, I mean it."

"Thanks for having us, and I sure will. Luke and I will come back and stay at your inn sometime."

"Oh, good. We'll plan to do something, just the four of us."

"That'll be fun. Y'all come see us sometime, too."

"Will do."

Chapter Seventeen

Jackson came and got the puppy back from Cassie on Sunday morning before they headed to the airport. He took Harry with him back over to Scarlett's, intending to get back in her good graces and tell her what he was. He'd given her three days to cool down. Hopefully that was enough time. He'd missed her in those three days since Thanksgiving night.

He'd been pleasantly surprised that he had been able to sleep through the night in human form with her. Usually angels who present themselves in human form can only do so for a limited amount of time before they have to change back into an angel. He did sleep, so maybe that was why he was able to physically do it.

He was waiting for punishment of his actions. It hadn't come yet, but maybe it started with Scarlett getting mad at him. He couldn't blame her for being mad. He had been dishonest with her. But it hadn't been all about sex, unlike what she had insinuated. She was his first sex experience…and what an experience it had been! It saddened him to think that he might never get to experience that again with her.

He rang her doorbell and waited. And waited. He saw her peek out the window once, but still she hesitated to answer the door, which meant she was still angry with him.

Scarlett, please let me in so we can talk, he thought in his head. He tried to see if she could read his thoughts again.

Finally, she opened the door. She had her short wig on again, had on light make-up, and wore a pair of casual black pants and a red half-zip soft-looking sporty top on. She looked radiant. The red top put a little color in her face, unless she'd been out in the sun that morning.

"Scarlett, I –"

Before he could say another word, Harry let out a yelp and jumped out of his arms and into Scarlett's. She caught him awkwardly and smiled at him when he licked her face.

"He missed you," Jackson said. *I missed you, too,* he thought.

Her eyes met his. Maybe she read his thoughts. If she did, she didn't show it. She didn't say a word nor did she move to invite him in the house.

"I'm sorry, Scarlett. Would you let me explain?"

"What is there to explain? You used me."

"I didn't..." He felt himself getting worked up, ready for an argument, but he didn't want to argue. He wanted to make amends. "I didn't mean to. Please, can I come in?"

She stared at him for a long moment, and then Harry looked at her and barked, like he was telling her it was okay to let him in. She looked at the dog and then stepped back, letting Jackson in the door. He picked up the crate on his way in and left it in the foyer.

She led the way to the family room where a warm fire was lit and the TV was playing what looked like a Hallmark movie. She picked up a remote, turned the volume down very low, and sat down on the sofa. He sat close by in a wide comfortable chair with big arms and many pillows.

How to begin, he wondered? He cleared his throat. "I really am sorry. I should've been truthful with you. Do you remember what I told you when we first met?"

She looked out towards the ocean and then back at him. *I'll likely never forget* he heard her think. "Yes," she said out loud. "You told me I wouldn't make it. That was the first time you made me angry."

It probably wouldn't be the last. "I know when people are going to die," he said.

"You mean you're psychic?"

"No. It's my job to tell people when they're getting ready to pass on."

"Your job?"

"Yes." He took a deep breath. "I'm an angel of death."

Her eyes got big. "You're a what?"

He knew she heard him, but he repeated, "Angel of death."

"You've got to be joking me."

"It's no joke."

"So you're telling me you're an angel?" she asked skeptically.

He nodded. "I help people cross over."

She looked back out at the ocean again, shaking her head. "I don't believe you. You're just trying to come up with an outrageous story so I would think you couldn't possibly be lying." She looked straight back at him. "Am I right?"

He shook his head. "No, I'm not lying." *How can I prove it to you?*

"How are you doing that?"

"Doing what?"

"Talking to me inside my head."

"You hear it, too?" He was hopeful.

She scrunched up her forehead. "I think I'm going crazy."

"You're not crazy. I am an angel, and I do have certain powers. Most angels cannot read human's thoughts unless they're guardian angels, but somehow you and I are able to do it. I've been hearing your voice from time to time in my head, too." She looked surprised but still skeptical. "I think it's because we have gotten so close," he continued. "I'm not really sure how we are doing it, to tell you the truth." He was as confused about that as she was.

She got up and walked around the room, stopped to look out the window at the ocean again, and came back and sat down on the sofa again. She put her hands together in her lap and glanced up at him. "Are you really an angel?"

"Yes." He let her process everything. "That's why I don't drive a car to get here. I just…appear."

She nodded her head.

"It's how I knew all about you and your condition."

"Which led me to believe you worked for my doctor."

"Right. I normally tell people right away who I am and why I'm there, but with you…well, you had so much determination. You told me off, that you were going to give it your all. So I left you alone for a while, let you do what you had to do. And then when you were told the cancer had come back, you lost hope. I knew it was time to see you again."

"And yet you still didn't tell me."

"No, I didn't. I saw you at that Halloween party, and you just looked like you needed someone to talk to, someone to share your sorrow with. I wanted to be that someone. You…touched me in a way no other human, no other woman, has."

She rolled her eyes, still unsure whether to believe him or not. "Are you the only one?"

"The only angel of death?" She nodded. "No, there are others. Some are not as friendly as me." Like the one he thought was troubling Skyler right now. "Some are very harsh and don't care about humans at all."

"But not you?"

"No, I enjoy interacting with humans very much. It's quite fun." He smiled.

"So, you're an angel pervert, is that it? You enjoy having sex with women?" Her voice was thick with disgust.

"No." He shook his head. "I only had sex with you – I swear it. I'm not saying I haven't had some fun with other women, but no sex…until you."

She looked at him curiously, still trying to figure out whether to believe him or not.

Is that the truth? she asked in his head.

"Yes," he said out loud.

She didn't look surprised, which meant she was still hearing his thoughts when he directed them to her.

"You really did know, didn't you?" she asked. He knew she was starting to believe him.

He nodded.

"So you really just came to tell me I'm dying?"

"At first, yes."

"And then you played with my emotions? How could you do that to my weak heart? In my condition?"

"I couldn't help it. I…I'm starting to fall for you, Scarlett. I know it's not right, but I can't help it."

"Stop," she said, holding her hand up. "I told you not to have feelings for me. Angel or human, you still can't have those kinds of thoughts for me."

"But I still do," he said softly. He laid his hand on top of hers. "You can't control my feelings."

"No, but I can control mine." She moved his hand off hers, got up, and walked towards the front door. "I think it's time for you to leave."

He slowly got up and walked towards her.

"Forget about feelings," he said. "Can't you just let me comfort you? You said yourself it was nice to be in my arms. Can't I be the arms you rest in?"

He saw tears in her eyes and emotion pass over her face. She swallowed hard and said, "I'll think about it."

He turned around to leave. She put her hand on his arm, and he turned back.

"Where will you go? What do you do when you're not here?"

He smiled inwardly, knowing she believed him now. "I go help other people or I go up to Eden and wait for other names to be given to me. I work the whole Tidewater area."

That is so weird, he heard her think. She nodded. "I'll get back to you. How will I reach you?"

"I'll keep tabs on you," he said, smiling. "I'll be back, I promise."

She nodded again.

He thought that all went fairly well.

Chapter Eighteen

Luke got the recording contract. Jen had whooped and hollered into the phone when he called her Monday night. He came home on Tuesday and was going to pack up and head back to Nashville the next day to start recording.

"They want to use both of my love songs that I wrote for you," he said to Jen. They were sitting outside on the upstairs covered balcony in the swing since it was a warm day for the first of December. He reached over and kissed her on the lips.

"Really?" She was all smiles. "That'll be so cool. Will I get to hear them on the radio?"

"Who knows? Maybe."

"Wow. I'm so proud of you, Luke."

She gave him a kiss and unzipped his jacket so she could run her hand up inside his shirt to run her fingers over his rock-hard abs.

"Oh baby, I've missed you," he said between kisses.

"Hey, Dad," Cassie said, coming up the stairs. She and Logan were coming home from school.

"Don't mind us," Logan said, passing by, snickering.

The two of them laughed briefly, kissed again, and then got up and went inside after the kids. Luke hadn't seen them all weekend.

"Until later…" Luke whispered in her ear.

She smiled and began to fix supper while Luke told them all about his exciting adventures in Nashville.

Luke's cell phone rang while he was telling them about Steve's luggage getting lost in Nashville, ending up on the wrong plane.

"Hello?"

"Luke?" It was Scarlett.

"Hey, what's up? Everything okay?"

"Yeah, fine. I was wondering if you and Jen could come over one night this week, maybe Friday, so we can tell Tyler that you're his dad. Is that okay with you? You still don't have to make any decisions about keeping yet him. I don't want him to grow up not knowing who his dad is."

Luke froze momentarily, both dreading and feeling excited about the prospect of having another son.

"That would be fine, but unfortunately, I can't this week. I'm going back to Nashville tomorrow. Did James tell you we got a contract?"

"No, he didn't. Congratulations!"

"Thanks."

"When will you be back in town?"

"I'm not sure. Maybe next week or the week after."

"Hmmm, that doesn't sound too certain. Would tonight be all right with you? I'm sorry to throw this on you at a busy and exciting time, but I don't know how long I have, and…" Luke heard her sob for a moment and then she cleared her throat. "I'm sorry. Would y'all like to come over for dessert? My neighbor Catrina made some éclairs that we can eat, and I'll make a pot of coffee. Do you have time?"

Luke felt sorry for her. She sounded desperate. It had to be hard, worrying about the future of your son when you knew you wouldn't be around to be there for him. "Sure, I'll make time."

"Great, I'll see you soon."

After hanging up the phone, Scarlett went to her son's bedroom upstairs. He was sprawled out on the bed doing what looked to be homework. Harry lay peacefully curled up beside him.

"Hey," she said, knocking on the doorframe.

He looked around. "Hey. I'm almost done with my math."

"Okay. I need to talk to you, so I'll just sit down and wait if that's okay with you."

"Sure."

He turned his attention back to his math book and worked out some more problems.

"Let me know if you need any help."

"Okay, I will."

He seemed to be pretty good at it. He didn't ask for any help and worked quietly.

Ever since arguing with Jackson, Scarlett had been thinking that she had gotten sidetracked and that she should be focusing more on Tyler. She hadn't told him about her cancer until this past weekend. He'd argued with her when she first told him.

"You can't have cancer. You can't die." He'd stomped his feet and screamed to the top of his lungs, and then he fell down on the floor and cried some more. She'd picked him up, curled him up in her arms, and rocked him like she had when he was a baby. "Please, Maman, don't leave me."

"Oh, mon cher. If there was a way that I could stay with you forever, I would gladly do it."

"I already don't have a father. What'll I do without a mother?" He stuck his thumb in his mouth and sucked on it, something he hadn't done since he was three years old. He popped it out to say, "Who's going to take care of me? Grand-mère already left us."

"I know, mon petit chou. As hard as it's going to be for you to get used to being without me, it'll also be hard for me to leave you."

"Comment fait-on? I don't want to live without you. Take me with you."

"Oh, my sweet boy. You cannot go where I'm going. I want you to live a long, full life. I'll find someone to take care of you, I promise."

He'd stayed in her arms the rest of the night and they watched his favorite cartoons, ate popcorn, and drank hot chocolate.

He'd been mad at her when he found out that she gave Harry back to Jackson, so on Sunday when he brought the puppy back, Tyler seemed to be doing better. Jackson was right about them needing a dog. Tyler would need him after she was gone.

Tyler finished his homework and closed up his book. He sat up and looked at her tentatively. "Are you feeling okay, Maman?"

"I'm fine. I wanted to tell you something very important. I know you've only just learned about my condition and that was some hard news to take, but I have some more news to tell you."

He looked scared. "Qu'est ce que c'est?" He picked up Harry and put him in his lap.

"I'm going to tell you who your father is."

His eyes got big. "My father? You know who my father is?"

She nodded. "I do. I apologize for not telling you sooner, but for years I didn't know how to contact him. I didn't know where he was. Well, I saw him a couple of weeks ago and I told him that you were his child."

"You did? What did he say?"

"He was surprised, of course, but he's very happy. He's coming over tonight so I can formally introduce you."

"Who is it?"

"It's Luke. Do you remember him? He's the one who played the guitar and sang on Thanksgiving?"

Tyler nodded his head, his expression unreadable.

"What do you think about that?"

"I don't know. Is he really happy that I'm his son?"

"He is."

They heard the doorbell ring.

"That's him now. Come on, let's go meet your papa."

They held hands as they walked down the stairs and didn't let go when Scarlett opened the front door.

"Hey, come on in," Scarlett said.

Luke and Jen walked inside and Jen closed the door back. All eyes were on Tyler.

"Tyler, this is Luke…your father."

Luke looked at her, surprised. He didn't know she was going to tell Tyler before he got there, but she thought it might be easier this way, in case Tyler was upset about it. Luke looked down at Tyler and squatted, leaning on his knees. "Hey, Tyler. I'm so happy that you're my son. I'm sorry I haven't been able to come and see you sooner." They shook hands.

Harry jumped up onto Luke's knee, and he petted him. "Hey, did you miss me?" He looked at Tyler. "Did you know he was at my house for a few days?"

Tyler looked irritated. "I thought he was with Jackson."

"Jackson couldn't keep him and he asked us to. I hope that was okay. We took good care of him."

Tyler picked the dog up and held him tight. "Yeah, it's okay," he said warily.

"Do you remember Jen?" Scarlett asked him.

He looked up at Jen, nodded, and smiled at her briefly. "Hi," he said.

"Hey, Tyler. It's so nice to see you again." She petted Harry in his arms. "And you, too."

"Come into the kitchen and have some éclairs and coffee. Do you like café au lait?"

"That sounds wonderful, and very French," Jen said.

Luke said, "Sure, I'll try some after I have one of these pastries." He looked at the éclairs. "Do you like these, Tyler? Are they any good?"

"Uh-huh, they are," he said, very matter-of-factly. "You should try one."

"Which one do you like better, vanilla or chocolate?" Luke asked.

"Chocolate," Tyler said, smiling. He put Harry on the floor, picked an éclair up and took a bite out of it. "Try it," he said, pointing to another chocolate one.

Luke smiled and picked it up, took a bite, and rolled his eyes with pleasure. "Mmm, this is really good. My compliments to the chef."

Jen and Scarlett both took a vanilla one, and Scarlett served cups of coffee for the three adults and a glass of milk for Tyler. They went into the family room and talked while they ate and drank for the next couple of hours, getting to know each other better. They talked about school, what Tyler liked to do for fun, and about the beach and how nice it was to be living here now. Before long, Tyler ended up sitting next to Luke and showed him a game he was playing on his Amazon Fire made for kids.

After a while, Jen got up and announced that it was nine o'clock and that Luke needed to get up early for his flight back to Nashville.

"Is that really the time?" Scarlett asked. "I apologize for keeping you so long."

"Not at all. I've enjoyed this," Luke said.

Scarlett and Tyler walked them to the door.

"Thank you so much for coming over on such short notice," she said to them before they left.

"You're welcome," Luke said. "Bye, Tyler. I'll see you soon."

"À bientôt!"

"Au revoir," Jen said.

"You guys will have to teach me French," Luke said, laughing.

Tyler surprised them all by hugging Luke before he left.

"Thank you for the hug, Tyler. I needed that."

Scarlett thought that Tyler did, too.

She kissed both of them on the cheek before they walked out the door. Closing it back, she felt a little bit better at the possibility that Tyler might get to spend the rest of his life with his real father. And he just might be happy about it. That would make her parting a little easier.

Chapter Nineteen

On Friday night, Cassie came home from Skyler's after having dinner with his family. She said hello to Jen, who was sitting on the couch in the living room. Her dad was still in Nashville.

"Hey, honey, could you take the trash out for me?" she asked Cassie.

"Where's Logan?"

"He's over at Emily's. He said he'd be home in about another hour."

"Okay."

"Thank you."

She pulled the bag out of the stainless steel trashcan, tied up the ends, and carried it outside by way of the back stairs. The big trashcans that the city emptied for them were kept behind the shed in the backyard. Remembering the last time she was back there at night, when she'd seen that creature, she flipped on the outdoor lights. She zipped up her jacket and walked boldly out to the shed, which was on the far side of the yard by the white picket fence.

It was a cold clear night with a half-moon and stars shining. She shivered and dumped the trash, replaced the lid, and listened for noises. Turning on her flashlight from her phone, she walked back around the shed towards the house when she heard a low growl. She froze and looked all around but saw nothing. It must be behind her, whatever it is. She slowly turned around and flashed her phone all around to help her see.

There in the other corner of the yard, on the inside of the fence was a big black creature of some sort. She blinked, thinking she must be dreaming. It was still there. Her first thought was that it was a bear. She was pretty sure she'd heard that bears could climb trees, but why would one come into their backyard? It must be looking for food. As long as it didn't think she was food, that was fine.

She slowly turned back around and walked slowly and carefully back towards the house. She turned around once and saw that the creature was following her. It had a big rounded back and walked on all fours, but she couldn't make out its face. She kept walking faster and faster, and turned to look at the creature again. It was right behind her. She felt like her heart leaped into her throat. She shined her phone's flashlight into its face. It was a face like she'd never seen before except maybe in a movie. It had black feathers and black beady eyes, which was weird since she thought it was a bear. It should have fur instead of feathers. If it had feathers, it might be able to fly. She couldn't imagine something that big being able to fly.

She took off running towards the house, nearly dropping her phone. Once she reached the staircase, the porch lights went out. She glanced around and saw the thing running towards her. She ran up the stairs quickly, and halfway up, she looked back and saw the thing fly directly at her. She screamed and raced to the top of the stairs on the balcony and ran straight into a figure. The figure grabbed her, and she screamed again. She shone her phone light and saw that it was Skyler.

"Skyler!" She threw her arms around him, trying to catch her breath.

"What's wrong?" he asked.

"There's a creature out in the yard." She peered over the balcony railing to see if it had followed her to the stairs. She didn't see it anywhere. She let go of Skyler and looked everywhere, even up on the roof. "Where'd it go?"

"What did this creature look like?" he asked her.

She described it to him, all the while looking all around the backyard and side yard, but it was gone.

"Whatever it was, it must've gotten spooked and ran away," he said.

He wrapped his arms around her, and she settled against his chest, trying to slow her heartbeat back down to normal. That was when she wondered why Skyler was there. His father had dropped her off at the house about half an hour ago. "What are you doing here?"

"I like to check on you sometimes. Old habits, you know?"

She thought that was nice but weird since he didn't have a car. "How'd you get here?"

"I got a ride."

She noticed that he smelled different. It reminded her of Jackson when she'd first met him…like the ocean. Why would he smell like the ocean? They hadn't been to the ocean; they'd had dinner at his house. Maybe it was just the outdoors she smelled since they had sat around a fire pit after dinner.

She looked up into his eyes. "With who?"

"A friend. Let's sit down over here and relax." He pulled her over to the swing. He took her cell phone out of her hand and put it on the table. "You don't need that right now."

He pulled her against his chest again. She sniffed him again and immediately thought about the erotic dreams she'd been having about him lately. She shivered and he pulled her closer.

"Are you cold?"

She nodded. "A little and also a little upset."

"I'll warm you up and keep you safe." He kissed her head. "I'll make you forget all about that nasty beast."

He pulled her head up and started kissing her lips, just like in her dreams. Her heart raced at his touch, both from an adrenaline rush from her encounter with that creature and also excitement from his kisses.

"I thought you didn't want to kiss because you're sick," she said. Ever since Skyler started getting sick, he claimed he didn't want to kiss her. He'd said, "I can't heal you now, Cassie, so all I can do is keep some distance when I'm sick. I don't want you to be sick." So him kissing her now made her curious. Not that she was complaining.

"I don't care about that right now. I haven't been able to stop thinking about kissing you."

She was thrilled, and he was right about it taking her mind off of the beast and warming her up. They get hot and heavy on the swing, caressing and kissing, until she heard the French door open and the security alarm chirp. Skyler abruptly stopped kissing her and said, "I gotta go."

Jen came out onto the porch and she immediately stood up. Jen asked her, "Are you all right? I thought you just went to take the trash out."

"Yeah, I'm okay," she said. She looked back, but Skyler had already disappeared – like he used to when he was an angel. That was weird.

Should she tell Jen that she had been talking to Skyler? Since he was being weird and sneaking around, she thought not. "I heard an animal and was trying to see what it was, wondering if I should open the gate so it could go back out."

"Oh," Jen said. "Is it still out there?"

"No, it's gone." She hoped so anyway. "And then Skyler called and I was talking to him." She picked up her cell phone that Skyler had placed on the table nearby. She was surprised to see a text from Skyler that read: *I miss you already. C u tomorrow.* She smiled. "I'm coming in now."

She went to bed wondering about the weird night she'd just had – first with the scary creature and then with Skyler's behavior. She drifted off to sleep with the memory of kissing him in her head.

Chapter Twenty

Scarlett began taking walks on the beach every morning at sunrise with Harry. This is where Jackson found her on Saturday morning as she was coming back. It was a clear beautiful morning, and the sun was shining over the water now in a long stream of yellow.

"Jackson!" she said when she saw him walking over the dunes near her house. "What are you doing here? Oh," she smiled, "I'm not supposed to say that when you come over, I forgot. I'm glad to see you."

"You are?" He looked surprised. He looked very fine in a white shirt covered by a gray sweater and dark jeans. The wind blew his hair, which at the moment looked golden in the sun's reflection, across his forehead, a look she had missed. She missed *him.*

"Yes. I've decided to forgive you and not be mad at you anymore. I need all the help I can get to see me through all of this." She wasn't sure what it meant to have an angel of death hanging around her, but whatever he was, she enjoyed being with him. He seemed to know exactly what she needed and provided it for her without her even asking. She didn't want to give that up.

He walked up to her and took her in his arms, something else she had missed. Though she was spending more time with Tyler, which she enjoyed, she realized that she needed Jackson in her life, too. He provided a comfort that her son just couldn't. He had touched a place in her – both physically and spiritually – that hadn't been touched in a very long time, if ever. She didn't want to let that go, no matter how little time she had left to enjoy it.

Harry tugged on the leash, which Scarlett was still holding. "Hold on a minute, Harry," she murmured against Jackson's chest.

I have missed you, she heard Jackson say in her head.

"I've missed you, too," she said out loud, raising her head to look up at him. He smiled and then kissed her lips.

She turned and linked arms with him and walked towards the house. Harry led the way. "Would you like some coffee and croissants? Catrina made me some and brought them over last night."

"Sure. So, are you walking every morning now?" he asked once they reached the back steps.

"Yes, I am. I decided that I want to watch every sunrise because I don't know how many of them I'll have left to see. And I thought getting some exercise would be good for me, too."

"I think it's working. I haven't seen you this radiant before. It becomes you."

"Merci." She blushed.

Once inside, she measured some coffee into the coffee maker and then took the cover off of the croissants. "Help yourself," she said. She walked to the fridge and pulled out some fresh Irish butter and some homemade apple butter that Jen had given her, made with apples from her backyard.

Jackson helped himself to a croissant with all the fixings and said, "Mmm, this is truly decadent."

She laughed. "It is, isn't it? The best part is I didn't have to make any of it. Everyone has been spoiling me so."

"That's good. You deserve to be spoiled."

Tyler came into the kitchen with bedhead and yawned.

"Hey, Tyler," Jackson said.

Tyler looked at him and said "Hey," and then he began looking for the dog. "Harry," he called. He found him drinking water in the kitchen and picked him up. He was rewarded with sloppy doggy kisses.

Scarlett fixed him a couple of the croissants and poured a glass of milk for him while Jackson poured them both cups of coffee.

"Do you want to go with us to see Santa Claus?" Tyler asked Jackson. "He's going to be at the mall today!"

"He is?" Jackson asked.

"Uh-huh." He put Harry back down on the floor and jumped up on a bar stool to eat his croissants.

"That sounds like fun," Jackson said. "I've never met Santa Claus before."

"Well, it's not the *real* Santa – he's way too busy to go to the mall. It's just one of his helpers."

Jackson and Scarlett both laughed. "That's good to know," Jackson said. "What time will you be going?" He looked at Scarlett.

"He'll be there from noon to four, so I guess we'll go at lunchtime. You want to come?" she asked, hoping he would. She didn't understand how an angel of death had so much free time to follow her around the way Jackson did, but she was happy that he did.

"I'd love to," he said.

She picked up her coffee mug and plate of croissants and headed for the balcony facing the ocean. "Let's have a morning picnic outside."

"Not for me," Tyler said. "Can I go ask Arianna if she's going to the mall?"

"You may call her. You don't need to be running down the street or the beach alone." She realized she'd been giving him too much freedom before and needed to keep a closer eye on him.

"Okay. Give me your phone." She raised her eyebrows up. "Please," he said, looking sheepish.

She handed him the phone, picked up her plate again and headed outside, turning to see if Jackson was following her. He was right behind her.

They sat down on the loveseat in companionable silence for a few moments, enjoying the beautiful morning, listening to the distant waves, eating and drinking. When Scarlett finished her croissants, she picked up her coffee mug and leaned back against Jackson. His arm came around her and he caressed her arm, which was snuggled up in an ecru warm sweater.

"Thank you for forgiving me," he said softly. "I know this must be hard for you."

She turned towards him and smiled, looked at his lips and longed to kiss them again. He reached down and kissed her before she could kiss him. Their minds had been thinking the same thing.

"Sorry for the coffee breath," she said.

"I have the same," he said.

She took another drink of it and then sat her mug down on the nearby table. "Do you know the date when I will pass?" she asked.

He was silent for a moment, reached his other arm around her and hugged her close. "Yes."

"Don't tell me. I don't want to know," she said. "Don't give me any hints, either."

"Okay," he agreed. He turned her head up to his and kissed her on the mouth again. "Let's go to Paris."

"What?" She would love to go to Paris but wasn't sure she should. He would know more than she would, though. If he thought it was all right to go, then it must be.

"Let's go see your father. Tyler, too. Has he ever met him?"

She got excited at the prospect of seeing her father again as well as seeing the country that she'd always been thrilled to visit and where she'd lived for a few years as a child.

"No. My father is not doing too good, health wise. I haven't been out to see him in many years, and Tyler was too young the last time I went. I refused to be one of those mothers who subjected everyone on the plane to a crying baby." She linked her hand with his. "You really think we should go?"

He smiled and nodded. "Security will be high right now after the terrorist attacks, but we'll be fine." She raised an eyebrow. "Trust me; you'll both live through it."

She nodded. There were advantages to having an angel of death as a companion. "Tyler doesn't even have a passport. That might take a while to process. Mine is still good."

"I'll see what I can do about getting his passport processed quickly. When would you like to go?"

"I don't know." She began to get excited. It was the first time in a long time that she was looking forward to a future event. "How soon do *you* think we should go?"

"Either before Christmas or after, your choice."

She sighed in relief. "That's good to know. I think this is a good idea. If you can help with the passport, then I'd like to go before Christmas."

"I'll do my best. If nothing else, I could fly you both over there for free."

Her eyes widened. "Are you serious?"

He laughed. "Mais, bien sûr." His expression changed and she swore he had a twinkle in his eye. "Would you like to go flying with me sometime? I could show you where you'll be living in the hereafter."

He'd shocked her again. "Oh, my. That sounds both scary and exciting."

"It's a beautiful, peaceful place, I assure you. I have special privileges and can take you there, just for a short visit. You just say the word when you want to go."

"How about we fly across the ocean first before we fly across the universe?"

He laughed lightly. "Deal. You know, I'm really happy you're talking to me again. I wasn't sure you'd want to. I wasn't sure you'd accept me for what I am."

She smiled. "I decided that I want to spend my last days with the ones I…" *love* she almost said. As foolish as it sounded, even to her, she thought she was falling in love with him. Could he read her mind? Would he think her insane? "…Care about," she finished instead.

He bent over and kissed her until she was breathless, and she ran her fingers through his thick dark hair.

About that time, Tyler ran out onto the porch. "Come on, let's go see Santa!" He stopped suddenly when he saw Scarlett in Jackson's arms. "What are you doing to my maman?" he asked Jackson boldly.

"Tyler," Scarlett scolded him.

"I care about your mother very much," Jackson said. "I promise you, I wouldn't do anything to hurt her."

Tyler seemed to take that into consideration while Scarlett stood up. "Are you willing to share me?" she asked him.

Tyler looked at the two of them alternately. "I guess," he said warily. "Come on, let's get going."

Scarlett relaxed and said to Jackson in her head so that Tyler couldn't hear. *I hope he doesn't give us any problems. He seems wary of you now.*

I'll be gentle with him, I promise. I'll win him over. If not, then I'll back off. I don't want anything to jeopardize your relationship with your son.

Scarlett covered her heart with her fist. *Thank you.*

Chapter Twenty-One

A week later, Luke was still in Nashville and staying at a Hampton Inn. He'd had a busy two weeks since the band got here, starting with recording the love song that Luke wrote for Jen and played at their wedding. It was called, "Take a Chance on Love," a love song about losing the love of your life, the miles separating you and then something happens and you realize if you don't make the effort, she will be lost forever. So he took a chance and told her how he felt, how much he loved her, and finally she was his again…because he had taken a chance on love. It had made Jen cry at the wedding, which made him so happy because he had poured his heart and soul into both the lyrics and the music.

James and his boss, Robert Sawyer, had loved it too, and so they recorded it in the studio. It took nearly a week to perfect it. After that, they had to get promo-ready. They went shopping for the right kind of clothes and then to a fancy men's salon and got new hairstyles, beards trimmed, and even got a massage and drank beer. It was like a spa for men. After that, they went to an old train station on the outskirts of Nashville that had been abandoned for years to get an album cover photo. They posed in front of the gray dilapidated building with Luke holding the neck of his old favorite guitar, which was standing up on the ground in front of him.

The song was going to be released Saturday morning and they were to make several appearances throughout Nashville including being interviewed at a local radio station. They would sign autographs at a mall, at a Farmer's Market, and then that evening they would perform a concert at The

Bluebird Cafe. They would have Sunday off and then start a tour around Tennessee for the next two weeks with a break for Christmas and New Year's. Then get back in the studio after the new year and start recording more songs.

He called Jen on Friday night before the release of their song.

"Luke, hey!" she said excitedly when she answered the phone. "How's it going?"

"Hey, baby. It's going great. We just finished our photo shoot this afternoon, and tomorrow morning our single comes out."

"Wow, I still can't believe your song is going to be heard by everyone in America on the radio! The song you wrote for me!"

"I can't either. My head is spinning. Hey, can you fly out here tomorrow? I'd love for you to be at our first concert tomorrow night. It's a small little place, but it would really mean a lot for you to be here."

"Won't that cost a lot of money, this late?"

"I don't care. I want you with me. I miss you like crazy."

"I miss you, too, but…tomorrow? It's Cassie's birthday."

"Oh God, I completely forgot. I'll have to celebrate with her at Christmas. I only get Sunday off and that wouldn't be enough time to spend with her, plus flying time. And if she flew out here, it wouldn't be fair to Logan."

"Yeah, and we can't afford three airplane tickets this late."

"Anyway, I was thinking that if you came, I could show you around Nashville on Sunday before you'd have to fly back home. We go on tour Monday for two weeks, right up until Christmas Eve."

"Will you be home for Christmas?"

"Supposed to be. I'll probably have to fly out late on Christmas Eve. We'll be home through New Year's and then have to fly back here to do some more recording."

"So this will be the last time I can see you until Christmas?"

"Yeah, I think so. It'll be the easiest because I know where I'll be this weekend. I have no idea where we're going on tour except that it's in Tennessee. Come on, Jen. Use our saved money from the sale of my old house."

"Luke, I'm not going to use our emergency fund."

"Please? I'll be getting paid as soon as our record hits the radio airwaves tomorrow. We'll be rolling in the dough in no time. Everything is happening so fast and I need you to keep me grounded. I can't stand being away from you like this."

Luke's phone in the hotel room rang. "Hold on a minute, Jen, I've got to answer my room phone."

"Okay."

Luke picked it up. "Hello?"

"Luke, it's James. Meet me downstairs in the lobby. We're going to have dinner at the Capitol Grille with some important people in the business. You might recognize one or two of them. Dress nice; it's at the Hermitage Hotel."

"Okay. What time?"

"In ten minutes."

"I'll be right down."

He hung up that phone and picked up his cell phone again.

"Where are you going?" Jen asked before he could say anything.

He told her what James told him. "I'm sorry, but I have to hang up now. Will I be seeing you tomorrow?"

"Yes, I'll be there," she said. "Don't drink too much tonight. Two drinks, that's it."

She knew him well. He'd had a history of getting drunk in the past and making a fool of himself.

"Two drinks, I promise. I'll see you tomorrow." He smiled, couldn't wait to see her. "I love you."

"I love you, too. Bye."

Jen bought her plane tickets online as soon as she hung up the phone with Luke. She was excited to see him but dreaded paying all that money…$569.00! She immediately packed a bag with what clean clothes she had, as she usually washed on the weekend. She packed Luke's favorite black lingerie of hers and hoped they would have some alone time. She told Cassie and Logan that she was going and then took a bath, washed her hair, and shaved her legs and armpits.

She left strict instructions to the kids that their friends were not allowed to come over, no parties, and if they went somewhere, they had to contact each other. They were advised to be on their best behavior and not to spend the night anywhere else besides the house. She gave them phone numbers for emergencies and codes for the security system, and then called Maggie and asked her to check on them.

"I'm leaving them alone for the first time, and they both are involved in romantic relationships. I know how easy it would be for them to be tempted to do something they might later regret," she told Maggie.

"I hear you. I'll drive by and check on them tomorrow night."

"That'd be great. Thanks, Maggie."

"I wish I could go with you, but," Maggie hesitated, "I've been throwing up."

"Oh, no. Are you getting sick?"

"I don't think so," Maggie said. She cleared her throat. "Can you keep a secret? I haven't even told Steve yet."

"Of course I can."

"Do you remember me telling you why Steve and I divorced?" They had divorced five years ago after only being married for five years.

"Yes, you said you lost a baby."

"I did. I had a procedure after that, and the doctor told me I most likely couldn't get pregnant again. Steve and I drifted apart after that. I was devastated that I couldn't have any children." She was silent a moment. "Well, I think the doctor was wrong."

"What? You think you're pregnant?"

"I suspect it, yes. Steve and I made love back in September after the house next door was robbed, remember that?"

"Oh yes, I do. That was the night you let me and Luke have some alone time."

Maggie laughed. "Yes, that's right."

"This is so exciting! Isn't it? Will you be able to carry another child?"

"I don't know. It's kind of scary. That's why I haven't told Steve yet. I don't want to get his hopes up yet until I know for sure. He was really disappointed when I lost our first child. He loved Emily but said he really wanted to have a baby with me."

"I understand that. I won't say anything, I promise."

"Okay. I have an appointment on Monday and I'll find out for sure then. I'll let you know what he says."

"Please do. I'll talk to you on Monday."

"Have fun, girl."

"You know I will."

Chapter Twenty-Two

The next day, after Jen had left for the airport, Cassie was picked up by Skyler and his family. It was her birthday and she spent the day with them in Williamsburg, walking around the Colonial area, Christmas shopping at Merchant's Square, and eating lunch at Seasons Restaurant. They also tried ice-skating at the new Liberty's Ice Pavilion. It was a lot of fun, even though she fell down a lot.

On the drive back to Virginia Beach, Cassie sat in the backseat between Skyler and Danielle. She and Skyler held hands in the dark, and she leaned her head against Skyler's shoulder, trying to think of other things besides kissing him since his family was in the car. Christmas music played in the background, and her mind drifted to her dad, who had missed her birthday. It wasn't the first birthday he'd missed spending with her over the years. Since he used to travel a lot for his job, he was often out of town for birthdays and holidays. She wondered if he'd be home for Christmas.

When they got to Cassie's house, Skyler walked her around the house to the upstairs back door. His parents knew about Jen and her dad being out of town, so Skyler was not allowed to stay.

"Have you had a good birthday?" he asked her.

She nodded. "I have." They walked up together, swinging their hands back and forth. "I really wish you could stay," she said when they reached the top of the stairs.

"Me, too," he said.

"Will I see you tomorrow?"

"Yeah, after church."

"You have to go tomorrow?" He and his family attended sometimes but not every week.

"Yeah, I'm playing the bells."

"Okay," she said sadly. She moved to kiss him.

He coughed sideways, covering his mouth. "I still can't kiss you, Cassie."

"You didn't mind it last week when you were here," she said.

He looked confused. "I've already told you I didn't kiss you when you talked about it before."

She wondered what his problem was. It seemed that he didn't remember coming over, chasing the animal out of the yard, and comforting her. She was beginning to worry about him. He'd had all of these sick symptoms, and now he was obviously having amnesia. Either that or he was suddenly bipolar. She wondered if he was being punished again by the angels for something.

She turned to unlock the door, trying to brush off her frustration.

He pulled her in his arms. "I'm sorry. I just hate for you to suffer. I don't want you to cough like me," he pleaded. "Please understand?"

She held back threatening tears, refused to look at him. "It's fine."

He turned her face up to look at him. "You have to know I want to kiss you, too."

She impulsively pulled him towards her and kissed him. She wanted to end her birthday on a happy note. She didn't care if she got sick. She only had a moment before his parents began to worry and she didn't want to waste it. He looked surprised, but when she stuck her tongue in his mouth, he seemed to change his mind. She felt him pull her closer to him.

His phone buzzed and they broke apart.

She smiled brightly like a cat that just ate a mouse.

"You won't be smiling like that if you get sick."

"Admit it, you're glad I did that," she said.

He looked at his cell phone. "It's my dad. I gotta go." He turned to go back downstairs.

"Admit it," she called.

He turned around and smiled. "I am glad."

Once inside the dark house, she turned off the alarm system and started flicking on all the lights. Logan had gone over to Emily's house.

She texted him to let him know that she was home now. Alone. He texted back *ok*.

She fixed herself a peanut butter-and-banana sandwich and some hot chocolate and took it to her bedroom, listening to today's popular hits music on her phone. She found herself humming to a Taylor Swift song while chewing her food and looking at Instagram pictures.

She heard a noise outside her window like someone was throwing rocks at it. "What the…" she said out loud.

She put her sandwich down and looked out the window, which faced the backyard. She peered out and saw a figure. She suddenly felt scared that it might be the creature she'd seen last week, but the figure shined a phone flashlight under his face and she saw that it was Skyler.

What was he doing back here? He had a big smile on his face.

She ran through the house to open the back door, and he was already there.

"Hey," he said. "Can I come in?"

"Skyler, what are you doing here? How'd you get back here so fast?"

"I had my parents drop me off at a friend's house, and then I ran here."

She smiled at his sneakiness. "I can't believe you did that. Did they actually believe you wouldn't try to come here?"

He shrugged his shoulders, still smiling.

"Come in here," she said, pushing him inside, closing the door and locking it. She then turned the alarm system on. "This way we'll know when Logan comes home," she said, thinking they could have a seriously good time celebrating her birthday since they were alone in the house. "Do you want a sandwich?" she asked as they walked through the house, pointing towards the kitchen.

"Nah."

He pulled her towards her bedroom. Her phone was still playing songs, and a jamming Nico & Vinz song came on, making her want to dance. She started moving around, and Skyler joined her. They moved all around the room, doing a little dirty dancing before it was over. When that song ended, a slow romantic song by John Legend came on, and Skyler took her in his arms. They slow danced and then began kissing.

Somewhere during the song, they stopped dancing and just kissed. Their hands started roaming, and Cassie's private parts started tingling with anticipation. He took her sweater off first, began feeling her up through her shirt, which he took off next, and finally reached around to unhook her bra. His mouth was over her breasts, and she gasped. Things had never moved this fast with him before. Her erotic dreams came to mind once again.

She wanted to go all the way.

She briefly thought of her partying days before she met Skyler, when she nearly had sex with Kerrick, her former boyfriend. She was so glad now that she hadn't gone all the way with him. Jen had told her many times to save herself for the person she felt she couldn't live without, the guy she loved more than anything.

Skyler was that guy. He was her one true love…her soulmate, if you wanted to call it that.

She was overanalyzing this. She decided to let go of those thoughts and just enjoy the moment. This could be THE moment…the moment she loses her virginity. Would Skyler do it? Would he let them go all the way or would he stop them as he had so many times in the past?

When he unzipped her jeans, she gasped again, and she was naked a moment later. She quickly pulled off his t-shirt and unzipped his jeans, in turn. Another fast song came on, and they began kissing frantically to the beat of the fast song, hands exploring. They somehow ended up on her bed, the covers pulled down, and his hand turned her on until she felt a burning, a build-up of such passion she never knew was inside of her. She gasped and moaned until she reached a peak that was so high, she couldn't stand it. An aching urge was fulfilled in that moment.

He smiled at her and then pulled her hand onto his maleness, and she turned him on until he lowered himself over her.

"Are you sure?" she whispered.

His eyes were dark with passion, a look she'd never seen in him before. He had a wicked smile and lowered himself into her, as his answer. A different ache awakened in her, and yet it felt like there was an obstruction. Her virginal plug. She felt it being torn and then he thrust himself into her again and again until they were both sweating and panting. He reached a peak and cried out at the climax before he collapsed on top of her.

Her body throbbed from pleasure. "Oh my god," she whispered. "That was awesome."

He raised his head up and smiled at her. "I hope I didn't hurt you."

"It only hurt a moment," she said. "It was mostly all good."

"I'm glad to be your first."

"I love you, Skyler."

Suddenly they heard the alarm go off, alerting them that someone had come in the house, and then it was turned off.

"Hello?" Logan called out.

"Oh God," Cassie said. "You've got to hide." She got off the bed quickly, looking for clothes. "I'm in my room, but I'm changing clothes. Hang on a minute," she called out.

Skyler quickly got up and she slammed her door shut, as it had been left open. He was dressed in a flash and was already trying to open her window.

"Can you get out that way? Hold on a minute. Maybe Logan won't say anything."

"I'm not taking any chances." He was out the window in no time at all. Gone into the night.

She quickly pulled on some sweat pants and a sleep shirt and opened the door. "Okay," she called out. She picked up her forgotten sandwich and walked into the hallway. Her clothes tickled her private areas, which were still throbbing from being stimulated.

"You okay?" he asked. "You look a little flushed."

She tried not to look embarrassed. "I'm fine."

"Okay. I'm going to watch some TV. You want to watch Grimm with me? It should have recorded from last night."

"Sure." She went back to her room for her hot chocolate, which was cold now, and took it back to the kitchen to reheat.

Before she sat down, the doorbell rang. She hesitated answering it. Who could that be this late? Surely not Skyler. Or worse, his mom or dad.

"I'll get it," Logan said, already walking towards the French doors.

It was Maggie. "Hey, guys. I just came to check on y'all and make sure everything's okay."

"Yeah, we're fine. You want to come in?" Logan asked.

She walked across to the family room and greeted Cassie. "Happy birthday, Cassie." She handed her a bag from a nearby bakery.

"What is it?" she smiled, excitedly.

"I felt bad that your dad and Jen were both out of town for your birthday and thought this might cheer you up a little."

Cassie opened it up and saw a gourmet cupcake, complete with sugar sprinkles and a candle. She lifted it out and the smell of sugar hit her. "Mmm, what flavor is it?"

"Vanilla birthday cake."

"Thanks so much," Cassie said.

"Do you guys need anything?" Maggie asked, glancing at Logan.

"No, we're good," Cassie answered. More than good, she thought. She almost felt embarrassed, but reminded herself that no one else knew what she'd just done with Skyler. She realized that Maggie probably came by because Jen asked her to check on them. She had to play it cool so they wouldn't find out about it. It was weird to think that just moments ago, she and Skyler had been in the house alone and they'd made love, and how risky that had been! Even if her dad and Jen were out of town, there were still two other people there now that weren't there just moments ago. They could've been caught!

Maggie turned to leave. "I won't bother you guys anymore. Just wanted to make sure y'all were safe. Does your mom get home tomorrow?" she asked Logan.

"Yeah, I'm going to pick her up at the airport at six."

"Okay, see y'all later. Bye."

Logan sat back down to watch TV and Cassie joined him, relieved that Maggie was gone. She smiled, feeling different. She felt so grown-up now, and even though she had a birthday, she felt years older instead of just one.

All because of what she and Skyler had done. He'd really given her the best birthday present ever.

Chapter Twenty-Three

As soon as Jen closed her shop the next Wednesday evening, she drove herself and the kids over to Maggie's. Maggie had invited several women over for a little Christmas cookie exchange/tree decorating party. They were to bring an ornament to put on Maggie's tree to help decorate it and also a dozen cookies to share.

It was dark by the time they arrived, and Maggie already had blue and white lights on a real pine tree, which sat in the family room over near the kitchen bar. There were also strings of seashell lights all around it and a starfish at the top. The chairs that normally sat on that side of the room, facing the ocean, were scooted back against the wall, one on either side of the Christmas tree, and the table had been taken downstairs to Maggie's office until the holidays were over.

The house smelled amazing…like cookies…and jazzy Christmas music played in the background.

"I made chocolate chip," Maggie said when Jen sat her cookies on the bar.

"I brought white chocolate chip with macadamia nuts."

"Yum," Catrina said, standing up from the couch. She walked over to greet them. "Arianna and Tyler are downstairs playing foosball," she told Cassie and Logan. The two went down the stairs to find them.

"What kind did you bake?" Jen asked her, knowing it was something good since she did a lot of baking. The cake she had made for Jen's wedding was the best she'd ever had.

"I made sugar plum cookies, and Arianna made macadamia macaroons."

"Oh my gosh, those sound yummy," Jen said.

Scarlett was also there and joined them. She was all wrapped up in a thick hunter green sweater and what looked like black wool pants. "I made some chocolate gingerbread cookies, my mother's recipe," she said.

"I've never heard of putting chocolate and gingerbread together. That sounds good, too," Jen said.

"It is. Just a hint of chocolate. It goes well with the molasses."

"All right ladies, let's all grab a couple of cookies and have some drinks, and then we'll decorate the tree," Maggie said.

"Sounds good to me," Catrina said.

They all tried each other's cookies and drank hot cider and coffee that Maggie had made. They took their Christmas mugs and plates of cookies into the family room to sit and talk while they ate.

"These are really good, Scarlett," Maggie said, eating one of the gingerbread cookies.

"Thank you. They take a little bit of time to make, but Jackson helped me."

"How's that going?" Jen asked her.

"Really well." She smiled and blushed.

The other girls said, "Oooo, do tell."

"He's really wonderful to me," Scarlett said. "I couldn't have asked for a better person to come into my life at the most appropriate time."

Jen smiled. She suspected Scarlett might be falling in love.

"How've you been?" Maggie asked her.

"Pretty good. I have good days where I have a lot of energy and then other days where I have none." She paused. "I'm going to Paris!"

"You are?" Catrina asked.

"Yes, Jackson suggested that I go and see my father. He's been really sick for a long time now. We still keep in touch by phone and letters – he's very old-fashioned. He has a heart condition and doesn't travel anymore. Tyler is going, too. He's never seen his grandfather."

"He hasn't?" Maggie asked.

"No. The first time I was diagnosed with cancer, I was pregnant with Tyler. I started treatment as soon as he was born. My father was going to come and see us, but he had a heart attack and had to be in the hospital for a while, and now he has a nurse that takes care of him at home."

"So he's not able to take care of Tyler for you…?" Maggie asked, not finishing her thought, but everyone knew what she meant.

"No, he's not well enough to take Tyler."

"That'll be a nice visit," Jen said.

"Is there nothing else that can be done for your cancer?" Maggie asked.

"No." She cleared her throat and looked down at her plate.

"Are you doing any kind of treatment at all?" Catrina asked her.

Scarlett took a sip of coffee and shook her head. "No. I'm eating healthy, organic and all natural, like that. Jackson suggested it. Oh, and I take morning walks, do yoga, and take lots of bubble baths." She smiled and they all laughed lightly.

"Who's going to take care of Tyler since your dad can't take him?" Catrina asked.

Scarlett looked at Jen, and she nodded her consent to tell the others about Luke being Tyler's dad. "Jen and Luke might be," she said.

"What?" Maggie asked.

"Luke is Tyler's father," Scarlett told her.

"He's what?" Maggie asked, her voice high-pitched.

"It was just a one-night stand; we weren't in love or anything. We never saw each other again. By the time I found out I was pregnant, I didn't know how to get in touch with him. The first day I came here looking for a beach house, Jen and Luke were on their honeymoon, remember?" Maggie nodded and Jen smiled. "That was the first time I'd seen Luke since the night Tyler was conceived."

"Wow," Maggie said. She looked over at Jen, who raised her eyebrows and smiled. "So you told Luke?"

Scarlett nodded and took another drink of coffee. "Yes, I wanted him and Jen to have the option of taking care of Tyler, since he's the father. But they're under no obligation." She smiled at Jen.

"That's so sad that you might not get to raise him yourself," Catrina said.

Maggie and Jen agreed.

Scarlett said, "It is sad, for sure. I won't be here to see him do a lot of things in life, but I'm beginning to think that maybe I'll be able to watch from above, you know?"

"That's a lovely thought," Maggie said.

"You know what else is sad, maybe even sadder?" The others couldn't guess what. "I think I've met the love of my life, and yet my life is going to be cut short. It's such a shame."

They all looked surprised, except Jen, who had already suspected it. "Jackson?" she asked.

Scarlett nodded. "Yes. I can't tell you how wonderful he is to me. How comfortable I feel around him. How much comfort he brings to me…comfort and joy."

"Sounds like a Christmas song," Catrina said. They all laughed.

"Well, it's true," Scarlett said, blushing a little.

"You look happy," Jen said. "You're actually kind of glowing."

"I am happy, despite all of this. It's totally out of the blue, and no one is more surprised than I am. I've never been in love before. I almost married once but it wasn't true love. He was smart enough to realize that before I did and he broke it off."

"It's never too late to fall in love," Jen said.

"That's what I'm realizing. I just decided to enjoy what we have for as long as I can."

"I think that's wonderful," Jen said. They all took turns hugging Scarlett.

"Is he good in the sack?" Maggie asked.

The other girls snickered and Scarlett looked momentarily shocked, but Jen asked, "Well, is he?"

Scarlett recovered and smiled. "He is wonderful."

They all screamed with delight.

"Jen, tell us all about Nashville," Maggie said, once their laughter had settled down.

"I didn't get to see much of it, except from the plane," Jen said, smiling. She'd spent the majority of it in Luke's hotel room. She told them about the nice restaurant where they ate and that otherwise, she and Luke were taking advantage of some alone time together.

"Well, ladies, I say we get this tree decorated, and then we can watch a Christmas movie. What do y'all say?"

They agreed and got up and took out the ornaments they had brought, and started decorating the tree. Soon the tree was glowing with bright shiny colors, decked with beachy and nautical ornaments.

"What movie do you want to see? I have *Home Alone*, *Christmas Vacation*, and I also have a couple of old ones like *White Christmas* and *Holiday Inn*," Maggie said.

They decided on *Christmas Vacation,* and ate some buttered popcorn and drank hot cider. The kids all came up for the movie, too.

Maggie had to leave the room once, and when she came back in the room, the credits were rolling to signify the end of the movie.

"You missed the ending," Jen said.

"Seen it many times before. I almost forgot to tell you all." She smiled at Jen, who looked surprised and then smiled knowingly. "I just found out I'm pregnant."

"You are?" Catrina asked.

Jen hugged her. "I'm so happy for you. I hope it all goes well."

"Me too," Maggie said quietly.

"How wonderful," Scarlett said.

"I was hesitant to tell you," she told Scarlett.

Scarlett shook her head. "A baby is always good news. I think every woman should have at least one, if possible. I'm really happy for you."

"Thank you. Steve is thrilled, and we're getting married in January. Honeymoon will be in Cancun, where we spent our first honeymoon."

"Congratulations!" Jen said.

They each hugged Maggie and then packed up a variety of cookies to take home with them.

"Y'all should all come out and do this again at my house tomorrow night," Jen said, laughing. "I haven't had time to get my tree out yet."

"I can't make it," Scarlett said. "Going to Paris tomorrow."

"How could I forget?" Jen said, laughing. "Have a wonderful trip!"

Chapter Twenty-Four

The next evening, Skyler's mom dropped him off at Cassie's house in Pungo. Jen had invited him over for pizza with the family and Emily.

"I'll see you later, Mom," he said, getting out of the car.

"Okay. Text me when you want me to pick you up."

"Will do." He smiled as she pulled away, and he headed around the back and up the stairs since Jen had already closed her shop.

The past week had been…weird. Cassie had been extremely affectionate, kissing him more often, touching him more often, and kept saying how amazing Saturday night had been. That it had been everything she'd dreamed it would be.

He didn't know what the heck she was talking about.

He was determined to find some time alone with her tonight and figure out what she meant. He kept racking his brain, but all they did on Saturday was drive to Colonial Williamsburg with his family, did some shopping, ice skating, and had dinner. Then they'd driven her back to her house, and she had said she'd wished he could come in because her parents were out of town. They both knew that wasn't allowed, though, and he didn't want Jen on his bad side because he knew she would tell his dad.

Then she had kissed him, even knowing he didn't want to make her sick.

So he had no idea what had gotten Cassie so amorous or why she had been extra flirty. He was enjoying her attention; it was just confusing.

Cassie let him in, her eyes bright, and she looked around before smashing her lips into his and her arms squeezed him tight. "Hey," she whispered.

"Hey," he said. "That's some greeting. Did you miss me that much since I saw you at school?"

"No, since last Saturday night," she whispered. "It's all I can think about."

He wished he knew what she was talking about.

Jen came into the room, and Cassie reluctantly let go of him and closed the door.

"You guys ready for some pizza?" Jen asked.

"Definitely," Cassie said.

Logan and Emily came in the door a few minutes later with two pizza boxes, and they all sat at the dining room table and ate. They talked about school and how they couldn't wait to be off for Christmas break.

"When's dad coming back home?" Cassie asked.

"He said he'd be home by Christmas Eve, hopefully," Jen said.

Skyler wondered if that was why Cassie was so affectionate with him…because she missed her dad.

"I still haven't been to Christmas Town yet. When do y'all get out again?" Jen asked.

"We get out early next Wednesday," Logan said.

"I can't do that day. It'll be a pretty busy day, and then Christmas Eve I'll keep it open all day. Hopefully your dad will be back that night, and then it's Christmas. Maybe we can go with your dad the next Monday."

"But then it'll be after Christmas. Don't you want to see it before?" Logan asked.

"Nah, that's okay. It'll still be pretty to see after Christmas. I'd rather see it with your dad anyway."

They finished the pizzas, then Logan and Emily went to his room to watch TV, and Cassie excused herself and Skyler from the table.

"Be good," Jen called after them.

Cassie practically dragged him into her bedroom and shut the door. She threw her arms around him and began kissing him aggressively, leading him over to her bed and then pushed him down on it.

"Whoa, Cassie. Where is all this coming from?"

"You should know," she murmured. She kept kissing him while she pulled his shirt out of his jeans and ran her hands up under his shirt.

"Cassie, your stepmom is right outside the door. And what did I say about kissing while I'm sick?"

She stopped and looked at him like he was weird. "We did a lot more than kissing last Saturday," she said, frowning. "What's going on with you? Do you regret what we did?"

"What did we do, Cassie?" He pushed her off of him and sat up. "Because all I remember is going to Williamsburg with my family. That couldn't have been that exciting to you."

She looked at him dully. "Really? That's all you remember?"

"What am I supposed to remember? Please tell me. You've got me all confused."

"I've got *you* confused? We had sex, and all you can say is you don't remember it? Have you blocked it out of our head?"

"Wait…what? Had sex?"

She rolled her eyes at him. "I get it. You want to forget it ever happened." She stood up and paced the room. "I thought you loved me, Skyler."

"Hold up! You're serious, aren't you? You think we had sex?"

"Of course we did. Why would I make it up? And more importantly, why do you act so surprised?"

"I did not have sex with you, Cassie," he whispered, fearing that someone might hear what they were arguing about. "I'm pretty sure I would remember that. You must've had another vivid dream."

She got teary-eyed. "It was not a dream! How can you sit there and say we didn't have sex? It was the most beautiful moment of my life." She wiped her eyes with a corner of her shirt.

He hated to see her upset, but what was going on? None of this made any sense. She really believed the two of them had sex. He definitely did not have sex with her.

He started coughing again. "Calm down and let's talk about this," he said. "When did we supposedly do this? Saturday night?"

"Yes. You came back to my house after your dad dropped me off, about thirty minutes later."

"And you let me in the house?"

"Yes. You threw something at my window, and I came and unlocked the French doors." She sat back down on the bed, grabbed a tissue box, and blew her nose into a tissue. "Skyler, do you really not remember this? How sick are you?"

He was beginning to wonder the same thing. He couldn't have amnesia, could he? He had been wondering why he had gotten sick and now he wondered about this. Jackson said someone or something could be messing with him. What if it was another angel? Maybe an angel that had punished him in the past, who enjoyed punishing people? *Could it be Jackson?* What if Jackson was just throwing him off by acting like he didn't know who it was? Could Jackson have pretended to be him and had sex with Cassie? He felt himself getting mad.

"I don't know what's going on," Skyler said, balling his hands up in fists. "What happened after you let 'me' inside?"

She sniffed and said, "I turned the alarm on so I would know when Logan came back home. We were all alone. We came in here…" She looked around the room and at her bed, and then her eyes landed on his and burned into his. "And we made love. Please tell me you remember."

He shook his head. "I don't know who you had sex with, Cassie, but it wasn't me."

"How could it not have been you, Skyler? He looked like you, he talked like you, he smelled…" Her eyes widened. "He smelled like Jackson the first day I met him."

"That's what I was afraid of," Skyler said.

"You think I had sex with Jackson? That he morphed or whatever into your body?"

"That's what I'm thinking."

She stood up quickly. "Ew! He's so…crusty. He's old now."

"I suspect Jackson has been messing with us. I think he's been making me sick and has been flirting with you and…and had sex with you." He cringed at the thought. He was mad enough to kill Jackson.

"Why would he do that? I thought he had a thing for Scarlett. She's definitely in love with him," Cassie said.

"I don't know why. It doesn't make any sense. I can't protect you from him anymore. I feel so helpless as a human."

She looked across the room at him like she was frightened. "Skyler, I…I'm so sorry. I thought it was you. You have to believe me. I would never…"

"I understand." He reached his arms out, and she flew into them, rested her head against his chest. "I *do* love you," he said, remembering what she'd said earlier.

"That was the only thing about the whole thing that bothered me. I told you…him…that I loved you, and he didn't say anything. Actually, we were interrupted. Logan came home as soon as we…finished." She seemed embarrassed to talk about it now.

"I see," he said quietly. He was really mad, but it wasn't her fault and he didn't want her to feel bad. He kissed her on the top of her head and caressed her hair, still holding her tight in his arms. "Next time…" She looked up at him. "When *I* make love to you, I will tell you over and over again how much I love you."

"Oh, Skyler." She started crying.

"Shhh, Jen will hear you," he said. He felt tears come to his own eyes. Someone had violated his Cassie, his love. He was madder than hell, so mad he couldn't see straight.

"I'm so, so sorry," she kept repeating. "When can you and I do it for real? Maybe one day after school?" She looked at him hopefully.

"Cassie…"

"Please? Then I won't think about the first…the other time. I will know it's you. I know, maybe one day when we're out of school for Christmas break. Please, Skyler?"

He wanted her to feel better, but he wasn't ready to have sex yet. He was a virgin. They'd both been virgins and were going to wait until they got married. Now everything was ruined. But he loved her so much, he hated to see her so upset. "Maybe," he said.

He got the tissues, wiped her tears away gently, and then kissed her. Damn the sickness. He wasn't going to let Jackson take his girl away from him while he kept his distance because of some godforsaken cough and some stomach pains.

The next time he saw Jackson, God help him, he was going to knock the crap out of him.

Chapter Twenty-Five

The flights from Norfolk to New York and then New York to Paris were uneventful. Scarlett and Tyler had seats together in first class, something Jackson recommended. Scarlett had protested the steep fares, but Jackson insisted it would be so much more comfortable, and with a glass of wine in her hand and a warm towel to pat her face and neck with on the flight over from New York City, she had to agree with him.

Jackson had no money and no passport and told her he would meet her at the airport. She marveled at his choice of transportation – flying instantly – when she saw him at the baggage claim in Paris.

"Tue es ici," she said excitedly.

"Ma chère," he said, holding his arms out to her. "Of course, I'm here. Just like I said I would be."

They embraced and kissed each other on both cheeks. He and Tyler exchanged fist bumps.

Jackson said it would be too complicated to get a passport himself because they might suspect him a terrorist, and he didn't want to raise any suspicions, especially in light of recent events in Paris. He had been able to get Tyler's passport pushed through quickly, using Scarlett's cancer and her father's illness as reasons. It had worked.

Scarlett, in turn, would have to make the other financial arrangements such as the airfare, hotels, food, and taxis. She decided against driving a rental car. They could easily take the Metro around town and the train to Toulon where her father lived.

When Jackson first talked about her paying for everything, she said that she could easily think him a charlatan. "How do I know you're not an angel at all and you're trying to swindle me for money?" she'd asked him.

"I'm not asking you to spend money on me, am I? Of course, I'll share a hotel room with you, but all you have to do is get two beds and I'll sleep on the couch if you prefer."

She'd eyed him curiously.

"You don't believe I'm an angel?"

She shook her head while smiling playfully. "No, I don't. Prove it to me."

Jackson then asked her to hold out her hand, and he presented a beautiful bright pink and white Asian lily in her palm.

"Magic tricks," she said, though still smiling.

"What about the mind-reading?"

"Lucky guesses." She was still smiling.

He then made himself disappear and a moment later reappear.

Her eyes widened. "Okay, I believe you now."

He laughed at her and they continued making reservations.

Now at the airport, she realized he had done the very same thing but at a farther distance, disappearing from Virginia Beach and appearing in Paris. It was a bit sci-fi, like *Star Trek* or *I Dream of Jeannie.*

"Where did you…arrive?" she whispered to him while waiting for the luggage.

"The men's bathroom," he whispered back, pointing across the wide hallway.

"Very clever. I'm so glad to see you."

"Did you have a rough flight?"

She sighed. "No, first class was wonderful, as you recommended. I just…missed you."

He kissed her lips and she closed her eyes. When she opened them, she looked around to be sure she had her eye on Tyler. Jackson had a way of distracting her attention and making her forget everything else.

"He's fine," Jackson said, reading her mind. He moved aside so she could see him behind Jackson, jumping up and down, waiting on the luggage to roll around.

They decided to take the train to visit her father and stay with him for a week, and then spend one night in Paris before going back home. They took a taxi through the busy Parisian streets to the train station, where Scarlett bought them all tickets to Toulon. Jackson didn't need a passport to travel within France, so he was able to be with them on the train. They soon boarded and made the journey south to Toulon.

Tyler had a wonderful time on the train and marveled at everything. Scarlett was extremely happy she let Jackson talk her into this trip. It was good for her as well as Tyler. It would be a trip he would always remember, the time his mother took him to France. He would get to see and do all sorts of exciting things. She doubted he would get to come back to France anytime soon, whether he lived with Luke or with James. He might never see his grand-père again, so they would have to make enough memories to last his lifetime.

They arrived in Toulon by nightfall. They took a taxi to her father's house, seeing the last day's light shining across the water at the nearby harbor. Toulon was a small town on the Mediterranean Sea with a port, shops, cafés, fountains, and an open-air marketplace. Her father lived in an apartment in the middle of the historic part of town so that he could walk wherever he needed to go and it would be a short distance. It was the same place Scarlett had lived when she lived here from ages two to seven.

Scarlett knocked on the big wooden door, and a plump woman with graying blonde hair answered the door, beckoning them inside.

"Je m'appelle Scarlett," she told her. "Parlez-vous anglais?"

"Yes, I speak English," the woman said. They kissed each other on the cheeks in a brief greeting. "Your father told me you were coming. Pleased to meet you," she said. "I'm Odette."

Scarlett introduced Tyler and Jackson to the woman.

"Is my father awake?" Scarlett asked.

"No, he sleeps." Odette took their jackets for them and then showed them to a small bedroom with a full-sized bed, which Scarlett and Tyler would be sleeping in. Jackson would be sleeping on the couch, as he had offered. Scarlett knew he would most likely not sleep at all, so she didn't worry about him being uncomfortable. She wasn't even sure if angels of death slept, but she did think he'd spent the whole night with her on Thanksgiving night after they'd made love.

Scarlett used the bathroom down the hall and then carefully opened the door to her father's bedroom to look in on him. It was the same bedroom her parents had shared, and childhood memories came back to her of running into their room in the mornings to wake them up. She could hear herself saying, "Time to get up, Maman. Papa, let's get moving." They would begrudgingly get out of bed all sleepy-eyed and soon the three of them would make their way down the cobblestone street to a little café or patisserie where they'd eat fresh croissants and drink hot chocolate and café au lait. She smiled at the memory.

Her father had a CPAP mask on and the noise of the machine filled the room, as well as his heavy breathing. She carefully closed the door back quietly and headed for her old room. She found Tyler already sleeping peacefully with a furry white ball of fur nestled next to him. On closer inspection, she saw that it was a big fluffy cat. It was only mildly interested in her and looked up at her, meowed once, and then laid back against Tyler again and purred.

Scarlett took her clothes off, slipped into a silky nightgown and slid under the covers beside the cat. Lucky thing she wasn't allergic to cats. She had one when she was a teenager, but it died before Tyler was born. She drifted off to sleep, wondering what Jackson was doing, wondering how her father would act since she hadn't seen him in so long, and thinking of things they could do the next day.

She awoke the next morning and felt something tickling her neck. She vaguely rubbed at it, and it swatted her in the chin. Her eyes flew open and she saw that it was the cat's tail. She had forgotten where she was for a moment.

"Are you awake?" Tyler asked. He was looking at her.

She smiled. "I am now. What's this cat doing in our bed? I found him in here with you last night."

"It's a she, and she belongs to grand-père. Odette said she could sleep with me. She keeps grand-père up a lot, so she doesn't like Fleur to sleep with him."

"Oh, I see."

"Don't you love her name? Remember? From Harry Potter?"

They were currently reading book four in the series. "Ah, oui. The French girl from the all-girls school who was in the competition."

"Right. I think she likes me." Tyler petted the cat, which purred and licked his hand.

Scarlett yawned and stretched.

"What are we going to do today? Can we get grand-père up?"

"You're welcome to go see if you like. I bet Jackson is already up. I need to freshen up in the bathroom first."

Tyler hopped out of bed, quickly pulled on some jeans and a sweatshirt, his shoulder-length blonde hair bouncing. He then opened the door quickly and pulled it shut noisily. Ah, the energy of little boys.

She went to the bathroom, showered, brushed her teeth, and put on a pair of tan wool blend pants and a black turtleneck Cashmere sweater. She adjusted her favorite bob wig, and walked into the living room.

She found Jackson and Tyler sitting on the couch, looking at Fleur. She walked over and Jackson stood up by the time she reached him. He whistled appreciatively at her and she blushed.

"You look wonderful," he said, kissing her lips lightly, one arm around her back. *And you smell wonderful, too,* she heard him say in her head.

"Where's my girl?" Scarlett heard a deep voice say behind her.

She turned around and saw her father. He was much older than the last time she'd seen him, she guessed it had been ten years ago. He was still tall, but his skin was more wrinkled, and his short hair was all gray including a full beard, mustache, and bushy eyebrows. His blue eyes looked the same, and she saw that they were watering a bit.

"Papa," she said and rushed into his arms. They kissed each other's cheeks and then embraced.

"Mon petit chou. Tu es très belle." He rubbed one hand over her hair and then touched her chin.

"Merci, and you are as handsome as ever, Papa."

He laughed. "You are funny," he said. "Who did you bring with you, ay?"

Scarlett introduced him to Jackson first. "Papa, this is Jackson. Jackson, this is my father, André." Her father looked surprised and smiled brightly. The two men kissed cheeks briefly and her father gave him a hearty hug.

Then she introduced him to Tyler. "And this is your grandson, Tyler."

"Oh, come give your pépé a hug." They hugged, and Scarlett instantly felt guilty that she hadn't brought him over to see her father before now.

"I'm so sorry that you haven't had a chance to meet before now. I was pregnant and also had cancer, and then Tyler was too young to travel with for several years," she said. "Then Maman got sick." She felt her throat tighten.

Her father let go of the boy and looked at Scarlett. He shook his head and said, "I wished I could've come to the funeral. My doctors wouldn't let me leave the country."

Scarlett nodded. "I know. Then I got cancer again."

He hugged her again. "My sweet fille. If I could, I would take this from you." She wiped away a tear as he kissed her head. "There now, no more tears." He turned around and looked at his nurse. "Odette, do we have some nice breakfast to offer?"

"Yes, I just got back from the patisserie. Fresh coffee, baguettes, and croissants are waiting on the table." She pointed to the dining room. "I even bought a couple of pains au chocolat for Tyler."

"Merci!" Tyler said excitedly, already bouncing into the dining room.

They had some breakfast and talked about the cool weather and sunny skies. "Perfect for some sightseeing," André said.

"Papa, you shouldn't over-exert yourself," Scarlett said. "We don't have to go anywhere."

"Nonsense. I can do a little walking. I'll take my cane. My doctor told me to do a little walking every day. I would go stir-crazy if I didn't."

As they were walking out the door, Tyler tugged on André's arm and asked, "Does Santa Claus come to France?"

The older man smiled and said, "But of course. Let's go see if we can find him."

Chapter Twenty-Six

Scarlett and the guys walked up and down the streets of Toulon, catching some of the major tourist sites that they could walk to. They went inside the Toulon Cathedral with its tall bell tower and incredibly high nave on the inside with big arches, stained glass windows, beautiful dark wood and artwork. Then they walked down by the harbor and looked at the boats. After that, Scarlett wanted to let her father rest, so they went to one of the peaceful squares with a gushing fountain and found an empty table at an outdoor café.

They relaxed and ate soup, sandwiches, shared a cheese platter, bread, and some wine.

"Have you had enough tourism for the day, Papa?" Scarlett asked her father.

"I'll be okay after we have this long lunch. Maybe you want to do some shopping on the way back?"

"That sounds good."

They took their time eating and relaxing, and then made their way back to the cobblestone streets. They stopped at an open-air market and got some fruit for snacking and vegetables to take back home and cook with the evening meal.

They spent the next several days with morning walks, shopping in boutiques, strolling by the picturesque harbor, and always relaxing for a leisure lunch. They spent the evening meals at her father's either in the dining room or outside on a small terrace in the back where there was a metal and marble-topped table with matching chairs, covered with pillows, and a small bubbling fountain. Tall ivy topiaries stood in big planters, a long fabric-covered outdoor sofa with abundant pillows sat against a stone wall, and tiny white lights shined above their heads, strung all around the covered terrace. It was here that they discussed local politics, the meaning of life, and enjoyed lots of French wine. They also played card games with Tyler until he couldn't keep his eyes open, and Jackson usually would have to carry him into the bedroom at night.

Her father and Jackson were getting on famously, although she suspected Jackson had the ability to get along with anybody he wanted to. Oftentimes, the two would still be talking and smoking cigars outside when everyone else had gone to bed for the night. Scarlett tried to stay up with them but usually started dozing off and had to stumble inside when she was too tired to listen to them anymore. Odette prepared the meals and ate with them, but she was relatively quiet and kept to herself a lot.

One morning, André insisted that Scarlett and Jackson go off and enjoy themselves without him and the garçon slowing them down. They decided to spend the early part of the day on a local beach and took a taxi to Mourillon. There they basked in the sun, and Scarlett read a magazine while Jackson distracted her by stealing kisses and talking about funny things her father or Tyler had said.

"This is so relaxing," she said. It was 63 and sunny, and it felt positively heavenly. They were sitting on comfortable beach lounges with pillows behind their backs, and Scarlett wore a thin white ruffled blouse with comfortable floral-printed Tommy Bahama slacks. Jackson wore dark casual pants and a lightweight gray sweater halfway unbuttoned over a white shirt. A light warm breeze blew his dark hair across his forehead, and she grabbed his hand, taken by his handsomeness. He leaned over and kissed her again.

She sighed happily. Hearing the bells of occasional boats as well as from a church nearby, she looked out on the water and said, "I haven't been on a boat in years."

"Would you like to?" Jackson asked.

"Yes, that would be nice."

"Where could we go?" he asked, though she suspected he knew the area well enough but just wanted to know what she would like to do.

She smiled and said, "We could take it down to Porquerolles. I saw that on a brochure and it looks just lovely. It's pretty secluded, too." *Maybe secluded enough to make love on the beach,* she thought. Would he read her mind?

He studied her eyes intently. His were burning with fresh fire. "If that's what you desire, then we will do it," he said quietly. His hand was gripping hers tightly, and she reached up, caressed his face, and kissed him.

I do, she thought. "It sounds wonderful," she said out loud. "How soon can we go?"

"If we could, I'd go right now," he said, "but maybe tomorrow would be better. We can stop by the harbor when we get back to Toulon and make reservations."

"Do you know how to sail a boat or will we need a guide?"

He smirked at her, and she knew he could do anything. "Of course I can sail a boat."

They relaxed some more, kissed some more, and then got hungry. They found a little café close by right on the beach and ate a big midday meal, drank some wine, and looked forward to the next day's boat trip. Some musicians were playing nearby, a tall man playing an accordion and a slim shorter man with a Tambourin, who played Christmas songs and sang in French.

While they were sipping on wine, a man walked up to their table. "Scarlett?"

She turned and saw a handsome man about her age with sandy brown hair, green eyes, and no facial hair. "I'm sorry, do I know you?"

"It's me. Tristan."

She looked closer at him and finally recognized the man her childhood friend had turned out to be. "Tristan? Is that really you?"

He laughed, and she stood up and they hugged. He and his parents and younger sister had lived right next door to them ever since she could remember. They used to play quite a bit in the square nearby. He was a couple of years older than her.

"Look at you, you're breathtaking!" he said.

"How on earth did you recognize me?" she asked. "I've changed quite a bit." She fluffed her short hair.

"I'd recognize those eyes anywhere," he said. She was flattered. "Besides, my mother told me you were coming to town."

She laughed. "Won't you join us?" she asked, looking at Jackson, who looked decidedly jealous of the newcomer. "Tristan, this is my…" *soul mate,* she wanted to say. She glanced at Jackson to see if he read her mind. He stared at her with longing so she thought he did. "Boyfriend, Jackson. Jackson, this is an old childhood friend of mine, Tristan."

The two men shook hands. "Are you sure I'm not intruding?" Tristan asked. He looked at Jackson for an answer.

"Not at all. Please, have a seat," Jackson said.

Tristan pulled out a chair and looked back at Scarlett. "So, how've you been? You haven't been to this part of the world in years, have you?"

"No, I haven't. I wanted to come and see my father one last time before I…" She cleared her throat and glanced at Jackson. "I have terminal breast cancer."

"Oh no, Scarlett." She could tell he was shocked. "C'est impossible." He reached over and hugged her again. "Is there nothing to be done? I could call my friend; he specializes in oncology."

She shook her head. "Thanks, but no. How do you know this oncologist? You're not sick, are you?"

"No. I'm a doctor. We met in med school."

"Oh? What kind of doctor are you?" She was glad to be steering the conversation away from her illness.

"Pediatrician. Do you have any kids?"

"Yes. I have one son, Tyler." She pulled her phone out of her handbag and looked for a picture. "He's seven." She showed him a picture of Tyler.

"He's handsome. Are you the father?" he asked Jackson.

Jackson shook his head and said, "No."

Scarlett said, "I never married." She then showed him a picture of her with super long hair – her favorite picture of her and her maman together in the backyard of her house in Pungo.

"Wow, this is a beautiful pic. How is your mother?" he asked.

"Didn't your mother tell you? She passed away last year. She had breast cancer too."

"Oh, I'm so sorry."

Their mothers had become good friends, especially when André was out to sea.

"She was a sweet lady and used to crack me up learning to speak French in her southern American accent," Tristan said.

"She got pretty good at it over the years," Scarlett said. "I used to make her sing the French national anthem every night before going to bed and then we'd sing the American anthem in the morning."

He and Jackson both laughed.

"I think she had a pretty singing voice – a lot better than me. I think Tyler inherited some talent from her and from my papa's father. He was a street musician in the '50s." She realized he must've also inherited some talent from Luke, his own father.

"I see your dad on occasion when I'm over at Maman's."

"Do you?" Tristan nodded. "How is your mother?"

"She's still alive, widowed. My father died eight years ago."

"I'm so sorry. I don't remember much about him."

"Thank you."

"What brings you down to the beaches?" Scarlett asked.

"Same as you, I suspect. A little relaxation."

"Ah, oui. Did you ever marry?"

He smiled. "I did, although it took me a long time to get over you," he said, smirking.

She laughed. "Sure, probably about two weeks, right?" She was seven when the family moved to America.

He laughed this time.

An attractive woman with black curly hair and olive skin walked up to them. "Tristan, are you ready?" She looked and talked like she might be Italian.

"Ah, here she is now. Scarlett, meet my wife, Isabella. Bella, this is an old friend, Scarlett, and Jackson."

They all greeted one another, and Tristan stood up. "I'm afraid I must be going. It was so good to see you," he said to Scarlett. His eyes suddenly welled up in tears, which he fought like mad to hide. "One moment, s'il vous plaît," he said to Bella and Jackson. He pulled Scarlett away a short distance so they could talk privately. "I can't believe this might be the last time I'll ever see you," he said. "Are you sure I can't call my friend?"

She blinked, touched by his kindness, tears welling up in her own eyes. "I'm sure," she said. She'd decided since Jackson came into her life that she would try to not be afraid of what lay ahead as long as he was there to help her. She hadn't quite welcomed death yet, but she had accepted that it was her fate.

He hugged her once more and then walked back to stand with Bella. He said good-bye to Jackson, and blew a kiss to Scarlett as he walked away.

"I almost got jealous," Jackson said when she sat back down at the table.

She dabbed her eyes with a napkin, took another drink of wine, and smiled at him. "You know you have no need of that."

"Yes, I read your mind…" He stared into her eyes, passion close to the surface once again. "But this feeling of jealousy is new to me. I've never had it before, not once."

"I'm flattered."

"You should be." He grinned at her then, and she laughed.

Chapter Twenty-Seven

The next day, Scarlett was getting ready to leave with Jackson for their boat ride, and she asked her father once again if he was sure about leaving Tyler with him again.

"Of course, I am sure. Go and enjoy yourselves. Tyler and I will go look for Père Noêl."

"Who's that, Pépé?" Tyler asked.

"Ah, he's the French equivalent of your Santa Claus. He looks the same, and he brings toys to children on Christmas morning instead of Christmas Eve night. The French children leave their shoes out by the fireplace the night before, and in the morning, Père Noêl leaves candy and small gifts."

"Why in the morning?" Tyler asked.

"That way, the sneaky children won't stay up late at night for a chance to see him."

"Ahhh," Tyler said. His pépé tickled his ribcage and he started laughing.

Scarlett was glad to see the two getting along and was once again glad she made this trip with him.

"And then we'll go get un sapin to decorate. Do you know what that is?"

"Yes, a Christmas tree. Can we chop one down with an axe?"

André laughed. "Maybe it would be safer to let some other Frenchman do that. Or Frenchwoman," he said, looking at Scarlett and grinning.

"All right. You two have fun," Scarlett said. "You have my mobile number if you need me."

"Yes, I do," her father said.

Scarlett and Jackson took a taxi to the harbor, and Jackson got the thirty-foot long sailboat ready and steered them out into the sea towards Porquerolles Island. Porquerolles was a small island to the south of Toulon, in the region of Provence. It had pristine beaches, pine forests, vineyards, and a big portion of the island was a protected National Park.

"Are you sure you know how to sail a boat?" Scarlett asked him once again, smiling.

"I can, and I can do it with no hands, see?" He demonstrated by waving his hand to steer the boat where he wanted it to go.

"You're still technically using your hands," she teased.

He smiled, "You're right, but they're also free to do whatever I want. Like this…" He took her in his arms and kissed her deeply, moving his hands all over her body, tingling and tickling her. "Admit it, you're impressed."

"I am," she said softly. "You're quite an impressive…being."

"Mmm," he said. He kissed her again.

The wind blew up around them, and Jackson looked towards the sails and adjusted the boat accordingly with a wave of his hand. The air was warm at times and then cold at other times, like it might be changing soon, and halfway across, it started clouding up. By the time they reached the harbor at Porquerolles, it was raining lightly.

"Oh no," Scarlett said. "This ruins everything."

"Nonsense, ma chérie. We'll just have to change our plans, that's all."

Scarlett tried not to sulk about her disappointment in the weather while Jackson tied the boat up at the docks. They disembarked at a charming village consisting of a beautiful church, shops, and cafés, surrounded by lush vegetation. Jackson led the way into one of the nearby stores.

"Stay here, I'll find out where we can go," he instructed her. He left her by a potted palm near a rack of dresses and walked over to the register. He came back a few moments later and led her outside.

"Where are we going?" she asked.

"We'll go find a dry place to relax at a more secluded part of the island."

They got into a shuttle bus.

"You're going to love this place. It's called Le Mas du Langoustier, and it has its own sandy beach and gardens amidst pine and eucalyptus trees to walk through, should the weather improve."

"We're going to a hotel?" she asked.

"Yes, well, we can't exactly *do* much out in the rain, can we?" he said in a low voice. There was also another couple inside the shuttle, sitting across from them.

He smirked at her and she knew exactly what he was talking about. Her heart began to race at the thought of making love to him again. They hadn't done it since Thanksgiving night, and then she'd gotten so mad at him the next morning when she found out he had lied to her.

He continued, as if she needed more convincing. "We'll have a nice meal at one of the restaurants, drink some wine, then go to our room and sit by the fireplace, and…relax." He whispered the last part.

"Sounds perfect."

They arrived at the beautiful C-shaped hotel with red roof tiles and a matching exterior among the trees and dying vines still clinging to some of the walls. They quickly walked inside and looked around. While Jackson made arrangements for a room, using her credit card, Scarlett called her father and explained to him the weather situation and what they were doing.

"We're going to relax here at a nice hotel. I don't know how long the weather will be like this."

"Stay the night, Scarlett. Let yourself relax a little with Jackson. You need it. I'll take care of the boy, no worries, eh?"

"Are you sure, papa? He has an awful lot of energy."

"Absolument. Enjoy yourself. You deserve it. My treat – give them my credit card number so I can pay for it."

"No, papa. It's fine; I'll pay for it."

"No, no, no. Let me do this for you. It'll be my Christmas present, okay? I insist. Let me talk to the desk clerk."

She didn't want to argue with him, get him upset, so she relented. She was touched at his generosity. "All right. Thank you, Papa."

She took the phone over to the check-in clerk and explained to Jackson about using her father's credit card instead of hers. She gave the clerk her phone so he could talk to her father. He handed her the phone moments later, and she said good-bye to her father.

"I'll see you tomorrow," she said.

"You're all set," the clerk told them, handing them keys to their room along with brochures and other information. "This weather will soon pass, and maybe you can enjoy supper with a nice sunset out on the terrace."

"That would be wonderful," Scarlett said.

They walked around the resort, and in one of the common areas, they saw a beautiful Christmas tree decorated in all green lights and decorations with hints of gold. Someone was playing Christmas songs at a piano nearby. They also passed a spa in another corridor, and Scarlett looked at it longingly.

"The spa sounds relaxing," she said.

"I could give you a massage…and a bath…like before," he said.

She felt the blood rush to various parts of her body at the thought of how erotic his care for her had been. She now realized he really wasn't just doing his job, since he didn't work for hospice. His feelings and his care for her were real. Her heart thumped, and she grabbed his hand and kissed it. "I would love that."

He stopped in the hall and kissed her lips.

"Let's get to our room," she murmured.

They made their way to their second floor "elegance" room, which was decorated in shades of red, tan, and brown. There was a king-sized bed, two chairs facing a small square table between them in front of oval-shaped terrace doors and a view of the trees beyond. There was a desk, a dark chair, and shelves full of books along with a TV along the wall across from the bed.

Once the door had closed, Jackson took her in his arms. "Before we do anything else," he started.

"Make love to me," she finished.

His eyes grew dark. "You read my mind."

They tore each other's clothes off hurriedly while standing up, and then he swiftly picked her up and took her to the bed. They kissed and caressed in a rush, making love like they did the first time.

"How are you doing this?" she asked him in the middle of it all.

"I'm in human form. I can do anything a human can right now."

They continued making love, Scarlett crying out, "Mon Dieu, oh Jackson," when she came. He followed soon after, and then they collapsed in a sweaty heap.

They cleaned up and then lay across the bed beside each other.

A thought occurred to Scarlett. "What if the weather doesn't get any better? How will we sail back to Toulon?"

Jackson pushed some of her wig hair out of her face. She bravely pulled it off and fluffed her hair. He smoothed it all out and looked at her lovingly. "I'm an angel, remember? If I had to, I'd transport us back magically. However, if you don't want any confusion about what happened to our boat, then you'll have to trust me that I can get us back safely and with no injuries, okay?"

"Okay." She smiled. She forgot for a moment what he was, and marveled at the things he could do.

She turned onto her side and looked towards him, started rubbing his back. "What do you do at night? When you're not with me?"

"I have other clients I tend to."

"Anyone I know?"

He laughed. "No."

"Did you stay all night with me on Thanksgiving night or did you have to…work?"

"I stayed with you. That was the first time I've ever done that in human form. I actually slept a lot – well, when you weren't wearing me out with your insatiable appetite for sex."

She laughed at him.

"Are you hungry yet?" he asked.

"I've had my fill of you…for now," she said, "but I am kind of hungry for food."

He laughed. "Let's go see what we can get to eat, shall we?"

Jackson marveled at his situation, at the many sensations the human body gave him. Humans really took it all for granted, he thought. Being with Scarlett like this gave him unspeakable joy, like he'd never known before. He knew that he loved her, and he longed to tell her the next time they made love. That he didn't want to live without her, if that was possible.

He still had not been punished for having sex with a human. He was stunned, didn't know what to make of it.

The two of them got dressed and headed for one of the restaurants, La Pinède. They had a late lunch/early dinner of locally prepared chicken, herbed potatoes, and green beans, along with cheeses, bread, and lots of wine. They sat in a well-lit dining area overlooking the terrace and gardens just outside the windows.

The sun finally made an appearance in time for sunset, and they walked down to the beach and sat on lounge chairs, wrapped up in a blanket together to watch the sky turn all shades of pinks and purples over the turquoise water. By the time the sun was down and the sky darkened, the Fort du Langoustier across the bay was all lit up with outside lights, which glowed and reflected across the dark waters. They walked back up the hill, past tables with candles where a few couples sat and talked quietly, drinking wine and smoking.

In a room near the bar, a man was playing the piano again, and people were singing Christmas carols. They stopped to listen to one song, and then went back up to their room.

Once they got to the room, Jackson's urge to make love to her again increased. He didn't want her to get overtired, though, so he offered her that massage he had promised.

"Are you sure you want to?" she asked. "You're not too tired?"

"Of course not. What else have I done today? Nothing strenuous." She raised her eyebrows at him. "Well, nothing so strenuous that I can't give my girl a massage."

She smiled at him. He had her strip down to nothing and had to force himself to concentrate on the task at hand and not making love to her unless she wanted it. He laid some towels across the bed and Scarlett laid on top of it. He got out some of his special massaging oil with ylang-ylang scent and rubbed every inch of the back of her body from her fingers all the way down to her toes. She was nearly asleep when he'd finished. He told her to turn over, which she did, and he rubbed oil over the front side of her body, too, though with greater efforts to control himself. She'd taken her wig off again, and he noted that the hair had grown a bit since Thanksgiving.

He tried to distract himself with a little conversation. "Your hair has grown. When are you going to stop wearing a wig?"

Her eyes popped open, green orbs gazing into his. "Not everyone will think it's as lovely as you do. I'm still not used to it yet. Maybe when it reaches my shoulders, I'll stop wearing the wig. I'm not up to looking like a pixie." She scrunched her nose in an adorable way, and he reached down and kissed it.

Scarlett wanted the oil gently cleansed off of her, so they decided to take a shower together, washing each other with a rose-scented lotion the hotel provided. Scarlett played more of the sensual French music in the background, and when they dried off, she asked him to love her again. They went back to bed and made love a second time, this time more slowly, more delicately. He ached with longing for her, even after it was all over.

"I love you, Scarlett." He saw tears forming in her eyes. He went on, "Don't get mad at me for saying so."

"Jackson, I know I told you I didn't want you to have feelings for me, but the truth of it is, I love you, too. As much as I tried not to, I do. Whatever you are, your soul, your essence…that's what I love."

"Oh, Scarlett." He kissed her with a new intensity. She actually loved him back. *Him.* A dreaded angel of death that everybody feared and nobody ever wanted to see. She didn't fear death any longer – he could feel that – and she didn't fear him. Rather, she longed to be with him, and most of all, best of all, she loved him. That was the best feeling he'd ever had.

"Is there any hope for us?" she asked. "After I pass, will I see you?" she asked, looking hopeful and yet desperate, longing for him to say yes.

"It is my greatest wish…to spend eternity with you," he said. "Whether that will happen or not remains to be seen."

Chapter Twenty-Eight

Scarlett and Jackson enjoyed sleeping in each other's arms. They ordered room service to bring up a nice breakfast, and they took it out onto their private terrace to eat, wrapped up in blankets to ward off the morning chill. The sun was up, and it was going to be a beautiful day for sailing back to Toulon.

They got dressed and caught the shuttle back to the harbor of Porquerolles where their rented sailboat was. They had an uneventful trip back and relaxed on a soft covered bench, watching some dolphins swim by and drinking mimosas. They'd purchased some oranges in the little square and a bottle of champagne, and Jackson made them on the boat.

They got back to her father's apartment and were greeted with the smell of sugar.

"What is going on here?" Scarlett asked upon entering the kitchen. Flour, sugar, and numerous other ingredients were scattered all over the kitchen countertops. A couple of dozen cookies were resting on a cooling rack, and a Bûche de Noël cake – or yule log cake – was sitting out on a big oval platter.

"We're making thirteen desserts," Tyler said, running over to hug her, flour on his fingers.

She laughed. "Thirteen? Are you celebrating Christmas Eve already?" It was a tradition in Provence to celebrate Christmas Eve by having a big meal and then following that with thirteen desserts, which represented Jesus and his twelve apostles. They were traditionally set out on the table on Christmas Eve and left there for three days.

Her father turned around and greeted her with kisses on her cheeks. "Yes, we worked hard yesterday getting them started so they would all be ready tonight."

"I can't wait to have thirteen desserts!" Tyler said.

"All in one night?" Scarlett asked.

"I know we're supposed to let them sit for three days, but you will all be leaving us soon, and I wanted to celebrate with you while I can." Her father's eyes moistened and he blinked twice to get rid of it.

"Oh, Papa." She hugged him, touched by his sentiment. "It's a wonderful idea. What can I do to help?"

"Me, too," Jackson said.

They spent the next several hours mixing, baking, icing, and covering up many more desserts, to include some flatbread topped with grape jam, white and dark chocolate nougat candies, gingerbread with a hint of hazelnut, a big bowl of fruit, as well as some bread made with olive oil, citrus zest, and orange flower water.

"We also have to make some chocolate gingerbread cookies," Scarlett said, "like Maman used to make. Do you remember?" she asked her father.

"Ah yes. Those were some of my favorite. Yes, let's make some of those. Do you remember the recipe?"

"Oui. I just made some for a friend's party."

"Good. What do we need, besides the molasses?"

They worked on making those next, and as Scarlett was working closely with her father, she got the urge to ask him what had happened between him and her mother. She looked around at Tyler, who was cutting some candies with Odette, and realized she'd better not talk about this in front of him.

I'll take him for a walk, she heard Jackson say in her head. She looked over at him and he was looking at her. She nodded her head and said *Thank you* in her head.

"Hey Tyler, why don't we go take a walk? Maybe we can find Père Noêl or his reindeer in one of the squares."

Tyler looked excited. "I already saw him with Pépé. I can take you to him if you want to see him."

"Really?" Scarlett asked him.

"Uh-huh, and I told him what I wanted for Christmas. I would tell you, but he said I had to keep it a secret."

The others laughed lightly. "Okay," Scarlett said.

"Let's take a carrot for the reindeer," Jackson said, trying to stir up the boy's imagination.

The two left, and Scarlett looked over at Odette, wondering how much she knew about her father and his family. She wondered if she had a family of her own, since she seemed to be living with her father in order to take care of him. She probably didn't. She would never get to see them, if she did.

"Papa," she began.

"Hmm?" he asked, mixing some eggs into the flour in a big bowl.

"What happened between you and Maman?"

Her father stopped what he was doing and looked up at her suddenly. He then glanced at Odette, who washed her hands and quietly left the room.

"I didn't mean to make her leave," Scarlett said.

Her father finished stirring and then placed a towel over the bowl. "Why don't we go out onto the terrace and talk? Maybe get some wine and cheese."

She agreed and got out some Brie cheese and a loaf of bread while he got a bottle of Sauvignon Blanc and two glasses.

The sun was still warm and covered part of the terrace, so they scooted the table over into the sunlight.

"What did your maman tell you?" he asked when they'd settled into their chairs.

"Not much. She wouldn't talk about it, just that you were a horrible man."

Her father laughed lightly. "I deserve that. Did she tell you about the baby we lost?"

"Yes. She said that you drifted apart after that."

"She was devastated. I told her we could try again in six months or a year, but she got more distant and wanted to move back to America."

"Oh, she had the miscarriage in France?"

"Oui. Only it wasn't a miscarriage; he was stillborn."

"Oh. I didn't know that." She'd only known it was a boy. That must have been devastating, to carry a child for nine months, go through the delivery, and then to find out the baby had died.

"We moved to America, I bought her a beautiful big house out in the country like she wanted, and we were relatively happy for a little while, raising you. But she still had the blues." He paused for a moment and took a drink of wine. "On a visit alone back here to Toulon to bury my mother, I met an old girlfriend from school. She was a nurse and had taken care of my mother before she passed." He looked away, seemingly ashamed. "I had an affair with her."

Scarlett scrunched her forehead. "You did what?"

"Your mother didn't deserve it, I know, and I didn't mean for it to happen. I loved your mother very much, but she had become so distant and this woman was very attentive." He fidgeted with the buttons on his sweater nervously. Scarlett tried to be patient. "That nurse is my nurse now."

"You mean Odette?"

"Yes," he confessed. "We had a brief affair and after I came back to America, I confessed to your mother."

"You had an affair with Odette?" Scarlett couldn't believe what she was hearing. She looked towards the back door and saw Odette had been listening to their conversation. She moved away from the door when she saw Scarlett looking her way.

"Yes. Your mother pitched a terrible fit, threw me out of the house and divorced me. I came back here and Odette and I married. So you see, she's not just my nurse. I'm sorry, I should have told you, but I was afraid you wouldn't come and see me if you knew the truth of it."

Scarlett tried to absorb all of this. Such a string of terrible tragedies in her mother's life. Losing a child, then losing her husband, and last of all, developing a terminal illness. It was a bit like her own life, and the realization of it left a bitter taste in her mouth. She'd never been in love or married before Jackson, but if they had been married and he'd had an affair, she wasn't sure she could forgive him either.

"I wanted to stay with your mother after the affair, but she wouldn't have me anymore."

"I can't say as I would blame her." She was a little perturbed with her papa just now.

"I know. I'm not perfect," he said.

"You deserted us…for *her*."

"I didn't desert you. I tried to come back and see you, but she wouldn't let me. So after the divorce, I did what I could. I gave your mother a large sum of money for the two of you every month."

"I should hope so."

"More than the law required, Scarlett. A lot more."

She was quiet, realizing how she and her mother were able to afford so many luxuries. Her mother did have some money from her own family, but now Scarlett realized that part of it had also come from her father. That huge house was completely paid for. "Very well, but still, I needed a father. Did you have to move all the way over here? Couldn't you have lived in America?"

"Odette's father was ill and she didn't want to leave him, and also…"

"Yes?"

"Odette and I had a son together. His name was Stefan."

Scarlett's eyes widened. "I have a half-brother and you never told me? How could you do that to me?"

"I am truly sorry. I thought perhaps your mother told you, but I see now she told you nothing."

"Where is he? Does he live here in Toulon?" She felt excitement at the thought of having a sibling.

He shook his head sadly. "No. He was killed in a car accident when he was sixteen."

"Oh." Her excitement quickly faded to sadness.

"When your mother found out that we had Stefan, she told me she hated me over the phone. She felt cheated that her son – our son – had died and now I was getting to raise another one. She told me to never come back to America to see you after that."

So that was the reason why he never visited her. Her mother had said he was in poor health. "Did I ever meet Stefan?"

"No. He was away the first time you came to visit, when you were finally old enough to come see me on your own. The second time you visited, Stefan had already passed."

"How long ago did this happen?" She knew her last trip here had been before Tyler was born, but she wasn't sure how many years it had been. At least eight.

"Nine years ago, in 2006."

She took a drink of her wine. "That was right after your heart attack. Do you mean that…?"

"Yes, I had the heart attack after Stefan was killed."

She felt sorry for him. "How terrible. Maman nearly talked me out of that visit. I thought you were in bad health, but I had no idea you were also grieving. Why didn't you tell me any of this then?"

"I was ashamed of the affair, and then I was afraid you'd never come to see me again if I told you about Stefan."

"I can't believe Maman never told me any of this. Even after I was grown up and had a child of my own. Why would she keep it a secret from me?"

"I suspect it hurt too much. I broke her heart, something I'm not proud of. I loved her as much as she would let me and we had a few good years, but in the end, we couldn't make it work. I'm just glad I was able to provide for you any way I could and that I was able to be with my son for sixteen years. I enjoyed mes enfants."

She tried to see reasoning from her father's point of view, but it was hard. She couldn't believe he'd had an affair and then had a son who'd died. She wasn't sure how she felt except that she was angry that no one told her and sad that she never got to know her half-brother.

"Do you have any pictures of Stefan?"

"But of course." He went inside and came back out a moment later with a 5x7 picture frame. When Scarlett saw the teenage boy, she caught her breath. She couldn't believe what she was seeing. How could it be?

"This is Stefan?" she asked incredulously.

"Yes. He's quite handsome, no?" She looked up at him, and he smiled faintly.

"He is, indeed." She needed time to think about all of this. "I think I'll go for a walk, catch up with Tyler and Jackson," she said.

Her father looked at her sadly. "Je suis désolé, ma chérie. Can you forgive me, s'il vous plaît?"

"Just give me some time, Papa."

She gulped down the rest of her wine and went inside to find a sweater. Then she set out to find more answers.

Jackson and Tyler had just missed Père Noêl, so they went to one of the parks instead. Tyler was climbing a tree in the square when Jackson heard sniffling and felt Scarlett's presence. He turned around and saw her walking towards him. He read her mind and could tell she was both hurt and angry. She balled up her fists and looked mad enough to hit him. It reminded him of when she found out he had lied to her and started pounding on his chest with her fists. Any other person who did something like that in the past would have angered him to the point of punishing them, but with her, it fascinated him and stirred his heart to witness the passion igniting inside of her, whether it be about something good or bad. He was so in love with her, he couldn't see straight sometimes.

She walked up to him and said, "How could you do that?"

"Do what?" he asked, trying to clarify what she was thinking.

"How is it that you look like an older version of my half-brother?"

She knows. "You have a half-brother?" he asked, smiling sheepishly.

"You know very well that I do. How is that possible?"

He glanced over to see that Tyler was all right and not listening to their conversation. "I started taking on his form after he passed. He's quite a striking fellow, don't you think?" She didn't want to answer that. "It's a coincidence, I swear it." At least he thought it was. "I started appearing as him at the same age he was when he passed over, sixteen, to Cassie and her friends." Scarlett looked confused. "Luke's daughter."

"Okay. Why?"

"I had helped Stefan cross over, and he lived all the way over here in France. I didn't think it would be a big deal. I don't get into everyone's family histories when I help them pass over. I didn't imagine that anyone would know that person in America. Until I met you."

"But you didn't tell me anyway? This is not the first time you've lied to me. How can I trust you?"

"Scarlett, I'm sorry. I didn't imagine that this would matter. You never met him, so you didn't know what he looked like."

"I can't believe you never told me. I can almost understand why my parents kept this a secret, but not you. I thought we had something special, something…otherworldly," she said, whispering the last part. He saw tears in her eyes.

"Scarlett, please." He longed to hold her, but she was too angry with him. He didn't blame her for being mad at him. It would be quite a shock.

He was hoping she wouldn't find out, but by now, he thought she would understand that things with him worked differently. He wasn't human.

Tyler ran up to her and hugged her. "Hey, Maman. Look at this cool tree I'm climbing."

"I see," she said, wiping tears from her eyes while Tyler wasn't looking.

"Watch me, Maman," he said, running off to climb the tree again.

"Okay, I will." She watched him climb and then turned back to Jackson. "I love you, Jackson, but maybe you don't understand how it works with humans. When we care about each other, we don't keep secrets like this."

"You mean like the one you kept from Tyler…and Luke?"

"That was different. I didn't know where to find Luke."

"But you could have told Tyler, before now."

She stopped and watched her son in the tree again and smiled at him. She looked back at Jackson and said, "You're right, I could have."

"I'm truly sorry I didn't tell you. I'm new at being human, okay? I'm only in this skin because my wings would be too weird to other people."

She studied him, actually looked at his back, trying to picture wings on him.

"I helped your half-brother pass over. I asked him for permission to present myself in his body form sometime, and said he didn't mind, as long as it was far away from here." He laughed lightly. She didn't.

"Didn't you think my father would recognize you when you got here? He could've had another heart attack. He could've thought you were him and that he didn't really die."

"He was shocked, for sure, but we talked about it the first night we came here. I told him what I am."

"You did what? Did he believe you?"

"He did. I told him that I helped Stefan pass over, and he took great comfort in that. I told him his son was fine. Actually, I could take you to see your brother if you'd like to sometime. Remember me telling you that I could show you what your future would be like, up in Eden?"

She did remember. "Would I be able to tell the two of you apart? Won't he look just like you?"

"Not exactly. Humans keep their appearance in Eden at whatever age they want to, from toddler up to the age of their death. So your brother would still look sixteen, or younger if he chooses. Of course, I look twenty years older than he did, but I am trying not to be seen by too many people here in Toulon. That is why I didn't say much when we met your friend, Tristan. Your father recognized me, of course, so that is why I've been letting my beard grow out and wearing a hat when I'm out on the streets walking around." He pointed to his toboggan.

"What do you really look like then, as an angel?"

"I can't show you that until you go up to Eden with me."

"Why would I have to wait?"

"You know…the wings."

"Ah, the wings. What color are yours?"

"Black."

She looked stunned. "Black?" she whispered.

"Yes, I am an angel of death, after all."

"You don't have red eyes, do you?"

He laughed. "No. My eyes are exactly the same as they are now. They won't change. That was one difference between your half-brother and me. He had green eyes like yours."

"Oh." She looked away at Tyler again, who came bouncing up to them.

"Let's go to Pépé's and get ready for the soap opera."

"The what?" Scarlett asked.

"What's it called? It's a play – Pépé says we're going to see a bunch of people singing and dancing on a stage."

"Oh, the opera."

"That's it." He twirled around in a circle, humming a tune to himself.

She grabbed him in a hug. "Okay, let's go."

Chapter Twenty-Nine

Walking back to her father's apartment, Scarlett thought about everything regarding her father, half-brother, and Jackson. She only wanted to deal with one thing at a time, so she started with her father.

She was sad that he and her mother had lost a baby and could see how her mother would be depressed for a while. The fact that she didn't seem to get over it made her understand – a little – how her father would be tempted by another woman, especially someone he had had a relationship with in the past. It wasn't right, but she couldn't talk to her mother to get her side of the story, see why she couldn't let go of her grief. She knew her mother had remained bitter about her father, but she didn't know that she'd held on to her grief for so long.

Her father asked for forgiveness, and she would give it to him. He had been through a lot, and the fact that her mother kept him from visiting Scarlett disturbed her, but there was nothing she could do about it now. Life was too short – especially for her – to hold grudges, especially for something that happened in the past and that she had no control over.

When they made it back to the apartment, she found her father taking a nap in the sitting room. Odette quickly left the room after saying hello, and her father woke up.

"Ah, you have returned."

Tyler ran up to him, hugged him and showed him a bright red leaf he had collected on the walk.

"Can we talk?" Scarlett asked her father.

He nodded and the two went out to the terrace.

"I forgive you, Papa. I don't like the fact that you and Maman kept this from me, and I'm still sad that I didn't get to meet my half-brother," (although she thought that perhaps she could, with Jackson), "but life is too short for me to stay mad at you." She hugged him.

"Merci beaucoup, ma chérie."

"I'm so glad I made this trip to see you, and I'm sorry that I didn't come sooner."

"You've had it rough. I understand," he said. "I know all about what Jackson is. You need to forgive him, too."

She was surprised at his words. "You don't hold any resentment for him using your son's appearance?"

"No, of course not. It was almost like seeing the future, what my son could have looked like when he got older. He has a different personality than Stefan, so he's not the same. And his eyes are different, black as night."

She nodded. She loved those coal black eyes.

"You're going to need him," her father said. "He'll be with you when you need it most, when I won't be there and your mother won't be there."

He was right about that. She didn't think she could've made it this far and been this happy without Jackson…even though she was still mad at him for deceiving her. Again.

"Will you also forgive Odette? She thinks you hate her."

"I'll try."

"While you and Jackson were on the island, I bought us tickets to a choir performance this evening. Are you up to doing that?"

She nodded. It would be good to get together as a family and a good memory for Tyler.

He walked back towards the door. "Shall I send Jackson out?"

She nodded again. Might as well get this conversation over with. She had more questions for him.

He walked out cautiously holding a bottle of wine, two glasses, and a long loaf of bread. He sat down at the table and started pouring the wine out.

Scarlett started right away with her interrogation. "It was your idea that we come to France. Didn't you think I might find out about my half-brother and that you look like him?"

"Yes, I wanted you to find out about your half-brother, even if it would be uncomfortable for all of us. When I first started appearing to you back in May and then this fall, I thought it would be fine. I knew you didn't know about him, and I thought you would never know that I took on his appearance. But the more I got to know you, the more I wanted you to know the truth before you passed over. Before I knew it, we had become very close and then it was too late to change my human appearance."

"Didn't you think I would find it weird that I had fallen in love with someone who looked like my half-brother? That's kind of creepy if you think about it."

"Yes, but at first, I didn't think you'd find out about him. Secondly, I didn't know you and I were going to fall in love. That was all very unexpected." She had to agree with him there. She would never have dreamed that she would've fallen in love with a man at the end of her life, let alone an angel.

She picked up her glass of wine and took a sip. "If you helped Stefan pass over, did you not see my father then?"

"No, I didn't see your father, and I had a different appearance when I saw Stefan. He died quickly and I couldn't prepare him. I just helped him move on afterwards."

"Oh. I didn't know it worked that way."

"Sometimes, yes, if the death is quick or violent, unexpected."

She sighed, tired of thinking. Her head was starting to hurt. "I can accept your reasons for using his appearance, but where does that leave us? I don't think I can look at you the same way anymore." She pulled a piece of bread off, took a bite, and looked at him.

"Do you want me to change my appearance?"

"No…I don't know. I fell in love with you as you look now. Maybe if I saw your true appearance…"

"You mean with wings and all?"

She nodded and took another bite of bread.

"Okay, I'll do it. Whatever makes you happy. Do you want to go see your brother tonight? I can arrange it. Will that make you feel better?"

Would it make her feel better? She wasn't sure. It might creep her out even more. At least she would get to meet him, though, so she said yes.

"Then you can see me in my true form. My only fear is that you won't love me anymore…in that form."

That was a fear she had, as well.

Over on Boulevard de Strasbourg was the 1862 Opera House. Scarlett admired the beautiful outside architecture and sculptures, and once inside, marveled at the ornate red and gold interior, beautiful chandeliers, gold-framed paintings, and arched windows. She'd been too young to appreciate this when she'd lived here before.

The performance that evening was of a choir from Cambridge playing music for Advent and Christmas. It was very beautiful, and halfway through, sitting between Jackson and Tyler, she grabbed both of their hands and held them tight. Tyler eventually tired of holding her hand and let go, but Jackson kept holding on.

At the end of the performance, she excused herself to go to the ladies' room, and Odette followed her.

"I understand if you hate me," she said once they were inside the restroom.

"I don't hate you. It's just a lot to take in, a lot of surprises."

"Life is full of surprises. Makes life interesting."

"That it does," Scarlett agreed. "I'm sorry you lost your son. That must've been awful."

"It was. I am sorry we couldn't come and see you and tell you all about this sooner, but he really has had to take it easy since the heart attack."

"I understand. Honestly," Scarlett looked directly at her, "life is too short for hate. Especially for me."

"I'm sorry about that, too. I nearly came to your mother's funeral, just to see you in your father's place, but I decided it wouldn't be a good idea. I didn't want to cause you further distress."

"I appreciate the thought."

"If there's anything I can do for you…" Odette suddenly hugged her.

Scarlett smiled. "Thank you."

They all took a taxi back to the apartment and then had a nice big Christmas Eve dinner, finishing it off with the thirteen desserts. Scarlett looked around at all the happy faces of her family and Jackson, and smiled. And she tried every one of those thirteen desserts.

Before going to bed, Jackson discreetly told her to meet him on the terrace at midnight. She got in the bed with Tyler and Fleur and waited until the right time, and then she slipped out of bed wearing a black velour top and pants, and crept out into the night.

Chapter Thirty

Scarlett saw Jackson in the moonlight. In the shadows, she could see that he was in full angel form. His full black wings were taller than he was, arched high on his back. He wore no shirt, and as she crept closer to him, she could see rippled muscles like none she'd ever seen before except on statues or body builders. He wore a short black skirt reminding her of the Romans in the old Bible movies from the '60s. His legs were muscular, toned, and he wore no shoes. He had no hair on his body except on his head, which was black, straight like a raven's, and reached his shoulders. She walked over closer to him and looked at his chiseled face, which was pale and actually glowing, and more handsome than any man she'd ever seen in her life. He still had bushy eyebrows but no other facial hair at all. His eyes were the most spectacular thing on him – the same eyes she had fallen in love with. Those same eyes flashed like lightning for a moment when the moonlight hit them, and then looked down upon her with love.

He took her breath away. She gasped. "Jackson?"

He smiled. "Who else?" His voice was the same. That was a relief. He reached out his hands, but she was afraid to touch him. "Are you ready?"

She closed her gaping mouth and nodded.

He slowly turned her around and wrapped her up in his arms. She took a deep breath and held fast to his arms around her. They left the ground and flew – actually flew, rather than disapparating – up into the star-filled sky. The night air felt cold, and the wind nearly blew her wig off her head. They passed into a large cluster of clouds like a thick fog where she couldn't see anything. The moisture from the clouds stuck to their skin, making her fearful of slipping from his grips.

"I've got you," he reassured her.

It started getting brighter and brighter, and suddenly she could see the sun and blue skies, and looking down, the most beautiful garden. It looked like something from Jurassic Park or Noah's Ark – animals of every kind roaming around in harmony. People, too, walked around – naked but somehow not indecent.

Birds of all kinds chirped and flitted from tree to tree. There were waterfalls big and small connected by a long stream, in which several different animals were drinking, washing, and playing. A couple of red foxes ran by, chasing two rabbits, and when they caught up with them, they played with them rather than trying to eat them. Flutes could be heard in one corner of the garden where people sat around a fire.

They got closer and closer to the ground, and Jackson landed in a grove of tall palm trees very carefully. She looked up at his wings, which were straight up in the air so as not to get caught on any of the palm fronds or coconuts. Her feet touched the ground not far away from the water where she saw her mother talking to Jackson's look-alike. She couldn't believe her eyes.

Jackson let go of her, and she ran up to her mother. "Maman!"

"Scarlett?" They hugged. "It's not your time yet, is it, honey?"

"How would you know that?" Scarlett asked, pulling back to look at her. She looked a lot younger, like maybe her thirties, the way she looked when Scarlett was a little girl. "Oh Maman, I've missed you so."

"I've missed you, too, pretty girl. You're getting too skinny, though, without me cooking for you."

"Oh, you must know my condition. I'm eating only the best foods; that's what Jackson told me to do. Have you met him?" She looked behind her at the beautiful creature in the daylight. Her breath caught.

"Yes, I have," her mother said.

Jackson walked up to them and looked at the young man who had to be Stefan. Scarlett looked at him and was shocked how much he looked like Jackson and yet very different, too. His eyes were the most obvious thing that was different about him, as well as his age.

"Scarlett, this is your half-brother, Stefan," Jackson said.

She hugged him, not worrying about formalities. "I'm so glad to meet you. I didn't even know you existed until today."

Stefan laughed. "I'm sorry we didn't get to meet before now." He had a French accent. That was different, too.

They looked at each other for a long moment.

"How's our father?" he asked.

"He's doing pretty good. Did you know about his heart attack after your passing?"

"Yes, I felt bad about that."

"It wasn't your fault," Scarlett said. She realized Jackson was right in bringing her up here to meet him. It was helping already. "So the two of you know each other now?" She looked from Stefan to her mother.

"Of course," her mother said. "Everybody knows everybody up here." She laughed. "I'm sorry for not telling you about Stefan. Can you forgive me?"

"Yes, but I didn't know you grieved your first child so much."

"You mean Andrew?" She glanced around and Scarlett saw a blonde-haired boy of about three years old playing by the water.

"Is that?"

"That's your brother. He died as a newborn, but here in Eden, he has grown to be three years old now. He's such a joy."

"I had no idea," Scarlett said. She didn't even think about the lost baby being here, too.

They all talked a while more, and finally Jackson said it was time to go, that she needed to get some sleep.

"Forgive your father, too," her mother said upon hugging one last time. "And I'll see you here sometime soon." She winked at Jackson.

"Goodbye, Maman."

She hugged Stefan and Andrew and thought that it wouldn't be so bad to come up here when she passed. She would miss Tyler, for sure, but she had other loved ones here.

She looked at Jackson again, took a deep breath because he literally took her breath away. He reached his arms out to her and she walked up to him and turned in his arms to be picked up. And away they went, back up into the sky where it turned to night again. The chilly air would have frozen her, but she felt warm and secure in Jackson's arms. It was fun to see the world from up high and watch Toulon get bigger and bigger.

They landed back at the terrace gently, and Scarlett immediately turned around. Jackson folded up his wings on his back and seemed to be about ready to change human, but she stopped him.

"Don't change back yet. Let me look at you." She did, all over. "Mon Dieu, you are the most handsome creature I've ever seen!" she whispered.

"You really think so?" he asked. She could feel uncertainty in him.

"Yes, most definitely," she reassured him. "You're breathtaking. Can you stay in this form when we…fool around? From now on? It's a little weird that you look different. I mean, I knew you were an angel, but I had no idea you wouldn't look the same. It's like getting to know you all over again."

"We angels are able to take whatever form we want, even as animals. I can change when we're alone, but I cannot change what I look like around other people."

"I understand the wings part, but what about the rest of you?"

"The rest of me?" He looked down at himself.

"Yes, all those gorgeous chiseled muscles."

"Oh, you like that, huh?"

"Mhmm. If you can change into any form, why can't you be yourself all except for the wings?"

"I'm not allowed to show my full self to people other than those who are going to die soon. Have you heard of the saying, 'You can't look upon the face of death and live'?" She nodded. "Well, no one can see my true form – face, body, wings – unless they are getting ready to die. That's why I can show myself to you, but I cannot show myself like this to someone who is not dying, like Tyler, for example."

"I see. But you'll do it for me, won't you? When were alone?"

"Wings and all?"

Her eyes widened. "Yes, that would be kind of exciting. Maybe we could fly at the same time…"

"Be still my heart…"

He reached out to take her in his arms, and it felt a little weird because he seemed like someone else.

"Just look into my eyes," he said, reading her thoughts. "It's me – my essence, my soul, is the same."

She walked into his arms and he just held her. His wings spread around both of them, and she felt excited but calm at the same time.

"Thank you for taking me to Eden. It was wonderful. I don't think I would have taken this news of my father and Odette and Stefan as well if you hadn't been in my life, nor would I have taken this cancer and my imminent demise as well as I have either. I have come to accept my fate and actually look forward to seeing my loved ones again. You have helped me beyond measure, and I thank you for that. And I forgive you for deceiving me. I can see why this should be kept secret."

He pulled her back to look at her. "Thank you," he whispered, and he slowly lowered his lips to hers. It was perhaps the sweetest kiss they'd shared yet.

Chapter Thirty-One

The next morning, Scarlett got up early to prepare to leave. They had an early train to catch back up to Paris, where they would spend part of the day, then fly out at four o'clock in the afternoon to Atlanta, and be home by midnight. She had hers and Tyler's bags packed by seven.

Jackson would travel with them by train but then they would be flying back without him, the same way they came. Jackson was already up when she entered the kitchen with her bags. He was sitting at the table, drinking coffee with her father.

"Good morning," she said to them both.

"It's not a good morning when my beautiful fille has to leave," her father said sadly.

He stood up and she hugged him.

"Come with me, I have something to give you," he said.

She followed him, pausing to place a quick kiss on Jackson's lips when she passed him. Her father went to his bedroom and picked up a French officer's uniform. Turning around, he said, "I want you to have my uniform." He handed it to her. It was covered with a plastic dry-cleaning bag.

"Papa, are you sure?"

"Oui." He turned around, picked up a nice garment bag, and placed the uniform inside it. "Give it to Tyler as an inheritance. I know it could wait, but I wanted to give it to you now; it's easier. He will, of course, also inherit money from me."

"Are you planning to join me so soon?" she asked, teasing him, trying to make light of the conversation.

"No, but just so, I wanted you to have this and know that Tyler will be taken care of. "Do you need anything? What can I do for you?"

"No, I don't need anything else, Papa. You've given me and Mother plenty of money in the past, and Tyler will have more than enough."

"Who's going to take care of him?"

"His father maybe or perhaps cousin James."

Her father frowned at the mention of her cousin. "He's too busy. He rarely sees his own father. What about me?"

"I didn't want to ask you, Papa. I didn't think you were well enough, and then it would be such a drastic change for him, coming to a foreign country."

"Oui, I understand, but if his father cannot take him, I would take him if you needed me to. He's a fine boy; I'm very proud of him. You've done a wonderful job taking care of him." She wiped a tear as he continued. "You let me know if his father can't take him."

"Okay, I will. Thank you, Papa."

She took the garment bag and joined Jackson, Tyler, and Odette in the kitchen, and they said their goodbyes.

"Thank you for forgiving me," Odette told her. "I've enjoyed having you here with us."

"Me, too. Take care of my father."

"I will."

She hugged her father for a long time while Jackson took their bags out to the waiting taxi. "Are you sure you cannot stay longer?" he asked her.

"I would love to, but our tickets are nonrefundable."

"Ah, well then. Take care, ma jolie fille."

"Je t'aime, Papa."

"Je t'aime. Au revoir." They kissed cheeks. "God willing, we'll see each other again on the other side." She nodded and wiped her tears. "Tell Stefan hello for me."

"I will." She wanted so badly to tell him that she'd seen both of her brothers in Eden, but she thought perhaps that was something best kept secret. She didn't want to get Jackson in trouble.

The train ride was uneventful, and once again, Tyler enjoyed looking out the window at everything. The weather turned from sunny to cloudy and finally a little rainy by the time they reached Paris.

"What do you want to do first?" Jackson asked Scarlett after they'd gotten off the train and retrieved their luggage.

"Would you like to go up in the Eiffel Tower?" she asked Tyler.

"You mean that big tall tower over there?" he pointed excitedly towards the Eiffel in the distance.

"Yes, that's the one."

"Uh-huh, let's go," he said.

They stored their luggage in lockers and then hopped on the Metro and came out at Passy station. They crossed the beautiful Seine River, and then the big iconic tower loomed over their heads. Hordes of people were walking around with their cameras and smart phones, taking selfies in front of it, despite the sprinkling rain and cool temperatures.

"Let's go, let's go," Tyler said, tugging his mother's arm.

"Okay, we're coming," Scarlett said, laughing.

She paid for their tickets, and they made their way to the lift and took it up to the first floor. They got off to have a look around, as Scarlett had heard it had been renovated. It now had a transparent floor to walk on, through which you could see to the ground below, as if you were walking on air. Tyler loved it, but it made Scarlett feel funny in her stomach. She did see a gift shop that she wanted to visit later. They took the elevator up to the second floor and got off to have another look at the views.

"C'est très beau," Scarlett said. They walked around, took pictures, and then they got on the elevator taking them to the very tiptop of the tower.

Tyler was in awe.

Scarlett was terrified. The elevator had glass windows, and they could see all of Paris get smaller and smaller. "Mon Dieu, why am I doing this? I can't look."

She turned around and hid in Jackson's secure arms.

"Maman, you're missing out," Tyler said. "This is way cool."

She thought about it and realized he was right. She was missing out. What was the worst that could happen? She's dying anyway. What was that country song her mother used to listen to? *Live like you were dying* were the words. That's what she should do. Because she *was* dying. She decided to enjoy the life she had left, take risks, and do things she wouldn't normally do.

She turned back around, pulled Jackson's arms around hers and then pulled Tyler up close in front of her and away from the windows, and she looked out. She felt Jackson's warm breath on her ear, and he whispered, "You're doing great. Have you not been on this before?"

"Oui, but I was just a young girl. I am older and wiser now…and more afraid." She laughed nervously. "But I will do it anyway." *If I were to fall, I know you would catch me with your wings,* she directed her thoughts to Jackson.

He squeezed her and kissed her ear and answered, *Of course, I would, chérie.*

Actually, it was a bit like being up in Jackson's arms when they flew to Eden. Only it was daytime now when it was dark before, so she could see more.

When they reached the top, they got off, had a little bit of rosé champagne at the small bar and took in the views.

"C'est magnifique!" Scarlett exclaimed. "It's breathtaking – literally!" It was considerably windy up there on the top.

She and Jackson toasted each other, took a sip of the champagne, and then kissed.

She made Tyler hold hands with both her and Jackson – especially Jackson – while they looked around. The rain kept them in the covered area, and then they got on the elevator to go back down. Once they got to the first floor again, after getting off at the second floor and taking the stairs down to the first, just because Tyler wanted to, they went to the gift shop. Scarlett bought an Eiffel Tower Christmas tree ornament, and then they ate lunch in the 58 restaurant with splendid views at a more reasonable height, Scarlett thought.

There was a special ice skating rink set up on the first floor for winter, and Scarlett let Tyler do a little skating while she and Jackson sat, drank some café au lait, and watched the skaters.

Next, they made their way down the streets of Paris and did a little shopping. The rain had stopped but the wind was picking up. In one shop, there were beautiful barbotine porcelain bowls and earthenware that Scarlett just loved. She spent a lot of time looking at the beautiful pieces and marveled at how real the flowers looked. They were like 3-D.

Jackson walked over to see what she was looking at.

"Aren't these beautiful?" she asked him.

"Why don't you buy something? Maybe a small piece, something you love."

"What's the point?" she asked sadly. "I won't get to enjoy it long."

"You'll have it to remind you of our trip to France for the rest of your days, and then you can pass it on to Tyler. He'll remember his trip to France with his dear mother and how much she loved these porcelain bowls."

"Okay, you've sold me," she said, laughing. "By the way, I guess I need to make out a will."

"That would be smart but wait until you know who Tyler will be staying with."

"Right, okay."

She picked out a small bowl with mauve, yellow, and light pink roses with a beige background, and Jackson asked the clerk to ship it to the beach house for them.

"That way you won't have to worry about it getting broken on the trip back home, and it will give you something to look forward to after the excitement of the trip and Christmas are over," he told her.

She agreed that all made sense.

After that, they went back to the lockers and got their luggage, and then took a taxi to the airport. On the way, they passed a mass of flowers in the street for the victims of the recent tragedy in Saint-Denis. Scarlett wept and explained to Tyler what it was for when he asked.

Quietly, she asked Jackson, "Did you…help any of them?"

"Yes. I helped their spirits move on after their deaths since it was quick and violent."

Like Stefan, she thought.

These people had no time to prepare, not in the way she has. They didn't know that they would be taking their last breath that day. At least Scarlett had been able to prepare. *Thank you,* she said in her head to Jackson.

He kissed her hand as the taxi moved on down the streets of Paris.

They arrived at the airport and she reluctantly said goodbye to Jackson since he wasn't flying in the plane with them.

"Jackson, how are you gettin' home?" Tyler asked him.

"I've got another flight. I'll catch up with you in Norfolk." He winked at Scarlett.

"Okay, see ya."

"Goodbye, my love," Scarlett said. "À plus tard."

"Until later," he repeated, kissing her lips.

She walked away from him picturing his big black wings on his back, and she blew him another kiss.

Chapter Thirty-Two

It had been a weird two weeks since Cassie had sex with…whoever it was she had sex with. She thought it was the love of her life, Skyler, but he swore adamantly it wasn't him. She'd spent enough time with angels lately to know that anything was possible. If it wasn't Skyler, if it was Jackson or someone – some*thing* else – she felt just awful because she had enjoyed it so much and she'd been unfaithful to Skyler. She felt like a whore. She'd lost her virginity for nothing. Just one more mistake added to her long list. She was on the naughty list for sure this Christmas.

On the other hand, Skyler had been an absolute joy for the past week, showing even more attention than usual and was back to kissing her. He seemed to think it was his fault Jackson did this to her. Jackson had been gone to France all week, which was good because Skyler was so mad at him, she thought he would literally get himself killed over defending her honor.

She hadn't seen the creature anymore, so she hoped it was gone, whatever it was. It could have been Jackson or whoever – whatever – she had sex with. That was a scary thought.

It was Christmas Eve and she was in Maggie's car with her, Jen, Logan, and Emily. They were all headed to Chesapeake to see Luke and the band play at a local country bar, Eagle's Nest. Skyler said he had a family thing to do until later, and then he would meet her at Maggie's for dinner and present exchange.

Cassie had missed her dad a lot and couldn't wait to see him play. His song had been playing on the local radio stations, which was exciting. She still couldn't believe what was happening.

On the downside, she hoped they didn't move to Nashville. She wanted to finish school at Kellam and mostly, she didn't want to leave Skyler. She'd already told Jen she wouldn't go if her dad asked them to.

Which meant, of course, that her dad would be away from them a lot. Again. Just like it had been in years past when he'd traveled up to Wallops Island as a government contractor. She hated it.

She hadn't gotten Skyler's cough or stomach pains like he'd been having, but she did have nausea for the past week. She even threw up yesterday morning. She thought maybe she was coming down with something but hoped not. She listened to Maggie talking about being so nauseous she couldn't cook today, so she was just going to pick up some pre-cooked food from the Harris Teeter deli.

It hit Cassie suddenly that they didn't use protection. Whoever she had sex with, they didn't use a condom. What if she was pregnant?! Her dad would kill her if he knew she had sex, let alone got pregnant. Then again, hadn't he and Jen conceived Logan while they were in high school? Surely they would understand at least a little, if she were pregnant. If she ever had to tell them, which she hoped never happened. They would hopefully not be mad at Skyler either. She wouldn't let them. There was one problem…Skyler wasn't the one she had sex with.

So who was the father? She started chewing on the skin surrounding one of her fingernails nervously. Her heart started pounding. She was scared. She was too young to be pregnant.

She wondered why her new guardian angel would allow herself to be sucked in by Jackson like that, to be deceived, and now maybe pregnant. She texted Skyler: *Sometimes I miss you being my guardian. I never felt safer.*

He texted back, *R U ok?*

Yes, she texted back. *Just sayin.*

Do you wish I hadn't become human? he texted back.

No, of course not.

"We're here," Jen said excitedly.

Cassie texted to Skyler that she'd see him later. Before turning her phone off, she deleted all the messages between her and Skyler because of the subject matter. She didn't want any evidence of talking about things like guardian angels.

She tried to push her worries and fears to the back of her mind and concentrate on her dad and the band for a little while.

Jen was so excited to see Luke on stage. He'd flown home earlier that day, and she'd closed the shop early to go pick him up at the airport. Cassie had been over to Skyler's and Logan at Emily's, so she and Luke made love in a rush. They'd missed each other so much, they couldn't wait to get naked together. After that, they'd only had time to shower and get dressed before Steve and Darren picked him up to go to Eagle's Nest.

It had been a hard few weeks without him. Even the short trip to Nashville hadn't been enough. Here it was Christmas Eve already, and yet the two of them had hardly done anything Christmassy at all. It seemed like she wanted to stop time until he came back home so they could do fun things together. Every trip to the mall or Walmart, every time she went Christmas shopping anywhere, she'd missed him. She'd bought him a lot of gifts, clothes, guitar picks, hot sauce, anything that she saw when she was out that she thought he'd like.

They quickly ran inside the bar and saw Bridget and her kids, who had reserved a big table in the back. Jen and the others joined them at the table and ordered drinks. The band was playing an early set, for which Jen was glad, so they could all have some fun at Maggie's.

The radio stations had been advertising the band's appearance here all day. They were supposed to sign autographs afterwards. Finally, they came out on the stage and started playing one of their fast numbers. Just like when she saw them in Nashville, all the girls started crowding around the stage, cheering, whistling, waving, and taking pictures of the band…mainly Luke. She'd gotten jealous then and she was jealous now. Sure, he was making his dreams come true, and she was happy for him and very proud of him because she knew he was incredibly talented. But it was hard seeing the one you loved being fawned over by all these women. Pretty women. Scantily clad obnoxious women who were flaunting anything they had at her man. It was hard to watch.

They played a few more songs and ended with their last song, the one that had been playing on the radio, and all the girls started cheering and videoing with their smart phones. After he finished, he told the crowd that song was written for his beautiful wife, Jen, and he pointed her out in the crowd. That made her feels a lot better. All those obnoxious girls turned around to see what she looked like, frowns on their faces.

Luke then introduced the band members and thanked the audience for coming out to see them tonight. They put their instruments down and went to the area where they would be signing autographs and handing out CDs with their single on it.

"Did you see some of those girls?" Bridget asked them.

"Yes," Jen said, rolling her eyes.

"They better keep their hands off my man, that's all I'm going to say." She laughed loudly.

"I'm with you," Maggie said.

Jen nodded her agreement. She glanced at the autograph table and saw a woman ask Luke to sign her chest. She was wearing a low-cut shirt, so it looked almost like he was signing her boob. "Oh my god," she complained. "It's sure going to be hard sharing him, but I don't want to say anything to Luke about it. It's been his dream for so long."

"Steve's too," Maggie said.

"We'll just have to keep reminding them what they married us for," Bridget said suggestively, and then laughed uproariously.

Later at Maggie's, Luke was spending time with his family and friends and thinking that life didn't get much better than this right here. Being home. He'd missed Jen and the kids like crazy. Now he had another son, Tyler, and he needed to make a decision soon about whether to raise him or not. He still didn't know what to do. If he did agree to take him – and he should; he was his flesh and blood after all – with his new career taking off, it would really be Jen who would be taking care of him. She said she would do it for him, that he seemed like a sweet boy and favored Luke a lot, but he still dreaded doing that to her.

Then there was the living situation. James and Robert both advised all the band members to move to Nashville, that it would just make things easier. He'd talked to Jen about it when she came to Nashville, and she tried to look enthused about it, but he could tell she really didn't want to. She said she would do it for him, but she had her store and her mother's old house here in Virginia Beach. Her best friend, Maggie, would be moving, too, if they all decided to make the move. That would be easier on Jen. The kids would be harder to convince. They only had another year of school left, and to make them move now would be hard for them. They'd have to leave their friends.

The worst to convince would be Cassie. She'd have to leave Skyler. He hated to do that to her. He kept thinking about how he and Jen had separated when they were in high school, when he'd found out Cassie's mom was pregnant and he'd married her and joined the Navy. He'd been away from everyone – the one he loved, Jen, the one he tried to love, Josie, and his daughter, Cassie.

It would be the same now, traveling on tour, being away from home. He wasn't completely sure he was all in just yet. It was exciting, to be sure, with all the people cheering for them, asking for autographs, treating him like a celebrity.

He came out of the kitchen and walked towards the hall to go to the bathroom when Scarlett came up the hall from the other direction.

"Luke, can I talk to you privately for a minute?"

"Sure."

He followed her into one of the bedrooms that had a small Christmas tree in the window, and he closed the door behind them. He guessed she wanted to talk about Tyler.

"I just got back from visiting my father in Toulon, and he said if you don't want to take Tyler, he would be happy to take him."

"Oh, I see," Luke said.

"The choice is still up to you and Jen, but I'm weighing all of my options, in case you decide not to – and that's perfectly fine if you don't. I understand it's a lot to take on."

"Of course, I'm still thinking about it."

She nodded. "I'm thinking James won't have time for Tyler, and he is unmarried, so Tyler would be left alone a lot or in child care. My father would be more attentive. He's not as bad off as I had thought; he just cannot travel by plane as far as America."

Luke could understand her way of thinking, and it would almost be a relief if he let Scarlett's father take the boy, but is that what he really wanted? For somebody else to raise his kid, halfway across the world?

Scarlett continued, "My father has a nice place where he could walk and get to places, it's in a safe area, there's beautiful weather most of the year, and my father adores him. As it turns out, he is married and his wife is a nurse, so Tyler would be well taken care of and loved."

Luke felt deflated. She seemed to be making a good case for Tyler to go live with her father. He wasn't sure how he felt about that. He actually liked the kid, and besides, he belonged to him. He shouldn't take this lightly. "That sounds pretty nice, but I'm still thinking about it, so don't make any decisions just yet."

"Oh, I won't. Of course, you are my first choice, being the father. I just wanted you to know that I have a pretty good backup plan if you aren't able to take him. You could still visit him in France if you think you'll be too busy with your new career. Believe me, I would understand."

Luke nodded. "Okay, thanks."

Chapter Thirty-Three

Skyler had been anticipating this moment for a week now. Confronting Jackson. Ever since he'd found out that someone had had sex with Cassie. All this time, he'd been talking to Jackson about his sicknesses, and Jackson said another angel was messing with him. Another angel was right – Jackson. Who else could it be? Hadn't Jackson flirted with her when they first met? He'd even kissed her. It all made sense.

What didn't make sense was why? Was it just to mess with them?

He walked into the kitchen with Cassie and spotted Jackson on the other side of Maggie's house, over in the family room by the back windows. Skyler asked Cassie to stay put and walked purposefully in that direction, bypassing everyone else until he got to Jackson. He was talking to Scarlett and Tyler.

"Can we talk privately? Now?" Skyler demanded. He was already balling up his fists, preparing for a fight.

Jackson looked confused but said, "Sure."

Skyler led the way out through the dining area onto the screened porch and out to the back deck overlooking the big sand dunes and the dark ocean. He walked all the way down to the end near Maggie's bedroom so that hopefully no one would see them from the other parts of the house.

He spun around and said, "How dare you?" He couldn't hold his temper any longer. Damned being human! He hauled off and punched Jackson in the face, then shook his hand discreetly from the pain of hitting him.

"What the hell?" Jackson said. "What'd you do that for?"

He grabbed both of Skyler's hands and held them fast. There was nothing Skyler could do. He knew he was not nearly as strong as an angel, especially an angel of death.

"You had sex with a human, and you know you're not supposed to!" Skyler said.

Jackson's expression changed to a guilty one, and Skyler knew he was right.

"How'd you find out about that?"

Skyler was so flipping mad, he kneed Jackson in the nads.

Jackson used one of his legs to trip Skyler, and he fell against the railing of the balcony. "You need to calm down."

"So it's true? How dare you? Do you think you're above all the rules?" Skyler asked.

"No, but none of this is any of your business, however you found out about it. You'd best stop trying to hurt me; you're just going to hurt yourself instead."

"I found out from Cassie, obviously."

"Cassie told you? How would she know?"

Skyler looked at him dumbly. "How else would she know, you arrogant bastard?!" He stood up and was about to hit him again, but Jackson grabbed both his hands again.

"I have no idea how Cassie would know," Jackson said.

"Maybe you've got a little touch of amnesia, if you can't remember pretending to be me and having sex with her."

"Pretending to be you? Why would I do that?"

"So she would consent to having sex with you. She thought it was me."

"Why would Scarlett want to have sex with you? I'm confused."

"Scarlett? We're not talking about Scarlett here. We're talking about Cassie," Skyler said, getting a little inpatient with this conversation.

"Wait a minute. You think I had sex with Cassie?" Jackson asked.

"I know you did. Don't try to deny it. Who else would do that to me? What I want to know is why?"

"I'd like to know the same thing," a female voice said.

Skyler and Jackson both turned to see Scarlett on the other end of the balcony. How much of the conversation she heard, Skyler didn't know, but

Jackson looked like he was going to be sick. He let go of Skyler's hands and focused on Scarlett.

"I didn't, I swear it," Jackson said to her.

"I don't believe you," she said, walking away.

Jackson couldn't believe how messed up things had gotten so quickly. Scarlett obviously thought what Skyler thought – that he'd had sex with Cassie – which he did not. He saw the hurt in her eyes. Dear Lord, he had to get this under control and fast. Scarlett walked away, tearing up. He'd have to deal with her later. He needed to calm down an ex-guardian first.

"Skyler, look, I had sex with Scarlett, not Cassie. This was just a big misunderstanding. I thought you were talking about Scarlett."

"Am I supposed to believe you? Because I don't. You've always lied, you've always had your punishments and your snide remarks. You used to flirt with Cassie a lot, even in cross country. Don't think I didn't know about all of that. You made the mistake of telling me that some other angel was messing with me. I thought I was going crazy for a while there, but the other angel was you, wasn't it? You're just trying to throw me off track."

"No," Jackson said. "It wasn't me, I swear it. On Michael's honor, I swear I didn't have sex with Cassie – in any form. Some other angel is messing with you, but it's not me. I'll help you find out who it is and what they want if you'll do something for me."

"Why would I want to help you?"

"Please, just tell Scarlett you were mistaken, that it wasn't me that had sex with Cassie."

Skyler said, "You help me first, then I'll tell Scarlett. You have to prove to me that it wasn't you, which means you have to find out whoever did it and have them come talk to me."

Jackson agreed. "Give me all the details. When was this supposed to have happened?"

Skyler told him, and then Jackson said, "I'll do my best."

He went back inside to find Scarlett.

Country Christmas music was playing and people were laughing, talking, and drinking. He looked around but didn't see Scarlett anywhere.

He saw Cassie and decided to talk to her. "Cassie, I swear it wasn't me," he said quietly.

She looked at him like she was scared. He didn't think she remembered him being an angel, but he wanted her, at least, to be clear that he did nothing to her.

"Honest. I'm already in a doomed relationship with Scarlett. Please just believe me."

She kept silent.

"Have you seen her?"

"She went towards the front door," Cassie said, pointing in that direction.

"Thanks." He took off towards the front balcony.

She wasn't there. He went down the two flights of stairs and walked around the house to the beach access path, thinking that maybe she went for a walk on the beach. He tried to follow footprints since the sand was moist from a recent rain. He went to the right where the imprints led and found her down near the waves, walking away from him.

"Scarlett," he called, making sure it was her.

She turned and looked at him, then looked away and kept walking.

He looked around and, not seeing anyone else on the beach or outside at Maggie's, he zoomed up to her in an instant. She looked startled when he was right next to her.

Scarlett didn't know what to think about Jackson and the accusation she'd overheard. Here was this gorgeous angel that she'd fallen in love with, but he had more problems than any human she knew. She came to a kind of epiphany when she was in France. Seeing Jackson for what he was, in all his glory, had been exciting, thrilling. Taking her – flying her – to Eden, made it all real. She thought she finally understood his reasons for deceiving her and for taking over her half-brother's appearance. She loved him with all her might, but what was that going to get her? They had a limited future at best. She didn't think he'd have time to hang out in Eden, and did people even marry in Eden? She didn't know. She really didn't know that much about his world at all. She'd never loved another man as much as she did Jackson, but he wasn't even a man. They were doomed, star-crossed lovers.

Now, what was she supposed to think? That kid Skyler was accusing Jackson of having sex with Luke's daughter. Tyler's half-sister. How sick was that? Was it true? She didn't have a clue. But if he had sex with her, Scarlett, that means he could have sex with other humans, too, right? The thought that he might have done that to Cassie made her angry and sad at the same time. Star-crossed lovers, indeed.

She heard him call her name and she gave him a hurtful look, which he probably couldn't see in the dark, and then suddenly he was right there beside her.

"Scarlett, I swear to you, it wasn't me. Haven't I been with you almost constantly for the past few weeks? This supposedly happened two weeks ago."

"You're gone at night," she said. "I don't know what you do or where you go then, so I can't be your alibi."

"I know, but please believe me. I told you that you were my first – the very first human sexual experience. I wasn't lying. You were my first, my only, and you will be the last."

She desperately wanted to believe him, but she still had doubts.

He forced his thoughts into her head. *Can't you feel how much I love you? Why would I even look at another human? Can't you please believe me? I've admitted to you in the past every time I did something deceitful. I'm not lying this time.*

"Get out of my head," she said, and kept walking.

He pulled on her arm to stop her from walking. He turned her around to face him and tried to put his arms around her, but she wouldn't let him.

"Jackson you have to prove it to me," she said.

"Fine, I will," he said. "I'm going up to talk to the other angels and find out what the hell is going on."

She saw anger in his face, something she'd never seen before, and then he disappeared instantly.

Chapter Thirty-Four

Jen finished cooking up some buttermilk pancakes, sat them down on the dining room table, and called out to the others to come and eat. She then poured some orange juice in four glasses and added champagne to hers and Luke's. It was her first Christmas morning as a married woman, the first Christmas as a complete family, and she wanted to start the day out with a hearty homemade breakfast.

The night before had been fun, seeing Luke perform on stage, and then the party at Maggie's. Maggie had been too nauseous with morning sickness to cook much, so she bought food pre-made while Jen, Bridget, and Scarlett brought more food. It had been a nice time, exchanging gifts, singing Christmas carols while Luke played guitar, and then the two of them took a walk on the beach. The rain had stopped and the wind was light and warm. It was one of those warm Christmases in Virginia Beach.

Christmas Day was going to be spent with the family. Luke's mom and stepdad were coming from Tennessee and would arrive sometime in the afternoon, and then Jen's father, Tom, and his wife Evie would be coming the next day from Georgia.

Luke came into the dining room wearing red, black and white plaid pajama pants, a red super-soft sleep shirt, and fleece-lined brown moccasins, gifts she had bought him and let him open the night before. It had just been the two of them under the Christmas tree in the small family room. He let her open a gift, too, which was a necklace with an open-heart pendant. She had it on now with a soft lightweight red sweater and dark jeans.

"Morning, baby," he said. He kissed her lips and let them linger there until Logan came in saying, "Morning, Mom and Dad!"

Jen smiled as they lingered a moment longer and then broke off the kiss.

"Good morning, son," Luke said. They were still getting used to being dad and son when they thought they were uncle and nephew for sixteen years.

"Morning, sweetheart," Jen said.

Cassie came dragging in the room last, looking like she didn't get as much sleep as she should have.

"You feeling okay this morning?" Jen asked her.

Cassie looked up at her quickly. "Yeah, fine."

They ate the pancakes along with some hardwood-smoked bacon and the juice drinks. Then the kids wanted to open the rest of their presents under the tree. Jen had always let Logan open one present on Christmas Eve and the rest on Christmas Day. She was carrying on that tradition with her extended family now.

After opening presents, Logan receiving some video games and Cassie a running iPod, and clothes for both of them, Jen made some mulled cider and handed out Christmas mugs for each of them to drink along with some sugar cookies with colorful sprinkles on top.

After Cassie ate one cookie, she looked at her smart phone and then said, "Is it all right if I go over to Maggie's with Emily?"

"Can I come, too?" Logan asked.

Jen was a little disappointed, but she should know better than to think that a couple of teenagers would want to spend the whole day with their parents. It would give her more time to be with Luke before their parents came to town, at least.

"Sure, that's fine. Be back later this afternoon when Mimi and Papa Greg get here," Jen said.

The two agreed and headed out to Jen's Mini Cooper.

"Wait, before y'all go, I have another present for your mom," Luke said. He stood up and pulled on Jen's arm. "Come on out to the driveway and I'll show you."

Jen couldn't imagine what would be out in the driveway unless he had hidden something in his truck.

They walked out the back balcony and down the steps, and when Jen walked up the side yard and opened the gate, she saw a third vehicle in the driveway. It was a white Honda Pilot and had a huge red bow on the front window.

Jen gasped. "Luke! What have you done?"

He put his arm around her and urged her to have a closer look. "I've bought my wife a family vehicle."

The four of them inspected the whole vehicle, front to back, including third row seating option in the back.

"I thought we needed a bigger vehicle since our family is getting bigger. And the kids can drive the Mini."

Jen had tears in her eyes and threw her arms around him. "Are you sure we can afford this?"

"Absolutely. I got a huge check before leaving Nashville. I paid cash for this."

She kissed him enthusiastically. "Thank you, Luke. I love you so much."

They didn't hear the kids drive away in the Mini Cooper.

Scarlett sat on the deck overlooking the beautiful sunrise among clouds the next morning. She reflected on the terrible Christmas Eve of the night before. Though she had enjoyed being with her friends and Tyler, opening presents, eating good food, and laughing, the fight with Jackson left her feeling extremely sad and exhausted. She still didn't know whether to believe him or not. She wanted to and hoped he was telling her the truth. He had left in a great hurry, disappearing the way he did. She could picture him flying away from her with those big black wings and those strong muscles rippling over his perfect body. She couldn't help having those kinds of thoughts, even if she was still mad at him.

She wondered if he'd ever shown himself to anyone else. Like Cassie? She selfishly hoped she was the only one he had shown himself to like that. Didn't he say no one could see him unless they were about to pass on? So maybe Cassie hadn't seen him that way. That thought gave her some comfort.

She was hoping he would come over today but she wasn't sure since he'd left in an agitated, almost menacing mood. She'd seen a fierceness in him that she'd never seen before and it was a little frightening.

Just when she was thinking of him, Jackson appeared at her front door. She heard Tyler let him in, and the two of them found her on the deck. Jackson had a box of doughnuts in his hands, a big red poinsettia, and Tyler had a gift in his.

"Come inside, Maman. Jackson brought me another present!" Tyler said.

Scarlett smiled at her son. "That's nice."

She stood up and smiled faintly at Jackson, who looked at her hopefully and kissed her cheek. "Thanks for the poinsettia," she said. She took it from him and put it on the middle of the bar.

They both watched Tyler open his gift, which was a treasure chest, and inside was an ancient looking scroll of paper to write on, a black feather and ink to write with, and a journal. Inside the journal were souvenir pamphlets from places they had visited while in France.

Scarlett wondered if the feather was one of Jacksons, and she looked at him. He smiled at her and nodded.

"Wow, this is cool!" Tyler said. "Look at this, Maman!"

"That's a special gift," she agreed.

"I thought you could have a special place to keep memories and also write down new ones. There's a secret decoder in there, too, if you wanted to make secret messages.

"Cool!"

He played with his new things while Scarlett went over to the kitchen.

"You want some coffee?" she offered Jackson.

He nodded. "I wanted to get you something nice, but I knew…you wouldn't have it long." He looked troubled.

"The poinsettia will be nice to look at. I love it."

"I suppose the trip to Eden was my big present to you."

She smiled. "It was a wonderful present." She turned away to pour the coffee, thinking she needed to get herself together so she wouldn't break down and cry in front of him. The beautiful memories of that whole trip seemed a long distance away, now that they were arguing. She handed him the cup. "I wanted to get you something, but I didn't think you had any place to keep anything." She kept her voice low so Tyler wouldn't hear.

"Your understanding, your trust in me is all I want for Christmas, Scarlett."

Her heart leaped for a moment. She wanted to give it to him. She searched his thoughts but didn't feel any deceit there, no guilt. Only sincere love and an incredible desire for her to believe him. She could feel that he desperately wanted things to be the way they were in France. It was weird because she used to only hear his thoughts sometimes but now she could feel what he was feeling. She could maybe understand why he would be able to do that with her, but how was she doing it with him? She had no super powers.

"Can you feel my love for you, Scarlett? I can read your thoughts." His eyes searched hers. "I can feel your confusion. Won't you believe me? Have faith in me?"

She considered it. He still hadn't proven to her yet that he didn't do it, though. "Why would Skyler suspect that you did this to Cassie?" she asked.

"He knows what I am." He hesitated and she thought he might be thinking up a lie to tell her, but his thoughts instead were of Skyler with white wings on his back.

"Look, I'm going to tell you something but you must never speak of it to any other human." She agreed and he said in a low voice, "Skyler used to be Cassie's guardian angel."

"What?" That must've been the reason for the white wings.

"Read my thoughts, I'm telling you the truth. I had to punish him a little and at the same time, I helped him turn into a human." Scarlett then saw that Jackson was thinking about somebody named Grant but he looked like Skyler.

"Who's Grant?" she asked.

Before he could answer, the doorbell rang.

It was Cassie.

After Cassie and Logan got to Maggie's, Cassie said hello to everyone and then said she was going to walk down to see Tyler for a minute. She walked on the beach, thinking about everything. She still didn't know what to think, who she had sex with. She knew what Skyler thought. He had a sore hand the rest of the night from hitting Jackson. He came back inside after Jackson left and told her all about their exchange. Jackson seemed pretty adamant about it not being him, though, and Cassie really couldn't see a reason why Jackson would do that to her anyway. Sure, he had punished them in the past, or tried to, but she didn't think he would do this. Since she had sex with some other being, not Skyler – and not Jackson – she wondered who it could be and why. How many times had she seen him, thinking it was Skyler when it wasn't? It reminded her of when Skyler had a "twin."

Several months before, she'd begun seeing two Skyler's, and it was later explained that one of them was her guardian angel Skyler, and the other one was human Skyler, waiting for guardian Skyler to turn human and go back in time.

Could something like that be going on again? Who would his "twin" be this time? Future Skyler? Did he decide to go back to being a guardian after all? She had a headache from not sleeping well the night before, with all these thoughts running through her head. She decided that she needed to talk to Jackson on her own. She had the excuse of giving Tyler another present as to why she would be coming over.

She hoped Jackson was there so they could talk privately. She didn't know if Scarlett knew anything about him or Skyler being angels. Surely Jackson told her about himself, since he was an angel of death and was supposed to be preparing her for death – at least that's what Skyler had told her.

She rang the doorbell and Scarlett answered it.

"Cassie, what a nice surprise. Come on in."

"Hi. I brought Tyler a Christmas present," she said.

"That's sweet. So, has your father told you that the two of you are related?"

"Yes, he told us. It's cool I have another half-brother."

Scarlett let her in the door and closed it back, and Cassie looked around and saw Tyler in the family room where the Christmas Parade was playing on the TV. Then she saw Jackson in the kitchen. Suddenly she felt nervous. How was this going to play out? If she talked to Jackson about having sex with someone who looked like Skyler, then she would also have to admit that she remembered everything about the two of them being angels. She wasn't supposed to remember that – it had been part of her punishment for Skyler having a relationship with a human while he was still an angel.

What would he do to her when he found out she still remembered? She bit her lower lip nervously and decided to talk to Tyler first.

She walked over to him and handed him the present. "Merry Christmas, Tyler," she said.

His eyes lit up. "Wow, another present!" He opened it up and showed his mom a new Star Wars Lego set. "Awesome!"

"What do you say, Tyler?"

"Thanks!" he said excitedly. He quickly tore the box open and started putting the pieces together.

That should keep him occupied for a while, Cassie thought.

She took a deep breath and walked into the kitchen. "Could we talk privately for a moment?" she asked Jackson. She hesitated doing this, but she would risk further punishment because she needed to know what was going on.

"Are you here to accuse him, too?" Scarlett interrupted.

Cassie's eyes widened. "Well, yeah, maybe. I'm not sure." She was more confused than ever. It seemed Scarlett was defending Jackson.

"Why don't we go outside on the deck?" Jackson suggested.

The three of them walked out and sat down in chairs. Scarlett had her coffee cup in her hand and sat beside Jackson on a loveseat.

Scarlett asked Cassie, "Why do you think it was Jackson?"

Jackson looked at her suspiciously. "What do you remember about me? Or about Skyler for that matter?"

Cassie looked at Scarlett and then Jackson, wondering how much Scarlett knew but figured she must know. "I remember all about the two of you being angels. Your little mojo didn't work."

Scarlett looked confused and Jackson told her, "That was part of the punishment. I tried to erase her angel memories." He looked at Cassie again. "I just told Scarlett about Skyler being your guardian before. How is it possible that you still remember? It's never failed before."

Cassie knew it had, with Skyler's mother, Juliet, but she kept her mouth quiet. She didn't want to get her in trouble.

"True love," she said. "It doesn't work with true love, that's what I think."

"Very well," Jackson said. "I haven't been given any orders to punish either one of you further, so it must be kosher. I was just up there last night looking for answers after Skyler accused me. I swear to you Cassie, it wasn't me you had sex with. I just don't know how to prove it." He and Scarlett looked at each other.

"If it wasn't you, who else could it have been? I just want some answers," Cassie said.

"Why don't you start by describing the person you were with? What did he look like, besides looking like Skyler? Was there anything different about him? Anything at all?"

Cassie had been thinking about the whole sex scene since Skyler said it wasn't him, and she'd been trying to remember if there was anything different. She pictured how quickly he had gone from kissing her to the two of them being naked. "He, uh, he moved faster along than Skyler does. He undressed quickly like he was in a hurry."

Suddenly she pictured his naked body, and besides blushing, she realized something important. The person she had sex with didn't have Skyler's tattoo on his left upper arm. Skyler and his dad Brad had gotten tattoos of a nautical star that stood for being a positive guide, something that would remind both of them that they used to be guardian angels. "I just now remembered that he didn't have Skyler's tattoo on his arm," she told them. "I hadn't thought about that before now."

"Good. That's good," Jackson said, looking slightly relieved. Scarlett put her hand in his and smiled encouragingly at him. As if that proved it wasn't Jackson. Jackson wouldn't have left out a detail like that. He was too smart. "Anything else?"

"He smelled the way you smelled the first night I met you at the beach party. Like the ocean. I thought you must've been a surfer that night, before you even offered to surf."

Jackson looked at Scarlett. "Do I smell that way to you?"

"No." She looked at him curiously.

"Have there been any other strange encounters?" Jackson asked.

"There have been white feathers on my pillow when I wake up in the morning. Also, I don't know if this is related or not, but I've seen a strange creature in the backyard twice. The second time, he actually flew over my house. And then…" she said thoughtfully, "…Skyler came over right away. As a matter of fact, he smelled different that night too."

"Any other encounters?"

"I think that's all for now." She felt slightly relieved at being able to talk about this to someone else. She'd had no one else to talk to, not even Juliet since she was Skyler's mother. "Is another angel doing this to me? Don't you have any guess as to who it might be?"

Jackson's expression looked grave. "I have my suspicions. The only entities that can hide from me are angels of darkness. Angels have a choice to be good or bad. The ones who are bad can hide in their own realm and not be seen. They like to wreak havoc on earth, play tricks on people and mess up their lives, especially when it concerns people who love each other. They are jealous that they cannot have this kind of relationship. They can also work together to distract your guardian temporarily in order to do things to you. Like have sex with you."

"Angel of darkness?" Cassie asked. That sounded scary.

"I can't say for sure right now, but that's what I suspect."

Cassie had another question for him that she dreaded hearing the answer to. "Is it possible that I could become pregnant?"

"Yes," he said. "That's how Grant was conceived. Brad was still an angel when he mated with Juliet."

Scarlett looked confused and Jackson said to her, "Brad is Skyler's dad, and he used to be a guardian, also." He looked back at Cassie again and said, "The baby would be part angel, just like Grant was."

"What does that mean?" Cassie asked.

"The baby may have some powers. Grant had the ability to heal people on a small scale."

"Would the baby's lifespan be shortened like Grant's was?" Cassie asked.

"No. That was punishment for his parents. The baby may actually live a very long time."

Cassie nodded. She hoped she wasn't pregnant, but this is what she would have to deal with if she did. "There's something else," she just thought of. "I didn't have that tingling sensation when we touched the way I did with Skyler when he was an angel. Are you sure this was an angel?"

"That's because Skyler was your guardian. You never felt that with me either, did you?"

She thought about it. "No, you're right. I didn't."

Tyler came out onto the balcony holding up his Lego Speeder that he'd already completed. "Look, Cassie!" he said.

"Wow, that was fast. You're good."

"It looks great," Scarlett agreed.

Cassie got up to leave. "Thanks for everything. I better get back to Maggie's before they start worrying about me."

Scarlett stood up and hugged her. "Thank you for coming over, Cassie. This talk has helped more than you know."

She walked her to the front door and saw her out.

Chapter Thirty-Five

Scarlett came back out onto the balcony where Jackson was still sitting, looking at the ocean.

"Would you like some more coffee? Another doughnut?" she asked.

"Sure, but I'll get it. You should rest. You've been a lot more tired since coming back from France, haven't you?"

She nodded and smiled. She was glad he could feel her moods. "Yes, I have," she said as she sat down.

He stood up and went inside. While waiting on him, Scarlett got a phone call from Jen.

"Hey," Jen said. "I was wondering if you and Tyler would like to come over for supper later. Luke's parents are going to be here around six o'clock, and they'd love to meet Tyler."

"Oh, that would be nice. Sure. Can I bring anything?"

"Not a thing. I'll even come and get you guys. Luke got me a new Honda Pilot for Christmas, and I can't wait to drive it!" Jen said excitedly.

"How wonderful."

"Jackson is welcome, too."

"Okay, I'll tell him."

"I'll come by at about 5:30 to get y'all."

"Sounds good. See you later. And thank you," Scarlett said.

"No problem. Y'all are family."

"Who are you seeing later?" Jackson said after she hung up the phone. He came out to the balcony carrying a tray and sat it down on the table in front of them. On it was a beautiful white Christmas teapot with a winterberry pattern of green leaves and red berries all over it, along with matching cups and saucers.

"Jen," she said. "She's coming to get us to take us back to her house for supper with Luke's parents. You're invited too."

"Oh, okay."

"What's this?"

"Well, I, uh, thought of something I could get you, and you can give it to Jen or something…later. I know how much you like to drink coffee and tea."

"It's a beautiful set." There were two teacups, saucers, and a matching plate topped with four doughnuts. "Thank you, Jackson."

He leaned over slowly, hesitantly, like he was asking permission to kiss her. She leaned in encouragingly and they kissed. His lips were warm on her cold ones.

"Are you cold? Would you rather be inside?" he asked.

"It's not as cold as it was in Paris."

"That's true," he said. He went inside anyway and came back out with a microfiber soft red blanket with white snowflakes on it, and placed it on her lap.

She looked down at it. "Another gift?" He nodded. "Ooo, it's so soft. Where do you get this stuff? Does it just appear?"

He gleamed and said, "Something like that."

"I hope you don't steal."

"Of course not. Sometimes my clients give me presents for helping them. I have a special place where I store them." His smile faded as he sat down and poured both of them some more coffee. "Are you still mad at me?"

Her heart jumped a little, and she knew that it was time to make up. "No. I believe you."

"Thank God for that." He put his arm around her and pulled her against his chest, kissed the top of her head.

"When Cassie said the man she had been with didn't have Skyler's tattoo, I could tell she didn't believe it was you then. I didn't believe it either. You're too smart to have left out a detail like that." She turned up to look at him. "Aren't you?"

"Well," he said and laughed. "I like to think I'm smart."

She reached up to kiss him and tugged on the red scarf around his neck to pull him closer to her. He responded quickly by putting both arms around her and kissing her. He whispered, "Je t'aime, Juliandra. Joyeux Noël."

She shivered and looked at him, wondering why he'd called her by her middle name. It was different, but she liked it. It sounded sexy coming out of his mouth. She searched his eyes, the eyes that would forever look at her the same way, whatever form his body took. "Why'd you call me that?" she whispered.

"You don't seem like a Scarlett to me. Juliandra suits you better. It sounds sexier."

"Coming out of your mouth, it certainly does."

He kissed her again until Tyler came out on the balcony. "Come play Legos with me," he said to both of them.

"In a minute," Scarlett said. "Have another doughnut and let me talk to Jackson for a minute, and we'll both come in and play."

"Okay." He took one of the doughnuts off the plate and ran back in the house, slamming the door behind him.

"What do I smell like to you?" Jackson asked her.

She remembered Cassie saying he'd smelled like the ocean when she first met him. "Hmm, to me you smell like…something delicious. Bold and mildly fruity like a red wine, smoky like a fine cigar, and exotic like coconut and rum."

"Wow," he said. He touched his lips to hers again. "Thank you for my Christmas present."

She looked confused but then remembered that he'd said he wanted her to believe him and to trust in him. She smiled. "I really didn't need Cassie to believe you. I felt the truth inside of you. How is it that not only am I able to hear your thoughts, but now I'm also able to feel what you feel?"

He caressed her cheek. "I'm not sure, but I think because we love each other." She looked at him, wondering. Could it be as simple as that? "No, seriously. You're in love with an angel here. Things are different. I've never loved another human before, so this is all new to me."

"To me, too. I've never loved another as I do you." She kissed his cheek, then his chin, and then licked his lips. "Je t'adore." She kissed his lips and then asked him, "Is Jackson your real name?"

"It's actually Raphael. You can call me Raph for short."

"Raph? Like the Ninja Turtle?" She smiled and he laughed. "Where's your bandana?"

"No bandana, but I do have super speed, strength, and agility."

"Ooo, that sounds sexy." She felt his strong arm muscles. "I like your real name. If you call me Juliandra, when we're…intimate," she whispered. "I shall call you Raphael."

She saw fire in his eyes and he kissed her, his hands rubbing up and down her arms. She could read his thoughts that he wanted nothing better than to change forms and make love to her. On the beach would be nice. At night. They could both imagine it together.

But she knew her son was just inside.

Jackson stopped kissing her and rested his forehead against hers. "I have something to tell you that won't make either one of us happy." She dreaded whatever it was. She could feel that it was rather heartbreaking to him. "I cannot come and see you as often as I have."

She felt panic well up inside of her. "Why not?"

"I have been told that I am to be punished after all. We cannot make love again…as long as I am angel and you are human."

She was right; it was heartbreaking. "What does that mean? That you would have to be human – a real human – or I would have to be an angel in order for us to make love?"

His dark eyes looked at hers intently. "Yes."

She swallowed hard. She knew it would make no sense for him to become human since she wouldn't live much longer. "Could I become an angel?" she whispered.

"You could."

She'd never thought about that. How did a human become an angel?

"You would have to give up Eden and being with your mother and your brothers, though," he said.

"So, in other words, I'd have to choose between you and my family?"

He paused, tentative, and said, "Yes."

"And you're saying we could have…we could make love if I was an angel?"

"If you were an angel of death, yes."

Her eyes widened.

They were interrupted by Tyler again. "Maman, look who's here."

It was Blanche, her housemaid.

"Blanche!" She stood up and walked over to hug her, touching Jackson's shoulder on her way over.

"I wanted to come see my girl on Christmas and see how you're getting along." She looked out across the dunes to the ocean. "My, what a beautiful view you have here, Miss Scarlett. I don't blame you for wanting to live here."

"I'll go in and play with Tyler," Jackson said. "Why don't the two of you stay out here and talk?"

"Thank you. Do you remember Jackson?" she asked Blanche.

"I do. Nice to see you again, Mr. Jackson."

"Nice to see you, as well."

"Sit down over here and let me tell you about my trip to France," Scarlett said, happy to see her dear friend.

Chapter Thirty-Six

Later that night, Scarlett slipped into a hot bathtub filled with peach-scented bubble bath and let the day and her troubles seep out into the water. She was so tired. She reflected on the evening spent with Luke and his family. Jackson didn't go; he said he would come back to her house later. Jen had been so sweet picking them up and then bringing her back home when she had gotten tired. She was thankful for her new friends and for Tyler getting to spend time with his dad and his other grandparents. Jen offered to keep him for the night so they could get better acquainted and so Scarlett could really rest, and she couldn't resist the offer.

Tyler had asked her, "Please Maman, is that okay with you?"

"Yes, if you really want to. It's fine with me," she'd said.

Luke's mother Connie, a nice lady with layered blonde hair, had asked her, "What does he call you?"

"Maman. It's French for mama. It's what I called my mother and now he calls me."

"That's very sweet. How good of you to teach him French."

They had talked more about French and Scarlett told to her some of the things they did while in France.

The hot water in the bathtub nearly made her fall asleep. She was drifting off and humming a French Christmas carol when she felt someone touch her arm. Startled, her eyes flew open and she saw Jackson standing over her.

"Hey," he said.

She smiled. "Hey."

"Can I help?" He grinned widely and her heart fluttered. She felt heat in her face suddenly realizing that she was naked in front of him underneath the disappearing bubbles.

"Sure," she said.

He got down on his knees and picked up a pouf. He poured some shower gel onto it and then washed her arms, chest, her legs one by one, and then her back.

"Where's Tyler?" he asked.

"He stayed at Luke's for the night."

"You mean we have the house to ourselves?"

"We sure do." She smiled broadly. "Are you sure we can't make love?" she asked seductively, alluding to the fact that he'd said he wasn't allowed to anymore.

He sighed deeply. "I'm sure, but you certainly aren't making it easy." He let go of the pouf, caressed her face, and leaned over and kissed her.

"What happens if we have sex again?" she asked. "What can they do to you?"

"They can separate me from you. I've already been with you way longer than I have any of my other clients. It's unprecedented."

"Will you get in trouble for being here now?"

"No. I'm allowed to visit in the late evenings and early mornings."

"So you could enjoy sunrises with me?"

He nodded while she leaned back against the tub again and yawned. "Yes, that would be nice," he said.

She looked up at his sheepishly. "Would you…change forms for me? I want to see the real you again."

He raised his eyebrows. "My wings are pretty big for this small bathroom."

She was disappointed. *Please?* she asked in her thoughts.

She could feel him caving.

"All right, you win. If I fold up my wings, it should be fine."

He crouched on his knees, spread his arms out wide, and changed into his angel form, his eyes never straying from hers the whole time. His clothes fell away, revealing his chiseled muscles, and his big black wings spread out behind him, brushing against the sink and nearly touching the ceiling before folding up on his back.

"Could you leave them out?" she asked meekly, smiling nervously.

"If you really want me to," he said. She nodded and he squatted down and spread his wings out again. She watched him with wonder.

"Mind if I join you?" he asked, pointing to the bathtub.

"No, come on in," she said, her heart hammering.

He slipped into the bathtub with her, skirt, wings, and all, sitting behind her. He pulled her against his chest, wrapped his arms and wings around her. He kissed her neck and said, "I wish I had the power to heal you, to at least help you feel better like guardians can. Are you in pain?"

She nodded. It gave her joy that he knew what she was feeling. "A little, but this helps. Being with you helps me so much." She turned into him and said, "I want to see you."

He loosened his now wet wings a bit. She bent her knees up over his legs and leaned one side against his chest. She looked at the long black feathers of one of his wings and touched them. They were soft like down feathers. She ran her hand all the way down the length of it and he started giggling.

"That tickles."

"Really?" He nodded and she laughed. "That's good to know."

She looked at his face – different and yet similar, the eyes always the same. She touched his smooth, non-wrinkled skin, and he closed his eyes, leaned down, and kissed her. She felt his love envelope her soul, and her heart leapt. She loved this…angel…so much.

She opened her eyes and looked at him again. "Would I have wings like this, too?"

He nodded, rubbed her short wet hair.

"Same color?" she asked.

"Yes."

"If I…"

"Yes," he said, reading her thoughts already. He knew what she wanted to ask, but she wanted to voice these questions out loud to help clarify her thoughts.

"If I become like you, what does that mean, besides I can't be with my family?"

"You can still visit your family on occasion; you just can't live with them in Eden."

"Okay." That made her feel better, that she would at least get to see her family on occasion. "Where would we live? Where do you go, if it's not Eden?"

"Heaven."

She raised her eyebrows. "Pearly gates and all?"

He nodded. "A section of heaven, I should say. And that's all I can say for now."

"Okay. What would I be doing? Helping people cross over? Same as you?"

"Yes."

"I notice you also deal with other angels, like Skyler. You were rather harsh with him and I saw a dark side to you I've never seen before."

"I apologize that you had to see me that way, but I was mad at being accused of something I didn't do."

"I understand that. It's very disturbing when you can't make someone believe you."

"You know you never have to fear me, right?"

She nodded and smiled. "I do know that."

"I would never hurt you. Ever."

She nodded and kissed his cheek reassuringly. "Do you ever have any free time to yourself?"

"Of course. How do you think I can spend so much time with you?"

"Have you ever…killed anyone?"

"I have been known to…help people pass over. Some people just give up the will to live and ask me to help them along. So in that respect, yes, I have helped people die before. But do I out and out kill people just because it's their time? No, I don't."

"If I chose not to be an angel, would I stay in Eden?" He nodded. "Would I ever get to see you?"

"I could visit from time to time, but we couldn't…mate together."

Oh. That made her extremely sad. Of all the things she would have to give up when she passed on, the one thing she didn't want to give up, the one thing she'd never had before now, was love. And sex. Even separately, those two things were pretty powerful, but together, they were the most wonderful thing she'd ever experienced, aside from having her baby. If she had to give Tyler up, she didn't think she could give up the other…love and sex…with *Raphael.*

"I…" she started to say.

"Don't make your decision right now," he said. "Just get some rest. Are you cold?"

She felt his wings wrap around her again, and she instantly felt warmer.

"I want you, Raph," she said in a raspy voice, her heart hammering inside, her breathing quick.

She could feel that he wanted her, too.

She couldn't feel any pain at the moment, only desire.

"Juliandra…I want to love you so badly…"

She felt tears in her eyes. The thought of losing him altogether kept her from begging him. She'd rather never have sex again than to lose him forever.

"What am I going to do without you?" she asked, and he knew she meant without making love with him and without being with him nearly every minute of the day as they had been for many months now.

He caressed her cheek. "Spend time with your boy, and I'll visit as often as I can."

"Every midnight and sunrise?" she asked.

"Absolument." He caressed her face and then slid his hand down her neck, down to her breast and sent shivers all over her body. Her breathing became heavy. "You know," he said, "just because we can't have sex doesn't mean we can't do other things." His eyes looked deep into hers.

She felt her woman parts tingle. "Truly?" He nodded and she asked, "Are you going to be naughty or nice." She grinned.

"How about both?"

"Ooo la la," she said breathlessly.

He kissed her lips and then let his tongue trace down her neck, down to her breasts, and he teased and sucked each one. She gasped and grabbed his wings. "Oh, Raph," she said, arching up to him. He then went down under the water and pleasured her until she thought she'd died and gone to heaven.

Chapter Thirty-Seven

"I think I might be pregnant," Cassie told Skyler.

It was New Year's Eve, and Cassie was in Skyler's bedroom. His parents were having a party with a lot of their friends and neighbors, and the two of them had snuck away to his room to talk.

"What?" Skyler's eyes widened.

Cassie nodded. She hadn't had a period in December, and she was still having nausea every day and had begun throwing up every morning. She felt miserable like she did when she was trying to get off drugs and alcohol last summer.

"I've been throwing up. Every day," she told him. She had done a pregnancy test the night before and it tested positive. She'd had a hard time hiding the pregnancy kit, giving Logan the excuse of stopping at the Red Barn convenience store to get a soda on the way home from school. She didn't open the bag until she got home but even then, she didn't work up the courage to do the test until she was in the bathroom getting ready for bed.

She could tell Skyler was both angry and hurt. "Oh God, I'm sorry, Cassie. I feel like this is all my fault."

"Why would it be your fault? You didn't do it. I did."

"I should've…I don't know, done something to prevent it. This other entity took on my identity, so I feel responsible."

"You're not."

He looked down at the carpeted floor. "I hate that you are pregnant by some other being."

She could tell lately that he was jealous of the fact that she'd had sex with someone else. He'd been having a hard time dealing with it. She tried to stress to him that she thought it was him, but that didn't make him feel any better. He still felt responsible for her since he had been her guardian angel in the past.

She just felt used and grossed out that it hadn't been Skyler, and the thought of being pregnant made her change her mind real quick about actually wanting to have sex with Skyler at the moment. "I know," she said. "Me, too. To tell you the truth, I'm scared," she said, whispering the last two words.

He took her in his arms.

"What's going to happen to my body?" she murmured against his chest. "How am I going to tell my parents? My dad will kill me, and you'll get in trouble for something you didn't do because I am *not* telling anyone that it wasn't you. No one would believe it was an angel."

She cried in his arms while he hugged her tight and kissed her head. "It's all right. You don't have to tell anyone right now. Wait until it shows. Then, I'll take the blame."

She let go of him and looked him in the eyes. "I can't ask you to do that, Skyler."

"You're not asking. I'm telling you. I can at least tell my dad about this. Maybe he'll help us figure out who did this to you and what we can do about it, and what to expect for the pregnancy."

"Could I talk to your mother about it? She was pregnant with Grant – who was half-human and half-angel. Maybe she could at least help me figure out what to expect with this type of pregnancy."

"But she doesn't know that I replaced Grant's body. She still thinks I'm half-angel, that I'm Grant."

Cassie hesitated about telling him the truth since she and Juliet had agreed to keep a secret, but circumstances had changed. She decided to tell him. "She knows. She knew the day of that car accident, that you weren't Grant."

"She what?"

"She told me the night of dad and Jen's wedding. Don't tell your dad. She wanted to keep it secret from him because she wanted him to feel like he was protecting her. Let her decide if she ever wants to tell him…or you."

He sighed. "I had no idea. She's even called me Grant on occasion. Now I have to wonder if it was an accident or if she was trying to throw me off."

"Maybe both, at different times." Cassie sat down on his bed. "So can I talk to your mom or just wait?"

"Wait for now and I will talk to my dad."

"Okay. How soon are these symptoms supposed to happen?" she asked.

"How should I know?"

"Don't you remember when your mom was pregnant with Danielle?"

"Not really. I'm sorry. Nine months, right? That's all I know."

She knew that much herself, but it seemed like her symptoms were coming on way too fast. She shouldn't even be a month along yet. Would she be throwing up so soon? She really felt like she needed to talk to someone about it. She was afraid to talk to either Jen or Juliet – afraid of their scorn and criticism, and Skyler getting the blame when it wasn't him.

Knowing Skyler, he would not have gone all the way with sex and she wouldn't be in this situation right now. She felt tears in her eyes again.

"I'm so sorry, Skyler," she said. She'd been apologizing to him nearly every day since she found out it wasn't him. She went into his arms again, and he patted her back.

"I know, Cassie. Stop beating yourself up about it. You honestly thought it was me. I understand. I'm sorry if I seem like I'm jealous or not supportive. I'll do anything you need me to do."

She nodded, feeling better, and wiped her eyes. She pulled away and looked at him again. "What if this guy comes around again? How will I know if it's you or him?"

"Look for my tattoo. Pay attention to his smell compared with mine. I'll make sure I don't change soaps or shampoos."

She sniffed. "Okay."

"We could also make a pact."

"What kind of pact?"

"I won't come over to your house anymore. You come here instead. That way, you'll know it's me and not him."

"That's a good idea."

"He would never come here and pose as me in front of my parents, I don't think."

"I don't think so either. Just be careful. Don't underestimate an angel, especially if this is a dark angel."

"I won't."

She wondered if Jackson was being honest with them when he'd claimed he was innocent and that it was a dark angel. "Do you think Jackson is telling truth?" she asked.

"I don't know. He can be devious, but he seemed like he was telling the truth. What do you think? Did he act in any way like the one you had sex with?"

She shook her head slowly. "No, not really. I don't know. He did really seem sincere about it."

"Then we have to trust him. He's the only angel we can talk to about any of this. If it bites us in the butts, then I'll get my dad to contact his guardian. He appears to him and helps him on occasion. I still feel funny about having my own guardian, but I could try talking to him maybe."

Cassie stood up and went to look out the window at the stars up above and partial moon. She had often looked to the stars for guidance, especially when she was a little girl. It had been Skyler, her guardian, who helped her.

She didn't hear Skyler come up behind her but felt his arms go around her waist and his lips to her head. She felt his warm breath through her hair. "I can't help you like I used to," he said, seeming to read her mind, "but I can marry you."

She turned around swiftly. "What?"

"I will marry you. You know I love you, and it has always been my plan to marry you someday. It will just be sooner than later now."

She got teary-eyed again. "But we're so young, Skyler. Where would we live?"

"We could live right here with my parents at first. They have the bigger house."

She wondered about being married. It was a scary thought moving forward so quickly. They were still in high school. She loved him but didn't feel ready for marriage. On the other hand, she wouldn't want to have a child without being married. A thought suddenly occurred to her.

"Since this is not your baby, maybe I should have an abortion. Then I won't have to tell anybody about it.

"I don't know," Skyler said, frowning. "I'm not sure you can kill an angel, or even half-angel."

"Could we ask your dad or Jackson?"

"You don't want to marry me?" he asked, looking disappointed.

"I didn't say that."

"It sounds like you would rather abort this baby than marry me."

"It's not yours, Skyler."

"I know that, but it's still a baby. Could you really kill a baby?"

She thought about it and realized he was right. She sighed and looked away. "No, I couldn't."

"Even if that baby was made by some other entity, it's still part of you. Your characteristics, your traits, maybe your color of hair or eyes."

She nodded, "You're right. I hadn't thought about that."

He continued, "And I will love it for that reason. Because it's a part of you and because I love you."

She nodded as he wiped away one of her tears.

"There's a purpose here, I just don't know what it is. That's the only reason your guardian would have let it happen in the first place."

"What purpose could it be? To teach me a lesson? No sex before marriage?"

"Maybe, I don't know."

"Jackson said the dark angels can work together and distract the guardian temporarily when they want to mess with humans, like having sex."

"When did he say that?"

"On Christmas Day. Remember me telling you I went over to give Tyler a present and talked to Jackson and Scarlett?"

"Right, okay." He brushed her hair back off her face and kissed her lips. "We don't have to decide anything right now. Just know that I will do anything for you, Cassie. Anything in my power." She smiled and nodded. "Don't do anything hasty, let me talk to my dad, and we'll figure out what to do. Okay?"

She nodded and he wrapped his arms around her again, making her feel better.

A knock on the door interrupted them. Danielle opened the door and asked, "Skyler, will you come down and play some songs on the piano?"

"Sure, we'll be right down."

Danielle closed the door back.

"Are you okay now?" he asked.

She nodded.

"Ready to go back downstairs?"

She took a deep breath and sighed. "Yes, I'm ready."

She wasn't sure what their future would hold, what this New Year would bring, but she felt reassured that she and Skyler would face it together.

Chapter Thirty-Eight

Scarlett felt like she was getting weaker by the day. She didn't even feel like going to a New Year's Eve party. Instead, she and Jackson stayed home, drank champagne, and watched the ball drop on TV with Ryan Seacrest. Jackson came by every night at midnight and every morning at dawn, which was around seven o'clock, to share breakfast and watch the sunrise over the ocean. On New Year's Eve night, he had to go away for a suicide victim, but then he came back and held her in his arms the rest of the night until sunrise.

About a week after New Year's, it was a rainy day, and she hadn't gone out all day, when Tyler came home with Jackson behind him. Harry barked and ran over to Tyler and begged to be petted. He growled at Jackson.

"Come on in, Jackson," Tyler said. He ran over to Scarlett with a painting he had made at school, which he explained was a picture of him, Jackson, and her. The stick figure that was supposed to be her had wings on it. It took her breath for a moment.

"Why did you put wings on my back?" she asked. She glanced at Jackson, who didn't have any expression on his face whatsoever. He was trying to pet Harry, letting him smell his hand.

"That's you after you go away," Tyler said. "You'll be an angel. My teacher told me so at school."

She let go of her breath then. "Oh really? That was a sweet thing to say."

"You can have that," Tyler said about the picture. He ran to the bathroom and said, "I'm going over to Brian's house for a minute," he yelled while using the facilities with the door open, "and then I'll come right back home and we can watch SpongeBob, okay?" He flushed the toilet and came back into the family room where Scarlett was sitting.

"That's fine." She smiled and he ran out the door. Brian was a new friend he had met who lived a couple of houses down.

"I'm surprised to see you here this time of day," Scarlett said to Jackson.

"Why's that?" he asked, looking confused.

"You usually only come at night and early morning."

He looked thoughtful and distracted, and Scarlett had to wonder what was going on with him. "Are you okay?" she asked.

"Of course." He leaned over and kissed her on the lips. He tasted different, smelled different. She wondered where he'd been. "I'm fine," he said. "Listen, I hate to tell you this, but I'm not going to be able to make my visits anymore."

"What? Why not?" She wondered if he was being punished further.

"I'm being sent away."

"You mean you're being punished?"

He sat on the couch next to her. "Yes, that's it. Your time is drawing near, and you don't need me anymore. They say it's best to get this thing over with and that it's time for me to let you go."

She was confused. She didn't think he would ever talk about letting her go. Hadn't he asked her to spend eternity with him? She felt tears in her eyes.

"Let me go? But what about…?"

"It's for the best. We've only been prolonging the inevitable."

"Is it really time? Right now? I haven't even figured out who is going to take care of Tyler yet. You told me to wait until Luke made his decision, that I had more time."

"Shhh." He stood up and offered her his hand. "Come, let's dance. Let's forget everything else and dance for a moment. One last time."

Jackson would never come suddenly and demand that it was her time. For nearly a year now, he'd been preparing her slowly. He wasn't acting himself. *Jackson, what's wrong?* she asked in her head. There was no response.

This couldn't be Jackson. She suddenly remembered all the talk about an angel of darkness and wondered if this could be him.

She took his hand carefully and he pulled her to her feet. She suddenly felt very woozy. More tired than she'd ever felt. She felt the room spin, and the tango music she had playing in the background seemed to grow distant, sounding like it was down in the basement rather than in the same room she was standing in.

"You're not Jackson, are you?" she asked wearily. Her voice seemed distant. What was wrong with her? Harry started growling at him again. No wonder he'd growled at him when he first came in the house. He'd never growled at Jackson.

He laughed lightly and said, "Of course I am."

"No. You're not. He would never take me suddenly like this. Who are you really?"

"It's me, Jackson. I swear it."

"Prove it to me. Show me your real form."

"You know I can't do that right now," he said. She heard an echo on the end of his voice.

"I know you're not Jackson. We can communicate telepathically."

"Ah, is that so? Good to know."

She hoped it wasn't a mistake to mention that. She stumbled as he clumsily led her around the room. "What have you done to me?" she asked. She felt more drunk that she could ever recall being.

"I'm dancing with you. You seem very tired, my dear. Would you like to go to bed?"

The bedroom. No, no, no. She remembered Cassie saying she'd been seduced by this dark angel, thinking he was Skyler. The same thing must be happening to her, too.

"Come to bed with me," he whispered seductively in her ear. It sounded raspy and distant. He led them towards the bedroom.

"No," she managed to get out. It sounded more like a croak.

She started falling, energy spent, and he leaned over and picked her up in his arms and carried her towards her bedroom. She suddenly felt cold all over, cold to the bone.

"I'm being punished and I'm being reassigned, so let us have one more time together," he said.

"No," she moaned, barely cognizant of what was going on. She barely heard Harry barking at the doorway.

She was frightened. She knew this was not Jackson. He smelled of the salty air outside, not like Jackson normally smelled to her. He wouldn't show himself to her, and he was trying to seduce her. She wondered what to do. She thought she would try contacting the real Jackson in her head.

Jackson, can you hear me? I need you. Now!

Within seconds, the dark angel disappeared before her eyes and another Jackson appeared on the other side of her bed. She looked at him worriedly, wondering if it was really him or if the dark angel had simply disappeared only to reappear and try to fool her again.

"What's wrong, Scarlett?" he asked anxiously, looking concerned.

Can you change into your angel form so I'll know it's really you? she asked him in her head.

Is Tyler home?

She knew it was Jackson then. He answered her telepathically. *No.*

He looked all around and she saw his clothes fall off and the black wings appear on his back, reaching up towards the ceiling, nudging her glass chandelier.

She sighed in relief. "Oh, Dieu merci."

She reached for him, and he lay beside her on the bed and took her in his arms. "What's wrong, ma chérie?"

She shivered and he wrapped his wings around her, too, warming her to her core. She felt her energy coming back. "That dark angel was just here, posing as you," she whispered. She held on tight to his back and wings.

"What?" He pulled away to look at her. "Here? What did he look like?"

"You."

"What did he say?"

Harry whined to be picked up, and Jackson leaned over and put him on the bed between the two of them. He seemed to know Jackson even in his angel form.

"Good boy," Scarlett murmured to the dog. "He said he wasn't coming to see me anymore, that my time was short and he was being punished and being assigned to someone else. And then he wanted me to dance and as soon as I touched him, I started feeling sick and so very tired, like I was drunk or had been poisoned or something."

Jackson looked at her worriedly. "You knew it wasn't me?"

She nodded.

"How did you know?"

"His smell. His words. His eyes. And he couldn't read my thoughts."

He took her back in his arms and wings again. "I cannot see the dark ones ahead of time. I'm sorry I couldn't protect you from him. It worries me that he came to you."

"Why would he come to me? He wanted to have sex with me."

She felt his muscles tense up. "He what?" he growled furiously.

"That's when I called for you in my head."

He looked at her worriedly. "You're all right? He didn't…touch you?"

"No, only danced, a kiss on the cheek, and he picked me up and brought me here to the bed."

She then remembered that he had come in the door with Tyler. She put her hand across her heart. "Mon Dieu, Jackson. He came into the house with Tyler. Please don't let him hurt my boy."

"I'll try, Scarlett. I'll talk to his guardian."

"I'm so glad you heard me when I called for you. You're my hero."

He smiled at her, such a beautiful smile, the new Jackson, the real Jackson, she was just coming to know and still getting used to.

"Of course, I did. You and I are bonded together. I believe you are my SpiritMate, the one I have been waiting for."

"What's a SpiritMate?" she asked.

Jackson wasn't sure if it was appropriate to talk about this right now, after she'd had a scare with this dark angel, but maybe it would help calm her down. He could feel her heart rate accelerated at a high rate and the blood rushing through her body quickly. "A SpiritMate is another soul – be it a human or angel – who is harmoniously joined in spirit with the one who he would spend eternity with."

He'd been looking for his for a very long time, a SpiritMate to share forever with, to love, to cherish, to make love to. It was only with a SpiritMate that angels of death were allowed to have sex. He finally figured out that this was the reason he'd not been punished for a while. He was told that they would be allowed to mate upon her death from her human body, but that they should not do so any further while she was still human, to make sure she had a fair choice of where she wanted to spend eternity. With him or with her family.

He'd been hoping she was his SpiritMate, hoping she would choose him, and the more he was with her, the closer they got to one another, physically and spiritually, he knew she was meant to be with him. Forever was a long time, and he'd never met another soul that he wanted to be with that long…until her.

"Is that like what we call soulmates?"

"Yes, but on a deeper more spiritual level. It only happens with angels of death. I think it's a consolation because of all the death and troubled souls we have to deal with. We are the only angels allowed to have a SpiritMate, the only angels allowed to mate…to have sex."

She looked deep into his eyes, and he could feel her heart beat faster. He could hear her thoughts about being joined with him forever and what a wonderful life that would be. "You think we're SpiritMates?" she asked.

He nodded. "I do, ma belle, mon coeur."

"Mon ange…my angel," she said, tracing his face with her fingertip.

His face leaned down closer to hers and he touched and tasted her lips with his, such a sweet kiss. Their souls intertwined and his heart leapt with unspeakable joy.

"Je t'aime, Juliandra."

"Je t'adore, Raphael."

They heard the front door open quickly.

"Maman." It was Tyler.

Jackson changed back to his human form quickly, got off the bed, and walked towards the door, quick as a lightning. He heard Scarlett thinking that he was as quick as a superhero in one of those shows she watched with Tyler.

"Hey, Tyler," Jackson said, walking out of the room.

"You want to watch SpongeBob with me? Where's Maman?"

"I'll be right out, Tyler," she called.

"She's been resting," Jackson said as Tyler ran into her bedroom.

"Look at my new guy – the Flash. Just like on TV."

That was it. The Flash. That's what Scarlett thought Jackson was like.

"Did you want to see my painting again?" Tyler asked him, running back into the family room. He picked it up off the coffee table and handed it to him.

Jackson smiled at Tyler. "This is very good. I like the way you painted your mother. She is an angel, isn't she?"

"She's a pretty good mom," he agreed, looking slightly embarrassed.

Mon ange, he said to her silently.

She smiled and he suddenly had a very good idea about what decision she was going to make about her afterlife.

He just had to figure out what dark angel was trying to seduce Scarlett and Cassie. If it really was a dark angel.

It could be an incubus.

Chapter Thirty-Nine

Luke had been busy for the past two weeks in Nashville recording more songs. They had recorded Luke's other ballad, "Stay," and had been working on an upbeat song for the past week. By the end of that week on Saturday, he could hardly think straight, he was so tired.

James invited the band to come to his treehouse in the outskirts of Nashville. It was attached to the main house by a bridge and stairs. The house was in the middle of tall trees and was big enough to have a second level with a bedroom for overnight stays. James wasn't married, but he wanted a retreat to come to so he could relax and also bring fellow musicians to visit. It even had a corner dedicated to recording music, including an acoustic alcove with walls made of cork.

"Man, this sure is nice," Luke said when he'd had a tour of both the house and then the treehouse. He and James lingered in the treehouse while Steve and Derek droves James's car to pick up some pizzas.

"Just think, you could have something like this for your wife and kids to come to," James said.

"That would be sweet."

"You should see it in the summertime when all the leaves are on the trees."

"I bet it's nice. I'm guessing it's brilliant in the fall, too, right?"

"Oh, it's gorgeous."

Jen would love that. Luke noted how barren the trees looked outside a big picture window, trying to imagine how they would look with leaves. A flock of black birds flew in groups, landing from this set of trees to the next, seemingly all at the same time. He wished he could get himself and his family all on the same page like all those birds were. He wished they were here with him now.

"Are you doing okay, Luke? You seem a bit distracted and…lost sometimes. Is this all too much for you?"

Luke turned and looked at him. "Nah, I just miss my wife and kids."

"Have you thought anymore about moving out here?"

"Of course I've thought about it. I'm just not sure Jen or the kids are willing," Luke said, looking out the window again. The boy in him would love to have something like this, a playhouse of sorts, in the trees. Wouldn't Jen and the kids love it, too? Especially Tyler.

Tyler. What was he going to do about him? He still hadn't decided. He was of his own flesh and blood, though, so he hated to dismiss him to his grandfather all the way over in France. He'd never get to see him if he did that, except maybe once a year if he was lucky. He couldn't abandon the little guy. Jen had said she would do whatever he wanted, which meant that she would have to take care of Tyler while he was traveling, touring, making records. It would all be Jen, and the child wasn't even hers.

She would be helping him raise yet another child that didn't belong to her, as she did with Cassie. Was it fair to ask that of her? Even if she was his wife now, it didn't seem to be.

His own parents would also miss out on seeing their grandchild, although with them living in Tennessee, he might be able to see them more if they lived here in Nashville.

"If you all don't move here," James said, stirring Luke from his thoughts, "it's going take a lot of your money to fly back and forth between here and Virginia Beach. You've got to make a decision. We're spending a lot of time and money getting a record made here. This is a once-in-a-lifetime opportunity, and you shouldn't blow it off."

Luke sighed and ran his fingers through his hair. "I know."

"You could move your family here and build an escape like this for down time, a place to be with your family. Or you could go back and see if there are any recording studios in Virginia Beach and stay there until tour time, but I'm telling you, it'll be much harder to make it from there. There's a vibe here in Nashville that you don't get anywhere else. The fans would love to see you and the band – and even your families – walking up and down the streets, maybe playing at some of the local venues now and then as a surprise. They eat that up and then go buy your records and tell their friends. That's what you want."

"Of course, I understand."

"You're under contract until the end of May, at least, to stick with it."

"Right." They had signed a six-month contract to begin with, so they could all see if it's something they really wanted to do and where they would live while doing it.

James got a beer out of the little refrigerator and offered one to Luke, which he accepted. Just one, he told himself. James handed him the cold bottle and said, "You can stay as involved as you want to or hide away until your tour starts, but the fans like getting to know you which means you have to get out there and connect with them."

"Man, I just got married. Jen and I just recently realized we were crazy about each other after first hooking up in high school. I lost her for many years in between. Did a lot of bad things too." He took a drink of the cold beer. "She grounds me. The fame, the fans, the drinking," he held up his bottle, "it could all get the best of me if I'm not careful. I can tell you right now that being on the road and lack of sleep will weaken me. I need her more than ever. But what can she do, go on tour with me? She might find that fascinating in the beginning but for how long? How long before she resents me, gets tired of traveling, gets tired of the fans?"

"It does take strong willpower to resist all the things that come with fame," James said. He sat down on a brown leather chair and Luke sat down nearby on a matching couch.

"Then there are the kids," Luke said. "I just found out about Tyler being mine and Scarlett dying of cancer. She told me at Christmas that if I couldn't take him, her father in France has offered to take him. I guess he's your uncle?" James nodded. "Am I supposed to just let his grandpa take him far away where I'll never see him? He needs his father. I've missed seven years of his life already. I don't know, man. I'm not sure this is the life I want. I thought I did, but I don't know anymore. The timing stinks."

"Maybe you should ask your family what they want to do, including Tyler. They might surprise you."

"That's true. I should ask the kids. I've talked to Jen about it, of course. She said she'll do whatever I want, but I hate to take her away from her shop that she's worked so hard to get. Then there's her mother's house that we're living in. I'm sure she doesn't want to give that up."

"You could rent the house out, and she could open a shop here in Nashville or one of the smaller towns just outside of it. You'll still have a place in Virginia Beach if you wanted to go back to visit from time to time."

"Where, if we're renting her house out?"

"In Pungo. Scarlett's house."

"I'm not following you," Luke said.

"You do know that if you take Tyler, you'll get Scarlett's house, too, don't you?"

"What? No, I had no idea."

"Maybe I wasn't supposed to say anything about it, but yeah. She offered it to me, but I have no desire to own a house in Virginia Beach – no offense. I have no family there besides Scarlett and Tyler, and no connections. My father wasn't interested either – he and my mom live up in Quebec. I don't believe her father is interested in it, either. He has plenty of money and no need of another property to have to sell or rent. I understand he's not even allowed to fly across the ocean."

"I don't know why she'd give the house to me. Why doesn't she just sell it now?"

"She wants an inheritance for Tyler. You should talk to her more about it, but I'm pretty sure she would want you to have the house if you choose to take Tyler, and save it for him until he's grown."

This was all news to Luke. More to think about and worry about. How could he manage a rental property, plus another property to maintain and save for Tyler's inheritance, and then be living all the way over here in Nashville? It would take money to hire some property management company to handle it all for them, unless he wanted to make more trips back and forth a lot. Which would be more money again.

"There are good schools here for your kids," James said. "I could help out with Tyler, too, if you needed me to. Of course, I do spend half the year in Quebec with my family. I have another house up there and another studio."

"Good to know all of that."

They heard a car arrive outside, which was Steve and Derek back with the food.

James pointed towards them. "You might want to ask the rest of the band what they want to do, too. You should all be in one accord, one way or another."

"You're right. I'll ask them."

Steve and Derek came in with the pizzas and they all gathered in a small dining area to eat, shoot the breeze, and talk about the last song they'd been trying to record.

"I think that last cord should slowly progress down to a C before it ends," Derek said.

"That's a good idea," Luke said.

"Are you still going into falsetto the last time through the chorus?" Steve asked him.

"Why, does it sound bad?" He looked at James. "Did it sound bad, James? Be honest."

James smiled. "No, I think it was great. You were in perfect pitch."

"There, see," Luke said.

The others started laughing.

James finished off his bottle of beer and got up from the table. "I'm going up to the house for a minute." He looked at Luke pointedly. "Let you boys do some talking."

After he left, Steve asked, "What did he mean by that?"

"You got something on your mind?" Derek asked.

Luke sighed. "It's just the families. Moving here. Do we really want to do this? Are we ready to change our whole lives for this?"

"I've already talked to Bridget," Derek said. "She's all in. She said she would take care of selling the house if I wanted her to. The kids are a little reluctant to move away from their friends and school, but they'll adjust, make new ones, right?"

"I hate to take my kids away from their friends, too," Luke agreed. "Especially Cassie. She and Skyler are like joined at the hip. I'm afraid she'll hate me if I make her move away."

Steve was quiet.

"What about you, Steve?" Luke asked.

Steve sighed. "Well, I didn't want to say anything, because I'm so excited to be a part of this, making our dreams come true, but Maggie and I just got married and she's pregnant with a baby now – her first – and I'd really like to be around for it all, you know? They grow up so fast." Steve and Maggie had taken a plane to Las Vegas and gotten remarried on January 1, stayed in the Paris Hotel for two nights, and then she flew back to

Virginia while he flew to Tennessee. "We didn't even get a real honeymoon," Steve said.

"I've got Tyler to think about, too," Luke said. "He's only seven, so I'm almost starting all over with him. He's got a lot of years of growing to do."

"So what are you guys saying?" Derek asked. "You want to give all this up and go back home?" He sounded a little miffed.

"I don't know what to do, that's why I'm asking y'all," Luke said.

The other two didn't seem to know what they wanted either, or at least Steve didn't.

"I say we do our six months and then see how we feel about it," Derek suggested.

"Sounds good to me," Luke said.

Steve agreed.

"Good, then it's settled. Give me another slice of pepperoni," Luke said.

Chapter Forty

That same weekend in the middle of January, Cassie was in her bedroom listening to the HOT radio station, studying for a history test. It was getting dark, and Jen was still downstairs in the shop and Logan was over at Emily's house. He saw her best friend now more than she did since they started dating. It seemed a little weird sometimes, but she was happy for both of them, and besides, she was a little preoccupied with Skyler and her pregnancy.

Her belly had gotten a lot bigger in the past week. It was getting ridiculous. She was only a month along and shouldn't be showing this soon, should she? She wanted to go talk to Jackson about it again.

She texted Skyler. *Can you come over and get me? I wanna go talk to Jackson.*

We agreed that I wouldn't come over there, remember?

Jen is still working in the shop, and I don't know if she'll have time to take me any time soon. Logan is at Emily's. I wish I had a car.

Ok, I'll come over. C u soon.

While waiting on him, she looked at herself in the mirror. She turned sideways and pulled her shirt against her belly, seeing a small baby bump. She would have to start wearing bigger clothes to try and hide it.

She didn't hear Skyler come in but saw him in her mirror behind her.

She turned around swiftly and then glanced at the door, which was closed.

"Hey," he said.

"Hey. That was fast."

His eyes opened wide and he looked down at her belly. "You're really pregnant."

She frowned at him. "You know that I am."

"You're showing."

"Yeah, tell me about it. That's why I want to go talk to Jackson about all of this."

"Why do you want to talk to Jackson?" He said Jackson's name like it was poison.

"Because he knows more about it than we do," she said.

He walked over close to her, reached down and put his hand over the baby bump. "My child," he whispered. He looked into her eyes and said, "We had a good time, didn't we?"

She was shocked at his words and that's when it hit her.

This wasn't Skyler.

This was the dark angel.

Her heart beat faster, from fear this time. She forced a smile, trying to play it off and act normal, though she suddenly felt really nervous. He leaned over to kiss her, but she turned her head at the last minute and his lips landed on her cheek instead. He put his arm around her and she shivered. "Come on, Cassie. Kiss me," he whispered.

She looked up at him. He still looked like the one she loved, and she suddenly remembered how it felt being with him, his hands all over her body. She couldn't keep up the farce any more. Otherwise, she would have to kiss him. He would think it strange if she didn't kiss her boyfriend. So she would have to call his bluff.

She cleared her throat, pried his arms off her and said, "I know you're not Skyler."

He frowned and said, "I am the real Skyler. I'm the one you fell in love with."

"No, you're not. You smell different."

"That's because I'm an angel, remember? Your guardian."

"Oh no. Don't even try that."

"I swear, Cassie, it's me. I've seen you with the other version of me. That's Grant. He never died. He's trying to fool you by pretending to be me."

"No," she said. "That's the real Skyler. He became human and he and his dad got tattoos. She pulled up his shirt sleeve, his eyes focused on hers. "Where's your tattoo?"

"I don't have a tattoo because I'm still your guardian. I never stopped being your guardian." He pulled her into his arms and said, "I love you, Cassie."

She was confused for half a minute. This guy was good. He could almost fool her, but then she thought about how sad the real Skyler was when he'd found out she had sex with someone else. She could also see the happiness on his face, the love, when she told him at her dad's wedding that she remembered everything about him being an angel. She also remembered that when she and Skyler had touched when he was an angel, she felt tingling on her skin. She didn't feel that now. She knew Skyler had changed and that this dark angel, whoever he was, was lying.

She suddenly had a thought – maybe this was Grant. He just mentioned him, didn't he? She had forgotten all about Grant. Could he have become a dark angel after he passed over, when Skyler the angel took his body?

"Stop it," she said, pushing him away.

That made him mad. "How would you like it if I told your dad and stepmom about this baby? *My* baby?"

"Are you threatening me?" She backed away from him. This was one of those times when she missed being able to talk to Skyler in her thoughts. She could talk to her new guardian. *Guardian, whoever you are, I need some help. Get this…being…away from me. Please.*

"It's just a warning," he said stiffly.

Cassie heard a car horn out front and the angel looked out towards the windows. She seized the moment to run towards the door and opened it. She turned back around, half expecting the dark angel to stop her, to be right behind her, but he was gone. He had disappeared. She ran down the hall and over to the family room and looked out the windows. Brad and Skyler were sitting in the black car. Skyler's window was rolled down, and he waved to her.

She ran back to her room for her purse and then went downstairs to tell Jen where she was going.

When she got outside, Skyler got out and opened the door for her. "I'm getting a new car for my birthday," he told her.

"You are?" she said. She was still shaken up about her encounter with the dark one and glanced in the front seat at Brad.

"How are you, Cassie?" he asked.

"Fine," she lied, faking her best smile.

Brad waved at the house and Cassie saw that Jen had come out to the front porch with a broom and waved back. "Okay, off to Miss Scarlett's," Brad said.

Cassie looked at Skyler. She pulled her phone out of her jeans pocket and started texting Skyler since they couldn't talk out loud.

The dark angel was just here.

She looked at him and pointed to his phone. He heard a ding and then read it. He looked at her quickly, panic on his face. She pointed to his phone.

He texted back, *R u ok?*

She nodded.

"This has been a crazy warm winter, hasn't it?" Brad asked, making conversation.

"It sure has," Cassie agreed.

What did he say? Skyler texted.

He wanted to know about the baby. He tried to kiss me.

Skyler looked mad.

"It's supposed to get cold next week, though," Brad said.

"Yeah, we've been spoiled, for sure," she said.

I told him I knew he wasn't the real Skyler, she texted.

Skyler looked panicked again. *You have to be careful, Cassie.*

I know that now. He tried to convince me that he was you, that he was still my guardian, that he never changed into a human, and that you were Grant.

Skyler looked at her and then looked at his dad, thoughtfully.

I need to ask my dad about this. I still haven't told him what happened to you. Is this why you said you wanted to go talk to Jackson?

No. This just happened right after I texted you. He just left when you pulled up.

He looked worried again. *Let's talk to Jackson first.*

Cassie nodded.

They reached Scarlett's beach house and said good-bye to Brad.

"Cassie, Skyler, what a nice surprise," Scarlett said when she opened the door. Harry jumped up on Cassie's legs, barking excitedly. Scarlett laughed. "Come on in."

She'd been watching a Disney movie with Tyler when the doorbell rang.

"Sorry to bother you," Cassie said. She looked nervous.

"No bother. Can I get you something to drink? Some cookies that Jackson baked me this morning?"

"No thanks," Cassie said. "Is he here right now?"

She shook her head. "No."

She led the way back to the family room and sunk back down on the couch. She seemed to be more tired with each passing day.

The two teens walked in and greeted Tyler and then sat down on the floor, looking at the TV. Harry barked and licked both their faces before settling down on Cassie's lap.

"Do you need to talk to him?" Scarlett asked.

They both looked at her and nodded.

"Okay. I can contact him."

"You can?" Cassie asked, eyes widened.

She nodded and picked up her cell phone since Tyler was in the room. "What's your cell number?" she asked. "I can give your number to Jackson."

Cassie gave it to her and Scarlett texted her, *I can talk to Jackson in my head. Don't ask me how, but we can do that with each other.*

Cassie showed her phone to Skyler, who nodded, as if it made perfect sense to him.

Cassie texted back, *Skyler and I used to be able to do that when he was my guardian.*

Oh, Scarlett texted back. She learned something new every day about these angels.

Jackson, she thought in her head. *Cassie and Skyler need to talk to you. Can you come visit?*

Immediately, the doorbell rang.

"Again!" Tyler said. He got up quickly and said, "I'll get it this time, Maman. You sit there."

She smiled. He was such a good boy.

Jackson was at the door, of course. Tyler pulled him into the family room.

"It's Jackson!"

"Hello, Jackson," Scarlett said, happy to see him again. She missed him being with her all the time like he used to be. She wished he could bend the rules.

He looked at her and silently said, *You know I wish I could, too.*

She smiled and patted the couch beside her for him to sit down, which he did.

"Tyler, would you do me a favor and run over to Catrina's and ask her for the croissants she said she had baked for me?"

He got up quickly. "Sure. I might be a few minutes, though, I want to talk to Arianna."

"All right, that's fine."

"I'll walk him over," Jackson said, getting up. "It's dark outside."

Scarlett nodded. "Merci."

While he was gone, she turned the Disney movie off and turned on some soft jazz music on her phone.

"Is everything okay?" she asked them.

"Cassie saw the dark angel again," Skyler said.

"Oh my. Wait until Jackson comes back so you won't have to tell the story twice." The teens nodded. "How's your dad doing in Nashville, Cassie?"

"Okay," Cassie said. "He stays busy, so I only get to talk to him on the phone for a minute every night. I think he and Jen talk for an hour or two. She's a little selfish about phone time."

Scarlett laughed. "Ah, well, I guess that's because they're still honeymooners and miss each other a lot." She could only imagine how hard it would be to stay away from Jackson like that, and they weren't even married.

Jackson came back and walked right in.

"Okay, so what's going on?" he asked. He sat back down beside Scarlett, put his arm around her, and played with her hair. It was shoulder length now in wavy layers and she quit wearing the wig. She never felt so free.

She noticed Cassie looking at the two of them, and she smiled at her.

"Are you guys SpiritMates?" Skyler asked.

"How do you know about that?" Scarlett asked.

"What's a SpiritMate?" Cassie asked.

"It's like soulmates," Skyler answered. "I've heard of them, of course, but I didn't know if it was true or not. Only angels of death can have one. It's pretty special."

"I'm surprised you knew about that," Jackson said.

"I still remember most things about being an angel," Skyler said.

Scarlett asked him, "Do you miss it? Being an angel?"

He glanced at Cassie and said, "I only miss being able to communicate with Cassie telepathically like you and Jackson do, and being with her all the time. That's all I miss, honestly. I'd rather be with Cassie as a human than anything else on heaven and earth, for however long we can be."

Scarlett thought that was sweet.

"So you're allowed to be together?" Cassie asked.

"It's a little more involved than just soulmates," Jackson said. "Each being, either two angels of death or an angel of death and a human who would soon die, would forever long for his or her other half, the other half of their soul. When the two find each other, there is an unspoken understanding of one another. They feel unified and would lie with each other in unity and know no greater joy than that." He looked at Scarlett and she nearly melted in a puddle at his feet. That was exactly how she felt. How was it said in that movie with Tom Cruise?

You complete me, Jackson said in her head.

Exactly. She looked at him longingly but remembered that Cassie and Skyler had come to talk with him, and so she turned her attention back to them.

"So then, tell me what happened," Jackson said. "You had another visit?"

"Yes," Cassie said. She told them all about the interchange, about her showing the baby bump, how he claimed it was his, how he tried to kiss her, and then got mad when she called his bluff. "Before he left, he threatened to tell my parents about the pregnancy," she said.

"Maybe you should tell them, so he can't use that against you," Jackson suggested.

"But that would mean getting Skyler in trouble," she said, looking at Skyler sorrowfully. "He also tried to convince me that he was the real Skyler, that he was still an angel and had not become human, and that this

Skyler," she pointed to Skyler, "was really Grant, that he didn't die in the accident, and that he was fooling me. Do you think this dark angel could be Grant?"

"I have been wondering that myself. It was a toss-up between that and an incubus. Do you know what that is?"

"Besides being the name of a rock band, no," Cassie said.

"It's a male entity that seduces women, has sex with them, makes them pregnant, and then the baby would have special powers. Very similar to a guardian angel having sex with a human. But now that you said he has actually mentioned Grant, I'm willing to bet that it *is* Grant."

"So humans can become an angel after passing on?" Cassie asked, looking at both Jackson and Scarlett.

Scarlett wasn't willing to tell anyone else that she was thinking very seriously about becoming an angel of death after she passed, so she remained silent.

"Yes," Jackson answered. "His soul went to Eden, but being part-angel, he was given a choice to remain in Eden or to become a full angel, whatever angel he chose to be. He was an angel of death for a while but then he dropped out of our view, off the radar so to speak. That's when he must have joined the dark angels. They are the only entities that can hide from us. Angels have a choice to be good or bad. The ones who are bad can hide in their own realm and not be seen."

"Why do you think Grant would want to impregnate me?" Cassie asked.

"Most likely to create a being with special powers that they could control," Jackson said.

Cassie looked at Scarlett. "How soon does a woman start showing pregnancy?"

"Oh, about four or five months along, I'd say," Scarlett said.

Cassie stood up and smoothed her shirt against her belly. "Is there a reason why my pregnancy would be accelerated? I shouldn't be showing at one month, right?"

Scarlett's eyes got big and she looked at Jackson.

"It's because the baby is half-angel. You have a very unique being inside of you, and it has special powers. Grant had healing powers, right?"

Skyler nodded.

"That baby inside of you will have some special abilities, too." He looked at Skyler. "I'm sure Juliet went through this with Grant. It's a shame you can't ask her about it."

Cassie looked at Skyler like she didn't know what to do. Scarlett felt sorry for her but was glad she had Skyler to support her and Jackson's knowledge, even if it was limited.

"Should I go to a doctor? What would he say about how far along I am?"

Jackson frowned. "No, don't go to a human doctor. I know someone who can help you, someone I had forgotten about. She's half-angel, half-human, and she's a doctor. I'll see if I can get her to come here for a visit."

"Thank you, Jackson," Cassie said.

Chapter Forty-One

"Do you know who this half-human, half-angel doctor is?" Cassie asked Skyler.

It was two weeks later, the last weekend of January, and Skyler was driving the two of them to Scarlett's beach house.

He'd gotten a new black Honda Fit as an early birthday present. It was actually Grant's birthday, which was now Skyler's birthday. He was born on February 13, the day before Valentine's Day, but his dad gave him the car early.

"No, I have no idea," Skyler said.

"It's getting harder and harder for me to hide this baby," she said, looking down at her belly. She had stopped throwing up in the last week, which was a nice relief, but now she was having backaches and saw the beginnings of stretch marks across her navel.

Skyler looked over at her and reached for her hand. "I know. I'll marry you whenever you want. Just say the word."

She laughed lightly. It seemed ridiculous to be thinking about marriage at seventeen. "I know." She smiled.

They pulled into Scarlett's driveway and saw a dark green sedan.

"She must be here already," Cassie said nervously.

"Don't be nervous. She's going to help you."

She nodded and Skyler got out quickly, and while Cassie was getting her purse, Skyler opened her door for her. He took her hand and helped her out. "Thank you." He was being extra-nice since she'd gotten pregnant.

Jackson let them in the house, and Harry greeted them. They saw a woman sitting at the kitchen bar. She had dark brown-and-reddish wavy hair that reached below her waist and the clearest light green eyes Cassie had ever seen. She was gorgeous. She wore a green dress with crisscross ties across the front like something worn in the seventeenth century. She stood up to reveal her tall height. She looked to be in her twenties, Cassie thought.

She walked towards them smiling and shook their hands. "Hello, I'm Dr. Adeline Brelane, but you can just call me Adeline," she said in a high-pitched European accent. Cassie shook her pale hand, which had silver and gold rings on all of her fingers, and introduced herself.

She shook Skyler's hand, and the three of them went to the bar and sat down. Cassie looked for Scarlett and saw her lying on the couch, her head already in Jackson's lap. She excused herself to go over and said hello to her.

"Are you feeling okay, Cassie?" Scarlett asked.

"I was going to ask you the same thing," Cassie said.

Scarlett smiled and reached out and squeezed her hand. "I'm just tired. This is my best medicine right here," she said, snuggling against Jackson's chest.

Cassie smiled and said, "I'm okay. I hope to be better after talking to the doctor. Where's Tyler?"

"He's at a friend's house. I made sure he would be away for the doctor's visit so that you could all talk openly."

Cassie nodded and then walked back over to the bar and sat down.

"Tell me about your pregnancy, Cassie," Adeline said.

Cassie told her all about it from the moment of conception to now, describing the dark angel and their conversations in detail. Not the embarrassing details, of course. She also told her about her encounters with the flying animal in the backyard and the feathers she'd found in her bedroom.

"I'm going to examine you now," Adeline said. She stood up and walked into the family room. "Could we use your bedroom, Scarlett?"

"Of course. It's right in there," she said, pointing the way. "There's an adjoining bathroom if you need it, too."

"Thank you," Adeline said.

Cassie followed her into the bedroom. It was just the two of them.

"I know this is embarrassing and you may think it's weird for someone like me to come all the way here from New England, but Jackson told me you were young and scared and needed someone who knew what you were going through. That's me." She smiled reassuringly. "Just take off your clothes from the waist down so I can see what's going on in your belly, okay?"

"Okay."

It did feel weird doing this in someone's house instead of at a doctor's office. While she undressed, Adeline went into the adjoining bathroom to wash her hands. She came back with a towel by the time Cassie was undressed.

Adeline put the towel on top of the bed. "Lie down on this."

"Okay." Cassie hopped up on the bed.

Adeline turned some music on her phone, which sounded like spa music or garden music that Jen liked to listen to sometimes. This song had an American Indian flute playing and some wind chimes tinkling. "Some people relax better when listening to this kind of music," Adeline explained.

She put gloves on, got some ointment out of a tapestry-covered doctor's bag and proceeded to examine Cassie's abdomen, inside and out. It was not comfortable. Cassie had never had a female exam before.

"I'm sorry, I know it's uncomfortable," the doctor said. "Try to just relax and let your legs fall apart like you're doing a yoga stretch."

Cassie tried to do that. She took a deep breath in order to try and make herself relax.

"How long have you known Skyler?"

"He was my guardian angel my whole life, but I didn't start actually interacting with him until last August."

Adeline continued the exam while talking to Cassie. "I can tell that the two of you are very close."

"We are," Cassie nodded, "but apparently not close enough for me to figure out it wasn't him when another angel came and pretended to be him."

"Don't beat yourself up about that. Dark angels can be very deceptive. It's what they do."

"So you're half-angel?" Cassie dared to ask, hoping she wouldn't be offended at the personal question.

"Yes, I am." Adeline finished the exam and took the gloves off. She went back to the bathroom, washed her hands and brought back some tissues. "You can get up now, all done." She handed the tissues to Cassie. "You can use the bathroom and put your clothes back on now, and then I'll tell you all about myself when you're done."

Cassie picked up her clothes and went to the bathroom to clean up and get dressed. Sitting on one of the shelves was a picture of Scarlett, Tyler, and an older woman, who she guessed was Scarlett's mom. Scarlett had really long brown hair very similar to Adeline's. She was so pretty. Cassie wondered if her dad was going to take Tyler and thought it must be painful for Scarlett to have to leave her child behind.

She thought about her own baby, but it was hard to think of it as an actual baby since she couldn't see it. She did feel it move just that morning which had been both scary and wild at the same time, to feel something moving inside of you that didn't normally belong there.

She came back out and the towel had been removed and the bed straightened back up, and Adeline was gone, the bedroom door closed. Cassie went back out to the family room where the others were gathered.

"Have a seat, Cassie," Adeline said, pointing to a love seat where Skyler was already sitting. Cassie sat down. "A pregnancy between a human and an angel is unique, obviously. The angel part makes the baby grow faster. You will be due around the beginning of May rather than the usual nine months associated with a human pregnancy, in which case you would have been due in September. It takes half the time. I myself am half-human, half-angel, as you all know. I was born in Norway. My father was a guardian angel and my mother human. My father didn't turn human the way you did, Skyler, because my mother died at my birth."

Cassie gasped. "Oh no, that's so sad."

Adeline nodded. "I was raised by my grandparents, my mother's parents. My dad comes to see me once a year on my birthday. He looks like a human, of course; I've never seen his angel form.

"My grandparents soon found out that I had special powers: the ability to heal. I understand that the dark angel who did this to you was once what I am. Grant was his name?" She looked at Jackson, who nodded. "I can heal people, but many times I choose not to. It becomes a burden to have such a gift because when people hear about it, they come from all over to be healed. That happened when I was a little girl of about ten years old. My grandparents decided to move to America to get far away from everyone in Europe who had heard about my abilities. They asked me not to use my healing powers except on certain special occasions so that I wouldn't be harassed. So I learned how to become a doctor, and like I said, sometimes I heal people."

"How have you been able to live a long life when Grant only lived six years?" Cassie asked.

"Grant's life was shortened as a human because of part of a punishment to his parents, Jackson tells me. There was no one to punish in my case. My mother had died and my father didn't become human. He was assigned another human to be guardian for. They were true star-crossed lovers. They don't even get to be together in the afterlife, although he does go and see her sometimes in Eden."

Cassie thought that was really sad, and once again, she was grateful for Skyler to have become human for her. It just showed her how very much he loved her. She squeezed his hand, and he squeezed hers back.

"You cannot go see a regular doctor. They wouldn't understand why the baby is growing so fast. If you'd like, I would be happy to speak to your parents and answer any of their questions, to prove to them that you have a doctor."

"I, uh, haven't told my parents yet," Cassie said.

"Well, you're not going to be able to hide it much longer, so you might want to do it soon," Adeline said. "You could also ask your parents about being homeschooled if you don't want the embarrassment of being pregnant in high school."

Cassie nodded. "That's a good idea." She already had to find excuses not to run in her PE class.

"I can come and see you once a month to check on you, and then I'll be here for you in May when you deliver. You can go to a real hospital for the delivery. Being a real doctor, I can get special permission to come to a local hospital and deliver the baby for you, if you'd like."

"Yes, that would be nice." Cassie felt safer delivering at an actual hospital, though she didn't mind the visits here at Scarlett's. It was a lot more private.

Adeline opened her tapestry bag, pulled out some brochures, and handed them to Cassie, along with a book. "These pamphlets have just some basic information about being pregnant. This book is a special book, one I helped write myself. I have two children. I am married to a human, and my pregnancies were a little different, just like yours will be. I also don't age quickly. Once I reached your age, seventeen, it was like my body stopped growing at the rate it used to. I'm actually forty-five years old."

Cassie's eyes bulged. She did *not* look that old, not even close.

"I still age, just at a much slower pace. My two girls are around your age now, sixteen and twenty. Since my pregnancy and my rate of growth are different, I wanted to write this book to help others like me. We are rare, but there are others out there. And of course, my two girls will hope to marry someday. They are only one-quarter angel, but they still have slight powers and may have the decreased growth rate, as well. They're still too young to tell right now."

"So at first, the growing rate is fast and then it slows way down?" Cassie asked, confused.

"Yes. I know, it's weird. My girls didn't have the rapid growth rate after they were born, but my pregnancies were half the time. Any other questions?"

"When will you be back here to meet me?"

Adeline looked at her phone for a minute and then said, "The third week of February works for me. Is this the best location to do this?" she asked Scarlett.

Scarlett nodded. "Yes. I'll mark that on my calendar and make sure my son is away again."

"Good, then it's settled." Adeline pulled a business card out of her tapestry bag. "Here's my card. Call me if you have *any* questions, or if you would like me to speak to your parents. You're welcome to show them my card when you do tell them."

Cassie looked at the card. It was white with a healthcare insignia in the upper left corner that had green vines and leaves on it as well as little red flowers, and a globe sat on the very top. The words written were *Adeline Brelane, M.D., N.D.* and on the next line, *Medical Doctor and Doctor of Naturopathic Medicine.*

"One more thing, are you having any nausea or other symptoms?" Adeline asked.

"Not anymore. I quit throwing up this week."

"That's good. Let me know if you start to have any other symptoms. I can send you some herbs to take."

"Scarlett, would you like something for your pain?" Adeline asked later.

Cassie and Skyler had gone, and it was just Scarlett, Jackson, and Adeline at the house.

"I'm taking some morphine if the pain gets really bad, but it makes me really tired and nauseous, so I try to avoid it and just take ibuprofen."

Adeline nodded and reached into her medicine bag. She handed her some bottles. "Here's some MSM and colloidal silver you can start taking, and some moringa oleifera." She brought out a bottle. "And this is some blue-green algae you can take every day. These will help you deal with pain in a more natural way."

"Thank you so much," Scarlett said.

"I'll see you next month."

Jackson showed her to the door, then came back and sat down with Scarlett again. She placed her legs across his lap, her arms around his waist, and her head against his chest. Harry settled down in front of the roaring fireplace.

"I miss my long hair," she said wistfully. "It was very similar to Adeline's."

Jackson played with her hair. "I know you do, but you'll get it back after you pass."

She looked up at him. "Truly?"

"Yes."

"Even if I become…what you are?"

"Oh, yes. Whatever you become, you can keep your hair. What age would you like to look like?"

"I'd like to look like I did when I had Tyler. My boobs were bigger and I had nice hips."

He smiled. "I can picture that."

"I'm glad to see you today. How long can you stay?"

"Just a few minutes longer." He cleared his throat. "Your time is coming soon," he said quietly.

"Jackson, I told you I don't want to know the date."

He wove his fingers into hers. "You have a little while yet, I will tell you that."

"Is it time to see a lawyer about my will?"

"Soon, yes."

She would have to talk to Luke and see what he wanted to do about Tyler soon, before she could make up her will.

"About the afterlife…as much as I would love to be with my family up in Eden, I can't stand the thought of losing you, of not seeing you every day. Not loving you."

He leaned down and kissed her. *Mon amore,* he said telepathically. "That makes me so happy, I can't begin to express…" He kissed her again, his lips moving over hers, and she felt her insides move with desire for him, her heart skipping a beat.

"So what would I have to do to become an angel of death?" she asked. "Is there training to go through?"

He smiled. "No. I will show you everything you need to know, when the time comes."

"Are there other humans who have become angels after passing over?"

"Yes, of course. It is an option. A lot of humans want to become guardian angels of someone they left behind, particularly of their children."

She could see wanting to watch over Tyler. "That makes sense. Has anyone besides me wanted to be an angel of death?"

"Yes. Grant was. Of course, he was half-angel to begin with."

"Are there a lot of other angels of death who have SpiritMates?"

"Yes, there are several that I know." He smoothed her hair away from her face. "No more questions until tonight. I must go."

He kissed her one last time, and then he disappeared, leaving behind a black feather. She picked it up and smelled it, pressed it against her face, and smiled.

Chapter Forty-Two

Luke flew home Valentine's weekend in February to spend Valentine's Day with Jen and for Logan's birthday, which was on the thirteenth. It would be the first birthday since he found out he was Logan's father, so it was important for him to be there. He'd already been out of town for Cassie's birthday in December, so he felt like he couldn't miss this one. He blew off a performance that evening at a local bar just to be here with his family. Jen didn't even know he was coming.

He took a taxi home amidst falling snow and arrived just in time for a birthday party that was going on for both Logan and Skyler since they shared the same birthday. He peeked in the windows before opening the door and saw a big group of teenagers inside.

"Luke!" Jen shouted when he let himself in the house. She ran up to him, flung her arms around him and kissed him. He squeezed her back. "What are you doing here?" she asked.

"I wanted to be home for Logan's birthday…and for Valentine's."

She kissed him again. "I'm so happy. Come on, let's find Logan."

They found him in the family room opening up presents. He and Skyler were taking turns opening gifts. Modern pop music was playing and dirty paper plates of half-eaten pizza were scattered around the dining and family rooms.

"Dad!" Logan hollered when he saw him. He got up, walked over and gave him a quick but heartfelt hug. "Thanks for coming home," he said, grinning from ear to ear.

"I didn't want to miss it for anything," Luke said.

His cell phone buzzed since he'd had it on vibrate for the plane trip. He looked at it and saw that it was his producer, Robert. He ignored it. He knew he was in trouble for missing the gig tonight, but he didn't care.

A few of Logan's friends asked for his autograph. It was embarrassing, really. He didn't want to take the attention off of either Logan or Skyler, but the guys didn't seem to mind sharing the spotlight with him for a moment.

Cassie came out of the direction of her bedroom or the bathroom, and he was shocked at how much weight she had gained. He hadn't seen her since New Year's, but she hadn't looked that heavy then. How could she have gained so much weight so quickly? Maybe it was the loose top she was wearing, but he thought she looked heavy in the middle.

"Hey, Dad," she said, walking cautiously over to him.

"Come here, sweetheart." Luke pulled her in for a hug.

"It's cool you're here," she said. Then she walked over and sat down in the floor next to Skyler.

He and Jen sat on a loveseat that a couple of the kids gave up for them, and they watched the boys open the rest of their presents. Then Jen went to the kitchen to get the cake and ice cream. She served them on plates and Luke helped her pass them all around.

Brad, Juliet, and Danielle came in and apologized for being late. "Sorry we couldn't make it sooner," Juliet said.

"How did the ballet recital go, Danielle?" Jen asked.

"It was good," Danielle said.

"It's good to see you, Luke," Brad said, obviously surprised to see him.

"You, too. I didn't want to miss Logan's birthday," Luke said. "I heard that Skyler got a new car."

"Yeah, he did. I know, we're spoiling him." Brad laughed.

"I'm sure it makes it easier for you guys, not having to drive him around everywhere...like over here." Luke laughed.

"Yeah, it does, although it makes it harder to keep an eye on them," Brad said, his eyes turning to look at their kids.

Luke's phone buzzed again, and he glanced to see it was Robert again. He sighed. "I better take this; it's my producer."

"Sure, no problem," Brad said.

Luke walked over to the back door and went outside onto the balcony to answer his phone.

"Luke, where the hell are you?!" Robert said before Luke could say anything.

"I'm home, Rob. I'm sorry, but I didn't want to miss my son's birthday. Or Valentine's Day with my new wife. Fire me if you want to, but I had to be here."

"It makes it real hard to make other people happy when the lead singer bails. It also doesn't look good for me. Don't do this to me again or I will pull everything – the songs off the radio, the rest of the album, the whole tour – everything."

"I understand." Luke clicked off the phone before Robert could say anything else.

"Is everything all right?" Jen asked when he went back inside. She was serving some cake and ice cream onto plates for Brad and the ladies. They had gone over and sat down in the family room.

"Yeah, uh, I was just getting blasted by Robert. I blew off a performance tonight and he wasn't too happy about it."

"Luke, why'd you do that?"

"I don't care, Jen. I'm getting tired of being told what to do, where to go, and who to have dinner with." He sighed. "I know I shouldn't complain. It's a once-in-a-lifetime opportunity, but it's hard being away from my family."

He walked over and ran his finger down the thin wispy sleeve of her off-white silky blouse. She looked up at him with fire in her eyes. "I'm not complaining," she said, laying the ice cream scoop down. She wrapped her arms around his neck and pulled him in for a deep kiss. His knees got weak. She was all he ever wanted. Why was he chasing his dreams when all he'd ever wanted since he was eighteen was her?

After the party was over, Cassie came over to Luke. "Dad, I didn't know you were going to be here, but I had already planned to go out to dinner with Skyler and his family. Is that okay?"

"Sure, baby. I'll see you when you get back. I wanted to talk to both you and Logan tonight about something important."

"Okay, Dad. See ya." She quickly kissed his cheek and left with Skyler and his family.

Logan walked up to him and said, "Uh, Dad? I was planning to take Emily out for dinner. Actually, she wanted to take me out for my birthday. That okay with you? I can cancel since you came all this way…"

"No, don't cancel. I'll see you when you get back. I have something important to talk to you about."

"Okay. Later, then." He fist-bumped Luke.

"Later, dude," Luke said, which caused Logan to chuckle.

After everyone else was gone, Luke helped Jen clean up the house. Then they took a shower together and made love while they had the house to themselves for a while.

They were dressed again and snuggled up together on the couch watching TV when both kids came back home later.

"What did you want to talk about?" Logan asked. He was sitting in a chair by the fireplace, and Cassie sat on the loveseat.

"It's about my career. If I do this, I have to do it all the way, which means we should probably move to Nashville."

"Aw, Dad," Logan said.

"Absolutely not," Cassie said.

"Guys, listen. I know it's not a convenient time, what with only one year of high school left, but my producers say I need to be in Nashville if I'm going to make it in this business."

"I'm not thrilled about moving," Logan said. "I'm a little tired of moving around. I moved up here from Georgia and I kind of like it here. And then there's Emily…"

"Yeah, and I'm not leaving Skyler," Cassie said.

"I know this is terrible timing but you'll both meet new friends in Nashville, I promise."

"You don't understand, Dad," Cassie said. The look on her face was almost terrified. "I'm not leaving Skyler. I can't. I…" She looked around at the others. "I'm pregnant," she whispered.

"You're what?!" Luke demanded.

Jen gasped.

"It's Skyler's and I can't leave him. He said he would marry me. He said we could live with his parents. You go on and move to Nashville, but I'm not going."

Dear God. She did the same thing her mother and Jen did…gotten pregnant as a teenager. "Cassie, my God."

"Didn't I warn you against having sex as a teenager?" Jen said.

"The same thing happened with you guys, remember? How many years did you have to be apart before you could be together the way you were meant to be? I'm not waiting sixteen years to be with Skyler. I'm not raising this baby without him."

"What about school, Cassie?" Luke asked.

"I want to be homeschooled. I can look for a teacher. I know Jen can't do it. I'll pay for it myself and get another job if you can't use me enough in the shop."

Luke was shocked and realized that his baby girl was growing up and he was still missing out on things. He'd missed her last birthday, now she had fooled around carelessly and gotten pregnant. Maybe he should quit this music business. By her next birthday, she would most likely be married with a baby. If that wasn't enough to keep a man at home, he didn't know what was.

He wanted to be angry with her, but he'd done the same thing at her age – to two different women. He knew Jen would probably think part of this was her fault, since Cassie had been in her care while he was away, but it was his fault. It was all his fault for not being there when his children needed him.

Chapter Forty-Three

Late that night, Jen and Luke were naked in bed talking. They were stretched out facing each other, leaning on pillows and elbows.

"I'm sorry for not watching Cassie more," Jen said. "I can't believe she's pregnant."

Luke smoothed his hand over her arm. "That's not your fault, baby."

"I feel like it is. I feel like I let you down."

He kissed her shoulder. "You didn't. It's my fault for not being here."

"I hate that she has to go through this at her age. I know exactly what she's going through. I was homeschooled too, down in Georgia."

Luke sighed. "Yeah. At least Skyler can be here for her. And as soon as May gets here, I'll be here for her, too. Things are going to change."

"What do you mean?"

"I don't think I can do this anymore."

"Do what?" Jen looked worried.

"Be away from you all. It's killing me. And then there's the partying and all the women."

Luke had called her drunk one night a week ago, and he'd told her that a woman nearly made him break his vows. She wanted to hop on the next flight to Nashville but decided not to. She couldn't babysit him or tell him what to do. He had to make his own decisions when it came to things like that. She just hoped he was faithful. She'd kill him if he wasn't. She would never recover from that. She hoped he loved her enough to remain faithful and she could trust him enough to believe him if he said he had been.

"Tell me about that woman, now that you're sober."

"Steve, Derek and I were at the hotel bar, and a group of three women came over to the bar and started hanging all over us, making advances towards us. I had already drunk three beers – I'm sorry, I know I shouldn't, but I'd had a tough day recording. They wanted to change everything about one of my songs. Anyway, the one who was hitting on me kept putting her hands all over me. She was beautiful, but I put her off, told her I was happily married. She didn't care. She was very forward, and I was a little drunk, and she tried to take advantage of that. She kissed me, I can't lie, but I pushed her away. I swear to you, it's the truth. Finally I told Steve to get either me or this woman out of the bar. The other two girls already left when they realized they didn't have a chance, but this one didn't. I don't know how they figured out where we were staying, but this one was obviously an obsessed fan. Steve told the bartender that the woman was drunk – which she was – and that she was harassing us, and security came and escorted her out. She wasn't a guest at the hotel, so they called her a cab. The three of us went up to my room after that and complained more about the session. I swear to you nothing happened. You believe me, don't you?"

She caressed his cheek. "If you tell me nothing happened, then I believe you."

Luke looked relieved. "Thank you for trusting me. I'm sorry for drinking too much. That's just one of the reasons why I need to get out of this business."

Jen was surprised. "Get out of the business? Are you serious?" She knew it was something he'd always wanted to do, but she would secretly be happy to have him home again.

"Yes. Alcohol is around me and the band constantly. We have drinks while we're playing, drinks with business associates, drinks late at night after recording sessions or concerts to mellow out. I also drink at night because I miss you so much. Drugs are offered – to help us sleep at night and others for energy during the day, but I don't take any of them. I just drink too much. Then there are girls hanging all over me. It's flattering to be sure but this is not what I wanted. At all."

"But Luke, it's been your dream for so long. How many years did I hear you complain about getting out of the government contracting business so you could just play music?"

"I know, but sometimes what you wish for is not what's best for you. Traveling, being away from you and the kids all the time, it's just not worth it. Besides, my biggest dream was to have you, and now I do." He leaned over and kissed her lips. "So what do I need this music career for? You are my life. I don't want to lose you over some stupid career."

Her heart melted and she leaned over and kissed him. "I was your biggest dream?"

He smiled and nodded. "You were. Ever since that night behind the bleachers."

"You were mine, too," she said.

"I'm sorry about quitting."

"Why are you apologizing to me? I never told you that you had to do this."

"I know but I wanted to make you proud."

"Luke, I am proud of you no matter what you choose to do in life. As long as you do it with me." She kissed him again. "You got to have a hit song on the radio. How many people can say that?"

"Yeah." He laughed lightly. "We may have to be a one-hit wonder. I'm fine with that. I'm glad I had the opportunity to do this, but I can see that I'm just not suited for the lifestyle. Maybe when I was younger or when I get older, but I don't like being away from you and the kids like this anymore. Now with Cassie being pregnant and then there's Tyler, our family is getting bigger. Do you realize we're going to be grandparents soon?"

"Technically just you. I'll be a grand-aunt."

"Jen, I hope you know I consider you to be Cassie's mom by now. True, you didn't give birth to her, but you have half raised her. She's as much your daughter as she was Josie's. And you've been here for her more than either me or Josie has."

"Oh, Luke." She ran her hand down his chest and then along his hip.

"Which means you'll be a grandmother soon," he teased her.

She tickled him with the hand that was on his hip, and he tickled her back along her ribcage, causing her to squeal.

His tickling turn into caressing. "I also want to take care of Tyler, if you're okay with that."

"Yes, absolutely. He's your son."

"That's another reason I want to be home. I feel a strong responsibility for him and I don't want to mess that up. I haven't been there enough for either Cassie or Logan, and I want to do better for Tyler. You've done a great job with them, but it's not fair for you to have to take care of all of my kids for me."

"But that's what I signed up for when I married you," she said, caressing his back.

"So are you okay with me quitting the music business? I am contracted to stay until May, but after that, I'm coming home for good."

"If that's really what you want to do, it's fine with me."

He seemed relieved, like a load was lifted off his back. "Good. Now come here." He pulled her closer to him and kissed her deeply, pressing his manhood against her. Her leg went over his.

"You know, maybe you could still write songs and sell them," she said between kisses. "Then you're free from the stress and traveling, but you'd still be making money."

"Hmmm, that's a great idea. We'll talk more about it later."

They made love slowly under a pile of blankets on the cold winter's night.

They woke up in the morning to Luke's cell phone ringing. He had it on vibrate, but he had it set to make exceptions for Jen, his kids, and his band members.

He reached for the phone on the nightstand and looked at it briefly to see that it was Steve. He slid the answer button over.

"Morning, Steve. What's up?"

"Man, it snowed here overnight. Two or three inches. When are you supposed to fly back?"

"I haven't made a reservation yet, but I was going to fly back this evening. Are they canceling flights?"

"What's wrong?" Jen asked, rubbing her eyes.

Luke put his arm around her and pulled her next to him. "I'm putting you on speaker. Jen's right here." He looked at Jen. "It's Steve. It snowed in Nashville."

"Oh no," she said.

"Hey, Jen."

"Hey, Steve."

"Yeah, Luke, they're canceling flights."

"Maybe I should drive. I could take my truck. It should be able to handle a little snow."

"Maybe. The roads are pretty bad here right now, but they might melt later."

"I could stay overnight at my mom's in Gray, Tennessee, and then make my way over to Nashville tomorrow morning. Maybe the highways will be cleared by then at least."

"Yeah, that sounds like a good plan. Then you'll have a truck here and we won't have to rely on these other guys and taxis to get anywhere."

"Means I'll have to quit drinking so much, which is a good thing," Luke said, laughing. "Listen, is Derek there? I need to talk to you both about something important."

"He is. I'll put you on speaker." There was a pause.

"Hey, Luke," Derek said. "Man, Robert sure was pissed when he found out you left town. I've never seen him so mad."

"Yeah, by the way, thanks a lot for ditching us," Steve added. "We could've come with ya – we have families there, too."

"I know, I'm sorry, but my boy had a birthday and then today is Valentine's – my first one with Jen since we got married." He squeezed her. "I couldn't miss that."

"I know what you mean," Steve said. "I'm going to have to miss my baby's ultrasound tomorrow. That sucks."

"Listen," Luke said. "I've decided I don't want to continue in the band after our contract ends in May. I know we agreed to wait until May to decide, but I've already decided. I hope y'all don't get too mad at me, but I just found out that my girl Cassie is pregnant."

"Oh, man," Derek said.

"Wow," Steve said.

"I'm just starting to spend some quality time with my son Logan, and now I have Tyler to raise. I don't have time for touring. Plus the temptations are too much for me. I don't need the fame."

"Are you serious?" Derek asked. "Man, that sucks. Wait till May, at least. You might feel differently."

"I don't think I will. I'm sorry. It's been quite a ride so far, but it'll soon be time for me to get off."

"It's fine with me," Steve said. "I've got a new baby to raise."

"We're supposed to start touring tomorrow," Derek reminded them. "We've got a gig in Knoxville. Maybe you could just meet us there."

"Hey, that'll work out even better. That's a lot closer than Nashville. Send me the address and other details, will you?"

"Sure thing."

"See y'all tomorrow night then. Bring my guitar for me."

Chapter Forty-Four

Luke hung up the phone and he and Jen started making plans for a Valentine's meal. They decided to have a big brunch at Tradewinds as a family. Tradewinds was a restaurant at the Virginia Beach Resort Hotel that sat on the Chesapeake Bay. It was a cold but clear day, and the view of the bay was beautiful through the floor-to-ceiling windows. There was an all-you-can-eat buffet with every breakfast food you could think of, even a banana fosters flambé that was lit on fire. There was a man dressed in a tuxedo playing the piano, creating a nice ambiance.

In the middle of the meal, Luke asked Cassie and Logan, "Would you guys mind it if I come back home and not pursue this music career anymore?"

Logan shrugged his shoulders. "I'd be happy to have you at home again." He smiled.

"Me, too," Cassie said. "I'm happy with no one moving to Nashville."

"Good." Luke relaxed a little. "Another thing I wanted to ask you about was Tyler. I told you both earlier that he is mine and that Scarlett has asked if I wanted to be part of his life. As you know, she is dying of cancer, and she has asked us if we'd like to take care of him. I would like to. Would that be all right with you guys?"

"Sure," Cassie said. "Tyler's great."

"Yeah, I'm cool with it. Does that mean I have to move downstairs?"

"Probably," Jen said, laughing. "Is that okay?"

"Sure," Logan said.

After they finished eating, Luke drove them all around, ending up in Pungo, just a relaxing Sunday drive on the back country roads. It had been a long time since he'd driven his truck or been with his family. He laughed at the silliest jokes they made. It felt so good to be home.

He decided he would just wait until Monday morning and drive straight to Knoxville so he could spend the rest of the day with his family. Driving around, he looked at the houses and wondered where Scarlett's house was, the one he would inherit. He still didn't feel right about inheriting a house, but technically it was for Tyler to grow up in. He didn't want to mention it to Jen or the kids until he'd talked with Scarlett about it first.

"Hey, is it okay if we drop by Scarlett's?" Luke asked the family.

"Fine with me," Jen answered. "You want to talk to her about Tyler?"

"Yeah, while I'm in town. I'd rather do it face to face. Kids, do you think you could occupy Tyler while we talk for a bit?"

"Sure," Logan and Cassie both said.

Tyler answered the door when they arrived and let them in the house. "Hey," he said. "You wanna watch the dinosaur movie with me?"

"How about you show me your Legos," Logan suggested.

"Yeah, I want to see what you have built his week," Cassie said.

Tyler led them upstairs to his room while Luke and Jen walked over to Scarlett, who was lying on the couch in the family room.

"Hey, what a nice surprise," she said. She used the remote to pause the movie. "Have a seat. Can I get you anything to drink?"

She swung her legs around to the floor, but Luke stopped her. "Don't get up. We're fine. I wanted to talk to you while I was in town for a short visit."

"Oh? What about?" Scarlett asked, stretching back out on the couch again.

"Tyler. I've decided – we've decided – we want to take him. I want to be in his life full time. He's a great kid. I have to tour until May, and then I'm putting my music career on hiatus. I need to take care of Tyler and my other kids." He motioned towards Tyler's bedroom.

Scarlett nodded her understanding. "That's wonderful, Luke, Jen. I'm so glad. My father offered to take him, and I'm sure he would've enjoyed spending time in a foreign country and could've learned a lot from my papa, but I was hoping you would want to take him. You'll inherit my house in Pungo, too."

"Yeah, James mentioned that. He said he might have goofed, telling me about it. I swear that the house had nothing to do with the reason I want to stay in Virginia Beach. It's all for Jen and the kids. I'm sure it'll be nice to have another house to live in and have Jen's house devoted solely to her shop. We can expand that a little. How many bedrooms does the house have, more than three, I hope?"

Scarlett smiled. "You will have plenty of room, Luke. It's a very big house of five thousand square feet with eight bedrooms, on ten acres of land. There's an old barn on the property we never used, so there's room for horses if that's something you'd like to have or your own music studio."

Luke's jaw dropped. "Oh my God. It's too much, Scarlett." He looked at Jen, who was also shocked.

"It's not. It's my gift to you for taking care of Tyler. I didn't tell you about it right away because I didn't want it to influence your decision about taking Tyler. I wanted to be sure you would take care of him and love him. I believe you will."

"I will, I promise."

"I would only ask that you remain in the house until Tyler grows up and is on his own. I want him to want for nothing and have a nice big house to grow up in."

"Of course."

"I also would like for you to take him to visit his pépé in Toulon once a year. My father is unable to fly across the ocean for health reasons, so it's better if you go there. I'll leave money in a fund for both his flight and yours each year until he turns eighteen. I don't want him traveling alone."

"You're too generous, Scarlett."

She smiled at him. "I just want Tyler to remember my father, not just from the one visit at Christmas. I want him to know where that side of his family came from. I don't know how much longer my father will live, but he will also have an inheritance for Tyler when he does pass over."

"I would be happy to take him to France once a year. Whatever you want me to do, I'll do it for you and for him."

"I'll also have a sum of money saved for Tyler when he turns twenty-five, but I don't want him to rely on that as his only source of income. Make sure he gets an education. I'll also leave money in a fund for college."

Luke nodded, hating that she was dying and couldn't be here to see Tyler through all of this, but she certainly was preparing. He couldn't believe the huge house that he and Jen would get to live in. Maybe they'd get to have their dream of having a horse farm, after all. And as it turns out, he won't even have to be in the music business to get it. "Thank you so much, Scarlett," he said.

"Would you like to go see the house while you're in town?"

"Are you sure you're up to it?" Jen asked.

"I'll be fine." She got up, picked up a little round pill container that had old-fashioned roses on it, and took some pills out. "Just let me take some of these vitamins to help me feel better." She walked over to the kitchen and got a glass of water to take them with.

Luke went upstairs to get the kids and told them they were going to see Tyler's other house.

Luke drove them all in his truck. Scarlett gave him directions on how to get there, and they drove deep into Pungo towards Creeds. She told him to turn down a driveway hidden by trees. Scarlett pressed a remote she had brought with her to open an iron gate to reveal a long winding paved driveway through the trees until they saw a huge Victorian house made of gray stone. Luke was awestruck.

"I didn't even know this was back here," he said. He couldn't believe this was going to be his house someday. "I had no idea you were so rich, Scarlett."

She smiled. "My parents were, not me. I inherited this from my mother. Papa let her have it when they divorced. Me, I just worked in insurance to have something to do."

They got out of the truck and looked at the huge house with its covered porch held up by pink marble columns. The porch stretched across the length of the house and wrapped around two turrets, one on either end of the house. Scarlett led the way onto the porch where a black wrought iron bench sat next to one of the turrets, and there were two wooden doors accentuated by black wrought iron door knockers.

"Come on, I'll show you my house," Tyler said, running up on the porch.

Scarlett unlocked the door and she and Tyler gave them a tour of the house including a library/study with dark wood and green walls, a pink and white parlor, a small blue parlor, an elaborate dining room with a large carved hutch, a well-appointed kitchen, and a red and yellow breakfast room. There were stained glass windows in many of the rooms, bright airy bedrooms with many windows on the second floor, and antiques all over the house.

They went back outside and Scarlett showed them the falling-down barn and then walked over to a gray gazebo that she said was surrounded by pale pink roses in the summer. Scarlett went inside it and sat down on a gray bench. Tyler showed them his swings nearby, but Jen lingered with Scarlett.

"It's a very beautiful house," Jen said.

"Are you sure you want to take care of another woman's child?" Scarlett asked her.

Jen smiled. "Yes, of course. He's a sweet boy and he's obviously Luke's. He looks so much like him. It'll be wonderful to care for him. I helped raise Cassie."

"Yes, but she belonged to your sister, whereas I was a one-night stand with your husband."

"I know but that was years ago and we weren't together then. I believe things happen for a reason, and you were meant to have that little boy who looks so much like his father, and now we are meant to help raise him. You're such a warm, caring person, how could I hold anything against you? Trusting us to take care your boy…giving us this house?" Her eyes started tearing up. She leaned over, hugged Scarlett, and said, "I can't thank you enough. I only wish…" She couldn't finish.

Scarlett knew what she was thinking; her face said it all. "I know," Scarlett said. "Me too. I had a wonderful housekeeper if you need someone to help you with this big house. It's a lot to take on, I know."

"I just might need to do that," Jen said, laughing lightly.

After leaving Scarlett's, Luke drove them back home and they all hung out at the house, talking, watching TV, just being a family. Both the kids had dates with their girlfriend/boyfriend that evening for Valentine's Day, so they soon got ready for that and then were out the door.

Luke took Jen to Il Giardino, a cozy Italian restaurant at the oceanfront where the lights were turned down low, candles lit the tables, and a piano was being played near the bar.

"Can you believe that house?" Luke asked her in the middle of their meal.

She shook her head. "I can't believe she's just giving it to us."

"Me either. I've been thinking since we left there that maybe we will have our horse ranch after all. The barn will obviously take a lot of work, but there's plenty of land and a big iron fence."

"Yeah, that would be great."

"We could raise horses and you could teach me how to ride well enough, and then I could teach other people," he said.

They had talked about it before, ever since going to her dad's ranch in Georgia last fall.

"I think this was meant to be," he continued. "I can still play music in your shop and maybe at local places from time to time, and write and sell some songs. That'll be enough for me."

"You could play for the horses, too," Jen said. "They would enjoy that."

"Really?"

"Sure."

They talked more about the house and the future and about Luke's tour.

After eating, they crossed the street and took a walk on the cold boardwalk by the ocean, walking arm in arm to try to keep warm. Then they drove back home and warmed up by making love in the bedroom before the kids came back home.

When they got back, Luke asked Cassie if she was getting the care she needed for the baby. "Do you have a doctor, baby?"

"Yeah, I have one already. Jackson told me about her." She went to her bedroom, brought back a card, and handed it to him. "This is her name."

"Okay. What are you and Skyler planning to do about it? Are you getting married or what?"

"He said he would marry me anytime, that I just had to say the word. I want to do it privately, though. No big wedding. I'd like to wait until you get back in May."

"That'd be nice, but if you'd rather be married before the baby is born, you can do it before May. I'll understand."

"So, you're really not moving to Nashville?"

"No. I want to be here for all my babies. Including yours."

She nodded. "Thank you, Daddy." She gave him a big hug and when she finally pulled away, she had tears in her eyes. He wiped them off her face.

"Don't cry, baby. True, you're growing up really fast, but Jen is here for you and I will be too, come May. Soon as we get Tyler…" and Scarlett passes on, he thought, "we can all move into that big house. There will be plenty of room for you, Skyler, and the baby, if that's something you want to do."

"I think I'd like that. It's nice and private, away from nosy neighbors."

He nodded. "I love you, baby. Good night."

"Night," she said, and he kissed her on the cheek.

The next morning, Luke packed his small bag and got the truck ready for the drive to Tennessee.

"Promise me you won't drink and drive," Jen said. "It's quite a drive to come see you in the hospital if you have an accident."

"I promise I won't."

He took her in his arms and snuggled his face in her neck and hair, taking in the smell of her shampoo and body wash.

"And drive carefully, especially if you run into snow." The snow they'd gotten on Friday had already melted.

"Yes, ma'am. I will."

"I wish I could go with you," she said.

"Me, too. But I'll be home for good soon."

Chapter Forty-Five

Scarlett looked forward to every morning and every night when Jackson would come and be with her. They fooled around every night when he came at midnight, and he would change into his magnificent angelic self and wrap his wings around her like a downy soft comforter. One night he had to disappear quickly when Tyler woke up from a nightmare and came into the bedroom carrying Harry.

Jackson came back every morning at dawn and they would lie on her bed and watch the sunrise. Like clockwork, he would appear on her bed and the blinds would lift up magically so they could see the ocean. She had asked him one morning to move her bed so that it faced the ocean, which he did effortlessly. She watched in amazement as things moved around the room seemingly of their own volition. She understood now how he had helped her move into this house so quickly since he had superpowers.

They often talked about her afterlife. She wondered how a human could become an angel. When she'd asked him how that happened, he explained that she would be leaving her human body, that her spirit would ascend and that after that, she had several possibilities. She could stay in a human-like body in Eden – which she recently found out he was one of the guardians over – or she could become whatever kind of angel she wanted. She could also go back into the body of a human on earth again, if the circumstances were right. God – or Adonai, as he called him – had to approve everything, and Michael, the archangel, was second in line and ruled over all the angels. Jackson said she would go straight to Eden when she passed and from there make her final decision.

He wouldn't give any further details than that, saying, "Only angels can know about the hows and whereabouts, so if you decide to stay with your family in Eden, you cannot know these things."

"Are there other women who have changed into angels after passing over?" she'd asked him.

"Yes, there are several, but female humans who become angels are rare because women usually want to be with their families, so they stay in Eden. They are more sentimental. Those who do change, it's usually because they have found their SpiritMate or because they don't have strong human attachments. They crave something different.

On Monday morning after Valentine's, after Jackson disappeared to help a teenage girl, Scarlett drove through more falling snow to her lawyer's office to make out her will. Now that Luke had decided to take Tyler, she wanted to get everything settled.

Her lawyer was surprised to see her and sympathized with her fate.

"I am sorry beyond belief, Scarlett," he said. He stood up from his squeaky brown leather chair and walked around the antique desk to give her a hug.

She accepted the hug briefly and then gently pushed him away. She didn't want to start crying.

He sat back down and started clicking away on his laptop, pulling up files and asking questions. She had already gone over all of these things with Luke the day before.

She was giving the Pungo house to Luke, of course, on the stipulation that it remain in his possession until Tyler turned eighteen. If anything happened to Luke, it would be Jen's responsibility, and if anything happened to Tyler, it would be up to Luke and Jen what they wished to do with the house.

It was set up that Luke would be the primary caretaker of Tyler, with Jen being the back-up, and Cassie as third back-up. She would be leaving money in a fund for Tyler's college education and a trust fund set up for him that he would receive when he turns twenty-five. She also would leave money in another fund that would allow yearly withdrawals without penalty so that Luke could take Tyler to France to see his grandfather.

He printed everything out and she signed them all, and his secretary witnessed and notarized them.

That evening, she was exhausted mentally and physically and in a lot of pain. When Jackson appeared at midnight in her bed, she was in so much pain that when he gently caressed her arm, she was nearly in tears.

"Ma chérie, what's the matter?" he asked.

She rolled over so she could see him – in all his angel glory – and he immediately enveloped her in his arms and wings. She let the tears flow onto his bare chest.

"Are you hurting?" he asked. She could feel his sadness.

Yes, she said in her head. *In my back.*

He rubbed her back gently. "I'm sorry. It seems that you're getting metastasis into your back," he said, referring to the cancer.

He kissed her, held her gently, and sang songs to her. She'd never heard him sing before. He had a beautiful calming voice. It helped. Finally, the pain eased. She didn't know how, but it seemed that every time he was around her, the pain would go away, especially lately.

"Feeling better?" he asked.

She nodded, and he loosened his arms and wings a bit and they looked at each other.

"How do you do that?"

"It's because we are so close. We are connected, so I can help you feel better when we're together. Your endorphins release, which can be healing."

"It seems like you are able to heal me to a certain degree. Sometimes when you're not here, it hurts so bad, I wish you could take me early."

He sympathized with her. "I know, and I would, but then your time with Tyler would be cut short. You should make the best of it. I'll get Adeline to recommend something else for your pain. Maybe I could fly you to some hot springs. They have healing powers. The effects will help you feel better for a little while."

"That sounds wonderful," she said. "Would this be in Eden or some place a little closer?"

He smiled. "There are some in Virginia. Is that close enough for you?"

"That'll do," she said, smiling, but her eyelids drooped. "How soon can we go?" she asked, yawning.

"Another time. You're too tired tonight. Did you make all of your final arrangements today?"

"Mostly, yes. I haven't been to the funeral home yet." That was a depressing thing to do, and she kept putting it off.

"No rush. You can do it next week. Do one thing at a time." He pushed her hair off of her face, wiped her tears away, and kissed her cheek.

"I was thinking…" she started to say.

"Hmmm?" he asked.

"I would like to get Tyler a little statue of an angel. Could you get one for me? He already thinks I'm going to be an angel when I pass, so I'll let him continue to think that and leave him something to think of me by."

"Sure, I could get you one. How about this?" He instantly produced a figure in his hand. It was a ceramic off-white female angel with long flowing hair wearing a long billowy dress that gathered well below her feet. She looked like she was designed to rest on top of something, her big wide wings ready to take off at a moment's notice. "You put her on top of a doorframe," Jackson explained. "Isn't she pretty?"

"She's beautiful. He could put her above his bedroom doorframe."

"I'll also get a big tall female angel for your grave. Where do you want your earthly body to rest?"

"I want to be buried beside my mother on the grounds of my house in Pungo. There is a little corner of the yard that's sectioned off with a little white picket fence. Then Tyler could visit me any time he likes. That's one of the reasons I had Luke to agree to let Tyler live in the house until he is eighteen at least."

She could picture a big angel statue covered in vines, something like purple vinca that bloomed in the spring.

"Then you should tell Luke or Jen what you want to do, as well as Tyler."

She nodded and he put the small angel statue on the bedside table and then she snuggled back up against his warm chest.

"I know you want to spend all the time you can with Tyler, and you should, but it's also important to let him get to know Jen and the kids really well before your time is up. It would be a smoother transition for him that way, because it will be devastating to him if he doesn't have a good support system in place."

"Yes, I understand what you're saying." She yawned again.

He caressed her head. "Go to sleep, my love. I'll stay with you until you fall asleep."

The next morning, Jackson was there with his arms and wings wrapped around her when she awoke. "Did you stay all night?"

"No, I just got here a few minutes ago."

It was wonderful going to sleep and waking up in his arms. The shades in the room had already been pulled up. She must've been really tired.

"It's a good day to travel," he said, pointing to the orange ball coming up over the deep blue ocean water. There were no clouds obstructing the sun. "You want to go to the hot springs?"

"Right now?" She raised up higher on the pillows, which Jackson fluffed for her.

"Are you feeling up to it? I'll fly the whole way, and then we'll just soak in the water, like being in a hot tub."

It sounded heavenly, but she realized she couldn't leave Tyler alone in the house. "Who would stay with Tyler?"

"How would you like to meet his guardian?"

Her eyes opened wide. "I would, very much."

"Put this robe on and I'll be right back."

He disappeared for a moment while she pulled on her red silky robe, and he returned in his human form with a tall tan man with blonde wavy hair pulled back in a ponytail. He was wearing a red, black and white plaid shirt, boot-cut jeans, and cowboy boots on his feet.

Scarlett stood up to greet him.

"Scarlett, this is Jesse, Tyler's guardian," Jackson said.

"I'm so pleased to meet you," Scarlett said, reaching out to shake his hand.

"It's my pleasure, ma'am," Jesse said in a country drawl.

"He has an affinity for cowboys, as you can tell," Jackson said, smirking.

Scarlett smiled. "Then you should enjoy living with Luke soon. I guess you know that's Tyler's father. He's in the country music business, at least for right now."

Jesse nodded. "Yes, ma'am, I am aware of that. He's got his guardian doing overtime, as usual. He was hoping Luke would settle down after he married, but now he's in Nashville living life on the edge."

"I think he's going to come home and take care of Tyler after May. At least, that's what he says he's going to do. So…you'll take care of my boy? Not just today but when I have to go away?"

"Of course, absolutely. It's my pleasure."

"All right, then. Should I change clothes?" she asked Jackson.

"Sure. Put on easy clothes to pull on and off, like sweats. And wear a bathing suit under it unless you want to be nude."

She put on a one-piece turquoise bathing suit with an emerald green velvet top and pants over it, and Indian moccasin boots with fleece lining on her feet.

"I'm ready," she said when she came back out of the bathroom. Jesse was still there, and Jackson was back in his angel form, holding a big black cape lined with black downy feathers.

"What's this?" she asked.

"Something to wrap up in for the flight so you won't get cold. My wings will be busy."

He wrapped it around her while Jesse opened the windows. Jackson gathered her up from behind and they took off out the window, over the ocean, and then turned west and rose high in the sky and across the fields and houses, higher until it looked like she was in an airplane. She had to close her eyes to keep from being so scared.

"I've got you, don't worry," Jackson murmured in her ear.

"Won't people see us?" she worried.

"Nah. I look like a big bird of prey when I'm up this high."

Finally they started getting closer to the ground again, and they landed softly among some tall trees in the mountains. Jackson changed back into his human form, picked her up, and carried her down the mountain.

"I don't want you to be tired, but I had to change forms where no one could see me."

"I understand. I love how you care for me. Are you sure you're not my guardian?"

He smiled. "I'm sure."

They stopped halfway down the mountain at a small natural pool that had steam coming off of it. The air around them was chilly in the thirties, but at least it was sunny.

"This is our own private pool not many people know about," he said. "I knew you would only want to be here for a short time, away from Tyler, and this way we don't have to pay or stay in the hotel that runs the big pool houses."

They both stripped down to their bathing suits – he wore a pair of orange board shorts – and got into the shallow pool up to their necks, sitting on a big smooth rock. It was so warm and relaxing. Scarlett immediately felt better. Black birds, black-capped chickadees, and cardinals chirped and flitted about in the trees around them. It was so peaceful.

"How long can we stay here?" she asked.

"About half an hour. Tyler will be up soon."

She leaned against his chest and felt the little bubbles of the mineral water making her muscles, joints, and bones feel better. All of her pain was literally gone while she was soaking.

"I feel wonderful," she said. "How long will these effects last?"

"A while." He kissed her temple. "Maybe a few days."

When it was time to go, they got out back into the cold air, and Jackson immediately wrapped her up in the cloak. "The feathers will help dry you off quickly," he explained.

She was dry in no time, and then she put her clothes and shoes back on and he wrapped the cloak around her again. He carried her back up the mountain, and then changed back to his angel form, and they flew home, just in the nick of time before Tyler came bouncing into her bedroom.

Chapter Forty-Six

In mid-March, Skyler picked Cassie up at her house and then drove back to his house. Since he had his own car now, he figured Cassie could tell when it was him versus the dark angel coming to visit. He didn't think the dark angel would be able to just pick up Skyler's keys and drive his car away. He kept them in his pocket at all times, just in case, except when he slept at night.

He told his dad about Cassie's condition the night before while they were washing the dishes. His mom had already gone upstairs to help Danielle with her homework. He told his dad the whole story about the dark angel posing as him, having sex with Cassie, and now she was pregnant. He took it surprisingly well, maybe because he had been an angel before and had gotten Juliet pregnant.

"Does she think it was you?" his dad had asked him.

"At first, yes. We had a pretty weird conversation the next day after it happened. Now she knows it was a dark angel. Dad, she remembers everything about me being an angel, about Jackson being an angel of death, about you, all of it."

His dad had been shocked. "She remembers? And she wasn't punished? Or maybe the pregnancy is the punishment."

Skyler frowned. "I don't think so. How could having a baby be a punishment?"

"Well, anyway, what are you going to do about it?"

"We're keeping it. I want to marry her. I know we're young, but it's part of her, you know?"

"Of course. Has she seen a doctor? Can she even see a doctor? I really don't know what Juliet did."

"We found a doctor who is half-angel, half-human who's been coming to see her once a month. We have our third visit tomorrow. We've been meeting at Scarlett's beach house. Apparently she knows all about Jackson, too."

"I'm glad you found someone to help Cassie. When is she due?"

"May."

His eyebrows shot up. "So soon? I thought you said this happened in December."

"It did. The thing is, well, do you know if mom had a short pregnancy?"

"Short, as in was he born premature?"

"No, did the baby grow fast? Cassie's is growing at twice the normal rate."

"Oh. I don't know. I wasn't around, and I had married Jen for a while before I knew your mom was even pregnant. I suppose she could have."

"Do you think we could ask her? Could we tell her about Cassie? She really would like to talk to someone who has been through this special kind of pregnancy before, besides Adeline."

His dad frowned. "I do not want to get into this whole angel thing with your mom. She doesn't remember any of that, remember?"

"Um, yes, she does."

"What?"

"Cassie said she didn't want you to be worried about more punishments. You haven't been, have you?"

"No, but…" Brad shook his head. "She's known all this time?"

"Yes. I just found out recently that she knew. Cassie has known since the night of her dad's wedding."

Brad sighed. "She's good at keeping secrets. So we have to tell her then?"

"If we don't, she'll think I was a bad boy."

"That's true. Okay, I guess we do this. What about this dark angel? Has he tried to hurt Cassie? Has he been back to see her?"

"No, he hasn't tried to hurt her that I know of. Yes, he came back to see that she was pregnant. She said he seemed happy about that and then lied to her about being me and saying that I was really Grant."

"Hmm, he sounds crafty. We need to keep him away from Cassie and the baby. What precautions are you taking?"

"Now that I'm driving, I'm picking her up every time we get together. Before that, she was having someone drive her over here. I don't think he would pretend to be me here in my own house, would he?"

"I don't know. That's another good reason to tell your mother about all of this, so she can be on her guard."

"Yeah." Skyler finished drying and putting away the last dish and said, "I feel cheated, you know?"

"Because the baby's not yours?"

Skyler nodded. "It's not fair. She's pregnant and I still haven't had sex yet. I missed out."

"It is unfortunate. But you love her, don't you?"

"More than anything."

"Then you'll get your chance."

"I also want to get a ring for Cassie. Would mom have one I could give her?"

"Maybe. What's Cassie going to do about school?"

"She's already being home schooled."

"We'll talk to your mom about it soon."

Now it was the next day, and they were all going to tell his mom about the dark angel and Cassie's pregnancy. Skyler helped Cassie out of the car and they walked into the house together. The smell of spaghetti and garlic bread hit their nostrils. His mom was cooking a big Saturday lunch for them.

When they walked in the door, his mom was in the dining room to the left of the foyer putting plates out on the table.

"Hey, guys," she said, smiling. While Skyler closed the door, his mother exclaimed, "Cassie! Are you pregnant?"

Cassie looked shocked. "Yes," she said meekly.

"Skyler! I can't believe this. Have you learned nothing from what your father and I did?" She covered her mouth. "I mean, getting your girlfriend pregnant when you're not married. When did his happen?" She walked around the table and joined them in the foyer. She folded her arms across her waist.

"I didn't get her pregnant mom," Skyler said. "If you'll just let me explain…"

"Cassie! How could you do that to Skyler?" Juliet scolded.

"It was a dark angel," Cassie said calmly.

Juliet stopped talking.

"Cassie," Skyler said. This conversation was not going at all like he'd hoped.

Skyler's dad, who had slipped up behind them unknowingly, groaned loudly.

"What did you say?" his mom asked. She looked scared and worried at the same time.

"A dark angel came to me and had sex with me, but he looked exactly like Skyler," Cassie said. "I thought I was having sex with Skyler." She bowed her head down in shame.

"Oh, Cassie," Juliet said. She looked at Brad.

"What are you thinking, Juliet?" Skyler's dad asked. "I know that you still remember about angels."

"You do?"

Brad nodded. "Skyler told me last night. Don't be mad at Cassie for telling Skyler. She felt that under the circumstances, we all needed to know what we're dealing with."

"A dark angel?" Juliet asked, looking at Cassie again.

"Afraid so," Cassie said. "At least that's what Jackson told us."

"Jackson!" Juliet rolled her eyes. "Let me go check on the sauce and then we'll all sit down and talk about this. Danielle is over at a friend's house, so we can talk freely. She does not know about any of this, and I don't want her to know, is that understood?" She looked at each one of them. "As far as she knows, she has two normal human parents, and that's all she needs to know."

They all agreed.

Cassie helped Juliet carry some of the dishes into the dining room from the kitchen, and they all sat down to eat. She'd had been mortified at the whole previous scene, watching Juliet judge her and Skyler about this pregnancy. It was so embarrassing to tell your boyfriend's mother that you thought you had had sex with her son, but actually it turned out to be a whole different creature.

She wouldn't have told her, but she felt like she needed someone to talk to about this whole experience, someone who had been through it before. Another human who had a half-angel baby. She only saw Adeline once a month – this afternoon would be the third visit – and that wasn't enough. She had so many questions. She could ask Jen some of them, but not the ones about how quickly she was progressing. Cassie wanted someone she could talk to about all of this angel stuff. She could talk to Scarlett, but she didn't know Scarlett as well as she did Juliet. This whole angel world was new to Scarlett anyway.

"So," Juliet said, ladling spaghetti noodles into her plate. "Tell me what happened. None of the gory details, but you know what I mean," she said, looking at Cassie.

Cassie told her how she got pregnant and about the conversations they'd had with Jackson, who thought it could be either an incubus or an angel of darkness. "He's leaning more towards dark angel. He says they like to play pranks on humans and that they can hide from the angels of death and distract guardians," Cassie said.

Juliet looked fearful. "I've heard Brad talk about them. Very scary guys, aren't they?"

Brad nodded his head. "They are. We had a hard time controlling them sometimes." He looked at Skyler, who nodded.

"So what are you going to do? Are you getting care?" Juliet asked.

Cassie told her about Adeline.

"That's good. I wish I'd had someone like that."

"Was your pregnancy quick? Did the baby grow fast?" Cassie asked.

Juliet nodded, swallowing a bite of garlic bread. "Yes, about half the normal time. I had no clue what was going on and why it was going by so fast. You look like you're about halfway thru, five months or so for a regular pregnancy."

"Yes, Adeline said I'm due in May."

"When you first walked in, I thought you had gotten pregnant while Skyler was still an angel. That's how far along you look to me. That's why I thought…well, at first I thought you had a half-angel by Skyler."

"I swear, that didn't happen, Mom," Skyler said.

She smiled at him. "I believe you."

"We wondered if he could actually be Grant," Skyler said. "Jackson said he became an angel of death after he passed over."

"No," Juliet gasped, clutching her heart.

"I'm not sure if I was supposed to tell you that or not," Skyler said, looking at her sadly. Cassie knew he felt inadequate for a son sometimes, as if Juliet would have rather raised the son she bore.

"I'm sorry," Juliet said quickly. "It's just shocking. Why do you both believe Jackson on this? He's never been the most reliable source."

"He's changed," Skyler said.

Cassie nodded. "I think Scarlett has changed him. He seems to be telling the truth. He's not snarky or sarcastic like he used to be."

"That would be a good thing," Juliet said. "When do you go see this angel doctor again?"

"This afternoon," Cassie said.

"Could I go with you?" Juliet looked at both of them.

"Sure," Cassie said. "That'd be great."

"I'd like to meet her."

Chapter Forty-Seven

Cassie held Skyler's hands as they walked up onto Scarlett's front porch, Juliet right behind them. Cassie was glad she was taking an active part in this whole pregnancy thing, but she couldn't tell what her motive was for coming to meet the doctor, if it was for curiosity's sake or if she really cared about what happened to Cassie. Maybe a little of both. They heard Harry barking behind the door.

Jackson let them in, and they greeted Harry. Cassie noticed that Juliet bristled upon seeing Jackson.

"Juliet…it's been a while," Jackson said.

"It has," she said stiffly.

"I take it that you're here because the kids told you what's been going on with the dark angel?"

"Yes, they told me. I wanted to meet the doctor."

"Of course, you would be curious since you went through the same sort of pregnancy."

"You look different," Juliet said. "Older."

Jackson nodded. "Yes, I have taken on an older appearance now, for Scarlett. Have you met her?"

He moved out of the way so that they could see Scarlett over in the family room, lying on the couch.

"Yes, I met her at Christmas," Juliet said.

They all greeted Scarlett and asked how she was doing.

"Tired," she said, smiling weakly.

Adeline walked inside from the back deck. "Hello, I see everybody's here." She hugged Cassie, then Skyler, and then looked at Juliet. "And who might you be?"

"I'm Juliet, Skyler's mom." They shook hands.

"Pleased to meet you," Adeline said. "I'm Dr. Adeline Brelane, but you can call me Adeline." She looked at Cassie. "I brought a hand-held ultrasound machine that hooks into my smart phone. I think you're really going to like this." She walked towards Scarlett's bedroom. "You can go ahead and get undressed and put that gown on over there. It has an opening right at the abdomen so we can do the ultrasound. We'll join you shortly."

Cassie obeyed her, went into the bedroom and changed her clothes, and then Adeline, Skyler and Juliet came in and gathered around her on the bed.

Adeline opened up her bag and pulled out a light blue and white instrument that looked like a microphone for children. It had a long cord on it that Adeline hooked into her phone and opened up an app, which showed a blank screen. Adeline pulled apart the Velcro at the opening on Cassie's gown and then got out some cold jelly and rubbed it over her abdomen. She shivered. Adeline then ran the wand over her belly while holding the phone in the other hand. She focused in on the baby and showed all of them on the phone. The baby was still little, but you could definitely see that it had a distinct head and body. Cassie had tears in her eyes. She squeezed Skyler's hand, wishing for all the world it was his.

"It looks like it's a girl," Adeline announced. "You did want to know what the sex was, didn't you?"

Cassie laughed. "Yes, that's fine. A girl?"

"Yes, and if I'm not mistaken…hang on." She moved the wand around some more, on what Cassie couldn't tell, maybe her back. "Cassie, I think this baby is going to have wings."

"Wings?" Her eyes widened. "What does that mean?"

"It means you can't deliver in a hospital. I'll have to deliver it privately, maybe in a friend's office. When it's close to your time, I'll come to town early. This is going to be a special baby. It's highly unusual for a human to give birth to a being with wings. I've never seen anything like it."

"Can the baby hurt Cassie, since it's part dark angel?" Juliet asked.

"I don't think so," Adeline said. "It's still very small. You might get sore and have some back pain in the next month, Cassie. With the baby growing so fast, you'll gain weight in your abdomen a lot quicker than a usual pregnancy."

"Yes, that happened to me, too," Juliet said. "I still have the stretch marks to prove it."

"You delivered a half-angel?" Adeline asked.

"Yes. My husband was my guardian when I conceived."

"Oh." Adeline looked back at Cassie, took a picture with her cell phone of the ultrasound, and then wiped the jelly off. "You can get dressed now," she said, putting her things away in her bag, "and we'll meet back out there so we can talk. I'll send you a picture of your baby, too. Your angel baby." She smiled reassuringly at Cassie and squeezed her arm.

Cassie got dressed again and went back to the family room. She sat next to Skyler on the love seat, Jackson, Scarlett, and Adeline were on the couch, and Juliet sat in a chair.

Juliet asked, "How can we protect Cassie from this dark angel?"

"I recommend that she not be alone at night," Jackson said.

"When are you getting married?" Scarlett asked Cassie.

"In April when everything is in bloom," she said.

"That's good. Then you'll have Skyler with you at night," Jackson said.

"I think you should do it sooner," Juliet said. "You could come and live with us. We'll all protect you."

Cassie didn't like Juliet telling her what to do. She felt like she was being forced into something. "I feel safe at home," she insisted. The dark angel or whatever he was had never tried to hurt her.

"Well, even if you do feel safe at home, your parents know nothing about this dark angel or what kind of baby you have inside of you. Your dad is in Nashville, so you don't even have a big strong man to protect you. No offense to Logan," Juliet said.

"She has a point," Skyler said.

"I want to wait until my dad can come and see us get married. He gets the weekend of April 9 off."

"Where are you going to have the wedding, Cassie?" Scarlett asked.

Cassie was glad for the change in subject. "I don't know," she said.

"Would you like to be married here on the beach? You can use this house," Scarlett offered.

Cassie looked out the window, wishing she could get married out on the beach like her dad and Jen did, how romantic that was, but there was no way she was going to do that on a public beach where any one of her friends from school could happen upon them and see that she was pregnant. "No," she said. "It's too public in my condition." She looked down at her belly.

"You can't just go to the Justice of the Peace," Juliet interjected. "That's not very romantic."

"You're welcome to have the wedding in the gardens at my house in Pungo," Scarlett said, again coming to her rescue from Juliet's pushiness. "It'll soon be your house anyway."

Cassie looked at her sadly, realizing she meant after she passed on.

"Seriously, the gardens are beautiful in April with all the dogwood trees blooming, the cherry trees, and the azaleas. You could be married at the gazebo or in the formal French garden on the other side of the property. I didn't show that to you guys the last time we were there. I was too tired that day. The garden is full of rose bushes, big heavy urns, white trellises, and even a water fountain. It would be a beautiful place to get married."

It did sound beautiful. Cassie thought about all the white blooms on the Bradford pear trees she saw on the drive over here and thought about how pretty it would be for the other spring flowers. She was still unsure, though.

"It'll be completely private," Scarlett said. "At least think about it. Go over there and check it out sometime."

"That sounds like a good idea," Juliet said. "A beautiful private place to get married. But it's up to you, of course."

Cassie felt a little better. It did sound like a romantic place to marry the love of her life. "What do you think, Skyler?"

"Whatever you want is fine with me," he said.

She grinned at his answer.

"If you don't have any more questions for me, I need to be going," Adeline said. She stood up.

No one said anything, not even Juliet.

"It was a pleasure meeting you," Adeline said to Juliet, shaking her hand.

Adeline hugged Cassie and said, "Don't worry too much. Keep it simple. You and the baby should be fine. I'll see you in a month. Maybe you'll be married by then."

Married. Cassie still wasn't used to the idea yet. She would need at least a couple of weeks to get used to the idea. She still didn't know where they would live, but she was leaning towards living in her own house where she felt the most comfortable. She thought that even though Juliet was nice, she would just make her feel uncomfortable. Ask too many question, give too many suggestions, and well, she just wasn't family. Even if her own family knew nothing about angels, Cassie still felt more comfortable living with them, and that's what she was going to try and talk Skyler into doing.

Adeline left, and Juliet said she needed to get back home, too. Cassie thought, here she goes again, telling them what to do and when to do it, since they drove together.

"Before you leave, I just wanted to say that at the next meeting, we need to come up with a plan," Jackson said. "I suspect the dark angel is going to try and take your baby, Cassie, but we can fight him."

Cassie felt a cold chill over her body. She would not let him take her baby away. She would do whatever she had to in order to keep him away from her, even if she had to give up her own life for her baby. *Her.* She was having a daughter…with wings. That sounded heavenly. She wondered what they could name her.

"I want to fight, too," Skyler said.

"No, Skyler," Cassie said. "I want you to stay safe. This baby girl will need you if something happens to me."

"Not on your life, Cassie. I'm not going to stay away. You and the baby are my life, and I will be there to protect you both in whatever way I can."

Chapter Forty-Eight

"Touring is so amazing, Jen." It was Easter Sunday night, and Jen was FaceTiming with Luke. "Singing and playing my guitar, something I love doing, and all these people are cheering for me, interested in everything I do and say, hanging on every word. It's intoxicating. A good kind of intoxication."

Jen started worrying that he might be changing his mind about continuing a music career. "Are you having second thoughts, Luke? Because you've got me all excited for you to be home and now you want to keep touring. Can you stop changing your mind back and forth?" She felt heat rise into her face. "Are you planning to live there by yourself? Or on a tour bus? I don't want to live in Scarlett's big house without you."

His smile disappeared. "I'm not changing my mind. It's just…" He sighed. "I just wanted to share some of my excitement with you. I'm sorry if that upsets you."

She felt bad. "No, I'm the one who's sorry. I just panicked for a minute. You should feel like you can share anything with me without worrying if it's going to upset me. I'm sorry."

He smiled again. "It's also okay for you to tell me how you feel about anything I do or say, so you're forgiven."

She smiled again. "Good."

He laughed out loud.

"What's so funny?" she asked.

"Nothing. I've just missed arguing with you."

She laughed.

"I'm coming back home in May, I promise."

"Okay, good. I called Bridget the other day to invite her to eat supper with Maggie and me. You know what she said?"

"What?"

"She said, 'No, I don't, Jen. I'm a little pissed off right now. Your husband is trying to mess it up for the rest of us. Why does he want to quit the band now? Nobody quits when they're just starting to get famous.' I was appalled."

"I'm sorry, Jen. I didn't know she was mad," Luke said.

"I told her I was sorry that she felt that way, that you wanted to be home with me and the kids. She said, 'You know what I think? You've got him wrapped around your little finger and you don't want to take care of that little boy by yourself so you're manipulating him so he'll come home. But you know what? Derek and I are moving to Nashville. We're going to make it in this business. Without Luke.' I told her, 'Good, I hope you do. I hope Derek becomes famous.' I tried to be calm and control my temper, and not say something I would regret. I didn't want to get you in trouble with Derek."

Luke made a noise of disgust. "Derek told me he wanted to stay in Nashville. He said he was going to talk to Bridget about it. I guess they made their decision. I'm sorry she fussed at you. You didn't deserve that tongue-lashing. I'm the one who deserved it."

"It's okay. I took one for the team." She grinned at him. "On a better subject, Cassie and Skyler decided to get married at Scarlett's house in Pungo. I still can't believe we're going to be living in that big house."

"Me either. I feel guilty about it."

"Me, too, but Scarlett is so nice about it. I drove out with Cassie, Skyler, and Juliet the other day to see it again, and there's this beautiful garden on the other side of the house that we didn't see the last time we were there. Cassie fell in love with it. It covers a big area and goes all the way to the back of the yard where a little graveyard is behind a white picket fence where Scarlett's mother is buried. Cassie called her and said she would love to be married there, and Scarlett said she was going to get her gardener to come and make sure it looks perfect before the wedding. She's also going to get her old housekeeper to clean up the house for the wedding in case we want to spend the night. She said Cassie and Skyler are welcome to stay in her beach house for their wedding night if they wanted to. Isn't that nice?"

"She's too nice."

"Are you sorry you didn't have more than a one-night stand with her?" Jen teased.

He laughed. "No, of course not, but that is one one-night stand I don't regret."

"Luke! If you were here, I'd smack you for that."

"Come on, look at that house. Plus, we get Tyler."

"You lucked out, for sure."

"You mean you did."

She laughed. "I miss you."

"I miss you more. I miss your stories, I miss your hugs, your kisses…"

There was a knock on Jen's bedroom door. "Come in," she called out.

Cassie poked her head in the room. "Are you talking to Dad?"

"Yes. It's Cassie," she said to Luke.

She walked forward a little. "Can I talk to him for a minute?"

"Sure sweetie." She patted the bed beside her and Cassie got up on the bed with her. Jen handed her the iPad.

"Dad, are you sure you'll be here April 9?"

"I'm sure. Two weeks from now, right?"

"Right. Can you give me away?"

"Sure, baby, much as I hate the way that sounds. You'll always be my little girl."

"Aw, dad. I'm not going anywhere, it's just a formality for the wedding."

"Skyler is a good boy. It will be my honor."

"Thanks. We're having it at Scarlett's house in Pungo. Wait until you see the gardens, Daddy. Very formal and the flowers and trees are starting to bloom."

"Sounds nice. I'm sure it will be real special."

"And private," Cassie said. Jen knew that was very important to her. "The day we went over there to see it, Skyler pulled out a beautiful diamond ring that his mother gave him and he proposed to me officially. He was so romantic." She lifted up her hand to show him the ring.

"Aw, that's sweet. You seem really happy. Are you?"

"Yes, Daddy, I am."

"I'm glad. That's all I've ever wanted."

"Guess what? Brad has offered to have a treehouse built for me on the property, the same guy who built theirs. It would give me a place to write if I wanted to. I still want to do that, like Grandma Evie."

"What a great idea. I told you about the treehouse I went to here in Nashville, didn't I?"

"Yeah, you did. With a bathroom and everything?"

"Yeah. You think Brad's friend would be able to do something like that?"

"Are you trying to take over my treehouse when it isn't even built yet? This is something Brad wanted to do for me, a wedding present," Cassie said. She was grinning at her dad.

Luke laughed. "Sorry, baby. It sounds great, bathroom or not."

"Okay. I'm going to bed now. See you in two weeks."

"Night, baby."

That week, Skyler wanted to get the gardens fixed up himself instead of Scarlett hiring a gardener. He asked Logan and Jackson to help him. So every day after school, they pulled weeds, pruned some trees, and added fresh mulch to the flowerbeds. Jackson came for about an hour each day and performed a little magic when Logan wasn't looking. He also added a big statue of a female angel in the graveyard.

"That's for Scarlett," he explained. "She wanted it for Tyler."

Skyler wouldn't let Cassie do anything but sit and watch. So she watched the birds, squirrels and rabbits, as well as the guys working hard, and sometimes offering unsolicited advice on extra things she thought they needed to do. She especially enjoyed watching Skyler when he took off his shirt, wearing nothing but his tattoo on his upper body. She was looking forward to their wedding night. She tried not to think about how her first experience had been with the dark angel but focus on Skyler and their love, and she knew it would be just wonderful between them. She did worry about her big belly protruding and how that would affect things. She also felt self-conscious about him seeing her new stretch marks.

She hadn't heard any more from the dark angel and was glad of it.

Emily came over one day and sat in the gazebo with her, and they talked about boys and babies.

"I can't believe you're getting married and having a baby," Emily said. "Do you remember what we were doing this time last year?"

Cassie didn't. "No, what?"

"I don't either." Emily laughed. "We were too high to think straight about anything. Look how far we've come."

She was right. They had changed a lot in the past year – for the better.

"How are things with you and Logan?" Cassie asked.

"Good, but we're not talking about marriage or babies yet."

Cassie laughed. "That's good. Enjoy your youth while you can."

"Do you regret having sex and getting pregnant?"

Cassie thought about that. Emily had no idea about the angel stuff going on, so she had to be careful what she said. "No. I honestly love Skyler with all my heart, so I'm glad I had sex." That much was true. "The pregnancy, of course, was an unexpected result, but it's not her fault. She's innocent in all of this."

"That's true. This time next year when you celebrate your one-year anniversary, she'll probably be walking and helping with the mulch."

Cassie laughed. "You're probably right." Or she might be flying in the trees with the birds, Cassie thought.

Chapter Forty-Nine

Cassie woke up with the sunrise two weeks later on her wedding day. She smiled and rubbed her belly.

"Today's our wedding day, baby," she said out loud. She'd embraced being pregnant, of having a being inside of her to take care of, one with tiny angel wings, and she'd begun talking to her like she was already with her in person.

"Do you think Daddy is as excited as we are?" She felt a little funny calling Skyler the baby's dad, but he would soon be her husband, so everything that was hers would also be his, including the baby.

The baby kicked at her hand, seemingly in response. Cassie laughed.

She stretched her arms overhead and sat up. The sun was shining, and when she got out of bed, she looked up in the sky and didn't see a single cloud anywhere. "Thank you, God," she whispered. She'd prayed every day since she decided to have an outdoor wedding that it would be a pretty day.

Jen insisted that they have a big tent set up just in case, where they could dance and sit at tables and eat for the reception. Cassie had helped as much as Skyler and her family would let her, stringing lights in the tent, putting tablecloths and candles on all the tables. Jen said she would get fresh flowers from the garden to put on all the tables that morning.

They had all spent the night at Scarlett's big house – Cassie, her dad, Jen, and Logan. Cassie had wanted Skyler to spend the night in his own room, too (there were plenty in this house), but Jen insisted it was bad luck for the groom to see the bride before the wedding, so he spent his last night of bachelorhood at his family's house. Scarlett's former housekeeper Blanche had spent the night in her old room in the big house after cleaning and cooking food for the reception. She had promised to cook Cassie a nice breakfast, too. Catrina was supposed to be bringing a strawberry-and-rose layered wedding cake. Cassie couldn't wait to see it.

She heard a knock on the door. "Come in," she called.

The door opened, and Jen came in carrying a tray of food. "Happy wedding day," she said, all smiles.

"Aw, thank you. You didn't have to bring that up to me."

"I know, but you're supposed to be spoiled on your wedding day." Jen sat the tray down on the bed and gave Cassie a hug.

"Okay, but I have to go to the bathroom first."

When she returned, she hopped back up on the high bed and ate her plate of eggs, bacon, and pancakes with strawberries and whipped cream on top.

"You can have the rest of the whipped cream for tonight, if you want it," Jen said and then started laughing.

"Jen!" Cassie was so embarrassed, she turned beet red.

"How's the baby doing this morning?"

"She's already awake," Cassie said.

"I'm going to go pick the flowers, and then I'll come back and help you get dressed," Jen said, picking up the empty tray.

"Okay, thanks."

The wedding was going to be at noon. They would have the ceremony, then eating and dancing, and then Skyler and Cassie would go to Scarlett's house for their wedding night by the ocean. Cassie couldn't wait. She just wasn't going to discuss it with her stepmom.

She took a shower and washed her hair, and by the time she was blowing it dry, Jen was back. She was wearing a light mauve dress covered in lace with long wispy sleeves. She helped Cassie curl her hair while Cassie put make-up on, and then Jen helped her into her own wedding gown. That was the "something borrowed." Jen had altered the dress so that the waistline was higher to accommodate Cassie's growing belly.

Emily soon joined them wearing a deep fuchsia calf-length dress. She was going to be her maid of honor and Logan would be Skyler's best man.

"Are Pops and Evie coming?" Cassie asked. The last she had heard, they were planning to come, but one of their mares had a baby the day before, so her Pops wanted to make sure mom and baby were okay before leaving Georgia.

"Yes, they are. They left at three in the morning, so they should make it by the ceremony, or at least the reception."

"Good. What about Mimi and Papa Greg?" she asked while Emily painted her fingernails a sparkly white color.

"They're on the way, too. Sarah called and said she was coming with her family, too."

"Great."

By the time Cassie was finished getting ready, it was a quarter to twelve, so they went downstairs for the ceremony. Emily went outside while Cassie and Jen waited in the big kitchen. Cassie saw her dad walk over and come inside. He looked handsome in his black tux and white shirt.

"There you are..." He stopped midsentence. "My God, you're an angel."

She smiled and thought to herself, *No, I'm marrying my angel.* "Thank you, Daddy."

"We have something for you. Something blue." He pulled a necklace out of his pocket. It was a blue sapphire pendant hanging on a silver chain. He showed it to her. "It was your mother's, and her grandmother's before that. So technically, it's something blue *and* something old."

"It's beautiful!" she said.

"Jen and I went through your mother's jewelry last night, and she thought you would like this one."

"Your dad has kept all of your mom's jewelry in a box inside a box all these years and forgot about it," Jen said. "I told him last night that you needed something for your wedding from Josie so she could be right here with you, in spirit, to see you get married. She would've loved to have been here for this."

"I love it. Thank you both." She hugged Jen and then her dad, and he clasped the necklace around her neck. He kissed her cheek and took her by the arm. "Are you ready?"

She nodded. "Yes, I'm ready."

"Take a deep breath and enjoy it all. Take your time," Jen said. "I'll see you out there." She kissed her cheek and went outside onto the back patio, and then disappeared into the bushes.

Cassie and her dad followed, and a moment later, the music started. Logan had brought an electronic keyboard outside and was playing Bruno Mars's song, "Just the Way You Are." Cassie started humming it, and then heard Logan start singing the lyrics. She didn't even know he could sing. He sounded great! He must've inherited that talent from their dad. She listened to the words and could hear Skyler singing those words to her, telling her how beautiful she was. He also had a beautiful voice – at least he did as an angel. She hadn't heard him sing since he became human, she just realized.

They walked slowly into the formal rose garden past big tall urns with carved angels filled with little purple flowers spilling out. In the courtyard area were manicured bushes as well as pink, yellow, and red tulips blooming in each corner. Above their heads, dogwood trees of pink and white reached the sky. A water fountain bubbled in the middle of a courtyard area, emptying out into a small pool. Cassie looked beyond the courtyard to a long path of stone pavers covered overhead by a long white trellis. Rose bushes flanked both sides, not blooming yet, but there were some fuchsia azaleas blooming nearby. At the end of the trellis stood Reed, the pastor at the church Skyler and his family attended, the same one who married her dad and Jen. Beside him was Skyler, who looked so handsome in his black and white tux, she got tears in her eyes. She saw all her family and Skyler's in the chairs that had been placed to the right of the path.

She walked towards the love of her life. He was smiling and smirking at her at the same time, like he knew a private joke. She wondered what he was thinking.

Her dad gave her away and Logan joined them at the front. She joined hands with Skyler and was surprised at how cold his were. She looked at their hands and then smelled the ocean. She looked into his eyes and thought, *Oh God. I can't do this.* He smiled at her reassuringly.

When the pastor asked if anyone objected to their union, Cassie quickly looked at him and said, "I do."

Everyone around them gasped, and Skyler looked surprised, confused.

"If we could just have a moment, please." She pulled him back through the garden, past many shocked faces, and into the house.

"What did you do with Skyler?" she shouted in the empty kitchen.

"What's wrong, Cassie? I *am* Skyler."

"No, you're not. How dare you come here and try to mess with me on my wedding day!"

"You're just having wedding jitters. Come on, let's go get married."

Before she could say anything, he pulled her hard against him and kissed her lips. Then he reached down and rubbed her abdomen where the baby was, and Cassie felt the baby kick at his hand. He laughed and then disappeared before her eyes. Her eyes widened when she saw another Skyler walk across the patio and into the house. This one looked a little disheveled, his hair messed up, and had grass on his clothes.

"Cassie! Jackson told me where you were," he said, looking anxious. "Are you okay?"

"Skyler? Is it really you?"

"It's me." He pulled his jacket halfway off and unbuttoned his shirt to show her his tattoo.

"Oh, Skyler. The dark angel was just here." She had tears in her eyes and she felt herself begin to tremble.

He pulled her into his arms and looked down at her. "What did he do to you?"

"He kissed me and touched by belly. On my wedding day," she cried.

"I'm sorry, Cassie. I can't believe he would have the nerve with all these people here. I went to the bathroom alone and came back outside and walked through the garden, taking it all in, anticipating seeing you. That's when I was struck in the back of the head. I just came to a moment ago – over there in the bushes on that side of the house."

"Turn around," she said.

He had blood on the back of his head.

"Skyler, you're bleeding. Let's go to the bathroom and put some water on it."

They got to the bathroom and she found some paper towels, got them wet and dabbed the back of his head. He made a noise of pain. "Sorry," she said softly.

"I didn't miss the ceremony, did I? You didn't marry him, did you?"

"No. It had just started. The pastor said, do you object, and I did. I knew it wasn't you. His fingers were as cold as ice, and he smelled different."

"I'm so sorry, Cassie. It was foolish of me to go off by myself like that. I didn't think about him doing anything to me. He makes me so mad!"

"Don't worry about it," she said. She finished washing his head, found a Band-Aid to put over the cut, and smoothed his hair over it to hide it. "It's all my fault." She started shaking again, and he turned around and faced her. "I almost married him, Skyler. What would he have done to me? Kidnapped me? Taken me off into the sky?" She felt tears, and he took her in his arms again.

"I won't leave you alone again, I promise. I'll even go to the bathroom with you." She laughed lightly against his tux. "I'm serious. After this ceremony, I'll be your husband." She looked up at him. "And I can stay with you constantly until the baby is born. I'll do anything to keep you and the baby safe."

"I can keep you safe, too," she said.

He kissed her and wiped her eyes. Then he got a paper towel wet and said, "Hold still. Your eye makeup is running down your face." He threw the paper towel away and said, "There. You're perfect again." He looked down at her necklace, her dress. "You're so beautiful, Cassie," he said softly. "You're the angel now."

She smiled and wiped the corner of her eye.

"Come on, let's go get married," he said.

They walked back out together through the garden and down the aisle arm in arm. Logan had been playing music, and he got up and followed them down the aisle. Everyone got quiet again and watched the couple closely.

Cassie apologized to the pastor. "I'm ready now." Now that she had the right groom.

She looked over at her dad who looked confused, but she reassured him with a smile and a thumbs-up.

And this time no one objected to them being joined together.

Chapter Fifty

Cassie and Skyler greeted the guests after the ceremony while standing by the fountain in the formal garden. "Somewhere Over the Rainbow" by Iz from Hawaii was playing from an iHome. It was Cassie's favorite version because it was just Iz and his ukulele, something she loved to play. The words meant a lot to her, too…wishing on a star and dreams coming true…her wishes and dreams had come true by marrying Skyler this day.

All of her grandparents were there and greeted them enthusiastically. Jen had already told them her condition before they came so they wouldn't be shocked. Cassie felt a little awkward and dreaded judgment from them, but they were all very gracious. Her cousin Sarah, Tori, Jason, and Grayson were there, and Scarlett sat with Jackson. She looked like she was having a good day.

"I'm so happy I got to see this," Scarlett said when she hugged her.

"Did you notice the visitor we had earlier?" Cassie asked Jackson when he hugged her.

He nodded. "I figured it out when you pulled him down the aisle. I found Skyler and told him where you were."

"Thank you for that."

Maggie and Steve were also there. Steve had flown home with Luke. Maggie's pregnancy was going well, and she looked about the same size as Cassie. They had their picture made together with their baby bumps showing.

After more pictures under the trellis, by the tulips, the azaleas, and the fountain, they all went to the big tent where food was being served by

Blanche and her daughter. Cassie's stomach growled looking at all the good food: fried chicken, spinach salad, finger sandwiches, and best of all, a mashed potato bar – that was the best idea Cassie had heard of and wanted to have it at her reception. It started with mashed potatoes and then you could add whatever you wanted to on top of that – cheese, bacon, onions, gravy, basil pesto, chives, corn, fried onion straws, guacamole, chopped ham, salsa, and even wasabi. It was served in a martini glass.

Catrina's strawberry and roses cake was beautiful and delicious. It was a three-tiered white lattice cake covered with cascading deep pink roses – both real and iced – from the top to the bottom along with green leaves – also both real and iced. The inside was a layered butter cake with a strawberry cream filling in the middle, complete with strawberry slices. It tasted as good as it looked.

After eating and drinking some sparkling cider for the young adults, champagne for the adults, it was time to dance on the makeshift dance floor on the other half of the tent. Cassie and Skyler danced the first dance, which started out as a slow song and ended up in a forties number. They swing-danced just like they did at her dad's wedding, just like they did for the first time in her bedroom one night when he told her that he'd had a previous client who was a dancer in the forties.

The others joined in on the dancing after that, and Cassie and Skyler just slow danced so Cassie could recover from the swing dancing. She made sure some of the songs that meant a lot to her and Skyler were played for the reception, including *Starlight* by Muse and *Just The Way You Are* by Billy Joel. Skyler sang the lyrics to the Billy Joel song, just like he did in the car that day many months ago. He'd been a complete mystery to her then, but she'd already known that she was falling in love with him.

"You still have your beautiful angelic voice, I see," she said to him.

He smiled. "Yeah, but I have to practice now."

"Will you sing with me later? I wanted to play the ukulele on a song."

"Of course. I'd love to. Will I know the lyrics?"

"I think so. It's a popular song on the radio."

Her dad played guitar and sang a couple of his love songs while Logan played the keyboard. Cassie sat down at hers and Skyler's special decorated table close to a big azalea bush while Skyler went to get them some water to drink. While he was gone, Cassie's grandmas both came over and talked to her about the baby.

"When are you due?" Mimi Connie asked her.

"The first week of May."

"I heard it was a girl. What are you going to name her?" Evie asked.

"We've been talking about Madison, Davina, or Arielle, or maybe a combination of two of those."

"Those are pretty names," Evie said. "How's the homeschooling going?"

"It's not bad. I miss my friends, but I seem to be able to finish the day quicker and have more free time.

"That's good," Mimi said. "Because after the baby comes, all your free time will be taken up." She and Evie both laughed.

"Yeah, if I were you, I'd try to finish up the whole year before the baby is born," Evie said.

"That's what my teacher said, too."

"Who's been teaching you?" Mimi asked.

"A lady that Jen knows, Melissa Townsend."

Her Pops also came over and talked to her about horses and the big house they would be inheriting.

"This is a mighty fine house," he said. "I hate to hear how you'll be inheriting it." He looked over at Scarlett, "But you'll have plenty of room for horses, won't you?"

"Yes, and Skyler's dad has a friend who is building us a treehouse."

"A treehouse? That sounds like fun for the baby, in a few years, of course."

"It's for me initially. I'm going to be writing in there, just like Evie does."

"Well, isn't that something! Did you tell Evie that?"

Cassie shook her head. Pops brought Evie back over and they talked about treehouses and writing. Evie said she liked the idea of a treehouse to write in, and she asked Pops if he would build her one, too.

"Now, you've done it," he said to Cassie. "You've got me in trouble. I'll have to start working on it as soon as we get back to Georgia." They all laughed.

Skyler came over then and asked if she was ready to do her song. She nodded and went inside to get her ukulele. She came back out and started playing *Sweet Pea* by Amos Lee, and Skyler started singing once he recognized what it… "Sweet pea, apple of my eye…you're the only reason I keep on coming home." They finished the song and sat back down at their table and she realized he would be coming home to her now. They would live together from here on out. Her heart swelled with joy and longing.

After a second helping of a glass from the mashed potato bar and another piece of cake for Cassie, the day turned into twilight, and Skyler whispered in her ear that it was time to go. She looked over at him and smiled. "I think you're right," she agreed. She was excited for the honeymoon.

Scarlett invited any of the guests to spend the night if they wanted to. She and Tyler would be there, as well as Cassie's dad, Jen, and Logan. Scarlett insisted there was plenty of room and that Blanche and her daughter would also be staying to cook breakfast for everyone in the morning. So all the grandparents decided to stay the night, too.

Cassie and Skyler said good-bye to everyone and Scarlett handed them the keys to the beach house.

"I even brought Harry here so you won't have to worry about taking him out to do his business," Scarlett told them.

Harry came bouncing out of the crate she'd brought and greeted everyone before peeing by one of the azaleas.

Cassie and Skyler went inside to change into something more comfortable, and then they walked to Skyler's car while being pelted with birdseed. The car had a Just Married banner across the back and wedding bells painted on the back windows. White bells and streamers trailed behind them as they drove off.

They found a buffet of food and drinks waiting for them in Scarlett's kitchen, with a note to enjoy that and more from the fridge and freezer. Chips and dip, popcorn, crackers, sliced French bread, doughnuts, homemade croissants, iced cookies, and a big bowl of fruit including apples, oranges and bananas were on the bar. The fridge was filled with grapes, different kinds of cheeses, deli meat for sandwiches, jalapeño pepper jelly and cream cheese to eat with crackers, and bottles of water. The freezer had different kinds of ice cream as well as frozen waffles and pancakes to pop into the toaster for breakfast.

"How lucky are we?" Cassie said. "We don't even have to cook for ourselves."

"Are you hungry?" Skyler asked her.

"Not for food," she said, grinning.

He grabbed her hand and they took off towards the bedroom and saw a big fluffy white comforter with red rose petals strewn across it. Beside the bed was a wine bucket on a tall stand filled with ice around a bottle of sparkling cider. Two wine glasses were on a side table.

They both looked at each other.

"Maybe later," Skyler said.

"Yeah," Cassie agreed.

They both started undressing quickly. Cassie started humming the words, *this is going to be the best day of my life* and started laughing. She was so happy. She had worried earlier about comparing this experience with her first one, with the dark angel, but she was determined to put that out of her head. She didn't want to be disappointed or disappointing to Skyler. She looked at Skyler's naked body with the tattoo on his arm and realized this is the angel she loved before, the man she loved now, and he was now her husband. As long as they both lived, they would have each other to do this with again and again. She was certain that her first experience with the dark one would eventually become a blur in her memory. She would pretend that this was their first time, since it was Skyler's first time anyway.

"God, Cassie. You're gorgeous."

She looked down at her belly. "You think so? Even with this?"

"Especially with that. You're positively glowing, and you're carrying a life inside of you. How miraculous is that? Angels can't do that, you know."

She nodded. She remembered that he'd told her before that guardian angels didn't get married or have babies.

He stepped close to her and rubbed his hand over the baby in her abdomen, then leaned over and kissed it. He stood up and caressed her arms, looked down at her breasts.

"I'm all yours," she whispered, "to do with as you wish."

His eyes burned with passion and he pulled her into his arms and kissed her with as much passion as he ever had. As any being ever had. "I've waited so long for this," he said. His hands caressed and explored everywhere on her body, starting at her shoulders, caressing her breasts, then he suckled them. They felt so engorged and he was so aggressive, she was surprised he didn't get any milk out. It tingled inside of her all the way down to her toes. She'd not felt that during her first experience. It was way better this time.

He picked her up and placed her on the bed in the middle of the rose petals, and then stretched out beside her. They kissed again urgently, and his hands roamed down to her nether regions and explored until she was burning, until she released with a climax. She cried out to him with pleasure. When it was over, she was sweating behind her knees and pulled her hair up away from her shoulders, spread it out onto the pillow behind her. She smiled at him dreamily, and he kissed her nipples. After she caught her breath, she said, "Come here, it's your turn."

"I'm already enjoying this immensely," he said. "More than I dreamed I would."

"Honey, you ain't seen nothing yet," she said, smiling.

She kissed and licked his chest and abs, and pleasured him until he said to stop, that he wanted to finish inside of her. She pushed him onto his back, and he cried out a little from the pain in his head.

"Oh, I'm sorry. I forgot."

"If that dark angel thought he was going to mess me up for my honeymoon, he was crazy."

"You're right, he is. There's an easy way around this," Cassie said. "You can be on top."

"Won't that hurt the baby?"

She shook her head and leaned back, pulling him onto her.

He entered her, and they both experienced so much pleasure, Cassie knew it wouldn't take long to climax.

"I love you, Cassie," he said, and he continued saying it as they made sweet love to each other, reminding her of what he'd said before, that when he made love to her, she would know he loved her because he would say it to her the whole time. He cried out then, and she was so pleased that he had reached his peak for the first time. She got tears in her eyes.

He collapsed on top of her and then quickly got back up, remembering the baby.

"No worries," she said, smiling, squeezing his back.

He rolled onto his side anyway, and she turned sideways against him, resting her arm over his waist and crossed one leg over his. "I will never forget this moment, our first time."

"Me either," he said. "This is worth becoming human for. This…with you. I know I could have done it as an angel, but…"

She interrupted him, "No, you couldn't. You are good. You always have been, and I love you for it."

She kissed him, and he said, "I'm glad I waited. It was so much better than I dreamed it would be."

"And we have the rest of our lives to practice it," she said, smiling.

"Yes, we do. Maybe a few more times tonight?"

"Yes," she said, her eyes widening with surprise and then pleasure.

"I just need a little break first."

"Of course," she said. "Thank you for marrying me and wanting to take care of a baby that doesn't belong to you."

"I know it still bothers you, but if he looked like me when you conceived, surely the baby will be like me, too."

"That's a good point." One she hadn't thought about. "But she has wings already. That part is not like you – not anymore."

"I'm sure I will love her just the same. Have we decided on a name yet?" He caressed her hip.

"I definitely want Arielle to be in her name," she said. Arielle was the female version of Ariel, which had been Skyler's middle name when he was a guardian angel. The name meant angel of protection, as well as lion or lioness of God, and one website said it meant angel of nature. "I don't know why, but it feels right. Mostly because it was your name," she said. "And now that we know she has wings, I think it's even more appropriate."

"I agree with that one. What about the other name? Is it going to be Madison or Davina?"

Madison meant gift of God, and Davina mean beloved, according to an angel name website they had looked at.

"I'm not sure about Madison," she said. "I'm sure she will be a gift, but the way I conceived her doesn't seem like a gift. I like to think more that she will be loved, so I'm leaning more towards Davina."

"I agree. I like Davina."

"Arielle Davina, then?"

"I think so. A beloved angel of nature. That sounds right," he said.

"It does."

She kissed him and he slid down and kissed her belly. "Did you hear that, baby girl? Your name's going to be Arielle Davina Garrett. What do you think?"

The baby kicked and moved in such a way that they could see something move across Cassie's belly.

"Whoa!" Skyler said. "What was that?"

"I don't know. An arm or something?"

"That's awesome! Has she done that before?"

"No, this is the first. I mean, I've felt her kick before, but nothing like this. That was unreal."

"I think she likes her name," he said.

"I think she likes her daddy's voice."

He looked at her and smiled. "I am going to be a daddy, aren't I?"

"Darn right, and you're going to help me change diapers and feed her and everything."

"I am?"

She nodded. "You are."

He smiled. "I will be happy to." He scooted back up and put his head back on the pillow beside her again. "So where will we be doing this baby changing, on the short term? My parents' house or yours?"

"I would like to live with mine," she said.

"My parents have the bigger house until Scarlett…"

"Right, but I am pregnant, and I'm speaking for two people when I say I want to be comfortable, and I am comfortable in the house I've half-lived in since I was six years old."

His eyes got big while she was talking, and then he laughed lightly. "Okay, you win. I don't want to argue on our honeymoon."

She smiled. "Good."

He pushed a strand of her golden blonde hair behind her ear and said, "I meant it when I said I'm not leaving you. Not until after the baby is born. I'm not taking any more chances on him coming near you."

"What about school?"

"I'll get homeschooled like you."

"You'd do that for me?"

"Of course I would. We're married now, so there's no reason we have to be apart. We'll be together every night from now on. Like I said earlier,

I'll go to the bathroom with you and we can take showers or baths together, all of it. I'm all in. You're not getting rid of me now."

She answered him with a kiss, which turned into lovemaking session number two.

They got up afterward and had a midnight snack, and then fell asleep in each other's arms; and the next morning, they shared their first ocean sunrise together as husband and wife.

Chapter Fifty-One

Scarlett woke up the next morning in her big old house. She stretched and glanced over and saw Jackson lying beside her on top of the covers, in human form. She missed seeing Raph, but she guessed he didn't want to be in that form because of all the other people in the house.

"Morning, beautiful," he said.

She smiled. "Morning." She leaned over and kissed him.

"How does it feel to be in your old house again?"

"It's nice. I missed the gardens, but this house is much too big for me. I get tired going up all those stairs. It has some good memories but also some sad ones. I'll be glad to get back to my beach house, honestly."

There was a knock on her bedroom door. "Yes?"

"Pardon me, Miss Scarlett, but there's someone here to see you," Blanche said on the other side of the door.

"Who is it?"

"You'll have to come and find out," Blanche said. Scarlett could've sworn she heard her giggle.

"What in the world?" she asked Jackson.

"Don't ask me. I can't see through walls. At least not in this form."

She got up and went to her private bathroom, and then went to the closet to find some clothes to put on. She found some things she'd forgotten about and was excited to wear again, although they fit a little looser since she'd lost some weight. She picked out some black pants, a soft pink short-sleeved shirt and a matching long-sleeved sweater in the same color.

"You're losing more weight, aren't you?" Jackson said, startling her.

"What are you doing sneaking up on me like that?" She swatted him with the sweater that was in her hands.

"You seem to be feeling better, chérie."

"I am. I've had more energy for the past couple of days than I've had in a long time. Maybe it was the wedding getting me all excited." She put her clothes on while he watched, and the way he looked at her made her want to get undressed again. "Would you marry me, Jackson?"

"I would like nothing better."

"Maybe we could have a pretend ceremony on the beach one night."

"Maybe we will. We don't have time to talk about it right now, though. Let's go see who's here."

"I can't imagine who it would be. Nearly everyone I know is already here," she said.

When they got downstairs, the man she saw in the front parlor was not who she expected. She thought she'd never see him again on this earth.

"Papa! What are you doing here? How did you get here? Are you well?" She said all of this while rushing into his arms.

He laughed. "I am well, ma jolie fille. I flew here, of course."

"But you're not supposed to fly." She pulled away enough to look at him but kept her hands on his elbows.

"I couldn't bear the thought of never seeing you again on this earth. I had to come. Besides, I want to be close to my grandson. I don't want to only see him once a year. That's not enough. Life is short."

"Oh, Papa. He'll be so thrilled." She wiped away a falling tear. "Does that mean you're moving here?"

"Yes, I am."

Odette walked into the house, carrying a crate with Fleur inside.

"Odette, how did you let him talk you into moving over here?" Scarlett asked her.

"Once he made up his mind, there was no changing it," she said. The two women hugged. "I have no family left to hold me in France, and I've never been to America. He made it seem so glamorous, promising one big final adventure in our life."

Scarlett laughed. "I'm sure he did."

"I was paying the taxi driver," Odette explained.

"We would've been here sooner, but we had to update our passports and get everything in order," her papa said. He reached for Jackson, kissed his cheeks and said, "I'm glad to see you again, too."

"Same here," Jackson said.

"What are you doing here at this house?" her father asked. "And all of these other cars?"

"Luke's daughter Cassie got married yesterday. I invited Luke, Jen and their parents to spend the night. I don't know if they're up yet or not. They stayed up fairly late. I went to bed at midnight." She looked over at Jackson, thinking of their midnight rendezvous while hearing voices and laughter deep in other parts of the house.

"Ah, a wedding. How lovely. The garden is getting beautiful already, I bet."

"It is," Scarlett agreed. "You'll get to meet Luke and the rest of the family. I'm so glad. They're very nice people."

"I've been looking forward to it."

"He has," Odette added. "The whole plane ride over, he's talked of nothing else but meeting his new extended family. And about surprising you, of course."

"I worry they won't want to bother with this old French guy," André said.

"Oh, please. Who wouldn't love you?" Scarlett said. She hugged him again. "I can't believe you're really here. You're lucky I was even here."

"Odette reminded me that you didn't live here anymore, but I didn't know where the beach house was, so I asked the taxi driver to come here first, hoping someone would be here. Imagine my surprise when I saw all the cars. And Blanche is still here."

Scarlett nodded. "She came to help out for the wedding. Her daughter Jeanette is here, too."

Right on key, Blanche walked down the hall towards them and asked if they would like breakfast.

"That would be wonderful. Thanks, Blanche," Scarlett said.

"Give me ten minutes, and I'll have it ready. Most of it already is. I'll get the coffee going," Blanche said. She walked back towards the kitchen.

"Let's sit down," Scarlett said, sitting down on a beige-and-white striped Victorian sofa. Jackson sat beside her, and André and Odette sat in the chairs across the round table from them.

"How was the flight, Papa?" Scarlett asked.

"It was fine, fine. I know you are worried about my health, but I'm fine. I thought one flight across the ocean wouldn't kill me." He laughed.

"I kept my eye on him," Odette said, winking at Scarlett.

"That's good," Scarlett said. "Where will you live, Papa? I have already set up my will, giving this house to Luke and his family since they'll be taking care of Tyler."

"That's okay. I didn't want to live in a big old house anyway. I bought this house for your mother. She had quite expensive taste," he said, grinning.

"Sure, Papa. I would say it has a lot of your touch, as well."

"And you added your own, I see."

She looked around at a statue of a woman with long hair that stood on top of a pedestal over by the curved windows of the turret. "Yes, I did." She'd bought that after her mother passed, just a reminder of her beautiful mother, watching over her. She had a direct view of the front door from where she stood, so Scarlett thought she would like knowing who entered her house. It seemed silly to her now, knowing where her mother really was, but perhaps she was able to see what happened to Scarlett from time to time.

"I know a good real estate agent if you need one," Scarlett said. "Maggie. I met her through one of my co-workers from the insurance company I used to work for. She lives at the beach, too."

"You think we could get a beach house?" her father asked.

"I'm sure you could, but there is nothing close by to walk to, not like you had it in Toulon. How will you get around?"

"I'll get Odette to learn how to drive."

Odette laughed. "Oh, the adventures you get me into, mon chou."

"Have you ever driven before?" Scarlett asked her.

"Oh yes, when I was a youth, but not in the past twenty years." She laughed again. "I'll be fine. As long as I don't have to venture out too far."

"That's part of the adventure," André said, wiggling his eyebrows up and down. "Getting lost a few times won't kill us."

"It might in the wrong neighborhood," Scarlett said. She put her hand over her heart. "You're making my heart hurt with worry for you." She grinned at him, though, happy for his enthusiasm.

"I did used to live here, you know. I'll tell her where to go. I have not forgotten everything."

"All right, Papa."

"Breakfast is served," Blanche said, coming into the room.

They all ate breakfast in the big dining room. Luke, Jen, Logan, and the grandparents all came down two by two after Scarlett and the others sat down to eat. Scarlett introduced them all to her father and Odette.

When Tyler came down, he ran over to André and said, "Pépé, you're here! Everyone is here now! He jumped into his lap and gave him a big hug. "Can we all live in his big house together?"

Scarlett and her father both laughed.

"I don't know about everyone else," Jen's father Tom said, "but we have to go back to our house in Georgia today."

"And we have to go back to Tennessee," Luke's mother Connie said.

"Aww," a disappointed Tyler said. "Can you stay?" he asked his Pépé, eyes full of hope.

"As a matter of fact, I am moving to town to be close to you."

"Really? Ah, that's awesome!" Tyler said. He jumped down, reached for a croissant from the table, and started eating it.

"You'll have to help me find a beach house," André said.

"Sure. You'll love it. We can build sandcastles together! And learn how to surf!"

André laughed. "That will be some adventure, won't it?" He looked at Odette.

"Absolutely not," she said. "Not me."

André laughed again.

After eating breakfast, they went to the back of the house to sit and talk in the garden room. This room had two pristine white couches facing each other, a dark wood coffee table with a glass top, two walls of windows, a couple of other matching chairs and tables, and plants and trees all around the room. It was one of Scarlett's favorite rooms in the house. She and her mother used to sit in here and read and talk for hours.

They talked about the wedding and showed André and Odette some of the pictures and videos they had taken.

"She's a lovely young lady," André said.

"Thank you," Luke said. He took his phone back and looked at the time. Standing up, he said, "I'm afraid I'm going to have to get going. I've got to fly to New Orleans for a show tomorrow night." He shook André's hand. "It was an honor meeting you, and I look forward to getting to know you."

André stood up and gave him a hug. "The pleasure was all mine."

"I'll see you in about a month."

The others began to leave, as well, having flights to Georgia and Tennessee. Jen was going to drive them all to the airport, so she and Logan also left.

Jackson said he had to leave, too, so Scarlett walked him to the front door.

"I'm glad your father will be close to you now. What a surprise, huh?" he said.

"Yes, a wonderful surprise."

He took her in his arms, and they kissed before parting. "I'll see you tonight. Will you be here or at the beach house?"

"I think I'll spend another day or two here since my father is here. Then we'll have to get together with Maggie and find him a place on the beach."

"À tout à l'heure," he said. He walked out the door and disappeared before her eyes.

Chapter Fifty-Two

Two weeks later on a Friday night, Skyler followed Cassie to the bathroom again for the last time that night. The baby had gotten considerably bigger and so she had to go to the bathroom many times through the day and night. Jen interrupted him, though, on the way there.

"Skyler, would you be a dear and take this down to Logan?" She was carrying a tray of chicken soup, crackers, a glass of water, and a box of allergy medicine. "He's having a bad allergy attack and doesn't feel well. I'm waiting on Luke to call."

Cassie watched as Skyler turned and looked at her, not wanting to leave her alone.

"You two have to separate sometime," Jen said, laughing lightly.

Cassie guessed it must look weird to other people in the house, but Skyler didn't want to leave her alone even for a second. She nodded for him to go ahead.

He reluctantly took the tray and said, "Sure."

Cassie went on to the bathroom alone, relieved her bladder, and washed her hands. When she came back out, Skyler was standing there on the other side of the door, and he took her hand and walked back to the bedroom with her.

"See? Nothing happened," she said.

Once she closed the door, he pulled her to him and kissed her a little forcefully. She smiled, thinking he'd missed her in those few minutes they were apart, and he was feeling frisky. His hands moved from her back and down over her buttocks.

When she realized he smelled fishy, warning bells went off in her head. This was the dark angel. She broke off the kiss and pushed him back just as the bedroom door opened. Another Skyler walked into the room. She looked at him in shock, then back at the other one, wondering what was going to happen. They'd never seen each other before. Skyler quickly shut the door.

"Get away from her!" he said to the dark angel. He quickly put himself between Cassie and the angel. "I don't know who you are, but you have no claim over Cassie. She's my wife now. You can't do anything to her."

"Who do you think you are to challenge me?" He laughed an evil laugh. "I'm an angel while you're just a human now. You can't do anything to stop me from doing whatever I want to do with Cassie. That baby inside of her is mine."

"It's mine now," Skyler said. "She married me, and what's hers is mine. Her baby is my baby."

The dark angel pushed Skyler aside effortlessly and reached for Cassie. Skyler had fallen to the floor but got up on his knees quickly and pounced on the dark angel's legs to make him fall. He fell on top of Skyler and then rolled over, bringing Skyler with him, and then threw him up against the wall.

Cassie screamed, and the dark angel reached around and cupped his hand over her mouth to silence her. Cassie heard footsteps running down the hall and then Jen knocked on the door. "Is everything okay?"

The dark angel disappeared, and Cassie recovered herself and said, "Fine, sorry. I just saw a spider."

Jen said, "Okay. Must've been an awfully big spider!"

"It was! Skyler took care of it for me."

"Good. I'll see y'all in the morning."

"Night."

By this time, Skyler was on his feet and checking Cassie to see if she was hurt.

"I'm fine," she said, but she suddenly collapsed in his arms.

"Cassie!"

He picked her up and placed her gently on the bed, then lay beside her and caressed her hair.

"I'm okay, really. I think the shock of him being here and seeing him hurt you upset me. I had a big rush of adrenaline and then relief when he disappeared. I feel so tired now."

"No more helping Jen, I don't care what she says. I'll tell her what's going on before I leave you alone again."

She smiled. "I'm so proud of you for standing up to him."

"I didn't do a very good job, I'm afraid. I forgot how strong angels are." He rubbed the back of his head. I think he hurt my head again."

"After it just healed up?" she asked.

"Yeah."

She turned his head so she could kiss the back of it. "You stood up to him, told him off, stood your ground. I'm sure that doesn't happen to him very often."

"Maybe not, but he's getting bolder. When we go meet with Adeline and Jackson tomorrow, we need to tell them about this and come up with a plan. I don't think he'll stop until he takes you and the baby away."

"I think you're right."

The next afternoon, they met with Adeline again at Scarlett's beach house. Jackson wasn't there, but Scarlett said he would be there as soon as he could.

"He's with another client," Scarlett said, "who died suddenly in the ocean. Down the coast, not here."

Cassie was a little disappointed that he wasn't there. She wanted to come up with a plan for her baby.

Adeline hugged Cassie. "Hiyah, good to see you again. Before we get started, I just want to let you know that I cannot get away for a long-term visit like I had hoped. I have another client who is due in two weeks, and I have to help her out first. She's been throwing up her whole pregnancy, and she's really weak. She lives in Little Elm, Texas. After she delivers, I'll be able to come here for you."

"Okay," Cassie said. "We had another encounter with the dark angel."

"You did? What happened?"

Cassie told her and Scarlett what had happened, how bold he'd been coming into the house with other humans around, and how he fought with Skyler.

"Maybe we should take the baby a little early to throw the dark angel off," Adeline said. "What I can do is come next week, which would be a week before you're due, and we can do a C-section. I'll come here first and then go to Texas. I don't want to come earlier than the date of the procedure. That will give him time to plan. Hopefully if I steal away in the middle of the night, he won't pick up on it until after the baby is born."

"C-section?" The thought of being cut on made Cassie nervous.

"It's not as awful as it sounds, I promise. I can make an incision down in the bikini area, so you can still wear a one-piece bathing suit and it won't show."

"Won't it be too early to take the baby then?"

"You'll be far enough along that it will be fine. Women do this all the time. *I* have done this before, too. It will probably be for the best anyway since I spotted some little wing buds on her back."

Adeline brought out her hand-held sonogram again. "Would you like to take a look and see how much she's grown?"

"Could we?" Cassie was excited to see her baby.

"Sure. Let's go in the bedroom." She picked up her bag and headed toward the bedroom, then turned around. "You coming, Skyler?"

"Of course."

Cassie got undressed while Adeline got set up. She did an exam, and then turned on the sonogram and rubbed it over Cassie's belly.

"Oh look! She has little wings now," Adeline said

"Get out!" Cassie said, unbelieving.

"Yes. Do you see, Skyler?"

Skyler was speechless. "Oh my," he said finally.

Adeline laughed. "Isn't she the cutest? I've honestly never come across this before."

"Wow," Skyler said. "What are we going to do with a baby with angel wings? We won't be able to have her out in public. Ever." He might have been speechless a moment ago, but it was all coming out now. He was actually bringing up things she hadn't thought about before, things that were worrisome.

"Let's not worry about that right now," she said. She could picture a little naked baby with little wings on her back, lying in a bed of flowers like those pretty pictures she'd seen before. Now she'd have one of her very own. A little cherub. She couldn't wait to see her in person.

"You'll definitely want to have a C-section now," Adeline said. "I don't think it would be possible to pass those wings, if you get what I mean."

Cassie nodded. She did get it and the thought of it was painful.

"Could I ask Scarlett in to see?" Adeline asked. "I think she would love to see this."

"Sure, I don't mind," Cassie said.

Adeline opened the door and called her in. Jackson was still not there.

When Scarlett saw the baby's wings, she gasped. "Mon Dieu. She really is an angel, isn't she?"

Cassie smiled. "Yes, she really is."

"What are you going to name her?" Scarlett asked.

"Arielle. It means lioness of God and also angel of nature. Since she has those wings, it seems fitting."

"It does. That's beautiful," Scarlett said.

Adeline packed everything up while Skyler helped Cassie get dressed in the bathroom.

When they came out to the family room, Jackson was there.

"I hear the baby has wings," he said.

"Yeah. Wild, huh?" Cassie said.

"I also hear you had another encounter. Are you both okay?"

Cassie nodded. Scarlett must have already told him.

"What am I going to tell my stepmom Jen about delivering the baby?" Cassie asked Adeline. "Would it be possible for her to be here, too? I'm going to have to tell her and my dad eventually. I won't be able to hide her wings from them."

"I recommend you wait until after the baby is born. They might not believe you until they see her wings for themselves. Also, we don't know what the dark angel is going to do, so it's best to keep your stepmom safe. After Arielle is born and things are more settled, you can tell them the whole story. Is your dad still touring?"

"Yes. He'll be home Mother's Day weekend."

"Okay. Wait until he is back in town to tell him. Tell Jen and your half-brother first, after you bring the baby home. Your whole family is going to have to keep this a secret. Are you willing to keep this baby in hiding for most of her life?"

"Yes. She was created for a reason, and I'm willing to do whatever I have to in order to keep her safe."

"Okay, good. When she's young, you might be able to hide her wings under her clothes, but as she gets older, her wings will most likely grow, too. I need to find more like her so I can inform you better on what to expect."

"What will I tell my parents when they ask me about where the baby will be delivered?"

"Since we'll be doing it early, they don't have to know you're delivering until after it's over. Then you can explain that I had to deliver here at Scarlett's because of her having those angel wings. They'll understand when they see her." She picked up her bag. "I've got to go. I'll see you in a week – April 30. Be ready. Come here. Can your little boy spend the night somewhere, Scarlett?"

"Yes. My father has moved to town. He can spend the night with him."

"Perfect."

"I'll be here, too," Jackson said. "Just in case."

"Thank you," Cassie said. "I'll be ready."

Chapter Fifty-Three

Jackson fixed Scarlett another cup of raspberry tea with honey and brought it to her on the couch by the windows. She tried to sit up. She was barely able to do anything now. In the last week, she'd gone from having lots of energy to having none at all and she hurt all over. Jackson was there morning and night as usual and also came in the middle of the day for an hour. It was Saturday afternoon, and he'd come to make her some tea and sit with her.

She'd been thinking all day that she should move back to her Pungo house. Her father and Odette were still staying there as they hadn't found a beach house yet, and she would like to be close to them. They could help her with Tyler and maybe even Blanche could cook for them.

Jackson lifted her up from her supine position, sat down beside her and leaned her against him. He helped her take a drink of the hot sweet tea. It felt wonderful going down her throat. Despite it being nearly the first of May and quite warm, she was cold all the time. Hot tea and being next to Jackson always warmed her up.

"My time is drawing near, isn't it?" she asked him.

He didn't say anything, but she knew it was. She could feel it.

"I wish I could take you to the hot springs and make you feel better," he said. "Would you like me to draw you a bath? I could put in some of the salts and minerals that Adeline left for you the last time she was here."

"Maybe later. I've been thinking…I want to move back to my big house in Pungo." She had to clear her throat. It even hurt to talk sometimes.

"Oh, chère. If it's too difficult to talk, tell me in your thoughts."

She nodded. *Cassie will be coming late in the night to meet with Adeline, so I want to make sure we're all out of the house and out of the way so she can deliver. I'm worried my father will come over for some reason, right when the little angel baby is born.*

"I understand. That's a good idea. I'll do everything. When do you want to move?"

She shrugged her shoulders but then winced. That little movement caused her a lot of pain. Jackson gently rubbed her neck and shoulders and moved her hair aside to kiss her neck.

I wish I had the energy to love you…one more time.

"Shhh, no worries. We'll be together again and you won't be in any pain at all. Do you want some pain medicine?"

She shook her head. "Not yet," she said aloud. *Can we move now? Tyler will be home from school soon. If you could get all our things moved quickly, then he won't be around to see it when you do your magic. I know you don't want to do it the old-fashioned way, and you know I cannot.*

"Of course, mon amour. You just sit tight. I'll get it all moved for you."

"Leave the bed…for Cassie," she said. "And this couch for Skyler and Juliet."

"All right."

She watched him move like lightning all through the house, moving things back and forth instantly from the beach house to the Pungo house. Harry barked at him, wondering what he was doing. Scarlett called him to sit up in her lap, which he did. She held him while looking out the window at the rolling waves of the ocean on the other side of the dunes and regretted leaving such a beautiful place. She would do it, though, for sweet young Cassie. She had hoped to be present for the birth and see the little angel, but it made more sense for her to be out of the house altogether.

When Jackson was finished, he sat back down with her and wrapped his arms around her. The couch she was sitting on was the only thing left in the room.

Can you drive my car? When Tyler gets home? I do not have the energy.

"Yes, of course."

Tyler came in the door a few minutes later. "What's going on? Where is everything?" He picked up Harry and then walked over and hugged Scarlett. "Maman, are you feeling any better today?"

She looked into his hopeful eyes and hated that she was going to have to leave him soon. She shook her head. "Tyler, we're going back to our big house in Pungo, okay? Papa and Odette are still there and can stay with us. There is…plenty of room." She felt out of breath.

"Okay." He looked at Jackson. "Did you move everything all by yourself?"

"Sure did. I put all your things back in your old room."

"Can we go now? I want to see if you did a good job."

Jackson and Scarlett both laughed lightly.

Jackson drove them on the backroads to the other house while Scarlett called her father and told him what she was doing. He was concerned about her, naturally, but said he was glad they would all be living together.

"You want me to call Blanche?" he offered.

"Yes, please. That would be nice for Odette so she won't have to cook so much." Not that she would be eating much. She had no appetite at all. Tyler, on the other hand, ate as much as a horse.

When they arrived, Scarlett's father fussed over her and convinced her to stay in a downstairs bedroom so she wouldn't have to climb the stairs. It was the same bedroom her mother passed away in. She agreed, and Jackson moved some of her favorite things down into the room for her.

Later that night, she lay on a settee in the sitting area of the bedroom with her family and Blanche. Her father tried to keep the conversation light, and they watched comedies on TV. Tyler built things with his Legos on the floor by Scarlett.

Before too long, Tyler got sleepy and wanted to go to bed. He kissed his mother on the cheek and said sadly, "I'll be all alone upstairs by myself."

"You can sleep with me if you like," Scarlett offered.

He smiled and ran over to the bed and pulled down the covers. "Thanks, Maman."

"You need to actually sleep, though, okay? You've got soccer in the morning." Her father and Odette had already agreed to take him to his game.

Tyler yawned. "Okay."

Odette and Blanche both went upstairs, and Scarlett's father lingered. He turned the TV off and she turned on some classical music.

"You're hurting, aren't you, chérie?" he asked.

She nodded.

"Why do you not take something for the pain?"

"I don't want to be like a zombie," she said. "I want to be with…my loves." She gasped for air. It took such effort to talk or even to breathe. She had thought Jackson would be the one to care for her in the end, but it made more sense to be with the humans that she would be leaving behind, one last time. She would have eternity with Jackson, if she chose to be what he is. She was grateful she had moved back home and that her father had traveled all this way to be with her in these days. "Thank you for coming…to help take care of me."

"But of course. I wish I had come sooner," he said sadly. He reached over from his chair and squeezed her hand.

She smiled sadly. "You're here…now."

She awoke sometime later and her father was gone. Jackson sat in the chair instead. It had to be after midnight. The classical music was still playing but the light had been turned off, with only a soft nightlight shining in the room.

She reached for Jackson. Instead of simply holding her hand, he picked her up and took her into the adjoining bathroom. He sat her down on a vanity chair. He had already poured a bath for her in a nice big Jacuzzi tub by a big glass-bricked window. There were lit candles all over the bathroom, around the tub, on the counter by the sink, and in the linen shelves.

You want to take a bath, chérie? he asked her quietly, since Tyler was sleeping in her bedroom.

She nodded.

He carefully undressed her and then picked her up and placed her in the tub.

You too? she asked. *In all your glory?* She wanted him to be in his angel form.

He looked at the bathroom door, locked it, and changed into Raph, her beloved creature. He climbed into the tub behind her, his legs straddling her, and leaned her back against him. The tub was quite full with the two of them in there, and Scarlett was completely covered with water up to her neck. He turned on the Jacuzzi, and Scarlett closed her eyes, relaxing in the bubbly water.

Jackson caressed her belly, and she turned to look up at him, to kiss him. She could feel his manhood in the small of her back. She felt such longing and arousal for him, but she just didn't have the energy to do anything. He pulled her up closer to him while sliding down a little way so that she could rest her head right beside his, his arms and wings wrapped around her. She folded her legs up across his legs. He hummed a song for her, and as nestled and comfortable as she felt, she soon forgot about any pain.

What time do you go to be with Cassie? she asked him.

Three o'clock.

Tell Cassie where I am and why I didn't stay. Tell her to bring the baby here if she wants, once she is born. I will tell my father, and we can all help take care of her. She can get Jen and the rest of her family to come here, too.

You are such a generous woman.

It's purely selfish. I want as many people around me as possible. And I want to see that baby.

No, you're definitely not selfish. A selfish person would not give her home away. She would have sold it instead.

I wish you could stay the night with me, but Tyler…

You need to spend time with Tyler while you can.

She enjoyed a few more minutes with him, and then he told her it was nearly three.

I must have dozed.

I didn't want to wake you, but I must go help Cassie now.

Of course.

She opened her eyes and saw that all the candles had burned down except for a big one by the sink. She turned to give him one last kiss, and he picked her up, lifted her out of the tub and dried her off with a big thick towel that had been on a warming stand. He then dressed her, changed back to human form, and carried her to bed. He kissed her on the forehead and silently said, *Rest well, ma bichette.*

Chapter Fifty-Four

"Here's your pink teddy bear," Skyler said, handing Cassie her stuffed animal. It was the same one he'd given her when she was six years old after the car accident that killed her mother.

"Thanks," she whispered. They were packing things to take to Scarlett's beach house.

Tonight she would become a mother. For real.

Adeline told them to be ready to operate at three in the morning, so Cassie and Skyler had gone to sleep at seven and woke up at one. Well, she'd tried to sleep. It was hard. She worried about something going wrong. Any number of things could happen. They could be caught wandering around in the middle of the night and have to explain to Jen what they were doing. Cassie could have problems with anesthesia and start throwing up, or have back pain from the needle going in the wrong place. She could bleed out. The baby could rip her insides accidentally with her wings before Adeline could pull her out.

The baby could be a monster.

Worst of all, the dark angel could come and try to take it from her, or God forbid, kill the baby.

The whole time she tried to sleep, each of these thoughts entered her mind, one after the other.

"Here are your robe and house shoes," Skyler said, handing them to her. They were a gift from Jen in her favorite color, bright pink.

She put them in her overnight suitcase and zipped it up.

"I've got the phone chargers," he said.

They slipped out quietly to the car and pulled out of the driveway and down to the red light before turning the lights on. One worry down, a hundred to go.

"Are you ok?" Skyler asked, grabbing her hand and squeezing it.

She glanced at him. "Yeah."

"It'll be okay. I'll do my best to keep you safe. We all will."

"I know." She stared straight ahead as they traveled on the curvy road through the trees towards Sandbridge. "What if the anesthesia doesn't work and I can feel Adeline cutting on me?" she asked, her voice just above a whisper.

"She won't start cutting until she knows for sure you won't feel anything."

They passed by a quaint old church Cassie had always admired. "What if the baby is a dark angel instead of human? What if she is hideous or has black feathers all over her?"

"Cassie. I don't think that's possible. She will be part of you. She will look human. You've seen her on the ultrasounds. I didn't see any feathers except the ones on her back, did you?"

She shook her head slowly. "What if…*he* comes?"

"He won't."

"He might."

"I'll fight him as best I can. And so will Jackson."

"Did we bring the baby's first outfit?" she asked, thinking of it suddenly. She just wanted to get this all over with and hold a sweet little baby in her arms, no worries or problems.

"Yes, it was the first thing you packed."

Jen wanted to have a baby shower for her, and she was planning to do it this weekend, but Cassie talked her out of it, asking her to postpone it until the next weekend if possible. She couldn't tell her why; she just gave the excuse of waiting until her dad was home next weekend, Mother's Day weekend.

She would be a mother on Mother's Day. Hopefully.

They arrived to a dark house. No porch light or any lights on inside. Cassie started worrying. It was two o'clock, and they had an hour before Adeline was going to start operating.

They walked up to the porch and rang the doorbell. No one answered. Cassie wondered if Scarlett was okay. She'd looked pretty good the last time she saw her, more energetic. She hoped they had taken Tyler over to his grandfather's house as planned.

Something wasn't right.

"What's going on?" she asked worriedly.

"I'll call Adeline and see if she knows," Skyler said. He pulled out his phone and dialed a number. Cassie sat down in a rocking chair to wait.

He hung up the phone a few minutes later and said, "She's on her way. She said she didn't know why Scarlett wasn't coming to the door, but she had a spare key to the house."

"Okay."

He sat down beside her in another rocker and held her hand. Thankfully, it was a warm night. She felt the baby kick. She was ready to get this over with, too, it seemed.

Finally, Adeline came and let them in. She flicked on the overhead lights, and they were surprised by the lack of furniture in the house.

"What's going on?" Cassie asked.

"I don't know. Maybe Scarlett has passed on?" Adeline said.

"I don't think so. Someone would have told us. Jackson would have, at least."

"Maybe he knows. He's supposed to be here at three. He has fifteen minutes to get here."

Cassie walked into the bedroom, turned another overhead light and fan on, and saw a bed. "At least there's still a bed here," she said, relieved.

"Go ahead and get undressed and put this on for me," Adeline said, handing her a patient gown.

She went into the bathroom and did that. She looked in the mirror one last time at her reflection, thinking this would be the last time she looked at a girl's face. When she saw that face again in the mirror, she would be a woman, a mother.

When she came back out, Jackson was there in the room with Adeline and Skyler.

"Where's Scarlett?" she asked him.

"She wasn't feeling good and wanted to move back to her house in Pungo."

"Oh, good. I mean, I thought something might have happened to her," Cassie said.

"She sends her love and thoughts. She wants you to bring the baby to the big house after she's born to show her, and to stay there if you'd like. You, too," he said to Skyler, "as well as your family, Cassie."

"Okay. I can't think about that right now." She was too nervous to think about what they would do after the baby was born. She vaguely heard Adeline's garden music playing.

"Go ahead and lie down. I've got the anesthesia ready," Adeline instructed her. "I'm going to give you both regional anesthesia in the back and also general anesthesia so you can rest, okay?"

Cassie nodded. She got on the bed and stretched out. Skyler handed her the pink teddy bear. She grabbed it and held it against her tight with one of her hands. Adeline pulled a stretchy rubber tube around her arm and then put a needle into her arm at the elbow crease. She felt the cold fluid enter her veins. She took a deep breath and closed her eyes, felt Skyler's hand on her shoulder. She heard him whisper, "I love you," and then everything went black and silent.

When she woke up, she was groggy and disoriented. She rubbed her eyes and opened them.

"She's awake," Skyler said.

She heard a baby cry and realized it was her baby. Sitting up, she searched the room for her but couldn't find her.

"She's beautiful," Skyler said. "You won't believe how beautiful."

Cassie couldn't wait to see. Where was she?

Adeline came out of the bathroom holding a bundle wrapped in pink. She placed her gently into Cassie's lap, and she gasped. She was the most beautiful baby she'd ever seen. She was wearing the pink and white little onesie with flowers on it that Jen had bought, little pink booties on her feet, and the big pink blanket surrounding her. Her hair was brown and wet, her skin deep pink. Her closed eyes fluttered open, and she actually smiled at Cassie. She'd heard that if newborns smiled, it was just gas, but she didn't believe it.

"Hey there, Arielle," she said, tears filling her eyes. "Happy birthday." She kissed her forehead.

Arielle smiled again and made a cute noise with her mouth, which was puckered and shaped like a kiss. She was perfect. She turned her head then and began searching Cassie's chest for something, her mouth open.

"She wants to nurse," Adeline said.

She showed Cassie how to do it, and it only took a couple of tries for her to latch on. Cassie smiled at her success. It was painful, but she felt useful to be able to feed her own baby.

Skyler sat down beside her and put one arm around her and the other around Arielle.

"Where are her wings?" Cassie asked.

"They flatten out on her back so you can't see them at the moment. They're tucked away inside the blanket. When you change her diaper next, you can see them," Skyler said.

"How big are they?"

"About the size of my palm right now," he said.

"They'll grow bigger as she grows," Adeline said.

"Is Jackson still here?" Cassie wondered.

"No. He said he had to go," Skyler said. "He said Scarlett needed him."

"Okay," Cassie said. "Everything went well, then? No dark angel?"

"No. Everything was perfect," Skyler said.

"You will be sore from the incisions for a while, but the surgery went great, Cassie," Adeline said. "I'll stay here for a while in case you want to get some more sleep."

"No, I'm good for now." She looked down at Arielle and then up at Skyler. "I'm happy right where I am."

Juliet arrived at about the same time as when Arielle finished nursing. Skyler carefully picked her up and placed her in her grandma's arms. Juliet had tears. "She's so beautiful." She snuggled up against her face. "Are you doing okay?" she asked Cassie.

"Fine."

"Sorry I didn't come sooner, but I thought I'd just be in the way during surgery. I wanted to wait until she was born."

"What time is it?" Cassie asked.

"Five o'clock. Have you called Jen or your dad yet?" Juliet asked.

"Not yet, but I will," Cassie said. "I need to go to the bathroom."

Adeline helped her up, walked her to the bathroom, and then back to the bed when she was finished.

Juliet walked around the room with Arielle propped up against her shoulder to burp her.

Cassie decided to go ahead and call Jen. "Jen?" she asked when she answered.

"Why are you calling me Cassie? Are you not home?"

"No. I had the baby. You're officially a grandma."

Chapter Fifty-Five

Scarlett was in a deep sleep in the downstairs bedroom when a light flashed over her face. Jackson had talked her into taking a Morphine pill before he left so she could sleep through the night, so it was hard for her to wake up. Her eyes fluttered open and she saw Jackson's face. He was waving a flashlight above her, otherwise it was dark in the room.

She asked him in her head, *Jackson? What's wrong?*

No answer. Her eyes flew open wide and she panicked. It was the dark angel. Before she could think anything else, he lifted her limp body up in his arms and the room disappeared. They moved through space and time in darkness and then they were inside some small room with windows. She could hear distant waves. Where was she? She looked out the windows and saw the ocean far down below. They were up high somewhere.

She called out for Jackson in her head, *Jackson…Raph, I need you.*

The dark angel laid her out on the floor and leaned her up against something hard. She turned and saw that it was the old light in the center of the lookout room of the lighthouse. Why would he bring her here? Why would he even kidnap her to begin with?

She cleared her throat and tried to talk. "What do you want…with me?"

He still looked like Jackson. It aggravated her that he posed as him. "Ah, so you know it's not Raphael," he said. "And here I was ready to dance with you, maybe kiss you." The thought of doing that with him made her nauseous. Just being close to him made her nauseous, as it had before. "Ah, well," he continued, rubbing his hands together. "Let's get on with it then."

"What are you going to do…with me?"

"It's simple really. I'm using you to lure your boyfriend here. I need him to do something for me."

"What?" What would he need Jackson to do for him that he couldn't do himself? He could steal her away in the middle of the night and take her to another location in an instant, but he couldn't he do…whatever it was he wanted to do…by himself?

"You're new to this world of angels, so let me explain. I am an angel of death, but I cannot kill a human. Pretty ironic, isn't it? Actually, I'm not an angel of death anymore…I'm an angel of darkness. The power to kill humans was taken away from me because I supposedly abused my powers."

Scarlett's heart sank. What human did he want to kill? She was afraid to ask. Instead, she asked, "Who are you?"

"No one you know."

"You're the one who drugged me that day…pretending to be Jackson."

"Yes, that was me, but I didn't drug you. Maybe it's because of your illness that you feel…weakened around me."

"Raph is busy at the moment. He might not come." She hoped that he would, but she knew he was with Cassie, standing by in case he was needed while she delivered her baby. The baby. Did this dark angel want the baby? To kill it? She thought it would be better not to mention it, though, in case he wasn't aware that Cassie was delivering the baby right now. But how could he not know? He knew where to find her, so surely he knew where Cassie was.

"I'm betting he will do anything for you," he said. "You told me earlier that the two of you communicated to each other through your minds so I know you can contact him, if you haven't already."

"Maybe I have."

"I know he's been hanging around you a lot lately. Your time on this earth is drawing near an end."

"How would you know that?" she asked.

"I told you, I was an angel of death. You see, I've had this whole thing planned – the timing for everything had to be planned meticulously. It has all been boiling down to this moment. It all started with getting

Cassie used to me. I appeared in her dreams at first. I put a little spell on her so she would think she was sleeping, but I was really doing things to her. She thought she was dreaming. Then I started appearing to her in my animal form, to scare her a little bit. I wanted to make her have a reason to fall into my arms when I came to see her in human form. She did. Then we had sex, and that produced an heir. I knew that a half-human, half-angel would only take half the time of a human before it was born, so I planned it with the time of your death." Her eyes widened. "Yes, you will be dying very soon."

"What do you want with Cassie's baby?" she dared to ask.

"*My* baby. I have plans for her. As for your part, I appeared to you as Raphael to see how you responded. When I realized that you were weakened in body and also could communicate with him in your head, it made my plan even more perfect. I waited until the time my baby would be born, which happened to be close to the time when you would be at your weakest and you couldn't resist me. Like I said before, I need Jackson to do something for me, but I needed leverage."

He magically produced a lantern and lit it with the tip of his finger. "I have to go now, but I'll be back for you soon."

With that, he disappeared.

At Scarlett's beach house, Juliet was holding Arielle when Cassie came out of the bathroom.

Adeline was packing up to leave. "Are you feeling okay?" she asked.

"Fairly well, yes. A little sore and tired," Cassie said.

"That's natural. I left some herbs for you on the table. You can also take some Tylenol if you need something for pain, but remember that whatever you ingest, Arielle will ingest, so be careful. I left a list of foods you should avoid."

"Okay, thank you…for everything. It turned out beautifully."

"Yes, it did. Your little girl is very special. It's very rare for a half-human, half-angel to have wings, which means special things are in store for her. What was meant for evil has been turned into something good here." Cassie smiled, agreeing with her. "I'm going to take off now. Call me if you need anything."

"What about well-baby checks, shots and that sort of thing?" Juliet asked.

"I'll come back periodically for that. She will probably grow at a fast rate initially, so I will come once a month for a while. Then we'll play it by ear after that."

After Adeline left, Juliet changed the baby's diaper on the bed next to Cassie, and they both got their first look at Arielle's wings on her back. They were small, about the size of Cassie's palm, and pure white.

"Would you look at that?" Juliet said, smiling. "How adorable."

"She actually fluttered them a little bit when Adeline first pulled her out," Skyler said. "I was there for the whole thing."

Cassie reached for his hand and they watched Juliet change the baby's diaper. She instructed them on what to do. Arielle slept through the whole thing, so she didn't make a fuss or move her wings. Juliet then put a onesie on her backwards, leaving a space open where her wings were. She folded up her wings, wrapped her back up in a blanket, and placed her gently on Cassie's lap.

"You two should probably get some rest," she said to both Cassie and Skyler. "I'll stay up and keep a watch for anything."

Cassie scooted over and Skyler stretched out on the bed beside Arielle, keeping her in between the two of them. Cassie couldn't hold her eyes open for long and she drifted off to sleep.

Her eyes fluttered open not too long later when she heard arguing. She looked up and Arielle was still on the bed beside her, but Skyler was standing up arguing with the other Skyler, the dark angel.

He had come.

"Get out of here," Skyler said to him.

Cassie immediately put a protective arm around Arielle. "Stay away from my baby," she warned him.

Juliet came out of the adjoining bathroom. She froze when she saw the two Skylers. "What the…?"

"Mom?" the dark angel said. He seemed momentarily dumbfounded.

She looked from one Skyler to the other and then squinted her eyes at the dark angel. "Grant?"

Cassie gasped. So he *was* Grant! The human who died, became an angel of death, and then turned to become a dark angel.

He smiled. "That's right. Except I go by Samael now."

"What are you doing here?" Juliet asked.

"I came for the baby."

"You can't have her," Cassie said. "She's mine."

"She's mine, too. I am the one who impregnated you. Without me, you wouldn't even have a baby, and the two of you wouldn't be married."

"What do you want with a baby?" Skyler asked.

Grant became vehement towards Skyler. "Whatever I want. It doesn't concern you. You are my adversary. You took what was mine, and I want it back. Starting with the baby."

"What are you talking about?" Skyler asked. "What did I take that was yours?"

"My body. My life."

"That's absurd. You know I only replaced your body because you were going to die anyway. What difference did it make if I took over your earthly body? You had no more use for it."

Grant gave him a disgusted look. "I have an appointment with the dark angels. They want the baby."

"What do you mean by that?" Juliet asked.

"They can't have her," Cassie said.

Grant turned towards Cassie. "I made a deal with them. They get the baby, and I get…well, that doesn't matter right now." He looked down at Arielle and his face softened. "She is beautiful, isn't she? Look what we made together, Cassie."

As if in response, Arielle started crying. Cassie got scared. She pulled Arielle up into her lap and wrapped her arms tightly around her to soothe her as well as protect her. "I won't let you have her," she said softly but in a tone that let him know she meant business.

"If you come with me, Cassie, we could hide from the dark angels, raise this baby on our own. We'd have a cozy little family. We could be happy. I know you like me."

She shook her head. "No, I don't."

"It was me you fell in love with. My body. My face. You wouldn't have felt the same about *Skyler* without me."

She continued rocking Arielle in her arms and her cries faded. "No, you're wrong. It wouldn't have mattered what he looked like. Skyler has always been sweet and kind and good. He was my protector. All you ever wanted was sex. You don't love me so why would I go with you?"

"It's up to you, Cassie. Either you both come away with me or she goes to the dark angels. You have a choice."

Juliet tried to distract him. "The Grant I knew wouldn't have done this," she said. "He wouldn't have gone over to the dark side. What happened to you?"

Grant looked at his earthly mother. "I was mad. I wanted my life back again. I missed out on so much. Would you have me as your son again?"

"I would love to be your mother again," Juliet said, "but our time has gone. You have to accept what you are now. Go and join Jackson and turn yourself back around. I know there is good still inside of you. Don't do this to Cassie or the baby."

"I have to do this; it's the only way. The baby must be sacrificed."

Cassie was horrified. How could she protect Arielle? What could she do? There were three of them, but they were no match for Grant, unless…she suddenly remembered that Brad had given her some pepper spray a couple of months ago to protect herself with. She'd brought it to the beach house, just in case. It was in her purse, which was across the room. Maybe if she faked it, she could get it out of her purse. That would give them some time. Maybe Jackson would come back.

"Okay," she said. "I'll go with you." She stood up with Arielle in her arms.

"Cassie, no," Skyler said.

She couldn't tell him what she was planning so she didn't look at him. She just walked over to her purse. "Just let me get my purse." She bent over to pick it up, and while shifting Arielle, she put the purse on her shoulder and in the process, reached in and found the pepper spray.

"I'm so glad, Cassie," Grant said, smiling. "You won't regret it. We'll go away someplace where the angels can't find us. Someplace between heaven and earth…"

Before he could finish, Cassie walked right up to him and sprayed his eyes with the pepper spray.

He cried out and covered his eyes. "What did you do to me?" He backed away from her and instantly changed into the hideous creature she had seen in her backyard.

Cassie gasped and he lurched forward and grabbed Arielle from her arms. Skyler leaped at his legs but Grant spread his wings and kicked him into the bathroom. He raised one of his wings towards the window and it flung open. Arielle started crying again, tearing at Cassie's heart.

"No! Please!" Cassie pleaded. She reached towards her baby. "I'll come with you, honest. Don't take my baby away from me!"

He didn't say anything and she saw that his eyes were red and still watering from the pepper spray. Still clutching Arielle, he flew out of the room, out over the ocean and then disappeared.

Cassie blinked, not believing what just happened. She looked around for Skyler, and despite the pain in her stitches, she walked over to help him up. She could barely see because of all the tears filling up in her eyes.

"I'm sorry I couldn't stop him," Skyler said.

"I was too stunned to move," Juliet said.

"That was the way he looked when he scared me in the backyard," Cassie told them. "He took her from me." She was heartbroken.

Skyler stood up and helped her back in bed. "You should rest, Cassie. Don't worry. I promise to do whatever it takes to get Arielle back."

Chapter Fifty-Six

At the lighthouse, Scarlett heard from Jackson after the dark angel disappeared. *I'm coming.*

He arrived moments later in angel form and lifted her up into his arms. "How did you get here?"

The dark angel brought me here. He looked just like you.

"I just left Skyler and Cassie. She had the baby and everything turned out fine. The baby was a healthy girl with little wings on her back."

I'm so glad. She clutched his back, feeling the warmth of his body and his protection all over her.

"Are you okay?" he asked.

"I am now," she said hoarsely, looking up into his eyes.

A cloud of black smoke appeared in the lighthouse, and as it vanished, an ugly creature appeared which had a long beak, black feathers all over its body, black wings, and a body shaped like a bear. It stood on its hind legs and held a baby wrapped up in a pink blanket. She was crying and looked out of place in the clutches of such a creature. Scarlett reasoned that this was Cassie's baby.

"What do you want, Grant?" Raphael asked.

So that's who the dark angel was, Scarlett thought. Raphael gently leaned her back against the windows and stood up to face him.

Grant changed into human form again and laughed wickedly. "Hello, Raphael. So, you figured out who I am."

"How could I not, with you looking like Skyler?"

"You mean he looks like me! It was I who first looked this way. He took my life from me, my identity!"

"What did you care? You had the freedom of being any kind of angel you wanted. You could've become what your father was – a guardian, a good angel. At least in choosing to be an angel of death, you could fly, perform a little magic, see humans whenever you wanted to. What more could you possibly want?"

"My human life. My parents. My powers of healing. I was a special creature. Now I have made a special creature of my own." He looked down at Arielle, who was crying.

"What are you doing with Cassie's baby?"

"*My* baby. I am taking her to the dark angels. I made a deal with them."

"What kind of deal?"

"I was to kidnap the baby and bring her to them in exchange for becoming human again."

"How are they going to make you human again?"

"By taking my body back. Skyler has to die."

Scarlett gasped. So that was the human he wanted to kill.

"Why did you bring Scarlett here?" Raphael asked.

"I brought her here to make sure you would come. You're going to help me by killing Skyler since I'm not allowed to kill a human anymore. Otherwise, I'm going to take Scarlett early. She'll go with me and won't get to be your SpiritMate."

"You have no control over that," Raphael said, getting angry.

"I could take her with me and the baby to the dark angels. I'm sure they would find some use for her. She could help take care of the baby for them."

Scarlett started trembling in fear. She felt cold chills all over her body. *What can we do, Raph?*

Stay calm, Raphael told her. "All this trouble just to be human again?" he said to Grant. "A frail human? Skyler doesn't have the powers you had as a half-angel. It wouldn't be the same."

"The dark angels said they would give it all back to me."

"They don't have that kind of power," Raphael said.

"They have more power than you think."

"I can't believe you didn't learn your lesson when you were reprimanded by the angels of death. There are rules you have to abide by. You can't do whatever you want."

Grant made a noise of disgust. "That's why I left the angels of death. They wouldn't give me my human life back and reprimanded me for killing my first assignment. He was going to die anyway, what did it matter?"

"That's not how it works."

"I even tried killing Skyler myself but I only ended up making myself sick."

"The dark angels are deceiving you. They cannot give you your powers back."

"We'll see. At least I'll have my body back. So, let's get going. Let's go get Skyler. I'm sure he's pissed you off at some point."

"No. I won't do it. You must stop this. Leave these humans alone and accept who you are."

"Never!"

Grant rushed over towards Scarlett and picked her up with his other arm. She screamed in pain at his touch. She looked over at Arielle and knew they had to do something or the baby would be lost forever from Cassie and Skyler. *How can I help?* she asked Raphael.

"Let go of Scarlett and the baby," Raphael said. He pulled out a long sword and threatened Grant with it, poising it over his head.

Grant laughed. "Go ahead and swing. Maybe you'll hit your girlfriend. Or the baby angel. The dark angels would be pissed if you did that. You'd have hell to pay."

"You're the one who's going to pay."

Raphael aimed his sword at the top of Grant's head and swung, but Grant dodged and suddenly grew big black wings like Raphael's. He ascended up in the air and the three of them disappeared into blackness.

Scarlett felt like she was flying. She looked behind them and saw Raphael following them in a fury. Where were they going? She'd never been so frightened before in her life.

Raphael struck at the wings of the creature and hit one of them. It flopped sideways, lifeless. Grant shrieked in anger and pain. Scarlett felt them descend, and they landed on top of a mountain full of pine trees, back on earth, though it was dark now. They must be in another time zone.

Grant dropped her to the ground but held fast to Arielle. Scarlett hurt so bad, she couldn't move. She felt like every bone in her body had broken.

Raphael struck at his other wing, and it broke, too. Grant grew claws and scratched Raphael the whole length of his arm. It bled but then healed up quickly, the blood disappearing. Grant continued scratching Raph while still holding Arielle, and Raph continued to strike Grant with his sword, in the stomach, in the leg, at his neck, careful not to hit Arielle. Neither one of them would back off and neither one of them were fatally wounded.

They continued battling while Scarlett watched in amazement and fear. She felt so useless. She wanted to help.

Grant suddenly dropped the baby, her blanket falling off of her, and her wings exposed. Scarlett reached up to catch her. She caught her in her arms and held her fast against her bosom. Arielle stopped crying instantly and Scarlett was momentarily taken with her beauty and the precious little wings on her back. When she looked around, she realized she was hovering in the air. She felt strong and more alive than she'd felt in months. She looked down and saw her body on the ground among the pine needles while she floated above it in midair. Was she dead? She didn't know. She only knew she had to protect the baby and help Raph if she could. She rose higher to keep Arielle out of harm's way.

Raph looked up at her, hovering in the air with Arielle, and he yelled "Scarlett!" in surprise. Grant took the opportunity to claw his chest in a deep wound.

Raph was furious. "You can't kill me, you know."

"No, I can't, but I can do this," Grant said. He waved his arm in the air and Scarlett looked up in the sky and saw a multitude of dark figures flying towards them like a colony of bats. As they got lower, they all looked like Grant, human but with black wings and claws. They must be more dark angels. They surrounded Raph and started beating and scratching him incessantly with their claws. The wounds could not heal up quick enough for all the hits and scratches, and blood soon covered him. They tore at his wings so that he couldn't fly.

Scarlett cried out, "Stop!" She was still holding the baby, who opened her eyes and seemingly watched the scene before her. Suddenly she said, "No," not loud but firm and commanding.

Scarlett looked at her in amazement. How could this newborn baby talk? "Did you just talk?" she asked.

Arielle lifted up her arm towards the other dark angels, and they began to leave. Finally, they were all gone and it was just Grant and Raphael again. Raph's wings were restored, and he flew up to join Scarlett and Arielle. He reached out and touched Scarlett's hand and then Arielle's, like a high-five among three people, forming a trinity. Raph silently said, *I want you to picture a ring on my finger. Sterling silver with five points on it like a star and a big ruby in the center.*

Scarlett nodded her head and pictured it while whispering its description to Arielle.

Pray with me. See it, Raph continued saying while Grant continued to claw at Raph's back. Suddenly, the ring appeared on Raph's finger. The ruby in the middle of it glowed like red-hot lava. He turned the ring towards Grant, and its rays shot out towards him, striking him in the neck at his carotid, knocking him back twenty feet.

Raphael continued to point it towards him and yelled, "You are hereby banished back to the outer realm of darkness with the dark angels for a hundred years as punishment for interfering in the lives of humans and angels, two counts of kidnapping, and one count of attempting to murder an angel of death!"

Grant doubled over and coiled up, his wings became whole again, and he was whipped across the sky in a red streak, disappearing from their view.

It was over.

Relieved, Scarlett descended back to her body on the ground, feeling spent. As soon as she entered her body again, she woke up feeling like she'd been beaten, so sore and tired in body. She craved the energy she had just felt again, but it was not her time yet.

Arielle touched her face with her hand and smiled at her.

"Arielle, you are so precious," Scarlett whispered. "You have helped to save us all. Thank you."

Raph took them both in his arms and they flew through space and time, back to Virginia Beach.

Chapter Fifty-Seven

Cassie was distraught without Arielle. She tried to remain calm and rest, but she couldn't. It had been hours since she was taken. Juliet had gone out for some food. She'd tried to talk Cassie and Skyler into coming home with her, but Cassie wouldn't leave. This was where she lost Arielle, and this was where she would remain until she returned.

She hoped she *would* return. She tried not to doubt, to have faith, but it was hard.

She felt so tired, she couldn't have gone anywhere if she wanted to anyway.

Skyler paced the room until she asked him to sit down. He went for a walk on the beach while his mother was still there and came back discouraged that he didn't know how to help or where they had gone. He couldn't even get his guardian angel to talk to him, and his dad, who was an FBI agent, was on an assignment in DC, so he couldn't even talk to him. He did text him, but he just told him to leave it to Jackson and to have faith.

Skyler was sitting on the bed beside Cassie when they heard a noise in the other room. Thinking it was probably Juliet, Cassie closed her eyes again.

Skyler got up, went into the other room, and returned a minute later. "Open your eyes," he said.

She did and saw that he had Arielle in his arms!

"Arielle! She's back!" She reached her arms out for her, happy tears filling her eyes.

Skyler placed her in Cassie's arms, and she kissed her head, held her fast, and rocked her. Arielle sighed and made happy gurgling noises.

Cassie laughed. "Thank God you're back," she whispered.

Jackson came into the room carrying Scarlett.

"Is she okay?" Cassie asked.

"She's very weak. She was kidnapped, too. Her time is drawing near, but she wanted to talk to you both before I take her home."

Jackson laid her on the bed beside Cassie and Arielle. Scarlett reached out and held one of Cassie's hands. Arielle put her hand on top of both of theirs.

"Look at that," Cassie said. "She put her hand on top of ours."

"She's…very special," Scarlett whispered.

"Let me talk for you, ma chére," Jackson said.

Cassie was reminded that the two could communicate in their minds, and she felt a twinge of jealousy that she and Skyler couldn't do that anymore.

Jackson relayed to Cassie and Skyler what had happened, the kidnappings, that Grant wanted to give the baby to the dark angels and wanted to kill Skyler in order to get his body back. He told them about Grant calling on the other dark angels, and how they beat him and tore at his flesh. He also told them about Scarlett somehow coming out of her body momentarily to help him and saved Arielle from a fall. Finally, he told them about Arielle speaking, telling the dark angels, simply, no, and they obeyed her. They left.

Cassie was in awe. She looked at Arielle, who seemed to understand what they were saying. She looked up into her mother's eyes and smiled. Cassie smiled back. "My precious angel," she said.

Jackson then explained how he, Scarlett, and even Arielle helped him pray for the Pentalpha ring. "It's a five-pointed star with a ruby in the middle, used to subdue demons. It worked. Grant won't be bothering us for another hundred years."

"That's a relief," Cassie said. "What about Arielle seeing you and the other angels of death in your true form? Skyler told me that's not allowed since you're an angel of death."

"She's a special case. Since she's part angel of death, it doesn't affect her. She can see angels in their true form without any consequences. I think you'll find that she's going to live a long life. I talked to Adeline before she left, and she told me that she thinks because Arielle is part angel of death, she will live a couple of hundred years."

"Wow." Cassie was dumbfounded.

Scarlett had more to say to them, and Jackson spoke for her. "Scarlett wants you both to know that she is very glad to have known you, and happy that she was able to help bring your baby back. She hopes you'll all be happy in the big Pungo house.

"Arielle," Jackson continued. "This message is for you. Scarlett says she will come and visit you in the garden from time to time when you get to the Pungo house."

"That is so sweet," Cassie said. She reached over and kissed Scarlett on the cheek.

Arielle sat up by herself, looked at Scarlett and said very clearly, "Bye."

Jackson brought Scarlett to the back porch where her father and Odette sat, fretting. He placed her in a cushioned chair beside her father.

"Scarlett!" her father exclaimed. "Mon Dieux, I was so worried." He looked at Jackson. "Is she all right?"

"She's very weak. Her time is almost at an end."

André nodded, tears in his eyes. "I should have come sooner."

She reached over for his hand and squeezed it. She looked up at Jackson, who spoke for her, "She says, no, we will see each other again. She might not look the same, but she'll come and visit you from time to time."

André kissed her cheek. "How long does she have?" he asked Jackson.

"A few hours. Where's Tyler?"

"Inside making a sandwich."

Tyler came out with a tray of food and drinks and nearly dropped them in trying to get to Scarlett quickly. He handed the tray to Odette, who skillfully kept it from spilling, and he ran into his mother's arms.

"Maman! I thought you had died."

"Not yet," Jackson said, "but soon."

Scarlett spent the rest of the evening with her family. Jackson carried her to the downstairs bedroom where she lay on the bed with Tyler. In the evening, she said her good-byes to her father and to Odette.

"Je t'aime, ma fille," her father said.

She smiled through tears and placed her hand across her chest.

"She loves you, too," Jackson said.

"Say hello to your mother for me," André said.

Scarlett blinked and smiled, and then she closed her eyes. It was too much effort to do anything anymore.

"She's not dead, is she?" Tyler asked.

"No," Jackson said.

"Why can't she talk?"

"She's very weak and can't breathe well, so it takes too much effort for her to talk," he told the boy. He bent over to whisper in his ear. "I have a secret."

"What is it?" Tyler asked.

"I can communicate with your mother by reading her mind."

Scarlett scolded him in her thoughts, *Jackson, don't scare him.*"

"You can?" Tyler asked, his eyes wide open.

Jackson nodded. "Mhmm. I can't do it with anyone else, just your mom."

"That's cool, but…are you just telling me that to make me feel better?"

"No, I promise. She wants me to tell you something."

"What is it?" Tyler asked, looking at his mother and then back at Jackson.

"She says, 'You are my one great accomplishment in life and I'm so proud of you and thankful for the time we have been given together. I love you more than you will ever know.'"

Tyler got sad and started crying. He kissed his mother on the cheek and said, "I love you, too, Maman." He cried harder. "Please don't go, Maman. Don't leave me."

André also had tears in his eyes, and he scooted his chair over by the bed and picked up Scarlett's other hand. Odette also got emotional and excused herself from the room for a bit.

This is breaking my heart. He doesn't understand. Tell him that I won't be in pain anymore, Scarlett told Jackson.

He put his arm on Tyler's shoulder. "She's been hurting a lot lately, did you know that?" Tyler nodded. "Where she's going, she won't be in pain anymore. Isn't that good?"

Tyler nodded but still wasn't satisfied. "I want her here with me and not in pain. Why can't she not be in pain here?"

"That's just the way it goes sometimes," Jackson said. "She has a sickness that has no cure, so now she has to go to a place where she won't be sick anymore. She wishes she didn't have to leave you, but she will watch over you." Jackson dug into his pocket and pulled something small out. "She wanted me to give you this."

He handed Tyler a small silver female angel that was as long as his pinkie finger. "It's a little angel that you put in your pocket. If you always keep it with you, your maman will always be close to you."

Tyler wiped his eyes and kissed the little angel, and then folded his hand over it.

That was very sweet, Raph, thank you, Scarlett told him.

"She also left this angel plaque to go over your bedroom door." Jackson reached down under the bed to get it out and show it to him. "She will protect you and watch over you, and this will remind you."

"Okay," Tyler said. He looked at his mother and started whimpering again.

"It's okay to be sad, but I want you to know that I'm going to take care of her," Jackson said.

Raph, what are you doing? Scarlett asked him.

Trying to help him.

"You are?" Tyler asked.

"Yes, I'm going to show her around heaven and how to be an angel."

"You get to go too? Can I come?"

"No, I'm sorry. Just me."

"Are you dying too?"

"No. I'm like one of heaven's helpers. I can travel back and forth between here and heaven. I'll still be able to come back and visit you now and then. Would you like that?" Tyler nodded. "Your maman also wants you to do something for her."

"What's that?"

"Take good care of Harry." Jackson bent down and picked the dog up from his place in front of the warm fireplace, and sat him on the bed beside Tyler.

Tyler sniffed again and petted the dog. "Okay. You take care of Maman, and I'll take care of Harry."

"Sounds like a good plan."

Thank you, Raph, Scarlett told him. *That's the real reason you bought the puppy, isn't it?*

Mostly, yes. I knew he would need comfort.

"Who's going to take care of me?" Tyler asked.

"Your father, Luke, Jen, and Pépé, too."

"Okay."

Tyler picked up his mother's hand and snuggled next to her, leaning his head against her shoulder. He stayed that way for hours, talking to her about everything until eventually he fell asleep.

And then, at the stroke of midnight, as the grandfather clock chimed in the hallway, Scarlett's heart stopped beating.

Chapter Fifty-Eight

Scarlett felt as light as a feather and drifted up in the air. She leaned down, kissed her son on the cheek, and then ascended, looking down at her body. She blew a kiss to her father and Odette who slept in chairs nearby.

As she rose higher, she went through the house effortlessly, not feeling a thing, and looked around for Raph. He was behind her. He took her hand and together they flew through the night sky. She felt weightless and yet could feel the wind on her face and Raph's hand in hers.

"So, that's it? I'm crossing over now?"

"Yes," he answered.

"That was painless. Well, besides the pain in my heart."

"I gave you a little Morphine when you weren't looking. That's why it was painless."

"Oh." She had to smile. "Thank you. We never got to have that wedding on the beach, did we?"

"Ah, no matter, chérie. There is plenty of celebrating awaiting you, I promise, no matter where you decide to spend your afterlife."

She knew in her heart what she would decide, but she remained silent for now. She flew with him to Eden where the sun was shining and everything was bright and beautiful.

This time, there was beautiful music playing, which got louder and louder as they got near the ground. Trumpets blared like announcing royalty.

"What's all the music for?" Scarlett asked.

"It's your welcome."

They touched their feet to the ground.

"For me?" She felt so special.

"Yes. Follow me."

They walked past a group of angels in white, white wings glistening, playing instruments, and past a choir of women angels singing a beautiful ethereal song. White doves flittered around and landed on the angels' instruments to give a listen.

They came to a building made of gold and walked inside.

"What is this place?" she asked.

"This is where you get your immortal body. What age did you say you wanted to look like? Your twenties?"

Her eyes widened in surprise. "Yes, I suppose so." It seemed like ages ago when they had talked about the afterlife, and now here she was.

They stood in a line that moved quickly as each person walked up to a counter, much like going to a bank to withdraw money. When it was her turn, she was given a piece of paper with the name Angevin on it and under that, Undecided. She was then told to go through a door nearby.

"What's this mean?" she asked Raph, holding up the paper.

"Angevin is your new angel name. It's French for 'angel of wine,'"

"Yes, I know what that means. I didn't know I would get a new name."

"You do."

"So you won't be calling me Juliandra anymore?"

"I will if you prefer it, but your official angel name is now Angevin."

"Okay. What's the undecided for?"

"It means you might stay human or you might become an angel. I told you that you would get to decide. I want you to go see your mother first before you make your decision."

"All right."

She went inside the room alone. It was like a small telephone booth, very dim with dancing lights revolving around like a disco ball. She heard a noise, felt a buzz like a mild electrical shock go through her body, and she felt herself become solid, heavier. The door opened up again, and she walked out and looked down at her hands, her buxom bosom, wide hips, and some meat on her bones again instead of the skinny shadow of herself that she had become.

She looked good. She didn't even need a mirror to know.

Raphael smiled brightly. He reached around and pulled long tresses of brown wavy hair and laid it across her chest. It reached her navel. She gasped. She had her long hair again! She looked up at him and smiled.

He took her hand and they walked back outside. She looked at her arms, getting used to her new body. She felt human again but just not quite as heavy. She felt energy again, coursing through her. She wondered if she could fly.

"Not unless you get your wings." Raph answered her question.

She smiled. *You can still hear my thoughts.*

Yes, I can. His eyes twinkled.

They found her mother down by the river under tall palm trees, playing with her two boys. She was so happy to see her.

"Scarlett, you've finally come!"

They hugged and kissed each other's cheeks.

They took a walk through the garden and talked while observing waterfalls, all manner of flowers, and docile animals, even dinosaurs.

"How was your passing? Painful?" her mother asked.

"Not at all. Oh, I got plenty tired, weak, and pain to the point of crying before, but Jackson – Raph – slipped me some morphine just before I passed, so it was painless."

"That's good. Are you going to stay or be with him?" her mother asked, getting right to the point.

Scarlett knew she wanted to be with Raphael. While she loved her mother very much, she couldn't let go of the dream of having the love of her life. She'd finally found him, and if it were at all possible to spend eternity with him, she wanted to do it.

"This all looks wonderful and I would love to be with you and my brothers, and but I finally met the man of my dreams – well, being of my dreams – and I want to cherish this love forever. I don't ever want to be separated from him. Can you understand that? You and father loved each other once, right?"

"Of course we did. I always loved him, even after he cheated on me."

"If you could have him the way you fell in love with him for the rest of eternity, wouldn't you take him? I've never experienced this before."

"Yes, I would. I don't blame you one bit," her mother said, reaching over to hug her.

"Maybe I can still visit from time to time," Scarlett said, tears in her eyes. Even her immortal body could still cry and feel sad.

"No tears allowed here," her mother said.

They both laughed lightly.

"Go. Be with your SpiritMate."

"You know about that?"

"Raphael told me. It sounds very special. I'm a little envious."

"I'm sure there's no envy allowed here, either," Scarlett said, laughing.

She felt relieved. She could be with Raph now.

She found him chatting with her brothers, looking so regal and handsome with his big black wings. He had them open wide. He was showing off a bit.

She kissed her brothers on the cheeks and took Raph's hand.

"We should be going," she said. *I'm ready to be with you now.*

Truly?

She nodded.

"We shall," he said, smiling brightly. "First, let us drink from the River of Life."

He walked over to the water, cupped some in his hands and held it up for Scarlett to drink from. It was cold and tasted pure, better than anything bottled ever did or even the mountain springs.

"And now we go to the tree."

He took her arm in his and they walked down a different path around tall camellia bushes, spiky short palms, big fluffy snowball bushes, and different colored roses that trailed over long trellises. Finally Scarlett saw a huge tree as big as the Tree of Life in Disney's Animal Kingdom. She'd taken Tyler there a few years before. This tree was real, though, and had names carved in it, a few hearts like you'd find on a childhood tree with initials of you and your boyfriend carved inside.

"What's this?" she asked.

"It's the Tree of Life."

"The actual….the real Tree of Life?"

He nodded. "Once you eat of it, you will be like me."

The tree had a trunk so wide, it could cover a city block. Its limbs reached farther than her eyes could see towards the sky, and also spread out wide and some hung down low enough to touch. They were filled with all different colors of apples, oranges, mangos, peaches, apricots, papayas, even bananas.

"What's your favorite kind of fruit?" he asked her.

"How do all of these different kinds of fruits grow on one tree?"

"It's a very special tree. Only one of its kind. There are twelve different kinds of fruits on it. First I want you to choose whatever kind you want, and then I will pick the second one for you. So what'll it be?"

"Hmm, so many choices. How about a mango? That's one of my favorites."

"You got it." He picked a big one off, peeled the skin off easily, and handed it to her.

"It's not going to poison me, is it?" she asked, smirking, thinking of fairy tales and poisoned apples.

He laughed. "No, and it won't make you embarrassed to be naked either."

She hadn't even realized that she was, but she looked down and realized it was true. He fed her a bite of the sweetest, juiciest mango she'd ever tasted before. "Sensationnel! C'est tres bien!" She chewed it up and swallowed. "Does everyone here get to eat one of these?"

"Yes." He looked up at the tree again and picked off what looked like a peach. "This is a very special peach. It's the thirteenth fruit and it only produces this kind of peach every once in a while."

"What does this one do?"

"It makes you like me. While the other fruits make you immortal, this one makes you an angel…and not only that, but also my SpiritMate."

He handed the peach to her. She took it and bit into it. Again, it was some of the sweetest fruit she'd ever tasted. "This one was for me?"

"Yes. When I first started to suspect that you and I were SpiritMates, I came and checked the tree, and it had a bloom on it. It just ripened…last night."

She was amazed. "What if I had chosen to stay with my mother?"

"I had hoped you wouldn't. If you had chosen that path, then I would've been wrong. My SpiritMate would have chosen me over anyone else, family or otherwise. I would have been very sad because if you hadn't chosen me, I would not have been able to see you again, and would have had to keep looking for my SpiritMate."

That would have been sad indeed.

"Like I said before, it's rare for human women to become an angel," he continued, "because they want to stay with their families."

That somehow made her feel cold and indifferent, like she didn't care about her family.

"I know you love your family; I'm not saying that you don't. I'm saying it's a rare and special thing that you and I have found. I'm so glad you're my SpiritMate."

"I do love my family, but I love you more. I love you like no other." Her heart beat fast inside of her, making her still feel human.

He reached over, took her chin in his hand, and gently kissed her lips. "And I love you the very same. And look…" He reached up to the tree and pulled another peach off identical to hers. "The mate to yours. There are two identical peaches produced, one for each mate."

He took a bite out of his, and when he did, a swirling wind blew around the two of them, blowing leaves up and surrounding them until they could not see anything else except each other and the surrounding leaves. The wind picked them up off the ground. Scarlett reached for Raph, and he wrapped his arms and wings around her. They floated in the air and landed again on a sandy beach. The wind stopped blowing, and the leaves fell to the sand.

Scarlett looked around at a tropical beach with coconut palms and banana trees. The waves were gentle and soothing, like a bay. On the beach to her left was a small green cottage trimmed in white with a porch across the front of it and nice cushioned white wicker chairs to sit on. Flower baskets hung from the ceiling, and the door was covered by a Victorian style screen door.

"What is this place?"

"A special part of Eden. There's always a sunrise here. Only good angels of death can come here. There are always people dying somewhere at different time zones all over the world, so this will be the place we come to when we want to rest and be together."

"All the angels of death live in this little house?"

He smiled. "No, just you and me. It's our own little corner of Eden, our own little cottage on the ocean. It even has a beautiful garden that never needs tending."

"This is just for us?"

"Yes. We have to deal with a lot of sad people and this is our escape, our haven."

"Is this heaven?"

"Actually, for us it is."

"How wonderful! Did you live here before, by yourself?"

"Yes. This is where I stash my gifts that people give me."

"Aha. I see now. Have you cleared out a couple of rooms for me?"

He laughed. "There is plenty of room. A nice big bed…" Her mind filled with ideas involving a bed. "We share everything now. Our lives, our assignments. In addition to helping people cross over, you will help me guard the Tree of Life."

"That's one of your assignments?"

He nodded. "That's what I do in Eden."

"Then I will get to see my family. A lot."

"Yes, you will."

"That works out perfectly."

He took her in his arms and pulled something on her back. She felt something pop and felt a rush of wind at her back. She glanced up and saw black wings. On *her* back. She had always thought she'd have white wings. That's the color all the paintings and movies have for good angels. But ever since she met Jackson aka Raphael, she knew that white wasn't the only color of wings angels could have. She now realized that it was wise for angels of death to have black wings so that they could fly through the night unseen. They would also appear as big birds of prey when they flew in the daytime.

She was now one of those angels.

"Can I really fly?"

"Give it a try," he said.

She flapped her wings, jumped with her legs, and actually left the ground about five feet. She cried out in delight. Raph laughed and joined her. He grabbed her hand and the two of them flew up and over the ocean a little ways and then flew back to the cottage.

"That was so exciting, so exhilarating!" she said.

He took her in his arms and kissed her deeply. "You have made me happier than I ever thought possible. I get to share all of eternity with someone as wonderful as you. I've waited a thousand years for you. Tu es ma vie," he said.

"Tu es l'amour de ma vie," she said. They joined their arms and wings together around each other.

A paper fell down from the sky and Scarlett caught it. It was the paper she'd been given at the gold house with Angevin written on it, but below that, instead of saying "Undecided," it now said, "Angel of Death."

"Turn it over," Raph said.

On the back, it said, *I now pronounce you SpiritMates.*

"Are we married now?" she asked.

He smiled. "We are. On the beach and everything."

"What about a witness?"

"Look up."

She did and there was a multitude of angels dressed in white with white wings, and they began to play celestial music. On the other side, hovering over the ocean, was a group of angels of death with black wings.

"Is that enough witnesses for you?"

She laughed. "You may kiss the bride," she said.

And he did.

Epilogue

Three months later

Cassie walked through the lush, secluded gardens of their new estate that Scarlett had graciously given her family. It was summertime and everything was in full bloom, the trees full of green leaves. There were abundant flowers, the fountain was tranquil and bubbling, and birds chirped and flittered in the trees. It was like their own little Eden. Cassie was looking for Arielle, who loved playing hide-and-seek here.

She softly called her daughter's name, walked around a corner and found her daughter perched up on the railing of the treehouse built between three tall oak trees. Arielle was talking softly to a bird in her hand, her little white wings spread out behind her. She was wearing her favorite white dress and wore a garland of flowers around her head, which Cassie liked to call her halo. Her golden blonde curls reached past her wings down her back.

Everyone in the family learned of the secret of what Arielle was and of what Skyler used to be. There was no way around it. They were all pretty shocked about it but accepted it after seeing Arielle's wings. Jen was even more shocked to learn that her ex-husband Brad had also been a guardian angel. They agreed to keep it a family secret, and didn't think they would be punished since they had been entrusted with the care of a special half-angel like Arielle. For the moment, they lived their lives in privacy on the big estate.

The baby angel was adored by the whole family. She grew at a rapid rate her first few months of life. At only three months, she looked more like a three-year-old and was more angel-like than human at times.

"Mama," Arielle said when she saw her. She flew down to her mother and showed her the blue bird. It was skittish of Cassie, but Arielle whispered to the bird, "It's okay. That's my mama. She won't hurt you." Her blue eyes, much like her father's – for Cassie considered Skyler her father now since it was his physical appearance and attributes that helped make Arielle who she was – brightened whenever she talked to the animals. Cassie marveled at the way Arielle was able to communicate with birds and animals of all kinds. It was like they were naturally drawn to her. It made Cassie wonder if she would be a vet someday. It fit her name perfectly since one of the name meanings for Arielle was angel of nature.

Arielle continued to pet the bird and it chirped and looked at Cassie. "Isn't she beautiful, mama?"

"She is," Cassie whispered. "Adeline is here for your check-up," Cassie told her daughter. "Time to come inside."

"Okay. Good-bye, little birdie. I'll see you later. Don't let that sparrow get in your house again. I'll have a talk with her later and show her a new place to live."

The bird flew up into the trees, and Cassie couldn't help but marvel at the wonder of her daughter and wondered how she could've ever had the fleeting thought of aborting such a beautiful creature.

"It's okay, Cassie." Adeline said from behind her. She had followed her to the garden. "We can do the exam in the treehouse if you'd like, Arielle. My, how big and pretty you've gotten in the past month."

"Thank you," Arielle said politely. She flew up into the treehouse on her own, leaving Adeline and Cassie to walk up the steps.

"She has greatly improved her flying skills," Adeline said.

"Yes, she has. She practices incessantly and hardly wants to come indoors at all."

They climbed the stairs to the treehouse that was enjoyed by the whole family. Cassie planned to continue being homeschooled here until she graduated and also write a novel in her spare time. For now, she spent a lot of time with Arielle and Skyler here since Arielle wanted to be outdoors so much, and the rest of the family would join them in the evenings. Cassie's dad would play his guitar and sing, which Arielle loved. She had recently begun singing with him. Her voice was angelic, of course, a very high soprano.

Her dad had come home for good and made sure the property had a secure fence around the whole perimeter as well as big tall bushes, in case any crazed fans or the paparazzi ever found out where he lived. It was most important for the safety of the family, especially Arielle since she had such special gifts that they had to keep a secret. There was already a secure metal fence, which Tyler said had always been there, and plenty of tall pine trees and big holly bushes. Cassie's dad had some electric wires placed on the fencing and a security system, but he had to disconnect the wires when Arielle insisted that it hurt the birds, that he just needed to place some cameras around the property and that would be good enough.

Once Cassie and Adeline reached the treehouse, they all went inside and Adeline performed her usual well check on Arielle in the upstairs bedroom loft. She also gave her a shot, which she tolerated well but insisted she didn't need.

"It looks like you're growing very well, Arielle," Adeline said.

"Thank you, I think so, too," Arielle said.

Cassie had to laugh.

"Excuse me, please," Arielle said, and flew out the open upstairs window to a nearby magnolia tree.

Cassie sat on the bed and watched her.

"I wanted to let you know that I found another half-dark angel, half-human," Adeline said.

"You did? Where?"

"He's actually in your family."

"*My* family? Who is it?" Cassie wondered which one of her relatives had been keeping such a secret.

"His name is Jason Barnes. He's married to your cousin, Sarah."

Cassie wrinkled her forehead. "Okay, but he's not the one I'm related to; it's Sarah."

"Actually you are. He's actually the triple-great grandfather of your cousin, Tori, on her father's side of the family."

"Wait, what?"

"He was born in the 1840s. That's why I had a hard time finding him."

"So he's like…a hundred and fifty years old or something?"

"Yeah. He's lived a long time."

"Wow. Is Arielle going to live that long, too?"

"Maybe, who knows?"

"I'm guessing Tori knows?"

"I don't know, but I'm pretty sure that Sarah does."

"I had no idea. He looks so young. They've not been married long, so I don't know him very well."

"I think it's time you got to know them a lot better. Jason could be very informative on what to expect for Arielle."

"You're right about that. Am I allowed to tell Mom?" Jen wasn't her real mom, but she'd been like a mom to her for a long time, so she felt like it was time she called her that.

"I think that would be all right," Adeline said.

"Did you talk to him?"

"Yes, before coming here. I told him I knew of another incident between a dark angel and a human female, but I didn't tell him it was you. I'll leave that part up to you."

"Okay, thanks."

"I should be going," Adeline said.

"I'll walk you back."

After Adeline left, Cassie saw Tyler in the yard playing with Arielle and Harry near the family graveyard. Tyler often came to his mother's and grandmother's graves.

Since Arielle could see other angels, she often talked to Scarlett in the garden. She would relay messages to Tyler, and the two of them had grown close. As soon as she began talking at one month of age, Tyler started spending more time with her. She was tall even for a three-year-old and strong as a horse, and she often carried Tyler around on her back and flew around the yard. It was clear that Tyler enjoyed being with her, and they played for hours in the garden that he grew up in. Things had changed quite a bit for him, but it seemed like he was growing an attachment to Arielle in the absence of his mother.

Arielle said that Scarlett became an angel, just as Tyler's teacher said she would. This made Tyler happy, and her visits to the garden and talks with Arielle reassured him that she would always be close.

Sometimes when the visits were over, there would be a bottle of wine propped up by the grave along with a bunch of grapes. Arielle told them the grapes were for Tyler, and the wine was for the adults, gifts from Scarlett.

Whenever Arielle talked with Scarlett in the garden, Jackson would come in person and talk to them, especially to Tyler. His visits seemed to make Tyler feel better and helped him to adjust to life without his mother. When Tyler asked Arielle why his mother couldn't come too, she'd explained that his mother would have to change her appearance in order to see him, to protect him, and that maybe one day she would do that, but she didn't want to confuse him right now.

Harry started barking at something close to the big angel statue, and Cassie had to wonder if that's where Scarlett stood, invisible to humans but not to little half-angels and dogs. Sure enough, Jackson walked across the yard towards Tyler, who ran and hugged him.

Scarlett's father, André, and Odette, were coming over for supper that night, and Jackson often came to see them. André had found a house at Sandbridge on the bay side rather than the ocean, as it was cheaper, had everything they wanted, and was within walking distance of the ocean, a church, and a restaurant. They could also enjoy sunsets on the bay from their back terrace. Tyler often spent the night with them and was reminded of his last days at the ocean with his mother.

Tonight, Maggie and Steve would also be coming over with their new two-month-old baby boy. They had to tell them about Arielle also, since she had grown so much quicker than Stefan had. Stefan was what they named their baby, which was a variation of Steve, and also it was a way of honoring Scarlett by naming him after her half-brother.

Arielle flew over to Cassie to be held, and Cassie wrapped her arms around her. She was such a loving baby girl.

"Scarlett says hello," Arielle said.

"Okay, thank you. Tell her hello for me. Is Tyler doing okay today?"

"Yeah, he is. Scarlett told me she helped her first person cross over last night. It was a little boy and it made her miss her boy, so she came for a visit."

"That's nice. I'm so glad you are able to talk to her and give messages to Tyler like you do."

"It's my pleasure. It's what I was meant to do."

She was so profound sometimes.

She saw her daddy, Skyler, and flew over to talk to him. Cassie smiled at the two of them. Skyler had quickly grown to love her, even though he wasn't responsible for her being alive. He loved her as his own.

It seemed ironic to Cassie that all this time she'd had to hide what Skyler was, but now the whole family knew. They knew what Skyler did to be with her, how much they loved each other, and knew about the dark angel that impregnated her, resulting in the precious little half-angel girl who was more angel than human. They understood the struggle that it took to keep her and would do whatever it took to protect her. So far, they've been successful at keeping her hidden but in the future they would have to think about how to introduce her to the world and how to hide her wings. For now, she was content in her backyard, conversing with her family, the animals, and the other angels who often came to visit.

Acknowledgments

While I was writing this book, the terrorist attacks in Paris happened. I had already planned to write about Scarlett's visit to Paris but went back and added this incident into my story as a condolence to the victims of this terrible event.

I would like to dedicate this book to the memory of my mom, who died of breast cancer, and also to my cousin, Kristen Duncan, who is a brave and admirable survivor of this terrible disease. She's been disease free for eight years now.

I would like to once again thank my assistant and close friend, Sherrie Frontz, for her advice, encouragement, ideas, and help with editing this novel, as well as Lyndsay Hobbs and Christy Rankin, who helped with proofreading.

About The Author

Cheryl R. Lane was born and raised in Tennessee and went to college at East Tennessee State University before marrying her high school sweetheart and moving to Virginia Beach, Virginia. She started writing as a hobby when she was in college and continued writing on the side while working as a medical transcriptionist. She tried the traditional publishing route, but after many rejections, she finally decided to self-publish her first book, "Wellington Cross," on Amazon through Kindle Direct Publishing as well as in print through CreateSpace. She has since published book two "Wellington Grove," a novella, "A Wellington Christmas," and book three in the series, "Wellington Rose." She began writing "Starlight," as it was originally titled, after reading the Twilight series. She wanted to make angels the forbidden love in the story rather than vampires, and it was geared toward young adults. She put it aside for a few years to write the Wellington series before coming back to Starlight and decided to add an adult storyline to it, as well. She is currently working on her next book. She is still married to her sweetheart after twenty-seven years, and they have one son and a Havanese bichon dog who thinks he's human.

www.cheryllaneauthor.com

STARLIGHT WISHES

BOOK ONE IN THE ANGEL SERIES

Go back and experience the budding relationship between Skyler and Cassie when he was still her guardian angel and she was a troubled teen. Read about how Luke and Jen flirted with each other, dated, argued, kissed and made up, and finally realized they were meant to be together, despite jealousies and secrets.

"I loved this book so much! It makes you want to visit the beach with the one you love! Highly recommended!"
~ Lyndsay, Goodreads reader

WELLINGTON CROSS SERIES

Get swept away to a Virginia plantation on the James River in the late 1800s in this historical romance series by Cheryl R. Lane…

Wellington Cross review: "I really loved this book! Could not put it down, just had to see what was going to happen! I stayed up late trying to finish it. I would definitely recommend this! Good plot, loveable characters, romance and mystery all wrapped up in one." *Sandy, Amazon review*

Available on Amazon in paperback and Kindle, and at Barnes & Noble on request.

55735701R00220

Made in the USA
Charleston, SC
04 May 2016